THE
STITCHER
AND THE
MUTE

TALES OF FENEST

Widow's Welcome

THE
STITCHER
AND THE
MUTE

Book Two of the Tales of Fenest

D.K. FIELDS

HEAD
of ZEUS

First published in the UK in 2020 by Head of Zeus Ltd
An Ad Astra Book

9 7 5 3 1 2 4 6 8

A catalogue record for this book is available from
the British Library.

ISBN (HB): 9781789542523
ISBN (XTPB): 9781789542530
ISBN (E): 9781789542516

Typeset by Siliconchips Services Ltd UK

Printed and bound in Great Britain
by CPI Group (UK) Ltd, Croydon, CR0 4YY

Head of Zeus Ltd
5–8 Hardwick Street
London EC1R 4RG
WWW.HEADOFZEUS.COM

For our dads, John and John

PERLISH

CASKERS

LOWLANDERS

WEST PERLANSE

PERLA

RIVER TUN

RIVER CASK

FENEST

THE LO

THE

BORDAIR

THE RUSTI

DESERT

The Swaying Audience

Abject Reveller, god of: loneliness, old age, fish
Affable Old Hand, god of: order, nostalgia, punctuality
Beguiled Picknicker, god of: festivals, incense, insect bites
Blind Devotee, god of: mothers, love, the sun
Bloated Professional, god of: wealth, debt, shined shoes
Calm Luminary, god of: peace, light, the forest
Courageous Rogue, god of: hunting, charity, thin swords
Curious Stowaway, god of: rites of passage, secrets, summer
    and the longest day
Deaf Relative, god of: hospitality
Delicate Tout, god of: herbs, prudence, drought
Engaged Matron, god of: childbirth
Exiled Washerwoman, god of: sanitation, rivers, obstacles
Faithful Companion, god of: marriage, loyalty, dancing
Filthy Builder, god of: clay, walls, buckets
Frail Beholder, god of: beauty, spectacles, masks
Generous Neighbour, god of: harvest, fertility, the first day
    of the month

Gilded Keeper, god of: justice, fairness, cages
Grateful Latecomer, god of: good fortune, spontaneity, autumn
Heckling Drunkard, god of: jokes, drink, fools
Honoured Bailiff, god of: thieves, the dark, bruises
Insolent Bore, god of: wind, bindleleaf, borders
Inspired Whisperer, god of: truth, wisdom, silk
Jittery Wit, god of: madness, lamps, volcanoes
Keen Musician, god of: destiny, wine, oil
Lazy Painter, god of: rain, noon, hair
Missing Lover, god of: forbidden love, youth, thunder
Moral Student, god of: the horizon, knowledge, mountains
Needled Critic, god of: criticism, bad weather, insincerity
Nodding Child, god of: sleep, dreams, innocence
Overdressed Liar, god of: butlers, beards, mischief
Overlooked Amateur, god of: jilted lovers, the wronged, apprentices
Pale Widow, god of: death and renewal, winter, burrowing animals, the moon
Penniless Poet, god of: song, poetry, money by nefarious means
Prized Dandy, god of: clothes, virility, bouquets
Querulous Weaver, god of: revenge, plots, pipes
Reformed Trumpeter, god of: earthquakes, the spoken word
Restless Patron, god of: employment, contracts and bonds, spring
Scandalous Dissenter, god of: protest, petition, dangerous animals

Senseless Brawler, god of: war, chequers, fire
Stalled Commoner, god of: home and hearth, decisions, crowds
The Mute, god of: Silence
Travelling Partner, god of: journeys, danger and misfortune, knives
Ugly Messenger, god of: pennysheets, handicrafts, dogs
Valiant Glutton, god of: cooking, trade, cattle
Vicious Beginner, god of: milk and nursing, midnight, ignorance
Weary Governess, god of: schooling, cats
Wide-eyed Inker, god of: tattoos, colour, sunsets
Withering Fishwife, god of: dusk, chastity, flooding
Yawning Hawker, god of: dawn, comfort, grain
Zealous Stitcher, god of: healing and mending

One

Detective Cora Gorderheim had heard many stories that started with death. Now, here was another, set in a barn in East Perlanse. Which of the Audience would hear this story's end? The Mute? The Keeper? Or the Widow?

The sour air of the barn hit Cora as soon as she stepped inside. It caught the back of her throat. She swallowed and tasted sinta, but overripe: the point when the fruit had gone bad but there was still no sign on the skin. When it tricked the eater. She spat into the straw at her feet and went over to the bodies.

Four of them.

Only one was a stranger: an older woman in a driver's long coat. She would've held the reins of the prisoner transport that drove this sad party here. Cora had passed the empty coach on her way into the barn.

Two of the dead were constables in uniform – veteran officers Cora recognised.

And the last body, the one Cora knew well. Or had thought she did.

The Casker, Finnuc Dawson.

He was lying a little way from the other three, closer

to the door, face down in the straw with his legs stretched out behind him. Perhaps the Casker had realised what was happening and had tried to go for help. Or perhaps he was just trying to escape; that was more like him. Not that he would have got far anyway, what with the shackles at his ankles. It was a mercy she couldn't see his face. Given the state of the others, it wouldn't be pretty.

He'd been strong and handsome, and when he told a story there was a boyishness to his eyes. Now he was ruined. At the thought of it, Cora shuddered. But she forced herself to step around Finnuc's body, glad to have him behind her, out of sight for the moment. She squatted next to the dead driver.

The woman was on her side in the straw. Cora took a handkerchief from her coat and gently pushed the woman's hair from her face. Her lips were blistered, her cheeks dark purple and her eyes all but out of their sockets, the whites thick with red lines. Both these things told a story of forceful purging. And here was evidence of it, all down the woman's coat and in the straw around her face: green liquid shot through with clots of blood. The poor woman looked to have brought up half her lungs along with whatever had poisoned her.

'Widow welcome you, friend,' Cora said, invoking a member of the Audience. But opening her own mouth was a mistake, given how the sour smell was much worse this near the corpse. She gagged, briefly imagined her own eyes being forced from her skull with the effort of retching, and stepped quickly away.

Something rolled against her foot. She used the handkerchief to free whatever it was from the straw. A bowl. A few spoons' worth of orange liquid sloshed inside. A broth or soup most likely.

She checked the bodies of the constables and found a bowl beside each of them too, the same orange stains inside. The pair were lying together, the woman's arm hanging over the chest of her male companion like a tale for the Devotee. But Cora thought it less romantic than that. The story here was that he'd shown signs first and she'd sought to help, then been taken ill herself and purged her insides all over him before they both choked to death, or their hearts gave out with the effort of breathing. Either way, the ending was the same. And all because of Finnuc Dawson.

There were voices outside the barn, raised voices, one of which Cora recognised as the capable tones of Constable Jenkins. She'd told Jenkins to keep everyone out, to give Cora a chance to see what stories the barn told before other people came in and started telling their own. From the noise, it didn't sound like that was going too well.

A man barged in. He was tall and looked too thin for his frame. Way he was going, arms swinging this way and that, face red with rage, he'd be in the straw himself before too long.

'Can't you hurry up?' he said. He wore a dark green jacket with a ridiculously tall collar that clipped his ears, and more buttons than was sensible. Feathers streamed from his lapels. Perlish fashions never ceased to be a mystery to Cora. 'I've got a business to run!' he said. He glanced behind him, then back to Cora. 'And the customers are starting to notice.'

'Given the smell, I've no doubt they are, Mr...'

'Tr'stanton. Samuel Tr'stanton.'

Constable Jenkins slipped past him and into the barn, her blue jacket a sharp contrast against the yellow straw. Cora recognised the look on the young woman's face: the blend of annoyance and professionalism, carefully managed, that made Jenkins such an asset. Her mouth was fixed in a line that hid her usually prominent teeth from view.

'Sorry, Detective. He wouldn't take no for an answer.'

Cora waved away the apology. She needed to talk to the barn owner anyway. Might as well get it over with. Useful to see his reaction to the horrors still lying in his barn, which didn't seem to be *much* of a reaction, truth be told. His boots were closer to the dead driver's head than Cora thought was right.

'Well, Mr Tristanton,' she said.

'It's *Tr'stanton*, without the i.'

'Right, well, these folks aren't going anywhere until I get a stitcher to look at them. Speaking of which – Jenkins?'

'Stitcher's been sent for, Detective, and some local constables. Don't know how long they'll take though. Nearest station's a few miles off apparently.'

'We'll just have to wait then, won't we?' Cora said, and gave Tr'stanton an apologetic smile that was low on the apology, the kind loved by the Critic.

Tr'stanton's face grew even redder and spit shone at the edges of his mouth. 'On whose authority are you preventing me from earning an honest mark?'

She pulled out her badge and pushed it closer to his face than she needed to. 'Detective Cora Gorderheim, from Bernswick.'

'Bernswick?'

8

'One of Fenest's finest police divisions.' Even with Cora making an effort, the words still came out as mocking.

It was hardly a surprise. Chief Inspector Sillian of Bernswick had been trying to stop Cora from getting to the heart of this case since the first body had turned up and started this story: Nicholas Ento, the murdered Wayward storyteller. All Cora's hard work had led her to the killer, Finnuc Dawson, and she'd been the one to arrest him. Now, here was *Finnuc* lying dead in a barn in Perlanse. A murderer murdered. This would change things back at the station. The chief inspector would have to let Cora investigate this properly, because it couldn't be a random killing. Someone had wanted Finnuc dead, and Cora was certain she knew who.

Tennworth.

Cora had the name, and the fact Tennworth was a woman, but not much more. Finnuc gave her that information before he was taken from the cell at the station, as good as admitting it was Tennworth who had ordered him to kill the Wayward storyteller. And, shortly after his confession, Finnuc was dead. Now, Cora had to find Tennworth before anyone else was killed.

'Bernswick... Fenest... You're a long way from home, Detective.' There was caution in Tr'stanton's voice now.

Cora put her badge away and moved further into the barn. Further from Finnuc. 'Believe me, Perlanse isn't where I wanted to find myself today.'

'*East* Perlanse,' Tr'stanton said. 'You're in the eastern duchy and I would ask that you acknowledge the rightful—'

'There's plenty of work waiting for me back in Fenest, Mr Tr'stanton. My job is to solve the crimes of the capital.

9

Well, in one patch of it. I haven't got time to wander the six realms of the Union. Isn't that right, Constable?'

'There *is* an election on,' Jenkins said.

'As if I don't know about the election!' Tr'stanton all but shouted. 'We do get pennysheets out here, Detective. Life does go on outside the glorious capital.'

'I'd say "death" is more the word for what's happening in your barn,' Cora said dryly.

Tr'stanton's long arms were flailing again. 'If Fenest keeps you so busy, *Detective*, why are you even standing in *my* barn?'

'Because that man was a prisoner.' Cora nodded in the direction of Finnuc. 'My prisoner.'

'The death of a prisoner is hardly a cause of regret,' Tr'stanton said. He folded his arms, making the feathers crammed onto his lapels flutter. 'One fewer mouth to feed on the Steppes. The Commission spends too much money on them as it is; we should string them up and be done with it. There's been a lot of talk about it in the right-thinking pennysheets.'

'Not the 'sheets I read,' Cora said. 'These others gone to the Widow here, they committed no crime. Their only job was to take the prisoner from the capital to the Steppes.'

Jenkins was staring at the pair of constables. She, too, had recognised them.

Cora leaned against one of the poles that supported the roof and reached into her coat for her bindleleaf tin. She'd been trying to give up smoking but recent events had been... challenging. After everything that had happened, smoking seemed the least of her problems.

Jenkins gave a low cough and nodded towards the

straw-covered floor. With a deep sigh that was gruff with years of bindle-smoke, Cora put the tin away. Probably wasn't a good idea to set fire to the barn, though it would make life a lot easier to burn the place to the ground, the bodies with it. Especially Finnuc's. The smell was too bad to stay inside any longer anyway. She headed outside, to the courtyard, Tr'stanton tight on her heels.

'Make sure no one else enters,' she told Jenkins, and headed for the coaching inn that stood on the other side of the courtyard.

'Where are you going?' Tr'stanton said.

'It was a long ride from Fenest,' Cora said. 'I could do with a drink.'

She pushed open the double doors that were a headache-bringing mess of coloured glass worked into the shapes of birds and flowers. The barroom beyond the doors was little better. Polished brass gleamed in the midday sun streaming through the tall windows, many of which had more coloured glass plates. The room was divided into spacious booths, each decked out in a different cloth that to her eye clashed with their neighbours, and with the fancy clothes of the Perlish travellers who sat in them. Her head swam. At least she'd be able to smoke in here. That might help.

The barroom was half full, and it was silent – the kind of fresh silence that she knew well. A detective walks into a bar… But it wasn't her causing it today. The stinking bodies in the barn were responsible for that. She was the one who'd said the travellers couldn't leave though. *That* was her doing.

Tr'stanton was at her elbow. 'Nothing to worry about!'

he called to the huddles of concerned faces. 'This matter will soon be dealt with.'

Angry murmurs suggested the stranded travellers thought this unlikely. While Tr'stanton commanded free drinks to soothe tempers, Cora sank into the nearest booth.

She was tired. After Finnuc had been taken from the Bernswick station she'd gone to the Dancing Oak to distract herself from all the things she didn't want to think about, including the question of who Tennworth was, and how Cora was going to find her. Then, after a long night ringside in which she'd lost more of her pay than she liked to tally, the message had come: the prisoner transport had got into trouble on the road to the Northern Steppes. She and Jenkins had set off immediately. Even before Cora had stepped into the foul air of the barn she'd known what was waiting for her. That Finnuc would be dead. That didn't make it any easier to see him lying there.

Tr'stanton thrust Cora a glass of something silvery: Greynal. 'I don't drink,' she said.

Tr'stanton's eyebrows shot up; they looked remarkably similar to the feathers he wore. 'But you said you needed—'

'*A* drink. Something to rid my tongue of dust. That doesn't mean it has to be distilled.'

'This *is* the finest spirit to come out of the Lowlands.'

'Send it over to Jenkins in the barn. She'll need warming up after the journey.' Cora enjoyed the appalled look on his face. He kept the glass of Greynal for himself. 'I'll take a sinta juice,' Cora said, then thought better of it when the glass arrived and she caught the smell, just like the barn. She'd make do with a smoke.

'Tell me, Mr Tr'stanton, you own this place?'

'Yes, but I can assure you I had nothing to do—'

'Get many prisoner transports stopping for supper?'

Tr'stanton straightened his lapels. 'From time to time. We are on the main road to the Steppes.'

'A good road too,' Cora said, and lit a bindleleaf. 'Better than the roads in Fenest. With the Perlish controlling the Assembly, Perlanse has done well. What a surprise.'

'Which realm wouldn't take care of their own people?' Tr'stanton said, as if Cora was a fool. Typical Perlish.

'Those looking to stay in control of the Assembly for another term,' she said. 'Those who care about the *whole* Union, not just their own back yard.'

The Assembly was the seat of power in the Union. The realm that won an election took control of the Assembly and made decisions that affected all six realms of the Union, as well as the capital, Fenest. The person at the head of this power was the Chambers. Every realm had their own Chambers to represent them in Fenest, making them the most powerful people you could have the misfortune to come across. As if that wasn't enough, the only *other* thing Cora knew about Tennworth apart from the name, apart from that she was a woman, was that Tennworth was very likely a Chambers. Of all the people to be chasing for murder…

The inn owner was jabbering on about the good works done by the current Perlish Assembly.

'You won't hold onto the Assembly after this election,' Cora said, interrupting him, 'given the grumblings I've heard about Perlish decisions these last five years.' She puffed a big cloud of smoke across the table at him. 'Might have helped if your Chambers spent some of the Union budget in other realms. Caskers keep telling me the River Stave needs dredging.'

'If their storyteller did a good enough job to win this year, they can dredge it themselves,' Tr'stanton said, coughing. 'The Caskers have told their tale. The Lowlanders too. The Perlish 'tellers are next, I believe.'

'The wheel turns,' Cora said grimly.

Tr'stanton glanced behind him. 'Can we get on with the business at hand? These people are costing me a fortune.'

'Looks to me like business is good enough to bear it.' She stubbed out the end of her bindleleaf against the untouched glass of sinta juice and enjoyed Tr'stanton's grimace. 'So good you don't really need prisoner transports stopping here, do you? Might as well make them eat in the barn.'

Tr'stanton leaned back in his seat. 'I don't have a choice about the prisoners stopping here, though if I had my way they'd never darken my door. It's bad for—'

'Business, yes, I get the idea.'

'The Commission doesn't seem to care.' He looked like he would say more but then wisely stopped himself. The Commission were the civil service in Fenest, and Cora's employer. The Assembly made the decisions about life in the Union, and the Commission recorded every aspect of them in painful detail. 'I do what I'm told and give the prisoner transports food to eat and somewhere to sleep,' he said. 'But the Commission have no rules about *where* that happens.'

'That's not like the Commission,' Cora said, and something like a smile briefly appeared on Tr'stanton's face. Wherever you found yourself in the Union of Realms, you found the Commission at work. Some days, Cora thought *that* was what united the different peoples. That and the election.

Once every five years the Union held its breath for the few weeks the election lasted, during which each realm competed to win control of the Assembly. Control was by votes, and votes were won by the storytellers. Six realms, a teller for each – two for the Perlish duchies – sent to the capital Fenest to tell a tale and win their realm control over all the others. The Union was in the middle of an election now – another reason not to leave Fenest, and yet here she was.

'Was there anything unusual about this prisoner transport in particular?' Cora asked.

'Not that I saw. The coach arrived around ten o'clock last night and the driver asked for room and board for herself, two constables and a prisoner. She'd stopped here before and knew the routine.'

'You recognised her?'

'Yes, but I couldn't tell you her name.' The inn owner sipped his Greynal. 'I gave her the key to the barn and said the food would be brought over soon.'

'And was it?' Cora said.

'As far as I know. I told the kitchen and let them get on with it.'

'But you didn't prepare and serve the food yourself.'

Tr'stanton put down his glass with a loud clunk. 'I am the owner of this establishment, Detective. I *manage* people.'

Cora slid out from the booth. 'I'll need to talk to these *managed* people.'

Two

The plainness of the kitchen was a relief after the bright colours of the bar. Pale wooden counters hugged white sinks and black stoves, and, even though the knives and pans were gleaming, the light was more bearable. Or Cora's tiredness was starting to dull everything.

She hoped the local constables arrived soon to interview the stranded travellers. Cora had enough to do with the kitchen staff. Of the six people now in the kitchen, three had been working the previous night when the prisoner transport arrived. Those three plus Tr'stanton and the cook were the only staff still there by that time, given the lateness. Right now, the cook was on a break, which gave Cora the chance to speak to the others individually about how the food had been prepared.

'What food did you send to the barn?' Cora asked one of the kitchen workers, a skinny lad with a lisp and a weak leg.

'Soup and bread,' the lad said.

'Was it made special for them?'

'It was the same as was served to the others, them in the dining room. Same pot.'

And no one else had been affected.

'You didn't see the cook add anything special to the soup that went to the barn?' Cora asked. 'No final touches?'

The lad laughed. 'Chance'd be a fine thing. Cook don't really do *touches*.'

'What about drink?' she said, trying not to lose her patience. 'Did you take them anything from the bar?'

'They said they had their own.' The lad leaned against a counter top to ease the strain on his bad leg, which looked scrawnier than the other. 'It was only the soup and bread we gave them. Elis took it out to the barn.'

The same story was told by the second kitchen worker: the food was made in the usual way, the cook had shouted as much as she always did. Someone had dropped a tray of cakes and earned a cuff round the ear from Tr'stanton. It was like any other night. Everything matched, including that the serving boy Elis had been the one to deliver the soup. When Cora looked around the kitchen for him, he was nowhere to be seen. She didn't believe *that* was an accident.

The cook returned from her break then. Cora questioned her and found nothing in the old woman's answers that countered what her workers had said. There were no signs she'd chosen to poison the people in the barn, but Cora was certain her soup had been used to do it. That was a kind of guilt.

Tr'stanton was waiting for her in the bar, another glass of Greynal in his fretting hands. 'Well? Are you finished?'

'I need to talk to the serving boy, Elis.'

'He's in the kitchen,' Tr'stanton said, already turning away.

'No, he isn't,' Cora said firmly. 'I need you to find him for me, *now*.'

Tr'stanton pushed past her into the kitchen but was out again soon enough, calling for a search.

Cora stepped into the courtyard. The inn flanked one side, the barn the other. Next to that were the stables – plenty of them, and no surprise, given this was a coaching inn. There weren't many places for the boy to hide, if he was still close by. The road stretched into the distance on either side of the inn, open scrub land surrounding it as far as the eye could see. As the calls for Elis to show himself continued around her, Cora lit another smoke and allowed herself to imagine what Finnuc must have felt when the coach had arrived here the previous night. Had he any idea his life was in danger? When she'd last seen Finnuc, in the cell back at the station in Fenest, he'd seemed resigned to his fate. Maybe he knew what was waiting for him on the road to the Steppes, and yet he'd still chosen to tell Cora about Tennworth and confess to the murder of the Wayward storyteller anyway, risking his life. Perhaps he wasn't all bad.

Constable Jenkins was still at her post in the barn's doorway. Cora joined her there but kept her back to the bodies still lying in the straw.

'I thought it was over when we caught the Casker,' Jenkins said, sounding gloomy.

'The Audience knew better, Constable.'

'Who do you think we're looking for now, then?'

Cora rolled her shoulders: the ache of the ride from Fenest was still with her. 'I think you know the answer to that question.'

Jenkins looked away. 'Tennworth.'

'Exactly. Who is very likely a Chambers. The most powerful people in the Union. If we can find the person who did this—' Cora pointed at the barn '—we're a step closer to finding Tennworth.'

'This is hardly the kind of thing a Chambers would do themselves though,' Jenkins said, keeping her voice low.

'Of course not. We're looking for a lackey,' Cora muttered. 'Someone to do the dirty work and disappear. No loose ends.'

'The kitchen staff?'

Cora grunted. 'They weren't much help.'

She was halfway through telling Jenkins what she'd learned when a cry went up from the stables. A few seconds later the lad with the limp came out, clutching the collar of a weeping boy.

The boy Elis didn't look much like a cold-blooded killer. He was no more than ten and seemed to be crying more than he was breathing. It was a day for people running out of air. Cora feared he might join the Audience before she'd had a chance to question him, so she ordered everyone apart from Jenkins back inside the inn. That didn't mean people didn't watch from the windows though.

'Let's go over here, Elis,' Cora said, and pushed him, gently, into one of the stables, away from the view of the inn, and of the barn's doorway too. 'You, me and Constable Jenkins will have a little chat about your work last night.'

'I... I... didn't mean to. I didn't know...'

'All right, now,' Cora said gently. 'No need to fret. Sit yourself on that pail there.'

Jenkins guided Elis to sit, and then squatted in the straw

next to him. Cora stayed standing, her back to the stable door. Just in case he tried to make a run for it.

'Now,' Cora said, 'I want you to tell me what happened last night, when you took the soup to the barn, and do it nice and slow.'

The boy fumbled in the pocket of his trousers and brought out a mark. He thrust it at Jenkins. 'You can have it! I don't even want it!'

Jenkins took the offered coin and glanced at Cora. 'Is that from Mr Tr'stanton?' the constable asked the boy.

He sobbed again, wiped his hand across his nose, and shook his head. 'I heard Mr Tr'stanton say them people in the barn are dead.' He looked up at Cora, his whole body shaking. 'Is it true?'

'Let's start from the beginning, Elis, like you were telling the Affable Old Hand a story. Maybe we'll try to tell it together. Can you help me with that?'

Elis nodded.

'Good,' Cora said. 'Were you in the kitchen last night when Cook made the soup?'

Another nod.

'And did she make it like she usually does? Nothing special about it last night?'

'It was the same soup as always.'

'And then she asked you to take it to the barn?' Cora said.

'There was people staying in there. Going to the Steppes, Cook said.'

'And she was right. Did you take the soup by yourself, Elis?'

'I did, but... I couldn't carry everything in one trip so I took the bowls and spoons first, and the bread, and I gave them to the lady in the blue clothes. Clothes like yours.' He looked at Jenkins.

'What were they doing, the people in the barn?' Cora said.

'Just sitting. They had some cards. The man in the blue clothes, he was sitting with the other man, the Casker. They were far away from the door. I wanted to look at the Casker's tattoos but the driver said I had to hurry up. She was hungry. So I went back to the kitchen to get the soup. I was nearly back at the barn when he grabbed me.'

'Who was this, Elis? Who grabbed you?'

'I didn't know him, and I would have remembered him if I seen him before. He's funny-looking.'

'Funny-looking how?'

'His nose was bent.' Elis did his best to squash the end of his own nose onto his cheek and his voice shifted into nasal. 'Like this.'

'Like it had been broken?' Jenkins said. The constable had taken out her notebook and was scribbling away.

'Yes, and he weren't tall. No higher than my mum and she's only little.'

'And how old was he?' Jenkins said.

'Ummm. Old?'

'Old as the detective here?'

The boy shook his head vehemently. Cora supposed that, to a boy like Elis, forty-something was ancient.

'Your age,' he said to Jenkins, which meant close to twenty.

'And where was this man when he spoke to you?' Cora said.

Elis turned and pointed to the corner of the barn, to the right of the door. 'There. He come round the side.'

From where he'd have had a good view of the inn's main doors on the other side of the courtyard. He could have watched Elis make the first trip with the bowls, then waited until the boy came back with the soup pan.

'The woman with the flowers in her hair saw him too,' Elis said. 'She'll tell you about him. About his bent nose.'

'What woman?' Cora said, turning back to him.

'She stayed at the inn last night. When the man was talking to me she come out the doors to the barroom and she saw us. Then she went back inside. I know she saw him. You ask her.'

Jenkins was already heading for the inn.

'Tell me what happened next,' Cora said. 'The man with the broken nose said you should wait, and you did. Why?'

'He said he was meant to take the soup into the barn. He said it was his job, and he sounded like Mr Tr'stanton and like Cook.'

'What do you mean, he sounded like them? You mean the way they said their words?'

'No, like he told people what to do all the time. I asked him if Mr Tr'stanton had told *him* to take the soup and he said yes. Then he said he'd give me a mark for my trouble, and I wanted to laugh then because it *weren't* no trouble to me, was it, to give him the soup.' Elis laughed now at the memory, but not for long. He shrank against the stable wall. 'Then this morning I heard Mr Tr'stanton say the people in the barn were taken ill, badly ill. That they were… dead.'

'It's not your fault,' Cora said, but as she did so her mind was churning. The man with the broken nose – he was a new arrival in this case. Odds were he'd put something in the soup. Was this the lackey?

Jenkins returned and Cora joined her outside the stable.

'The boy's right,' Jenkins said. 'Woman in there, flowers woven into her hair. Last night she was looking for the privy and ended up in the courtyard. She says Elis *was* near the door to the barn, holding something that looked like a pan, and talking to a short figure. The woman can't speak to a broken nose, or what this man said, but she saw enough to confirm there definitely was someone else here, acting in the way Elis suggests.'

'Anyone still inside match the man's description?'

'No.'

'Thought as much. He'll be long gone. We'd better try the nearest town, wherever *that* might be.'

Cora turned to go back into the stable, but Jenkins caught her.

'That might have to wait, Detective. The stitcher's here.'

The stitcher was waiting just inside the barn. She was a woman close to Cora's age. The bag at her feet and her apron marked her role, but Cora was surprised to see the woman's shirt was plain – none of the lavish Perlish embroidery climbing the sleeves of those waiting inside the inn. Her trousers were of thick wool and her boots were sturdy. The woman's accent on greeting Cora with a curt *afternoon* confirmed it: the stitcher was a Seeder. *Lowlander*, Cora corrected herself. She'd been trying to stop using what Jenkins said was a slur to describe the people of the Lowlands. Old habits died hard, especially when southerners were concerned.

The stitcher introduced herself as Lett and held out her

hand to Cora, who was looking for farm soil on it before she realised what she was doing.

'Grim business, this,' Lett said. 'Where do you want me to start?'

'With him there, the one shackled.' As much as Cora didn't want to see Finnuc's face, he was the cause of this.

Cora told Jenkins to stay at the doorway and see they weren't disturbed.

'Can you say what killed them by looking at them here,' Cora called to the stitcher, 'or will you need to...' She had no idea what the alternative was. Back at the Bernswick station, she tried to have as little to do with the activities of Pruett, the station's stitcher, as she could.

Lett examined the bowl at Finnuc's side.

'Well?' Cora said, still keeping her distance.

'I have an idea of what it is.' Lett set the bowl back in the straw. 'The smell, the purging. Blisters on the lips will confirm it.'

'You've seen this before then?' Cora said.

'Poison's a popular way to kill in Perlanse.'

'You seem to know the place well.'

'Being a stitcher,' Lett said, rifling through her bag, 'gives you a certain kind of insight.'

'Different to stitching those from home, I guess. What brings you north to work? I can't believe the Lowlands are lucky enough to have more stitchers than they need.'

Lett's hands stilled, but she didn't look up. 'The things going on there, at home, the south... I couldn't stay.'

'What do you mean?'

The stitcher shook her head. 'I brought some constables

with me, as requested. I'll need one to help me in here, but the rest are yours.'

Cora told Jenkins to take the constables to the inn and question everyone there about the man with the broken nose.

'I want to know if anyone saw him arrive, if he went into the inn first. Anyone local, do they know him?'

Jenkins was away across the courtyard, the new constables stepping quickly into line behind her. Their jackets were the same shade of deep blue worn by the constables of Fenest. Seemed some habits of the capital were followed out here in the countryside. Jenkins' height meant she stood out in the sea of blue backs, as did the authority in her voice as she gave instructions to the Perlish constables. Jenkins would be giving Sergeant Hearst – Cora's commanding officer at Bernswick – a run for his money before too long. Short odds on *that* wager as to who'd end up in charge.

Back in the barn, Lett and one of her constables were turning Finnuc's body. The Casker was heavy and they had a job of it. Cora stepped forward to help but caught sight of Finnuc's face and had to turn away again. She concentrated on the sounds: Lett and the constable's heavy breath, the clank of the shackles as Finnuc's feet dragged along the floor, the crackle of the straw as his broad back was levered clear. A grunt of effort told Cora the job was done.

'Well?' Cora said, still looking away.

'It's Heartsbane, as I thought,' Lett said. 'The smell and the purging suggested it. With these blisters on the lips, you can't mistake—'

'Stitcher?' It was the constable. 'There's something tucked in his collar. Here.'

Cora turned. The constable was kneeling in the straw, Finnuc face up and lying in the man's arms as if he'd just been dragged from a river or some burning building. But too late, because his face—

The features she had known, now swollen and split. His lips bubbled with blisters. His poor, poor eyes.

Lett was fiddling with Finnuc's chest, her back to Cora. When she turned round she was holding something in her hand. No, two things.

'I can't think why these are here. There aren't any chickens.'

'Chickens?'

Two feathers.

One black, and one white.

Three

Lett wanted to fully examine the faces of the other bodies. Cora left her and the constable to it and went out to the courtyard. She leaned against the coach that had brought Finnuc here, and studied the feathers. One black. One white. The same colours as the stones used to vote in elections, when each realm sent their storyteller to Fenest and the capital's voters cast their judgement on the tales. When control of the Assembly was won or lost, depending on the number of stones won. Black for yes, white for no.

Cora stuffed the feathers into her coat pocket. It was no accident that these two colours had been left like this on Finnuc's body. The laces used to stitch the murdered Wayward storyteller's lips together, that *Finnuc* had used, had been black and white. That act was a message that the Wayward election story should be silenced, and surely this was the same: Finnuc was the one now robbed of his story. A loose end, tied up, marked with the colours of the election.

Stitcher Lett left the barn and joined Cora by the coach.

'I've seen all I need to. Heartsbane killed the four of them, administered in the soup.'

Cora had never heard of it. 'This is when you tell me it's hard to come by,' she said. 'I could do with a lead.'

'Sorry to disappoint you, Detective. Heartsbane is one of the most common poisons in Perlanse – both duchies. Well, not common as a poison. As a tool.'

'A tool?'

'All kinds of uses for Heartsbane,' the stitcher said. 'It thins liquids.'

'People's insides too, by the look of it,' Cora muttered.

'Dyers use it,' Lett said, 'and those in the laundries. Ink-makers too.'

'Ink is poisonous?'

'In Perlanse it can be,' Lett said. 'Only the finest *Perlish* ink, of course.'

They shared a smile.

'If you're looking to kill someone quickly and quietly then Heartsbane is a good choice,' Lett said. 'Odourless until the purging starts.'

'By which time it's too late to do anything about it.' Cora spat. 'The poison used to kill my prisoner, his driver and two constables is easy to come by and could be in half the houses in East Perlanse. That's what you're telling me.'

'I am, Detective.'

'No Latecomer's luck for me.'

'What had he done, the Casker?'

Would the stitcher believe Cora if she told her? An unforgiveable crime that Cora herself was still trying to understand.

'You read the pennysheets?' Cora said.

'When I can. *The Fenestiran Times* usually.'

'Then you already know.'

Lett's eyes widened. 'That's him? The man who killed a storyteller?'

Cora's silence was enough.

'He deserved to die,' Lett said.

'*Someone* clearly thought so.' Cora stared hard at Lett, who seemed to remember that she was talking to the detective trying to find the killer.

'What do you want done with the bodies?' the stitcher said quickly.

'The driver and the constables need to be taken back to Fenest. Far as I know, they're all from the capital, their families there. Wrap them and put them on a cart to Bernswick. Commission will pay for it. I'm sure there's a form, and Perlish ink to write it.'

'And the Casker?'

Cora fumbled with her cuff. 'Do whatever you do to dead prisoners in Perlanse.'

Lett was about to tell Cora what that fate was when the doors to the inn opened. Jenkins crossed the courtyard, her constable companions in tow. Lett told the local officers to help her in the barn. None looked pleased, and Cora didn't blame them.

'Well?' she asked Jenkins.

'No one knows anything about a broken nose. No one saw him arrive or leave. No one saw him at all apart from the woman with the flowers.'

'Any locals in there?' Cora said, nodding towards the inn's brightly panelled doors.

'One or two. They didn't recognise the description.'

'Which leaves us without a lead on him.'

''Fraid so, Detective,' Jenkins said, her voice heavy.

Cora smoked while she thought. The man with the broken nose had known where to find Finnuc, and found a way to murder him quickly, with an inn full of people only a courtyard away. But that man could be anywhere by now. Better to go back to Fenest and investigate from there: that was where this case began, and where it would surely end. If Tennworth truly was a Chambers, as Finnuc had suggested, then she would be in Fenest for the election.

'It's time we went home, Jenkins. We've more than enough waiting for us there.'

Including having to face Chief Inspector Sillian with the news that the person arrested for the murder of a storyteller was now dead himself.

They were untying their horses when they heard a shout from the barn, then Lett was in the doorway waving to them.

'Detective – wait!'

Cora and Jenkins hurried over.

'There's another one,' Lett said, 'hidden at the back. A constable saw it when he was moving your lot.'

'Another feather?' Cora said.

'Another body.'

The constables were huddled at the far end of the barn, their backs to Cora.

'Move!' she shouted.

The row of blue jackets scattered to reveal a deep drift of straw topped by a wooden pallet. A hand was just visible, clutching the pallet's edge. A hand raw with blisters. And the face, when the constables lifted the pallet and pushed back the straw, was as Cora suspected it would be: his nose was lumpen, squashed sideways into his cheek, just as the serving boy Elis had described. Cora ordered the Perlish constables to wait outside.

The man bore the same signs of forceful purging as the other victims, but worse, if that were possible. His skin was purple and hard as stone when Cora touched it. One of his eyes had left its socket and lay, deflated, on his cheek.

'This one yours too?' Lett the stitcher said.

'He is now,' Cora said.

'Why does he look in a worse state than the others?' Jenkins asked.

Lett held a cloth to her mouth and nose and leaned close to the man to look him over. 'Drank the Heartsbane neat, I'd guess. No sign of the soup near him, not like the others. Ah – there it is. His hand must have locked round it.'

She used the cloth to ease something from the dead man's hand, then turned to Cora with it. A small dark bottle. More of a vial. Cora made to take it, but Lett moved it out of her reach.

'I'd keep away from this, Detective. Not unless you want your flesh to end up like his.'

'He did this to himself?' Cora said.

'I'd say so. From the looks of it, he lay down in the straw, pulled the pallet over him, and drank. There's the "how". The "why" I leave to people like yourselves, Detective.'

'I've got a start on that,' Cora said. 'Give us a minute, Stitcher?' When Lett had gone, Cora turned to Jenkins and spoke quickly. 'My guess is this man was told to end his own life once he'd carried out the killings. Finnuc was a loose end. Once he'd been taken care of, there couldn't be any more.'

'*Told* to do it?' Jenkins said, in all but a whisper.

'Tennworth has a habit of getting people to commit horrific acts on her behalf. She had Finnuc Dawson kill the Wayward storyteller *and* mutilate his body. Help me check the pockets, but don't touch any of his skin. If the poison's still on him, you'll know about it.'

Carefully, they went through his clothes. The dead man wore narrow-legged trousers, the kind Cora had noticed on the men and women in the inn and which weren't cut with pockets. His jacket had two, and his shirt one, but none of them held anything – no papers, no keys. Not even a handkerchief.

'Nothing to identify him,' Cora said, moving away from the body. 'I suspect that was part of the instructions.'

'How can Tennworth make people do these things?' Jenkins said. 'It can't just be because she's a Chambers. That doesn't mean she can force people to kill themselves!'

'Which means that her power over this man had to be something specific,' Cora said, 'something personal. Debts. Family. It's leverage that makes a person do this to themselves. Leverage we're unlikely to learn now.'

'But why has he done this here?' Jenkins said. 'So close to his crime?'

'No one to meet him coming home smelling of something strange, to wonder at his absence. To ask questions.'

'We're asking questions though, aren't we?' Jenkins said.

'If I'm right and Tennworth told this man to kill Finnuc and the others, then to kill himself, Tennworth *wants* us to ask those questions. Finnuc's death, the feathers – it's another message. We've got to get back to Fenest.'

Four

As they rode away, Cora felt the pain in her foot return. In the last few weeks it had been getting worse, though the Zealous Stitcher knew there was little sense in that, given that she'd had the injury since she was a child. Surely the pain should *lessen* over time? The pain had returned because she'd seen Ruth.

Her sister was the reason glass got into her foot in the first place, all those years ago, on the night Ruth had left their home, and left the city. Where she'd gone, Cora had never learned. Her sister vanished. Until now, because Ruth was back in Fenest. Wasn't she? Cora had had a glimpse of a woman who may or may not have been Ruth, but she hadn't had time for such thinking: there was too much going on. Just as she'd solved one murder by arresting Finnuc, more bodies had arrived. The Audience loved stories with patterns. Cora tried to ignore the pain throbbing in her foot.

Jenkins, too, looked uncomfortable, but that was more to do with the aches of the journey to Perlanse. The constable was perched awkwardly, gripping her saddle's front bit – Cora had never learned the names of horse gear, never had need to. Jenkins' knees were locked, her toes pointed down, and her face was grey.

'Neither of us would make a convincing Wayward,' Cora said, thinking of the realm defined by their wandering, their moving of horses across great tracts of land.

Jenkins could only nod in agreement. It had become clear as soon as they'd left Bernswick station that the constable hadn't had much to do with horses in all her young years in Fenest, other than catching gigs. Cora wasn't much more experienced as a rider, but compared to Jenkins, she was doing well.

It had been Sergeant Hearst's idea to ride to the inn. Quicker, he'd said. That might have been true, but how long would it take Cora and Jenkins to stand straight again? There wouldn't be much time to rest when they got back to Fenest. The election was well underway and there was no stopping it. Two stories told – those of the Caskers and the Seeders – and four more to go, including that of the Wayward whose storyteller Finnuc had killed. The pennysheets had been rife with speculation about the replacement storyteller following Nicholas Ento's murder, but there'd been no official announcement yet from the Commission. Perhaps by the time she and Jenkins got back to the station that news would be shouted from street corners. If it wasn't, Cora knew a certain pennysheet seller who would keep her up to date with developments.

The road was a busy one, being the main route to and from Fenest, and the traffic was mostly going one way. Riders on horseback like themselves, carts and wagons, plenty of coaches, all heading to the capital of the Union.

'The spoked wheel turns and draws us all,' Cora found

herself saying. 'Would you do the same, Jenkins, if you lived here, in the glorious Duchy of East Perlanse?'

'Do what, Detective?'

'Go to the capital for the election. Because that's what they're doing, mark my words, even if they haven't a hope of hearing the stories. Every election there's more people who want to listen.'

Jenkins yawned, her large teeth seeming to grow even larger in her mouth. Cora rubbed her eyes. She must be more tired than she'd realised.

'Never had to think about it,' Jenkins said, and shrugged. 'My mother's job meant I always got to listen to election stories.'

'President of Election Offices, wasn't it?'

'Director of Electoral Affairs.'

'How could I forget that most *important* of Commission departments?' But Cora's mocking tone seemed to pass Jenkins by.

'My mother took me to every election until she retired because she knew it was important to hear the stories, to understand what it might mean for each realm to win. Just like all these people do.' The constable gestured towards the line of slow-moving carts in front of them.

'There's one story that someone doesn't want told,' Cora said. She tried to take her bindleleaf tin from her coat pocket but it was too difficult to manage with the reins. Her old horse looked docile enough but who was to say the animal wouldn't take off if it had a mind to? A smoke would have to wait. She tried to push the tin further into the pocket of her coat, but the pocket was too shallow.

This coat was new, or new to her, at least. Her old one

had seen her through many a case: long, red and carrying the grime of Fenest in its seams, with pockets deep enough for plenty of rolled smokes, betting slips, and pennies for the 'sheet sellers. She missed it, but after coming too close to plague victims at Burlington Palace, the old coat had to go. Her new one was shorter, the hem against her hips, and cut of deep black cloth. A whore had taken pity on Cora when, waking together one morning, they found the spring air had turned cold again, just as it was meant to start warming up. He made Cora take his coat, telling her he had plenty. A tailor came regularly to his bed and liked to dress him. The lad had more clothes stuffed under the bed than Cora had owned in all her forty-something years.

'I'm sorry, detective,' Jenkins said.

Cora looked over. 'For what?'

'That the Casker... that he's dead.'

Was Jenkins sorry for the case, or for Cora? After all, the constable had stood guard outside Finnuc's cell while Cora questioned him, back at Bernswick. How much had Jenkins overheard of the more 'personal' nature of Cora and Finnuc's relationship? The fact they'd spent more than a few afternoons together, talking about the election, talking about their lives? That they'd ripped each other's clothes off when alone on the Hook barge? Cora decided to ignore the possibility Jenkins knew about any of that. No need to encourage that kind of talk.

'A dead end is a dead end,' she said, urging her horse into a trot. 'Let's get ahead of these bumpkins.'

By the time they'd cleared the run of carts and Jenkins had recovered from the jerks of the faster pace, Cora had recovered her own sense of balance. And she'd also decided something else: she wouldn't tell Jenkins about Ruth. What was the need, when her sister's return was so unlikely? Cora had been mistaken in the winery carriageway; Ruth couldn't have been the woman with Finnuc. At the time Cora had thought she'd finally put all the pieces together. Well, some of the pieces. Enough, at any rate, to arrest Finnuc and learn the reason behind the killing of the Wayward storyteller, Nicholas Ento: that the south was falling apart. That the Wayward story Tennworth was trying to supress was one of change.

Change that some people didn't want heard.

The road climbed once more and their horses slowed. Cora couldn't blame them. They'd travelled many miles since leaving Fenest. She'd not spent much time in Perlanse before now – just the occasional visit to make enquiries in a case. She hadn't seen much of the Union beyond Fenest, truth be told. But all the realms came to the capital so was there any need to go out and find them?

She had to admit, the countryside of East Perlanse wasn't such a bad place to visit. Their journey to the inn had been in darkness as they rode through the night, but now, in the late afternoon spring sunshine, the woodlands and the bright rivers, the humped bridges and fancy market towns had a kind of charm. What would it mean to stop here, to not go back? To ignore the hunt for Tennworth, who was likely a Chambers?

The road rose and sloped and rose again – she lost count of the number of hills. They stopped once, for Cora to smoke and Jenkins to dismount and get the blood moving in her feet. The final climb gave a welcome sight from the top of the hill.

'Ah – there it is,' Cora said. 'Still standing, then.'

Far below them, Fenest sprawled across the plains. Cora pulled her horse to a halt and Jenkins followed suit.

'Don't get much chance to see it from a distance,' Cora said.

'It looks... bigger, somehow.'

'Because you're not jammed in some alleyway with a cutpurse at your throat,' Cora said. 'That can feel *very* cramped.'

Jenkins laughed. 'It's not all like that, Detective.'

'My part is.'

But that hadn't always been her part of the city, Cora thought. She shook that idea away, not wanting to think about the past, about her parents. About Ruth. That was over and done with a long time ago, and good riddance. She made herself look at the city, her city, in all its messy glory.

In the Casker election story, the main character, the Sanga, had described Fenest as a bloodstain, first time he saw it. That was seeing it from the River Cask though. From here, on a hill in Perlanse, Cora thought the city was like a giant spider, with more legs than was usual. Each leg a street, and from each of *them* sprouted alleys, cut-throughs, crooked lanes. The whole place crammed with people, the wealthy and the poor, the innocent and the whores, the chequers and their customers, the pennysheet sellers and their readers. The spider that was Fenest twitched with life.

And at the centre were the spider's twin beating hearts: the Wheelhouse, where the Commission was based, and the Assembly building, where the Chambers sat. Both were so huge that she could see them from here. The Wheelhouse was anything but round – a squat, square sandstone building covered in tiny windows. Close by, the Assembly building was easy to spot. Its glass dome caught the early evening sun.

'You all right, Detective?' Jenkins was frowning at her.

'Once we get back there, we'll be investigating the Chambers – the most powerful people in the Union. It's going to be... difficult. Dangerous.'

'I didn't join the police because it was easy,' Jenkins said. 'I'm sure you didn't either.'

'True. We'd better get moving then, hadn't we, Constable?'

Cora gave her horse a gentle nudge and headed down the hill. They were still hours away, but now that home was in sight, she knew she'd keep riding towards it. And towards the case.

It was late by the time they returned the horses to the coaching inn on the outskirts of the city. Jenkins was all for going to the station and starting work straight away, but Cora told her to get some rest. The constable made some half-hearted noises of protest, but she was too tired to really fight Cora's order.

'Tomorrow, the real work begins,' Cora said. 'We need to work out who Tennworth is.'

Jenkins took her leave and headed into the maze of streets to wherever it was she lived. Cora realised she didn't know. Likely for the best.

Cora was never one to follow her own advice: a catch-up with Sergeant Hearst would be helpful. Might as well confirm, sooner rather than later, the suspicions both had shared when news had come that the prisoner transport was in trouble.

The steps of Bernswick station were quiet, the lamps at the main doors lit to ward off the dusk. She'd be glad for their warmth inside, too; the spring evenings still had a bite and the station was known for its draughts as well as its many leaks. The Perlish-controlled Assembly hadn't spent anything to improve things for the police in the last five years. Would this election make any difference? Cora pulled the whore's coat tighter and headed inside.

The desk sergeant, Lester, barely looked up from his pennysheet. He was around her age and had been there for as long as she could remember.

'What tales has *The Spoke* for us?' Cora asked.

'That the world isn't ending quite yet.' Lester scratched his days-old stubble with a loud rasp.

'Black Jefferey had its fill, has it?'

'Seems so. Commission are keeping Burlington Palace as a hospital for the time being, but they've re-opened the roads around it.' Lester shook his head. 'What the Commission *should* be doing is keeping people out of the city.'

'Hard to do that in an election year,' Cora said.

'Hard to do it any time, the way people are coming up from the south these days. Why they can't just stay in their own homes, I don't know.'

He wasn't saying anything she hadn't heard before. A few of the pennysheet titles took the same view and spouted their anti-southern talk often enough, so people spread the same story. More regularly since Black Jefferey had arrived in Fenest. A plague carried by an election story, some said. By a southern Casker story.

'People wouldn't be coming to Fenest unless they had to,' Cora told Lester.

But Lester wasn't listening, his gaze firmly on the pennysheet. 'Some funny business with the Caskers, they're saying here.'

'At Burlington?' Cora had seen plenty of bargemen and women when she'd gone to see the trouble at the make-shift plague hospital.

'No, at Bordair,' Lester said, and peered closer at the 'sheet as if to make more sense of the story, as if *that* was likely with *The Spoke*. 'Saying they're drowning themselves.'

Bordair was the inland lake the Caskers called home, the place they sailed back to when they weren't travelling up and down the rivers of the Union.

'Says they're strapping stones to themselves before they jump into the water.' Lester shook his head. 'It's all rubbish. I don't know why I bother reading it.'

'That the latest edition?'

The desk sergeant nodded.

So news of Finnuc's death hadn't reached the city yet. That would be Cora's story to share.

'The girl dropped it off,' Lester said. 'The one with the loud voice, and the funny name.'

'Marcus.'

'That's it! Said she'd be telling the Bailiff about me if I didn't pay her quicker for the 'sheets. Where did you find *that* one, Detective?'

'You don't want to know.'

She made for the briefing room: the heart of the station, not least because that was where the coffee was. It was also where the constables spent their days, when they weren't out in the streets. Spent their night shifts, too, bedding down in the corners, and ate their breakfast there when Sergeant

Hearst roused them in the morning. The long room was all but empty now. A few constables were playing cards at the back, and she fought the urge to join them. Another was lying on a bench, her blue jacket rolled as a pillow and her snores breaking into the low chat of the card game. The election meant that most constables were doing double shifts, dealing with the inevitable rise in cutpurse attacks as well as managing the election story sites. She'd be pleased when it was all over.

Cora had barely lifted the still-warm coffee pot when Hearst found her.

'You didn't hang around to enjoy the charms of the Eastern Duchy of Perlanse, Gorderheim?' he said.

'Not much time, not many charms.'

'Ah.'

Her commanding officer was a foot shorter than her and slighter in build, but he made up for that with a presence. The constables jumped to attention as soon as he stepped into the briefing room. Unlike Cora, who wore plain clothes, Sergeant Hearst worked in uniform. But, just like Cora, his jacket was usually in need of a wash, not least because of the time he spent looking after the birds who lived on the station roof.

'How bad?' Hearst said.

'All four dead. Poisoned.'

Hearst rubbed his mouth with the back of his hand. 'You'd better pour me a cup.'

'You look like you need something stronger, sir.'

'So do you, Gorderheim. And you might be tempted to start proper drinking once the chief inspector hears the news.'

Cora swirled the coffee in her mug. 'She's here?'

'No, she's been tied up at the Assembly lately.'

'Guess I have *that* conversation to look forward to, then.'

Hearst smiled grimly. 'And in the meantime, we start looking for Tennworth.'

The trip to Perlanse had kept her awake far too long. Now the walls of the station were turning hazy. She needed some fresh air if she was going to achieve anything else that night.

She stopped on the station's steps to roll a smoke, then leaned against the wall to ease the pain in her foot, which was throbbing again. She'd ask Pruett, the station's stitcher, to have a look at it. The glass inside might be moving. She'd been told that might happen, back when her foot was first stitched, the night Ruth left. The stitcher who'd come to the house had done his best to pick the glass from Cora's bloodied foot after she'd stood on the broken pane of her parents' cabinet. Broken by Ruth stealing trading papers. Stitcher said if there was any glass left inside Cora's foot then it could take a fancy for shifting, try to get out. It might take years, but there was a chance. Cora had been in too much pain to understand what he was saying at the time. She'd been frightened by the blood too, and by Ruth's words before she slipped out of the window into the night: *the whole place is rotten, right through the middle.*

Now, outside Bernswick police station, after too many hours in the saddle and a daunting task ahead of her – was a Chambers truly involved in multiple murders? – she understood: nothing ever truly healed.

She took a drag on the bindleleaf. The street was busy. All the streets of Fenest were busy, until the election was over. She watched some harried-looking Fenestirans try to find their way through groups of Perlish who sauntered in their feathered finery, enjoying being looked at, thin blue smoke rising from their fancy cigarettes in fancier long-stemmed holders. Two Wayward rode on horseback, their many-pocketed cloaks pulled tight to their chins to keep out the evening's chill. Just behind them, a woman in a dark dress had to dodge a pennysheet seller waving copies of the latest edition. Cora caught the seller's voice – too high to be that of Marcus, her gruff informant, but just as determined to sell her 'sheets.

The pennysheet girl shoved one of the Perlish dandies into their companion and there was cursing, shouts of revenge loud enough to interest the Weaver. One of the Wayward horses started dancing about and the woman in the dark dress looked to be caught in the middle of it all. Cora was just about ready to go back inside the station when the woman in the dark dress came clear again. She turned, looked over to the station, and her gaze found Cora.

It was Ruth.

Five

There was pain in Cora's fingers and she shook her hand to be rid of it. Her forgotten bindleleaf had burned down and singed her. When she looked back at the crowd, the woman in the dark dress had gone.

Cora was tired, that was what it was. Hadn't slept right in days. No wonder she was seeing things. The woman could have been anyone, but she couldn't have been Ruth.

Cora had told herself the same thing after she'd arrested Finnuc at Tennworth's winery. The woman who'd been there with him and who had escaped in the old Commission coach had looked like her older sister. Or how Cora imagined her to look after all these years, when she'd allowed herself to think about Ruth. But since that glimpse in the winery, Cora had talked herself out it. Ruth wasn't back in Fenest. Ruth was anywhere else. With the Audience, even. Did Cora care? Ruth had ruined everything when she stole their parents' papers and gave the pennysheets the story of the Gorderheims embezzling Commission funds. Ruth had never even bothered to come back and witness the damage.

These thoughts were no help for anything. Cora went

back inside. Maybe she'd get some work done, or maybe she'd bed down on an empty bench in the briefing room.

Bellowing in the corridor woke her the next morning.

'One day until the Perlish story! Will it be tragedy? Will it be the funny the city needs? Find out in the first edition!'

'You can save that roar for the street,' Cora shouted back.

'Morning, Detective,' said a gruff figure, now looking down at Cora. 'Rough night? Them fights at the Dancing Oak get the better of you again?'

Cora winced at the noise. Surely the girl was louder today than usual? Marcus: named on Drunkard's Day and loud as the Brawler. A mean combination in the cut-throat world of pennysheet selling, and handy for other things too.

'Bring the 'sheets into my office. I wanted a word with you anyway.'

A constable grinned at Marcus as they passed, and Marcus glowered back, stomping along in her worn boots, her bare toes poking out the end of one.

'You'll like these numbers, Detective,' the girl said. 'Eight to one on the Perlish story. *The Daily Tales* says it's gonna be *racy*.'

'Do you even know what that word means, Marcus?'

'I know it don't mean people dying, like in them other two stories.'

'That would be something. Put the 'sheets on the floor,' Cora said, once they were inside her office. She leaned against her desk. 'Have you heard any talk about the new Wayward storyteller? Ento's replacement?'

'Not much, and I been listening. Really listening, Detective. You buying so many 'sheets off me.'

The girl looked around Cora's filthy office, the few sticks of furniture covered with old pennysheets, pastry wrappers, and over-flowing ashtrays, in something like wonder: a bad sign. Cora would have to get one of the constables in. The office had reached its annual crisis point.

'But there's been something?' she asked Marcus.

'Only the last few days. Girl I know, sleeps at Beulah's place like me – her cousin works the presses at *The Spoke*. Knows a hack there called Butterman. Do you know him, Detective?'

'Sadly, yes.'

'Well,' Marcus rocked backwards on her tattered boot heels, 'this cousin was at the 'sheet offices when Butterman comes in all excited. The cousin overheard him telling another hack that the new Wayward 'teller is from outside their realm.'

Cora started. 'What? Where are they from?'

'Dunno. Married in, Butterman said.'

'That's...' What? Unlikely? Illegal? She'd have to ask Jenkins. The constable was a fount of knowledge about elections. 'How did Butterman hear about this?' Cora said.

'Couldn't you ask him that, you being police?'

'You'd think so, wouldn't you? Hacks don't reveal their sources. Not willingly. Tell me what you know about it.'

'One of the sellers told me there was a note slipped under Butterman's door. No name on it, just the stuff about the new storyteller. But someone else said Butterman had some meeting at the Assembly building last week and that's when he was told.'

'Meeting the Wayward Chambers?' Cora said.

Marcus shrugged. 'Butterman goes there all the time for his stories. Likes the lunch they give him.'

'Because it's free,' Cora muttered. The story wasn't in the 'sheets yet. Someone was keeping this tale away.

'Well,' she said to Marcus, 'keep your ears open.'

'For you, Detective, they're never closed.'

'As long as I'm paying you.'

'Girl's gotta eat, ain't she?' Marcus grinned.

'And walk the streets.' Cora fished in her pocket and found a few pennies, which she tossed to Marcus. 'For your boots. You won't be much good to me if you can't keep up.'

In a blink, the coins had disappeared inside Marcus' frayed and grubby sleeve. 'Don't worry. I won't tell Beulah you've got some pennies left to pay your debts at the Dancing Oak.' She turned to go but collided with Constable Jenkins in the doorway. 'Partner take you!' Marcus shouted.

Jenkins raised her palms, as if facing a Seeder bandit wielding a knife.

'At ease, Constable,' Cora said. 'Marcus here was just leaving. Weren't you, Marcus?'

Marcus looked Jenkins up and down, then gave a loud sniff. 'No wonder you're needing help, Detective.' She headed down the corridor, no doubt ready to shout at Lester on the front desk.

'I *need* breakfast,' Cora said.

Jenkins produced a bag and the stale office was filled with the warm, buttery smell of pastries. 'Sergeant Hearst sent me out for them.'

'Hope you filled in the proper ledger for that purchase, Constable Jenkins,' Cora said lightly, and raised her eyebrows. 'Commission does insist on accuracy in *all* transactions, *all* of the time.'

Jenkins' face paled. 'I thought I did, but if you'd like to check, Detective, I can get—'

'Jenkins, it was a joke. So, Hearst sent you for breakfast, but he isn't here to eat it.'

'He said to tell you he's on his way.'

'Pigeons eating first again, are they?' Cora said. 'Coffee, then, while we wait for the sergeant to finish stuffing those flying rats with seed.'

The briefing room was busy, with the night shift bedding down and the morning constables getting ready to go out. Jenkins started talking to one of them, murmured names that meant nothing to Cora but she did hear 'Perlanse'. The other constable looked away, his eyes wet. Jenkins clasped his shoulder. This was someone who was close to the officers who'd been poisoned along with Finnuc. And what did Cora have to show for the constables' deaths?

She stepped away to let the constables talk. Last night's edition of *The Daily Tales* was on the table by the coffee pot. The print was heavily marked by mug rings but she could just make out a story that claimed a Casker had robbed a Seeder farm, killing the residents in the process. She picked up the sheet, but the paper fell apart in a wet mess of coffee. It wasn't worth reading anyway. There was more truth in a Perlish tax form than there was in *The Daily Tales*' coverage of life in the south of the Union.

Sergeant Hearst appeared then, and Cora called Jenkins. The three of them went into her office and she closed the door.

'So,' Cora said, looking at each of them in turn. 'We need to find out who Tennworth is. Let's recap what we know so far.'

Hearst cleared a corner of Cora's desk to perch on. 'Point one, Tennworth is the name Finnuc Dawson used for the woman who'd rescued him as a child.'

'And point two,' Cora said, 'Finnuc all but admitted to me that Tennworth was the person who told him to murder the Wayward storyteller.'

Jenkins took a pastry from the bag. 'Point three, Tennworth is a woman.'

'How sure are we about that point?' Hearst said.

'In all Finnuc's stories she was a woman,' Cora said. 'That was one of the few things that stayed the same: Captain Tennworth was a woman who helped him. When I arrested him in the winery, he stuck to that.'

'So that's point four,' Jenkins said, 'that Tennworth owns, or is at least associated with, a winery here in Fenest.'

'Yes, but point five is that Tennworth isn't her real name,' Cora said, and took her own pastry from the bag.

'Well that's wonderful,' Hearst said. 'We don't even know if it's her real name?'

'It might be one of her names, sir,' Cora said. 'I don't know. But we've got to start there. And we have to acknowledge point six: the fact Tennworth might be a Chambers.'

Jenkins seemed to shiver at this. Cora couldn't blame her.

'Though it pains me to have to say this out loud,' Hearst said, and glanced at the door to Cora's office as if to check it was still closed, 'where does the Chambers angle come in?'

'Well, Chief Inspector Sillian told me it was only the Chambers who knew the identity of the other realms' storytellers before the election,' Cora said. 'Therefore, logically it had to be a Chambers who ordered Finnuc to kill the Wayward storyteller, Nicholas Ento. I believe the same Chambers then ordered the killing of Finnuc in Perlanse.' She chewed on her pastry and let her words sink in.

After a while, Hearst cleared his throat. 'Right. If we go

down this road then we need to think about it practically. The current Chambers, three of them are women: those of the Caskers, Rustans, and Seeders.'

'None of whom are called Tennworth,' Jenkins said. 'So it's almost certainly not her real name.'

'And there's no record of her, or her winery, anywhere in the Wheelhouse records,' Hearst said. 'That in itself is odd. That the Commission should have no knowledge of her? How much can we trust that what this Casker Dawson told you is true?'

'I trust him on this,' Cora said quietly.

'Maybe the Casker angle is a good place to start,' Jenkins said, 'with the Chambers, I mean. Dawson was a Casker. He called Tennworth "Captain". People in charge of barges are called "Captain".'

'Seems as good a lead as any,' Cora said. 'What's the name of the Casker Chambers?'

'Kranna,' Jenkins said, without missing a beat.

'With the Perlish story tomorrow, we've got time,' Cora said, dusting the pastry crumbs from her hands.

'Time for what?' Hearst asked.

'To go to the Hook barge,' Cora said. 'Come on, Constable. I know how much you like seeing the Hooks.'

'I do, but... How does the *Perlish* Hook help us investigate Casker Chambers Kranna?'

Cora was halfway out the door. 'It's not the Hook we need to see. It's the Casker bargehands who manage the site. Finnuc Dawson's old friends.'

'And how do *you* know Dawson's friends, Detective?' Hearst said, but Cora was far enough into the corridor that she could pretend she hadn't heard him.

Six

The approach to the Hook barge was as busy as ever, the crowds keen to see the teaser of the Perlish story. Cora had to remind herself that the majority of people in Fenest – whether they lived here or not – saw the election as an exciting spectacle. It wasn't dangerous for *them*. They didn't risk *their* lives because of it. Cora stared grimly at all the happy, laughing faces around her. There were so many of them, bustling about the food stalls, browsing the hawkers' wares, and taking slips from the many chequers. Eight to one on the Perlish, and a lot of people liked them for this year, despite their term of penny-pinching in the Assembly. But then, elections were all about the stories each realm told on the day, when storytellers eclipsed all other goings-on in the Union. And the next tale, due to be told by the Perlish storyteller tomorrow? 'Racy,' Marcus had said. That should make for an interesting Hook at least, or so Cora thought. She hoped the Casker bargehands, too, might have something interesting for her.

But she had to get to them first.

Cora and Jenkins pushed through the knots of people until they got caught in what was clearly a queue: nothing else made people face the same direction as one another. Blue-jacketed constables stood at regular intervals along the queue, far more than had been posted at the barge for the first two Hooks. But it wasn't just the constables, with their gazes constantly moving amongst the crowd – there were more purple tunics around the barge than Cora had seen before, more than at a story venue even. Those tunics spent most of their time bellowing orders and looking busy, but doing what, Cora couldn't fathom. Purple was the colour worn by most Commission employees. For those involved in the election, their uniform was a long tunic of deep colour that made a flapping sound as they bustled by.

Cora could see over the heads of those in front of her, and the gangway that led onto the barge beyond. Lounging to one side of it were three heavily tattooed, burly figures. A man and two women.

'There's our bargehands,' she said to Jenkins.

'Do you recognise them?'

'Only the bloke.' Cora craned her head to see the rest of the barge but couldn't spot any more bargehands. 'There were more of them here before.'

'Looks like the Commission wanted to take over security,' Jenkins said. 'All these tunics, the constables too.'

'So someone wants the Perlish Hook to be a nice, ordered affair.'

'Don't we all?' Jenkins said, and she *meant* it. Unlike Cora, she wouldn't stoop so low as sarcasm.

'Come on, Constable. Clear the way.'

Jenkins took a deep breath. 'Bernswick Division, stand aside!' she shouted, and with her lean yet powerful arms, pushed a path towards the barge.

At the muttered oaths and hisses about queue-jumpers, Cora brandished her badge, and after only a few elbows in the ribs, they were at the gangway. A purple tunic strode over, scowling, but before the Commission man could open his mouth, Cora spoke loudly.

'All right, friend. Just needing a word with these fine people from the south.'

'The bargehands? But—'

'Official investigation business,' she said, 'Can't be more specific. Sure you understand?'

A shout from the gangway took the tunic's attention – a boy had slipped and nearly gone in the river.

'Best leave me to it, hadn't you?' Cora said. 'You too, Jenkins.'

'Fine, but be quick about it – you're obstructing the queue,' the tunic said, before hurrying away.

The female bargehands had barely looked up from their conversation at Cora's approach. But the man eyed Cora shrewdly, and in silence. She held up her badge.

'I'm here about Finnuc Dawson,' she said.

'Who?' one of the women said.

'You didn't know him?'

'Never heard of him,' the woman said, her friend shaking her head beside her.

'Think yourself lucky,' muttered the man. 'What he did to that storyteller…'

The bargehand had an inked spiral on his cheek which spun its way down his neck and arm. He wasn't as tall as Finnuc had been. Cora remembered him from when she'd come to the barge to see the Seeder Hook – the mostins – and this Casker had given her and Finnuc blindfolds to protect against the eye-watering fint. Finnuc had loomed over this bargehand.

'Give us a minute,' Cora said to the women. Without a word, they crossed the gangway onto the barge, scattering the crowd in their wake. 'Any more of Finnuc's friends here?' Cora asked the man.

'You won't find many in this city now who'll admit to that.'

'Those who knew him then. They here?'

The Casker shook his head and the spiral tattoo seemed to dance. 'Commission laid most of us off. All my old crew gone. I've not been paid for the last week. She says I won't be out of pocket, but I'd be telling stories to the Drunkard if I believed that.'

'She?'

'Our Chambers, Kranna.' The Casker spat, to cries of disgust from those in the queue nearby. 'She don't care about people like me. Didn't fight the Perlish Assembly to keep us working, did she?'

'Did Finnuc ever talk about her?' Cora said, trying to keep her voice even.

'Only to complain about wages. About her not sticking up for her own people. He was right about that.'

'Did you ever see him with Kranna?'

'With *Chambers* Kranna?' The Casker looked at Cora as if she'd hit her head on the way to the gangway. 'Finnuc was a coach driver! And before you ask, he didn't drive for the Assembly. Who'd want that job, having to work with *her* and her people? They got their priorities all wrong, what they're doing...'

'What do you mean?'

He glanced around. 'Why you asking about Kranna anyway?'

From the anxious look on his face, Cora decided no answer would be more useful than a lie. She looked back at Jenkins, and then waited.

'Do you know something about—' The bargehand shook his head. 'I shouldn't have said anything. Not about the Chambers. I got work to do, Detective.'

He turned to go but she grabbed his arm. His skin was hot, almost as if the ink were burning on his flesh.

'What about someone called Tennworth?' Cora said. 'Did Finnuc ever mention that name to you?'

The Casker shook his head. 'Finnuc – he wasn't much of a talker, was he? Didn't say much about himself.'

He did to me, Cora thought, surprised at how pleased she was by this. Unless it had all been lies.

'Finnuc kept himself to himself,' the Casker said. 'And now we know why, don't we? The things he did. Can't be right in the head. I hope he don't last long on the Steppes.'

Cora was about to tell him that Finnuc hadn't made it that far, but stopped herself. The news would be in the pennysheets before too long. Or some version of it.

The Casker loped into the queue and headed back towards Hook Square. She watched him go, and for a moment he was Finnuc. A moment too long.

Jenkins was waiting on the gangway, her gaze firmly fixed ahead of her towards the Hook, whatever that might be.

'Come on, Constable, we might as well see it as we're here. Save the whole trip being wasted.'

'No luck with the Caskers?'

'Not about Finnuc, but there was something he wouldn't

say.' Cora dropped her voice. 'About Kranna. He disapproves of something she's doing but he's too afraid to say what.' Cora became aware of the chatter around her which was growing more excitable. 'The Perlish Hook seems to have stirred everyone up. You heard anything about it?'

'A little. I won't spoil it for you.'

'Please do.'

Jenkins shook her head and grinned.

They moved further onto the gangway. It was wide – enough for eight to stand side-by-side, maybe. They'd built something extra since Cora had last been to see a Hook here. This new part of the barge was a huge square arch coming out of the water on either side of the gangway. Perhaps they were going to cover the approach? Cora imagined standing here in the Painter's rain would be enough to dampen anyone's excitement, even that of Jenkins.

'What's all this?' Cora asked the purple tunic standing nearby – a harassed-looking man no older than Jenkins.

'You'll see.'

'And what about them?' Cora gestured to a group of people who'd been stopped by more purple tunics, halfway along the gangway.

'They'll see too. You'll all see.'

'Can't *you* see, Detective?' Jenkins asked, as if Cora were fool enough for the Drunkard.

'I see myself losing my patience,' Cora said.

'No, *look*,' Jenkins said, pointing at the big arch.

'What?'

'That's the Hook.'

Cora turned back to the arch. 'That?'

'What does it look like to you?' Jenkins said.

It stretched so high, Cora's neck ached from trying to see the top, but the planks were thin – thin enough you might miss them as you walked through them, beneath them. 'Like someone was building something, but didn't finish,' she said.

'And what about the people under it?' Jenkins was enjoying herself, that much was clear.

They were still. All of them looking back along the gangway at Cora.

And then Cora saw it.

The arch was an enormous wooden frame. A picture frame.

She stared, open-mouthed, until the purple tunic told her to move forward. As she and Jenkins did as they were told, the group standing in the frame moved along too. Cora was stopped again, right under the frame, and then it was her turn to gawp back from the middle of the gangway.

So many people, from all over the Union, walking through an empty space that the Perlish had chosen to mark out as important somehow.

'Audience take me if I can see what this means for the Perlish story,' Cora said.

'Well… A frame is a way to hold something, isn't it?'

'But there's nothing inside this frame,' Cora said.

'That's not true,' said a man beside her. He scratched his long nose, which was beset by warts. 'We're in the Perlish frame, aren't we? Walking through it.'

'What have *we* got to do with the story?' Cora said.

Jenkins smiled.

'She sees it,' the man said. 'We look at what's in a frame, don't we? A frame shows us what's important.'

They were moved on by tunics for a third time, finally onto the Hook barge, but not to go inside. The single room where the Hooks were normally displayed was all closed up; heavy curtains blocked the windows, and bars crossed the main doors.

'Maybe they're still cleaning up after the Lowlanders' Hook, the mostins?' Jenkins said as they filed past.

'That wouldn't be a small job,' Cora said. 'Especially now the Commission have cut the number of bargehands.'

A smaller, thinner gangway – not much more than a few planks of wood lashed together – took them back onto dry land, and back to the crowds. Cora looked again at the square arch, at the Perlish picture frame. She was beginning to understand.

'I like it,' Jenkins said. 'It makes a kind of sense. We're in the frame.'

'But frames don't just show what we're meant to look at, Constable. They cut things out, too. What would the Perlish want to exclude with their story?'

'The pennysheets can't seem to agree. It's like the 'sheets are talking about separate stories. No two reports are the same, or anything like each other.' Jenkins sounded incredulous.

Cora grunted. 'So what's new?'

They made their way across Hook Square, fighting the tide of people surging to see the Hook.

'It's not like that, Detective. The way I read it, each pennysheet has been leaked a different tale. There's no way to link them.'

'The Perlish are just trying to get everyone talking about it,' Cora said, 'like *we* are now.'

'Maybe... *The Spoke* made a big fuss about a plant, some

kind of creeper, but then *The Fenestiran Times* said it was all about a game.'

'The whole election's a game,' Cora said. 'And there's one of our players.'

The bargehand she'd spoken to earlier was coming their way. He slowed his pace as he reached them but didn't stop.

'Dock forty-nine, Detective,' he said as he strode by. 'That'll tell you all you need to know about our Chambers.'

And he was gone into the crowd, back towards the barge.

Docks one through twenty were in central Fenest, not far from Hook Square where the barge was moored. But twenty-one through forty were on the other side of the quay, and forty-one onwards were further away still.

Cora and Jenkins made their way along a quay strewn with broken barrels and discarded pennysheets. The River Stave beside them didn't look too clean either, the water here brown and oily. Most of the docks were empty, and those barges or small sailing craft that were moored up seemed none too water-worthy.

'What would a Chambers be wanting with a dock here?' Cora said.

'Hiding something.'

'Something that bargehand didn't approve of, that's for certain. Not many prying eyes down here.'

'There are *some* eyes,' Jenkins said quietly, and inclined her head towards the corner of the street.

An ageing man leaned against the wall. His open shirt and rouged cheeks made his profession clear, as did the fact he tossed his hair and catcalled them as he watched their progress along the quay.

'If only I wasn't on duty,' Cora called back. 'Bernswick Division. You know it? The place with the crowded cells.' Suddenly the whore had somewhere else to be.

'The likes of *him* won't be near the Assembly building,' Jenkins said.

'Which makes me think that whatever's happening at dock forty-nine,' Cora said, 'the distance from the Assembly isn't an accident.'

'Business that Kranna doesn't want to share with the Commission?'

'Or someone looking for a Captain Tennworth. This might be our way to her, through her trade. The wares in the winery had to come into the city from somewhere. What number are we up to?'

Jenkins had been counting off the small signs displayed at each dock. 'Forty-six, forty-seven.'

The docks had become meaner and smaller the further they'd travelled from Hook Square. Now, the quay curved away from them, and as they rounded the bend, dock forty-eight appeared, and then, beside it, was a world of activity.

'Well,' Cora said. 'Would you look at that?'

There was a fleet of small barges crammed into the space of dock forty-nine. Each one was low in the water, and it was no wonder given the amount of barrels and crates being carried onto them by nimble bargehands.

She and Jenkins watched from behind a cart nearby, one that had been recently unloaded, given the traces of cabbage leaves and squashed sintas left behind.

'That doesn't look like wine to me,' Jenkins said, nodding towards the goods on the quayside.

It was fresh food going onto the barge, as well as sacks of flour and what might be dried figs – longer-lasting supplies for wherever this barge was going.

'But nothing anyone would have any need to hide,' Cora said.

'Unless the papers aren't in order,' Jenkins said, and started for the quayside, ready to demand the most common yet precious commodity in the Union: the appropriate paperwork.

But Cora held her back. 'If this is Kranna's business, and so maybe Tennworth's, plain clothes might be better. Keep yourself out of sight, Constable.'

Cora made her way casually to a heavily pierced young Casker woman who was ticking things off a list.

'Help you?' the woman said, without looking up from her paper.

'That depends,' Cora said quietly. 'You logged this with the Wheelhouse?'

The woman looked up in alarm. 'Who's asking?'

Cora gave the woman a glimpse of her badge then tucked it away again. 'No need for there to be a fuss. I just want to know where this lot is going.'

The woman swallowed audibly and the piercings in her cheeks seemed to jump. 'South.'

'And why aren't you declaring it?'

'She said the Assembly might stop it.'

'She?' Cora said. 'You mean Casker Chambers Kranna?'

The woman's eyes widened. 'How do you know—'

'Never mind that.' All around them, Casker men and women were moving the goods, packing them tight onto every spare inch of space on each barge. No one seemed to have noticed Cora talking to the woman. 'Why is Kranna moving all this south?'

'Because that's where it's needed!' the woman said, fierce now, her fear gone. 'People there, they're suffering, and our Chambers is the only one doing anything about it.'

'You're obviously a supporter,' Cora said.

'All true Caskers are!'

'Do you know her by any other name?'

The woman frowned. 'Kranna? No. Why would—'

A shout went up from one of the barges. 'We're ready, Aileen! Cast her off!'

'Please,' the woman, Aileen, said to Cora. 'Please. People are desperate down there. Our Chambers says we have to keep this secret. The Assembly mustn't find out.'

Cora waited a moment, making the woman think she might put a stop to this – she worked for the Commission, after all, and the Commission carried out the bidding of the Assembly. Then she nodded and stepped away, back to Jenkins. From their hidden vantage point they watched as, one by one, the barges left the quayside.

'South?' Jenkins asked, when Cora told her what Aileen had said. 'But surely all that food has just *come* from the south, from the Lowlands. The Lowlands feed the Union.' Jenkins was almost reciting her Seminary learning. 'Why send it back again?'

'Good question,' Cora said.

'And why is Kranna involved?'

'Another good question, Jenkins, but I think I have an answer for that one. You seen those stories in the 'sheets, about the trouble in Bordair?'

'Of course. Sounds terrible, people so hard up they're drowning themselves. You think Kranna is sending food to them?'

'Seems plausible. But here's a question for *you*, Constable. Why would that Casker bargehand be against feeding his own people in the south? Why would the Perlish Assembly be against it, for that matter? The pennysheets say that it's Bordair in trouble, but maybe there's something else going on here.'

'You mean Chambers Kranna is feeding people other than Caskers,' Jenkins said slowly. 'But who?'

'That's something we might need to find out. One thing is clear: those supplies are going south.'

Seven

The next morning, as Cora approached Z'anderzi's Kantina, venue for the Perlish election story, she wondered why she hadn't been to Z'anderzi's before. She'd heard plenty about it over the years. It was the only place outside the twin duchies of Perlanse where the dividing line between the East and West territories was officially observed. In her parents' day, it had been *the* place to be seen with a glass of something expensive in hand, with the favoured, fashionable side of the building – East or West – changing from week to week. Cora had memories of her father discussing it with his trading hall pals of an evening, the talk floating in the clouds of pipe smoke that filled the salon at the Gorderheim house. Looking at the place now, she could see exactly why it had been such a draw for Victor Gorderheim, in the days before Ruth ruined everything. It was just her father's sort of place.

Z'anderzi's was a tall, thin building that took up the corner of a wide street. The angle meant there were two front walls, each of which was made of smoky glass. One had red solder between large square panes, the other blue wooden frames around curved windows. Either side looked the kind of place drinks would be served in tall glasses with long, thin spoons, and food would glide around on silver trays, never served in pieces bigger than Cora's thumbnail. There couldn't be anywhere in Fenest more different to the Dancing Oak, Cora's favourite betting ring, than Z'anderzi's Kantina.

Each frontage had a pair of grand double doors, and each of *those* had a kenna bird designed in little bits of coloured glass above. *Mosaic*, her father had called it. A red bird for West Perlanse and a blue for the East. The birds were usually seen together; in the realm's symbol, their long necks wrapped around each other so that the birds could look into the other's eyes. Whenever Cora saw the sigil, she thought the West's bird was about to peck out the eyes of the East, unless the East got there first. To see the kenna birds separate like this, one over each doorway, was odd.

Were the Chambers inside yet? They would all be in attendance for the Perlish story, all sitting in whatever part of Z'anderzi's the Commission had sectioned off for the good and great of the Union. Except one of them wasn't so good. One of them was Tennworth. The Casker, the Seeder, the Rustan. A choice of three. Good odds and yet Cora felt far from ready to place a bet. Not yet. She needed to talk to Casker Chambers Kranna, find out the truth of what was behind the barges she'd seen yesterday. Find out if Kranna went by another name.

Cora chose the door that looked the least busy, paying no heed whatsoever to whether she favoured the East or the West. The pennysheet hacks posted inside would likely be noting the comings and goings of all who entered, and using that to speculate wildly on which of the duchies had the upper hand in Fenestiran life these days. It was all so ridiculously dull. Her mother would have loved it.

'Cora!' a man called. A man she knew.

Her hand stilled on the door. How long had it been? She took a deep breath and turned.

Investigator Serus jogged across the busy road, dodging gigs and puddles. His tall, lean frame was clad head to toe in a slip-dog hide coat, like many other Rustans. As Cora watched him, she thought for a moment that the fire investigator had cut off his long auburn hair since she'd last seen him, but as he turned to curse at a Wayward on horseback who'd nearly knocked him over, Cora saw that his hair was knotted up. Made sense for someone who spent their days walking into burning buildings.

'Perks of the job, eh?' Serus said as he reached her at the door to Z'anderzi's.

He stood close enough to Cora that she could smell the ash about him. And the spice of some kind of oil. Not the burning kind. The kind that kept his skin soft.

'Got to get something out of working for the Commission,' she said.

'We're certainly not doing it for the pay.'

Cora laughed. She couldn't remember the last time that had happened. She leaned against the window and her gaze caught the metal in Serus's face. Metal that had replaced the cheek bones he'd been born with; the plates were silver ovals in his flesh. Cora had wondered before why Serus had chosen this part of his body to change – body modification being a Rustan tradition. There didn't seem to be a purpose to Serus's modification, not like replacing a leg bone with something stronger. Perhaps it was vanity.

'You coming in?' she said, suddenly aware she'd been staring. 'I'm sure there's a seat in the Commission box for one of Fenest's fire investigators.'

Now it was his turn to laugh, his metal cheek plates barely moving. 'You mean a crate at the back?'

'That's where I'll likely be,' Cora said, and felt the cool slink of his slip-dog hide coat graze her hand.

'Sadly, I have somewhere else to be this morning.' Serus nodded up the street. 'Duty calls.'

'You don't look like you're rushing off to a burning building, Investigator Serus.'

'Can't get anything past you, *Detective*.' He pulled a wad of papers from his coat pocket. 'Safety check. Paperwork. You know how it is, Cora.'

'Only too well.'

'I'll have to read about the Perlish story in the pennysheets afterwards. Or perhaps we could—'

A gaggle of young and excitable Seeders were all at once between them, seemingly fighting each other to get inside the story venue. Whatever Serus was about to say – what Cora hoped he might say – was lost, and the last Cora saw of him was the wave of a slip-dog hide arm as he moved off down the street.

She let the Seeders sort themselves out, and then followed them inside Z'anderzi's, thinking of Serus.

He'd been the chief investigator in her part of the city for a few years now, but to Cora he was still the new investigator. That was what happened when you stayed in the same job as long as she had. Serus had been on the scene for some big cases, like the recent inferno at the warehouse in Murbick. The owner claimed there were only rugs stored inside, but men on fire had come streaming out like beacons in the night. Men who were forced to work for the warehouse owner to pay 'debts' he claimed they'd incurred when he brought them to work in Fenest. Work for no wages. Serus had been good to have on that case, as far as Cora was concerned: methodical, patient, refusing to jump to conclusions even when the Perlish-run Assembly put pressure on him to find easy blame.

To her mind, it made perfect sense to have a Rustan as a chief fire investigator. Rustans overlooked the Tear, a place of fire. But unlike the Torn, who seemed to have no problem with sudden bursts of molten rock, the Rustans, sensibly, feared it, and so they understood it. Understood it better than anyone in Fenest was likely to. She'd read 'sheets that called for Fenestirans to have the jobs in Fenest, but who went to pennysheets for sense? Cora preferred people who were trained to do their jobs.

Inside Z'anderzi's there was a central space that was vaulted up to the roof – at least three storeys high. She couldn't miss the thick line that ran down the middle of the floor. It looked to be made of brass or copper – whatever the material, it gleamed as it cut through the cream floor tiles. The line didn't stop where it met the public gallery, and it became a pole that connected with the balcony above, where it did the same, running on up the third and final level. Cora tipped back her head. The metal strip ran across the wooden ceiling and down the other side of the balconies, back to the floor.

But everywhere she looked new building work was clear to see, even to Cora's untrained eye. Pale, freshly cut wood made up the tiered levels of seating on all sides. The air smelled of sawdust and new paint.

Cora pushed her way through what felt like a maze of potted plants. She'd seen fewer trees in the streets *outside* Z'anderzi's than the small forests getting in people's way here.

The seating on the ground floor was reserved for the voters. Cora knew that if she counted the seats, there'd be fifty: one for every voter, each of them Fenestirans, who were the only people in the Union permitted to vote. The benefit of living in the capital and having no storyteller of their own. If that even was a benefit. The fifty voters for today's story were picked from the pool of three hundred selected for this election. No sign of them here yet.

'Morning, Detective,' Jenkins said, her uniform looking as freshly pressed and neatly buttoned as ever.

'Constable. This renovation work – you know anything about it?'

Jenkins looked around as if seeing the fresh wood and sawdust for the first time. 'Oh, that. There was some kind of infestation a few years back. The upper floors fell in. Z'anderzi's has been closed ever since.' She ran her finger across an exposed nail head. 'Termites, I think my mother said.'

'But the place is re-opened just in time for the Perlish story.'

'Would have cost a fortune, my mother says, given the state it was in.'

Cora shook her head. 'Isn't it amazing what the Commission can get cleaned up when they put their minds to it?'

'Almost makes you proud, doesn't it, Detective?' Jenkins said, with that pride clear in her voice.

'Not sure that's the word I'd use.' Cora glanced around her. 'If there's a difference between this side and that one,' she pointed across the line, 'I can't see it.'

'Neither can I, but I wouldn't go saying that to either of *them*.'

One of the Perlish Chambers had arrived, a slim, middle-aged man. He wore the brown robes of his office, but the gaggle with him were in strangely layered dresses and jackets, all of which seemed to have feathers and gold stitching on every last inch of cloth. The group were on the other side of the line. The red feather the Chambers had poking out of his hair was as good as a flag: this was the Western duchy.

There was a noise behind them, and she and Jenkins turned to the door. The second Perlish Chambers had appeared, another man, with a blue feather at each temple. The East had arrived.

The chatter in Z'anderzi's dropped away as the two Perlish Chambers eyed each other. Cora was put in mind of the times she'd stared down a cutpurse in an alley: who would blink first? Then the man from West Perlanse started to fold forward in a bow. The man from the East rushed to do the same so that his bowing would be quicker. He flapped his arms behind him in some sort of swimming motion, while the man from East Perlanse brought both arms over his head and made an arch, his fingers pointing to the floor.

'Are they making kenna birds of themselves?' Cora whispered to Jenkins, whose mouth had fallen open.

'Maybe it makes sense to the Perlish.'

'If only someone had a hat pin,' Cora said, thinking of the act that had started the War of the Feathers all those years ago.

'No shortage of hat pins in here today, Detective,' Jenkins said, then looked shocked at her own words.

Cora thought about teasing the constable for her murderous intentions, then remembered Jenkins' approach to a joke was the equivalent of having a hat pin driven through it.

'Go and find us somewhere to sit, Constable. This ridiculousness might go on all day.'

'Of course, Detective.' And Jenkins trotted off obediently to find a purple tunic.

Eventually, the Perlish display was complete and each of the Chambers and their hangers-on swept to the spiral staircase on *their* side of Z'anderzi's. Of course there were two staircases. People started talking again.

Each Perlish Chambers looked to have their eye on the other as they climbed: they were speeding up then slowing down before racing again, as if they wanted to make a run for it but couldn't. Cora caught sight of someone else watching the Perlish pair. Another in a brown robe: a woman, with red hair. This was Casker Chambers Kranna. Cora made her way slowly towards her, aware of the dark-purple-clad pair of tunics flanking her. Chambers didn't usually go anywhere without Commission watchers.

'Strange dance they do, isn't it?' Cora said.

As Casker Chambers Kranna turned to her, the watchers stepped forward and Cora felt herself hemmed in. She'd committed herself now, approaching a Chambers. Nothing else to do but carry on.

The woman was broad as a barge and weathered as most barges. Her eyes were bloodshot, her skin lined and veined enough to show that Kranna had enjoyed riotous Casker living alongside her official work.

'Have we met?' Kranna asked, but not coldly.

'Detective Gorderheim, Bernswick Division.'

'Of course.' Kranna took Cora's hand in hers in a hot grip. Kranna's sleeves had fallen back, revealing arms covered in tattoos, like most Caskers. The manacles on each wrist were all but lost in the swirling ink. Did the woman keep hold of Cora's hand a heartbeat longer than needed?

With a flick of her head, Kranna dismissed the watchers, who slipped away amid the pot plants. 'Most things the Perlish do are strange,' she said, her gaze returning to the progress the Perlish Chambers were making up the stairs. 'Both want to be first to their seats. Think it makes 'em seem better than the other, more powerful, but if they do that too quick then it looks *unseemly*.' She said the last word as if it were bitter-tasting.

'They do this in the Assembly building too?' Cora asked.

'Every day. I make a habit of being late so I miss it. Here he goes, look.'

The Perlish Chambers for the Eastern Duchy made a lunge for the final stair. The Perlish Chambers for the West saw this and alarm flashed across his face. He hoiked up his robes and dashed forward. With strangled cries, both careered out of sight in the middle balcony where Cora guessed they were wrestling over their chairs.

Important-looking people started climbing the stairs in the wake of the Perlish Chambers, and now the public were being admitted at either door. The ground floor was filling up and the air was now stuffy.

Kranna drew a large purple handkerchief from the depths of her robe and mopped the sweat beading on her face. 'You've been on a trip recently, Detective. Enjoying the sights of Perlanse.'

'That's right, your honour. Not much to enjoy on this visit though.'

Kranna's expression darkened and she stuffed the handkerchief back into her robe. 'I heard that too. Finnuc Dawson might have been a misguided man, but he was still one of my people – a Casker.'

'A Casker who murdered the Wayward storyteller.'

Cora watched Kranna closely, wondering if this was Tennworth. Was she even now talking to the person who had ordered the deaths of the Wayward storyteller and Finnuc?

'I've heard rumours that a bandit attack sent him to the Audience,' Kranna said mildly, toying with the leaf of a pot plant. Every so often she nodded to someone in the crowd. Cora was very aware of the two watchers who kept their gaze on Kranna. 'Likely be in the pennysheets soon enough.'

'All rumours end up in the 'sheets.'

'I've heard other rumours too.' Kranna looked at Cora. 'That Finnuc Dawson was poisoned.'

Was this a bluff, Kranna making out she knew nothing of the crime she herself had ordered? Only one way to find out – keep the Chambers talking. Cora held Kranna's gaze.

'I'm told that Heartsbane is a common enough poison in Perlanse,' she said, trying to keep her voice as flat as possible.

The sweat was back on Kranna's flushed face, and this time she made no effort to wipe it away. 'Either way, I suppose Dawson got the punishment he deserved.'

'Earlier than some would have liked. He missed out on a few back-breaking years on the Steppes.'

'Only the Audience knows when we're due to join them, Detective. And they know.'

'They also know about all the comings and goings in this city.'

'Daresay they do,' Kranna said, and chose that moment to produce the handkerchief again. To buy herself time?

'And the city's waterways,' Cora said quickly. 'Goods coming and going. The busy docks. Would dock forty-nine mean anything to you, your honour?'

'All docks mean something to me, I'm a Casker. I'm of the rivers.'

'What about goods leaving that particular dock without paperwork?'

Kranna swung herself to face Cora, closing the distance between them as she did so. 'You'd do well to keep your voice low, Detective.'

'Oh, and why's that?' Cora's mouth was dry. The Perlish plants seemed to have shifted closer to her.

'Because there are bigger forces at play here than you realise,' Kranna growled.

'The kind that make your people strap rocks to their chests before they throw themselves into Bordair? The Casker election story warned of plague. Your realm wanted Fenest to know about the disaster, and now I'm wondering: just how bad *was* your realm hit by Black Jefferey?'

'Come now, Detective. Weren't we just talking about how you shouldn't believe what you read in the pennysheets?'

'What should I believe then?'

'The truth,' Kranna said simply. 'Once you've found it.'

Casker Chambers Kranna swept into the sea of potted plants, heading for the staircase, her watchers tight on her heels. Cora took a moment to catch her breath amid the heat and the fierce pumping of her blood. Had she just been talking to Tennworth?

Before she had a chance to think through what she'd learned from Kranna, Cora caught a flash of gold at the corner of her eye. A manacle. Cora braced herself for Kranna's return, but this manacle belonged to another realm. This Chambers raised a hand, and that, too, glinted. A whole wrist made of metal. This was the Rustan Chambers – Cora hadn't approached this Chambers before, but the woman's appearance left Cora in no doubt who it was: one of the three female Chambers who could be Tennworth. The Rustan Chambers was perhaps twenty feet away, across the crowded room, but Cora saw the woman mouth a word at her, the shape of it all too familiar.

Detective.

Cora's blood had been hot, but now, in an instant, it seemed to run cold. The Rustan Chambers knew who she was. And wanted her to know. That couldn't be good. Why would—

'We have to go to the top floor, Detective.'

Cora spun round to find Constable Jenkins at her side. Jenkins with a face of concern, her large teeth far too close to Cora for comfort.

'Are you all right, Detective? You look like you've just—'

'The heat in here. What kind of venue is this, where voters might sweat to death before the story even starts?'

'I know, but the tunics, they say we have to go up now if we're going to listen.'

'Lead the way, Constable. Maybe there'll be some air up there.'

Jenkins set off through the pot plants. When Cora looked

back, the Rustan Chambers had gone. But with each step of the staircase, Cora felt as if someone was watching her.

There were so many people in Z'anderzi's now. The spiral staircases on each side were jammed. Just where the voters were in the building was its own little mystery; there wasn't room for a garbing pavilion here. Somewhere nearby they'd be donning their robes and masks, becoming the Audience, Cora thought, as she followed Jenkins up the staircase on the eastern side of Z'anderzi's. The noise was settling. Everyone was ready for the Audience to arrive.

As they came to the landing of the second floor, she looked across to the Commission box, where the Chambers and their aides, plus senior staff from the Assembly building and the Wheelhouse, listened to the election story. They sat on padded chairs with side tables set with drinks, purple tunics hovering close by to see to any need or demand.

The Chambers were all in the front row. All seven of them. The Rustan Chambers was staring right at her.

'Move along,' mumbled a purple tunic stationed on the landing.

She and Jenkins hurried up the stairs to the third floor to the public gallery. They'd just sat down when the bell rang and everyone else stood up. The view from that height was dizzying: three floors below were the cream flagstones divided by the brass line, surrounded by the chairs for the Audience.

As Cora watched and tried not to pitch forward, the Audience took their seats all that way below. She couldn't see where they emerged from.

Black robed, their masks a riot of colour, each voter representing a different member ready to be swayed, swaying as they massed together. A leering, weeping, cursing, heckling story-hungry mob. Everyone's eyes were on them as they made their way to their seats. For once, the over-sized masks looked small, but the colours were bright as ever as the Audience took their seats: the Stitcher and the Mute, the Child and the Liar, the Messenger and the Poet, the Dandy and the Keeper, and all the rest of that mob – the fifty members of the Swaying Audience, each with two stones in their pockets. The black and the white. The yes and the no. How would the Perlish fare? Incumbents for five unpopular years, but if the story they told was good enough...

The Master of Ceremonies appeared below, one foot either side of the brass line in what could only be a gesture of fairness.

'Audience, welcome,' he said, his voice as clear to Cora as if she were seated down there with the Keeper. Some trick of the building's construction, she guessed, for the sound to travel like that. 'In this, the two hundred and ninth election of our realms,' the Master of Ceremonies said, 'we give you *two* 'tellers who give you a tale.'

'The Audience is listening,' came the response. Jenkins mouthed the words along with the Audience. Cora suspected many others in Z'anderzi's were doing the same. There was a flash of something near her feet. A scuttle across the floor and the creature disappeared between two boards. The Perlish had better get a move on or the termites might send the floors crashing down again.

Jenkins jabbed her in the ribs, harder than Cora thought

was needed, but then the constable was excitable when it came to elections. Jenkins pointed over their balcony: the storytellers had arrived, one either side of the dividing line, *of course*.

The Perlish storytellers were both women, one tall, one short, but both with the same dark hair curling about their temples, and something similar about the face. Sisters? Each wore a soft, floppy hat in the colours of their duchy. They faced each other and bowed, thankfully much more simply than the fussy displays of their Chambers had been, then turned and bowed to the Audience.

'It's always amazed me,' Jenkins whispered, 'how two people can tell a story together.'

'They can't agree on being one realm, but every five years they find a way to tell *one* election story.'

'And one that so often wins!'

'This pair though,' Cora said, squinting over the balcony, 'they look so similar, they might actually be related.'

'A family divided across duchies,' Jenkins said in a dreamy voice. 'Perhaps this story is one for the Missing Lover. I'd like a romance, one with—'

The woman next to Jenkins told them to quieten down or she'd send them to the Widow.

Then the storyteller for West Perlanse, the woman wearing the red hat, stepped forward and said, 'This is a story that begins with an end.'

The Perlish story

This is a story that begins with an end. And it is an end that begins with a bright, warm day viewed through a window.

Cecil W'oventrout looked out from the third storey of his family's ancestral seat, looked out and despaired at the sunlit approach. He knew something was coming. A most dreadful thing, a thing he'd spent most of his life avoiding, would soon be making its way up the winding mountain road.

Foreigns.

He shrugged into his thick velvet house coat, not feeling any of the warmth the rest of East Perlanse was enjoying. There, in the gallery corridor, he felt the cold emanation of generations of W'oventrouts and their own encounters with... foreigns.

But we'll come to all that in good time. For now, we watch Cecil in his watching. He was a man in his sixtieth year, though with little prompting he would tell guests he was but forty-seven. A carefully chosen number that was plausible because it was an odd number – not a number likely chosen for a lie – and because Cecil had looked forty-seven since he came of age. He lost most of his hair soon after he saw his first naked woman, though Cecil had never equated the two events. He had lazy eyelids that gave him the hooded look of a man dozing his way through days. And why not doze? What need had a W'oventrout to be awake to life's worries, we may ask. What need, indeed?

Beneath Cecil's bare feet, the plush carpet and runner both needed some attention. The former sent up dust with every step, the latter was dulled and tarnished. The narrow window from which he watched was the former home of generations of spiders, but they, too, had moved on. Cecil was careful not to disturb the webs they'd left behind as he licked a finger to wipe the dirty window panes. He succeeded in moving the dirt – moving, but not *removing*.

'Perkins,' he bawled. This was simply unacceptable. Guests were expected. Foreign guests, yes, but even so. 'Liar take you, Perkins, where are you?' His voice echoing along the gallery was the only answer, that and the disapproving stares of W'oventrouts long dead. Cecil whirled, rushing to the portrait of his great great grandmother Darmst.

'Don't look at me like that! It's not my fault. How was I to know? Mother never told me.'

Darmst's gaze hardened.

'At least they're not *westerners*.' He ran a finger along the portrait's dusty frame. 'Perk—'

But Perkins was gone; most of the staff were. Cecil remembered, now. He had kept Chef, else he risked starving in those last months. But the others had gone one by one. Perkins' leaving he remembered distinctly. It was another sun-scorched day, there had been so many of late, and Cecil had stood in the scant shade of the coach porch, squinting as the butler wept. The tears ran from his comely cheek onto his pinafore and as he took a shuddering breath, his plaits swung across his breasts...

No. That was the head house-maid.

She had a name. Cecil knew that much.

'I know that much!' he told Great Great Grandmother Darmst. Such a particular-looking woman, darker of complexion and with a jawline that would be an asset to a craftsman's toolbox. In fact, she had something of the craftsman about her despite her ballooning layers of lace and satin.

The braying of a mule broke Cecil's reverie. For a moment he entertained the idea it was Darmst, and found he could believe such a sound might come from such lips. But then he remembered his purpose in the gallery in the first place.

At the window once more, Cecil barely allowed himself a breath. The mule aired its complaint again, closer this time. Mules! Really. Trust a foreign merchant. Cecil felt pangs of guilt in his breast, that he would be the one to see his family seat handed over to a man who drove his own mules. Pangs all the sharper as the guilt was not truly his own, but borrowed from his mother – a woman who knew more of borrowing than any other in this story. But her story is her own, and she shall tell it.

Never one to lack for imagination, Cecil's despair filled the still-empty approach with all manner of disturbing foreign paraphernalia. Tea chests, racks of foul-smelling spices, rugs woven to modern tastes, furniture made of light wood. He shuddered. What would this man do to Truss House? The depravity of a merchant could know no bounds, surely? And what would a merchant do with Great Great Grandmother Darmst? Hang her in the library? But even foreign merchants must understand portraits are not meant for libraries? They must.

But they wouldn't. Cecil had been a fool to take any such thing for granted. There simply was no *time*. Where had the time gone? He lifted Darmst from the wall. Taking a few awkward steps, unsure where he was bound or what he was about, he eventually leaned her underneath Great Uncle Henry. The two practically spat sparks at each other.

'Behave, you two,' Cecil said, 'or I'll give you to the merchant.'

He stared down the long gallery and wished, perhaps for the first time, that he did not come from such a long-established, illustrious, and heavily framed family.

He was wrestling with a distant cousin – one of the smaller works – when he spotted movement on the road below. He hurried to look, then rubbed his eyes in disbelief.

A cart!

With people sitting in the back, no less.

He laughed until the tears came. There was nothing else for it. Tears for the Amateur, who was sympathetic to tales of the wronged. Tears for the Drunkard, who enjoyed jests at the expense of fools. As far as Cecil was concerned, the two of them could fight over his tears from now until the end of his days under the Audience.

The little foreign merchant tribe plodded its way towards the house. Driving the cart was a portly man with a wide-brimmed hat hiding most of him – deception from the outset. Behind him, pointing and gawping, were a pair of younger folk. And between them, to no surprise of Cecil's, was a child. How merchants liked to breed!

Cecil watched in horror as the driver tried to angle his fat cart beneath the coach porch.

'The trades entrance is to the right. To the right, damn you! Do they not have coaches in your lands?' Cecil shouted to no avail. The mule's protests were more effective, and the merchant's disappointment was writ large on his fat shoulders. The children were up and out of the cart in a flash. They were... the front door. They were making to come inside. Inside.

'What was I thinking?' Cecil said. He should have been at the threshold, ready to repel the invaders. Or, at least be sure they wiped their grubby feet. He ran down the gallery as quickly as his bulbous, thin-skinned knees would take him.

His house coat flew open and he realised he was naked beneath it. In his fugue state he'd forgotten to dress himself. Or had his valet forgotten to dress him? No, no the valet was gone. They were all gone.

'I knew that,' he screamed as he left his gilt-framed ancestors behind.

Cecil's house coat was thrice tied when he stood at the front door of Truss House; he on one side, his future on the other. This was a future he was duty-bound to invite in, but he had no desire to do so.

He had also never opened his own front door before.

He understood the mechanics – he wasn't a dullard. But he also understood the symbolism of what he was about to do and how it encompassed, in one painfully efficient instance, his predicament. He was opening his own door.

Bracing himself against the weight of it, both literal and figurative, he pulled. He pulled with all his reluctant might. But it was lighter than he expected. The combined action of his arm and the door's own momentum dragged him to one side. He caught a glimpse of four surprised faces, with four sets of wide eyes, all arrayed at different heights before he disappeared behind the iron-studded oak.

A squeak, followed by a polite cough, saved Cecil from further, prolonged embarrassment.

'Yes?' he said, risking only his head around the door's edge.

'Cecil W'oventrout, I take it?' the portly man said.

What was this, by way of greeting? Already taking? Had this man not taken enough already?

'No you may not "take it",' Cecil said.

The little girl giggled. It was an impudent sound, and Cecil did not much care for it. He decided to close the door. Contracts and traditions and the Patron be damned to Silence.

But the man entered, his tribe following dutifully behind, each flashing Cecil a grin more mischievous than the last. He quailed behind the solid oak that his great grandfather Bertram hung after the great storms of so-and-so year.

'Commoner hear it, would you look at this?' the man said, taking in the cool marble floor and marble-edged grand staircase.

'It's not as big as the first one we looked at,' the woman said.

'Now, Rosamund, you know why we had to settle for Truss House.'

Rosamund muttered something about taxes and debts and small entrance ways.

Cecil was on the verge of apoplexy. *Settle* for Truss House? These dirt-encrusted foreigns, who had not the grace or education to offer greetings to their host, were to *settle* for his ancestral home? Foreigns with names as ugly as Rosamund? He began a coughing fit that shook him from top to bottom. That, at least, secured their attention. He was led out from behind the door and given a moment to compose himself.

'Welcome,' Cecil said without warmth, 'to Truss House. I am Cecil W'oventrout. The last of a Perlish dynasty, which dates back to the joining of the great houses of Wetovens and Trouts.' He anticipated four impressed faces, but was met with disinterest.

The man, still wearing his hat no less, introduced himself as Edwin Adlesworth.

'And your daughters, Edwin?'

This produced much crude laughter from the newcomers.

'This is my second *wife*, Rosamund,' Edwin said. 'Married just last week.'

Despite his years of comportment lessons, this revelation set Cecil's mouth all a flap.

'Look, Father, he *is* a trout!' the little girl said.

'This is my daughter, Florence. And this handsome chap is my ward, Gideon Owens.' Handsome, perhaps, but his handshake was rough and calloused, and his face spoke of many dreadful days out in the sun.

'Why is Cedric here, Father?'

'My name is Ce—'

'We talked of this, Flo-Flo, it's a Perlish tradition.'

'It's a foolish tradition,' Rosamund muttered again. She was a mutterer. Mother would not have approved of that. Not at all.

Edwin knelt to look Florence in the eye, his host quite forgotten, as if the little creature was just as important as anyone else present. 'When the Perlish sell their homes, they host the buyer for their final night.'

'But *why*?'

'I suppose it's a way to pass a home from one person to the next, and for everyone to feel good about it. Isn't that right, Cecil?'

'Well, I—'

'Trout,' Florence cried.

They laughed again. They laughed a lot, it seemed. As if their little merchant lives were just full of joy and wonder. Full of malice and greed, more like. Full of spite and deceit, more like. That was what edged their grinning mouths and wrinkled their beady eyes. Spite and deceit, Cecil marked them both in great quantities. There was little he could do about either.

86

'You must be tired after your long journey,' Cecil said, attempting to restore order. 'Allow me to—'

'Fenest is not so far. And no need, Cecil, we know our way,' Edwin said, and then proceeded to ably marshal his troops up the stairs to the terrace.

The front door was still open, the mule still in its traces, and the Adlesworths' belongings still in the bed of the cart. Cecil was caught between two competing horrors: the chance another visitor might stumble across the abandoned mule-led cart, and the marauding Adlesworths being amongst his private rooms. He left the door and took the stairs two at a time.

He found the family strewn out along the long terrace, each examining the adjoining rooms. And none more critically than the little Florence. With a hand, she stopped Cecil in his tracks.

'Whose room was *this*?' she said.

'Pardon me?'

'Why, what did you do?'

'I was not quite certain of your question. You wanted to know whose room this is?'

'Was,' Florence said, crossing her arms.

'Mother's,' Cecil said.

'Did she die in there?'

Cecil swallowed. 'Yes, she did. It was a very peaceful, beautiful thing.'

'In the bed?'

'That's right.'

'Father!' the girl caterwauled. 'I will need a new bed!'

To Cecil's relief, the girl's mother rescued him from further insult. Though as one young woman led another away, he wondered if such an assumption would lead him from one blunder with Rosamund to another: what was to say this *second wife* was the mother of the fork-tongued brat? Looking closely now at the two of them, there was little physical resemblance. Perhaps none of them were related? Perhaps merchants were not born of one another, but grown in pots, taken as cuttings from one master merchant and raised from vicious seedlings into full-grown constrictors.

'Cecil?'

He blinked away his nightmare vision, only to be presented with a rounder, fleshier one.

Edwin gestured to the master bedroom. 'I couldn't help but notice your belongings were still in the master.'

'That is correct. As tradition dictates. But there are plenty of guest rooms.'

The Fenestiran merchant sucked air through his teeth, making a noise akin to an angered goose. Cecil was so taken aback, he flinched.

'You see,' Edwin said, 'we were really planning on having our first night in the master bedroom. My wife and I. Our *first. Night.*'

Cecil was not a worldly man. He had never been married, not once, let alone twice. The mysteries of marriage were just that: unfathomable, unnameable, mysteries. That he had, in fact, lain with a woman would come as a surprise to anyone who might hear such a rumour. A cousin, more years his senior than he'd care to admit, had taken it upon herself to educate a young Cecil in the ways of the female body. Which is not euphemistic – education was the primary drive. Very little pleasure was had by either party.

'I see,' Cecil said. 'Perkins!'

The name echoed along the terrace, cutting through the jibber jabber of the young Adlesworths. The silence that followed was humiliating.

He gathered in his arms the few items of clothing he had yet to sell or store: his wigs, his night-time snuff, and his slippers. Then, passing the bed, he paused. Grimly he emptied his arms on top of his bedding. He pulled the corners of the bedsheet free one by one. He would not leave them behind to be soiled by a Fenestiran's *first night*. So encumbered by his remaining possessions, he waddled down the terrace to the furthest guest room. The Adlesworths watched on, for once silent, lost of their mirth and laughter. Somehow, that was far worse.

Dinner was to be served at seven. To his credit, Cecil worried for his guests. Perhaps they would not know the appropriate dining hour? Perhaps they would be so ravenously hungry as to lay siege to the kitchen, or to oust Chef as Cecil had been so ousted from his own bedroom? There was little chance of a Fenestiran merchant family knowing the saltberry fork from the salad fork, or their second course napkin from their third. But he was confident, as he adjusted his wig in the mirror, that any embarrassment would only be felt by him, and him alone. At least Chef would be spared any unintended insult, with no serving staff to relay the Adlesworths' behaviour.

Cecil gasped, realising that Chef would see such insults first hand, having to serve that most wretched of tables himself! Cecil would not look the man in the eye, of that he was certain. It would be too much. It was all too much.

'Now, now, Cecil. Tears before dinner spoils the potatoes.' Another of Mother's pearls of wisdom. He fanned his eyes, but still had to reapply his powders. Fortunately, the guest rooms were still furnished for... guests, and so he had all he needed to look presentable. Not that he had worried about such earlier that day. But dinner was an entirely different affair.

He had been unable to take his usual pre-dinner nap. Voices in the hall and on the terrace, so distant and yet so close, were like the ghosts of W'oventrouts past. At least behind a closed door those voices were softened, made anonymous almost. But his curiosity got the better of him, and, still in his house-coat, he wandered down the hall, passing the closed but silent door of his old bedroom. Somewhere distant Florence called for her father. A call repeated often, until there was no option but to relent. Cecil stopped by his mother's room, but regretted his quick glance as it alighted on chaos incarnate: drawers strewn across the room; wooden toys haphazardly arranged on the mirrored dresser; a small puddle of milk seeping towards the rug. He had to hurry on, or risk the abyss.

But in doing so, he saw what he was not supposed to. Something illicit – not necessarily in act, but in tone. Cecil, angled in a doorway that should not have been open, had a view that any portrait painter would envy.

He bore witness to a parting of hands between Rosamund and the handsome ward Gideon. She, sitting on a bed that hadn't been occupied since his Great Aunt Isabella died in childbirth. He, midstride, his hand trailing. And she? Looking on with an expression painted in foreign tones – too hard for love, too open for fear, too pleased for hatred. Such a look was beyond Cecil. Such a look has been beyond many better men throughout the ages and across the realms. Better to barely see that look, as Gideon barely saw it.

'Tonight, Gideon,' Rosamund whispered. 'We must do away with the old man tonight.'

'But...' He turned to her, and to Cecil's eye the boy softened. 'As you wish.'

Needless to say, witnessing such an exchange sent Cecil

scurrying back to his guest bedroom. He had known these southern invaders would not stop at evicting him from his own home, done through the Poet's own nefarious methods of entirely legal purchase, but to learn that they wished to 'do away' with him entirely!

But hold on now, you might say, what reason had these two to plot such a heinous act? By Perlish tradition, Cecil would be gone from their new home and new lives by morning. The old man in danger must be Edwin! And you would be right, clever audience that you are. Cecil, however, was neither clever nor particularly aware of the lives of those around him; two characteristics that were not required of an only child of a Perlish noble family. If anything of note was to happen, then, in Cecil's mind, it must be happening to him.

By the time the small bell rang in Cecil's room, which was Chef summoning him to dinner, his nerves were frayed beyond repair. He jumped at the chimes that came from above the door, and clutched a cushion to his breast as if it were a thick iron shield. Just the bell, dear Cecil, he told himself. Just the bell for dinner. And what could be so frightening about a good meal? Laughing thinly at his own folly, he brushed down his dinner jacket and patted at his spiralling wig. He stepped out to face his fate.

But rather than daggers in the dark, he found confusion. The elder Adlesworths were also out in the hall, looking from one another to their respective chamber doors.

'What is the bell, Cecil?' Edwin called from an undignified distance. 'Is it—?'

'Fire!' Like a cat with its tail alight, little Florence shot out of Mother's room with her bedpan held precariously in front of her. Before Cecil had a chance to give voice to the truth, she upended the bedpan over the terrace's marble rail.

All who looked on, even Florence herself, were somewhat taken aback. But none more so than Chef, who happened to be stationed below to offer guidance to the guests. His grunt of surprise, and nothing more, was the mark of a true professional.

'That is the chime for dinner,' Cecil said, joining the girl.

'It was mostly water,' Florence said. 'Mostly.'

The first to crack was, would it be believed, Edwin, though he had the presence of mind to turn from the terrace, from Chef below, before his bubbling laughter erupted. The rest were less kind. Florence laughed so hard at her own blunder that only the railing kept her upright. Rosamund ruined her powder and rouge – poorly applied in the first place – with streaks of mirth-fuelled tears. And Gideon's was a hearty belly-laugh that provided the percussion section in that orchestra of ill-manners.

Cecil blanched beneath his powders. He gave Chef a look he hoped expressed his regret, his sorrow, his guilt. But he lacked a woman's power in this regard.

'Come, come now dinner awaits,' he said, hoping to curtail the Adlesworths' cruel jesting. But they continued to chuckle along the hall and, should the laughter abate, one or other would say 'mostly' and they would begin again.

Cecil paused at the top of the stairs. 'After you,' he said, with an attempt at a gracious half-bow. But he eyed the staircase – had it always been so precipitous?

All but Gideon trooped down the stairs in their own ungainly manners.

'After you, kind host,' the boy said.

'No, no, I *insist*.'

'But I am just a ward. You do me too great an honour.'

Though it was true, Cecil swallowed his pride for the sake of his brittle old bones. 'Not at all. Ward now, but heir to Truss House one day.'

'One day *soon*,' Gideon said, patting Cecil solidly on the shoulder.

Cecil waited until the boy was fully on the stairs before checking the shoulder of his dinner jacket for stains.

Despite a thunderous dripping and the Adlesworths' poorly stifled giggles, Chef delivered them to the dining room with a stoic calm that Cecil envied. He did not know how old Chef was – certainly younger than his own forty-seven years – but then, he'd never thought to enquire. The man had a family somewhere in a nearby village. A son? Perhaps two? That had a ring of truth to it. Chef was a man built of square planes: from cheek bones and forehead to shovel-like hands and flat feet. You knew where you stood with such a man. Such a man was incapable of hiding anything – an important feature in a cook. He returned to the kitchens to bring forth the first round of apple slices.

The Adlesworths arranged themselves haphazardly about the dinner table, dragging placings as they went and so undoing much of Chef's careful work. Saltberry forks jumbled beside butter knives. Florence picked up a salad fork and brushed all others onto the floor. Cecil bit his tongue. Those were no longer his family's forks – the bill of sale included all furniture and household effects, apart from the few paintings he was taking. Let these incomers ruin everything, as everything was ruined for him.

Gideon had placed himself directly opposite Cecil. The boy was now intent on his fish knife, testing the tip with his thumb.

A vicious-looking thing, a fish knife, but not the sharpest. Which also aptly described the boy. The knife found its way to the boy's pocket, and Cecil almost choked on his water.

'Our host is in some trouble,' Edwin said. 'Do help him, Gideon.'

'No, no!' Cecil said, struggling to recover without offering his guests the second deluge of the evening.

'What's that?' Florence said, pointing her remaining fork at the painting above the hearth. All turned to look.

'That's a deer,' Edwin said.

'A stag,' Cecil said, correcting him. The majestic animal stood triumphantly at the centre of the large painting, while behind lurked the hunting party that would inevitably end its life. A distant W'oventrout was at the head of that party, though Cecil had forgotten which exactly. Many of his ancestors had enjoyed hunting, in the days when the family had a fully functioning stable.

'Is it the same *stag* as that one?' Florence pointed to the mounted head at the far end of the room.

'I do not know,' Cecil answered honestly.

'I don't like them. Father, take them down.'

'Not now, Flo-Flo.'

'Father!'

Edwin sighed. 'Gideon, would you?'

Gideon obliged. Or tried to. The painting was too big, too heavy for one man to take hold of. He even struggled to prise it away from the wall to get a better look at its fastenings. For this, he employed the fire's poker. He hefted the poker, feeling the weight of it in an appraising manner that Cecil did not like.

A manner Cecil did not like one bit.

To his relief, Chef brought the first meat course and

accompanying potatoes. The stags were forgotten amidst a barrage of questions and complaints and ignorant claims from all generations of Adlesworth.

The meal proceeded in this manner for some time. Chef's considered artistry of flavours and textures was, course by course, subject to rude degrees of disdain and appreciation alike. Florence hacked away at meat fillets and fish and creamed potatoes with the same blunt butter knife. The ring of debris grew wider around the girl with every new plate. Rosamund barely picked at her food. The two men didn't seem to breathe between forkfuls piled high enough to make chewing an impressive feat. All the while Chef said nothing unless spoken to, remained polite, and served those that were undeserving of his talents with grace. Cecil found himself struggling to emulate his soon-to-be-former staff.

What little conversation was afforded by such table manners was, to be sure, brutish. The Fenestiran family had no interest in the finer points of the arts – as Florence had quite succinctly illustrated – and even less interest in polite societal discussion. Cecil's attempts to draw their opinions on the recent marriage between Claudia Stanubins and Hubert Yowdly fell on ears as deaf as the Relative's. Evidently, they knew nothing of the neighbouring families. Though initially horrified, Cecil spent the final desert course in the grips of a vivid fantasy of the Adlesworths hosting the viperous Lady Stanubins – her tongue sharp enough to draw blood from Edwin with every lashing. So much blood as to paint the dining room bright red, as jarring and ill-fitting a colour as their modern tastes deserved.

When Chef came to clear his plate, Cecil realised they were all looking at him.

'Are you all right, Cedric?' The little girl was standing next to him, her expression one of cruel interest rather than concern. If he were an insect, he would have feared for his wings.

'Quite all right, thank you, Florence.'

'Well, we've all had a long day. Perhaps it's best we all retire,' Edwin said.

'No!' Cecil said. 'Not yet. Allow me one indulgence as your host for this last evening in my ancestral home.'

'What?' Florence asked flatly.

'A story.'

At this she brightened. 'A good one? With fighting and death and Torn magics, and no kissing?'

'Under the Audience, a good one indeed.'

'Not too long, I hope?' Edwin said, looking at his *second* wife, who would not meet his eye.

'A story takes as long as it takes.' Perhaps the story would take all night? And so engaged, there would be no opportunity for Gideon to use the fish knife that now made a bulge of the young man's pocket. Cecil planned to tell a story to save himself, and who has not found themselves telling such a story at least once in their lives? 'My family has always told its stories in the drawing room. Shall we?'

The Adlesworths were either too full or too preoccupied with their own troubles to argue. His only barrier to the drawing room was Florence.

'No. Kissing. In. The. Story,' she said, punctuating each word by stabbing his chest with her salad fork. Evidently the fork was a new and permanent companion for the little girl.

'No kissing,' Cecil confirmed.

He led the way to the more comfortably attired drawing room. Each Adlesworth found a suitable place to drape themselves, while Cecil preferred to stand at the lit hearth – as any good storyteller would. He cleared his throat and brought his audience to attention.

'My mother enjoyed many games. Some would say she enjoyed them too much, which might be true of one game in particular.'

It was a game that was slow in making its way to our beloved Truss House. Slow in winding its way up the mountain track. Slow in creeping its way across the Moral Mountains. But *not* slow in taking root in the social circles of both duchies, with their constant hunger for new and exotic distractions.

In her thirty-seven years Vivian W'oventrout had played every game worth playing, and many more besides. Thirty-seven – though she would admit this number to no one, not even her husband, Roderick, who believed quite certainly that she was twenty-six and had been for some years – was old enough, nay wise enough, to be disinclined towards the new. To have favourites for good reason: those games in which one had developed some skill approaching, but not reaching, mastery. Such as the game of Hounding the Horses she was trying to enjoy when all this talk of bones and the like had so rudely intruded.

'Meredith Yowdly said it is wonderfully complicated, a game of real skill. She swears it is the Latecomer's very delight,' said the hound to Vivian's right. At least, Vivian felt fairly confident in her deduction that the woman was a hound. She played like one. And she yapped like one also, but that was a dangerous way to be thinking.

'Meredith Yowdly swears entirely too much as it is,' said Vivian's fellow horse – a young gentleman who over-oiled his moustache.

Dutiful titters circled the table, as the players settled back to their hands. The game was entering its final stages, and all to plan. The hounds had flushed out one early horse, from the gentleman's hand, but were too ponderous in their collective play to close in on the final knight card that Vivian held. Which was in no small part due to her excellent dissembling. It had been, if she might say so herself, a truly dazzling display – made all the more spectacular by the lack of understanding shown by those at the table.

But this was only a social circle, not the serious circles that played for fortunes or the games that followed ducal invitations. At best it might function as light practice; to pick an analogy from the current game, it was like a horse trotting around a yard to loosen the muscles after a day in the stable. A far cry from the gallop of the hunt or the race.

At a lull – otherwise known as Judith Mon'butter's turn – Vivian rang for her butler. He appeared at her elbow, as swift and silent as all staff should be.

'I'll take my sherry now, Perkins. And for the table,' Vivian said.

This was met by a chorus of polite declinations and orders for other spirits. Perkins nodded and relayed as much to the bar-boy whose station was at the end of the games room. A dark wooden bar brooded there, with none of the garish, modern polished brass that festooned such rooms in Western Perlanse and further afield. 'A bar,' her father used to say, 'should be so dark the boy tending it should appear like a ghost, presiding over shelves of unknowables that he drags from the underworld to ours, at our bidding.'

Had her current company known Vivian better, or simply been more attentive, they would have realised the implied insult of calling for sherry before the game was finished. That she had three thousand marks riding on the horse in her hand was of little consequence, and about as safe as any rider who had ever taken to the saddle.

'I would still like to try it,' Judith Mon'butter said, finally laying her card.

'Then have Perkins bring you a glass,' Vivian said.

'No, the Torn Game, dear.'

Vivian schooled herself to calm. That 'dear' was as obvious as a sabre lunge, and she would not dignify such an ungainly manoeuvre with a response.

'I would also enjoy the novelty,' said a rather meek woman by the name of Georgina, who played as brazenly as a just-docked bargeman.

'Then we shall,' Vivian said, knowing full well she would never allow such a game at her table. What could the Torn possibly know of games? What room did they have in their hovels clinging to volcanoes for the sophisticated back-and-forth of strategy, of bluff and counter-bluff? Their grubby little lives were too short-lived to fully comprehend the long-term planning required to make a gaming circle, be it for social or financial gains. The thought of which served to remind her of the purpose of today's game.

'I hear the Lock'ambs are looking to marry their youngest,' Vivian said.

There was some shifting and fidgeting at the table.

Vivian allowed the silence to drag, despite their discomfort.

Eventually, the moustache-wearing horse, Georges Stanubins, cleared his throat. 'So young,' was all he said. But it was enough to breach the dam and bring forth the life-giving flood of gossip.

'I hear she has been nothing but trouble from the out.'

'They say no stable boy is safe.'

'I heard that was *itself* a fabricated rumour, started by Old Lock'amb to hide—' a lowered voice '— debts.'

'Such an ugly side to that family.'

'What is to be expected from generations of shepherds?'

'Are they so different in that regard?'

The table thought so, unanimously. All present company would not treat a daughter as one might livestock, to be sold to the highest bidder. No, they would be married off for their own good. To men of good, Eastern houses.

'Your Cecil is not so much younger than the girl, is he not?' Judith said.

Yes, thank you, Judith. Another lunge with the sabre, still as ungainly as a new-born.

'Not so much, but enough,' Vivian said. 'He has a few more years chasing butterflies in the garden before we make a match.'

'Be sure those butterflies do not find their way into the hay loft,' Georges said. 'We were all young once.'

'Some of us still are,' Vivian said, placing a hand on his arm just so, to the incredulous, hungry delight of the table. Sadly, the man did not have the good grace to blush. Instead, and without taking his eyes from hers, he lay his seed-sower card calmly on the table.

For a moment her touch turned to a hard grip, and then she was back to her own hand. He had cost her a share of the winnings, perhaps as much as two thousand marks, but no matter. The Lock'ambs were in trouble, and their youngest needed a husband. That was worth winning a little less.

She lay her final scoring card, the knight, and smiled fixedly at the cries of 'I knew it!', 'Surely not', and 'You crafty old mare!' as was tradition in hounding the horses. A little less emphasis on the *old* would have sufficed, but was to be expected from Judith.

The game finished, they retired from the felted table to the more comfortable tables about the bar. Tea was served. The hounds each discreetly made their way to Perkins and accounted for their losses. Collectively less than it might have been, and in the fortunes of East Perlanse's great houses these were drops in the oceans. Oceans that would dwarf Break Deep. No, in fact the real losers of that afternoon would not be revealed for some time. And though the seeds had been sown many, many years before this moment, they found fresh life at Vivian W'oventrout's table.

The weeks and months passed as dictated by the Audience: with barely enough stories of victories and defeats, loves and duties, scandals and monotony, to keep even the most attentive of them interested. For our purposes, those months contained an itch that, no matter how hard she might try, Vivian could not ignore. And like all itches, while there is short-lived relief in the scratching, little good comes of it in the end.

Let us touch briefly on that relief.

Vivian had four regular, weekly circles, and was moved on occasion to travel as far as Port O'Price in the east, or to dip a toe into Western Perlanse at the ducal table. Such invitations were hard to turn down: as much as the westerners were a bore, they were so dreadfully keen to lose their money. It was, Vivian felt, a result of having actually *earned* that money themselves – it embarrassed them. And rightly so.

It was on such a trip west that Vivian played her first game of Bouncing Bones. She had been right when she mollified that circle of associates: she would not bring the Torn Game, as it was called in more polite circles, to her table. Not at first. Instead she would, unknowingly, go to *it*. On this occasion she was formally invited by the Duke of West Perlanse to an evening of games at his palace, Westerly Strife; games that were not specified on the invitation. Vivian did not know she was to play the Torn Game. She travelled by coach and deigned to allow Roderick, her husband, to accompany her.

Roderick was not a player of games.

He was not, in her estimation, a man of any real passions. He drifted through his comfortable and carefree life as one might expect of the Perlish nobility. But Roderick was in possession of perhaps the rarest qualities of his station: contentment. He told his stories to the Luminary at a modest shrine in the lower gardens, doted on his son, Cecil, and did his best to keep out of his wife's way. He did not seek adventure, scandal, or excitement. His half-hooded eyes, which he shared with his son, had seen enough of East Perlanse – and what else was there to see? In short, he was finished with life and had the wealth for life to be finished with him.

Vivian could not imagine a more suitable husband.

He slept as they left the mountains of the east behind and wound through the low hills of the borderlands. They passed prosperous villages and towns. On the roads they saw men and women and children, some carrying more than a mule might, others hard at work at one trade or another. All jolly in their task, all happy in their station. The sun shone on Eastern Perlanse and in its warmth they felt the applause of the Audience. In the west it rained.

Vivian had not packed for rain. She elbowed her husband.

'I have not packed for rain,' she told him.

Roderick worked his mouth awake and his eyelids to their half-open zenith.

'Well, dearest, you won't be playing games outside, will you?' he asked, not to mollify, but because he was not always sure just what such games involved.

'Of course not! But I also do not wish to arrive at the ducal palace, if we can call it such—'

'We can.'

'— as bedraggled as a drowned rat.'

'Do rats drown?' Roderick asked, again not to frustrate but because he was not entirely sure if they could be drowned or not. He had never seen a rat drown. He supposed anything that breathed might drown, but—

'A tale for the Whisperer, no doubt.'

'Or the Widow.'

'Or the Drunkard! Roderick, really, what am I going to do about this rain?'

His blank expression said it all. There was nothing to do about the rain, except complain to the Painter – and he likely heard more stories than the rest of them combined. Except where it didn't rain, such as in the Tear.

Vivian was most worried for her carefully sculpted ringlets. They were, she knew, a devastating weapon in the west, where hair fell naturally straight.

But the Painter took pity on Vivian's story, and drew the curtain of his rains back from the Duke of Western Perlanse's eastern most palace, the aptly named Westerly Strife. Her ringlets were safe, her weapons primed, and her husband napping once more. Which was just as well, because the road to the ducal palace was busier than usual as they began the long, flat approach. Vivian felt a familiar pang of envy tighten her jaw at the wide, open, and imposing space that Westerly Strife enjoyed. In peacetime it was a flaunting of wealth and ownership of all that the palace surveyed. It stood just inside the border of West Perlanse, and during the War of the Feathers it changed hands more often than a deck of cards – there was no defending such a place. But that was so long ago now. Worrying over a house's defences felt dangerously unfashionable. She thought of her own Truss House, sitting impregnable atop a mountain with little more than a goat path as an approach.

'Would you look at those southern trees,' Vivian said, knowing full well her husband still slept. Tall, straight, like columns of stone rather than proper Perlish trees, they lined the long drive and they were an affront. The first of many that visit.

Their driver joined the queue for the coach porch. A queue! What was the realm coming to? Was the Duke inviting all and sundry to his palace? Was that the latest modern fashion that Vivian would have to disapprovingly adopt, to invite lesser houses to one's games? Suddenly that defensible goat path did not feel quite so lamentable.

Fortunately, at the very least a footman was on hand to help Roderick from the carriage and another to gather their luggage for the night. They entered behind a large woman in a dress of mourning and a gentleman who could have been, and if not *should* have been, her grandson. Vivian could feel the gaze of those arriving behind but stared straight ahead; as uncomfortable an entrance as she had ever experienced. The crowded entrance hall – crowded, despite its colossal size – did not help. But the Duke had made efforts to amply provide for his guests: staff moved amongst the small knots of travel-wearied nobles with trays of exquisitely made, overly flavoured western delicacies and flutes of sweetened wines.

As she was inspecting one such tray, Vivian caught a movement in the corner of her eye. Try as she might, she could not ignore it.

'Oh, Reveller spare me, they invited Judith Mon'butter,' Vivian said under her breath. 'Smile and wave, Roderick.'

'I am.'

'Hello, Judith!'

'I told Karl we would know plenty of people here,' Judith said. 'Did I not tell you, Karl?'

'You did,' Karl said. The voice of a broken man, who had been such for so long he had forgotten what it was to be whole. At least Judith had got that right. The husbands quickly dismissed, Vivian and Judith dispensed with the niceties.

'This time the Duke has evidently invited every house in the east,' Vivian said, taking a glass of wine from a passing tray. She had no intention of drinking it.

'I heard he re-appointed the main ballroom for tonight,' Judith said. 'I imagined it would be draughty and brought my fur shawl, but not my favoured fan.'

'Do not tell me you still use that moth-eaten rag you claim is liked by the Latecomer?'

'Oh, Vivian.' Judith sighed like a two-penny harlot. 'I know you still prefer those quaint card games we used to play. But with the Torn Game, all luck is to be coveted and nurtured.'

'I *prefer* games that covet skill, Judith.'

'How easily the ignorant equate the two, don't you find?'

'Only in certain company.'

'Quite.'

The two women glanced away as a form of brief respite, as two fencers might after a clash. Half a glance was spared for husbands engaged in their inane prattle, and then on to the crowd. So many eastern families were in attendance that Vivian wondered if she should be worried. One troop of Ducal Guardsmen could achieve what decades of warring did not. At least there were many faces she only partly recognised, and many others she did not. Their straight hair and oddly cut clothing gave her all the reassurance she needed.

'I *do* hope you manage to enjoy yourself, Vivian.'

Now, that was worrying.

'Win or lose, I typically do.'

'Yes,' Judith said, touching her arm briefly, before moving off with Karl in tow.

Vivian was in no small shock at such a display of... of what, she wondered?

'Are you all right, dearest?'

'Be quiet, Roderick, I am thinking.'

Pity.

It struck like a bolt from the Missing Lover. Judith had expressed that rarest and most mistaken of feelings: something genuine. She really did pity Vivian.

'You don't look well, my dear. Is it the wine?'

'Audience take me, Roderick, do not speak again until spoken to.'

He opened his mouth to acquiesce, but caught himself just in time. He was also somewhat rescued from tying his own noose by the ringing of bells. A silence descended in their wake, and the Duke's head butler ascended above the crowd.

'Welcome, one and all, west and east, to the Duke of Western Perlanse's Westerly Strife evening of games!'

Light applause.

'Your rooms are ready, if you would please follow your footman.'

The young man who had helped Roderick out of the carriage appeared by their side. For a moment Vivian imagined him with a cruel knife in his pocket, ready to break the ancient pact under the Audience between host and guest.

She hoped fervently the young man would reconsider, whatever his motives.

When he raised his hand, she flinched, but his palm was empty and only employed as a simple invitation. If he noticed her agitation, he was too professional to give any such indication. She followed and made an effort to calm her breathing. That calm was short-lived.

Judith had been correct in at least one regard: the Duke had furnished his ballroom with gaming tables, a bar against each wall, and a number of areas to which players might retire between games. These were, by and large, groupings of dark leather loungers and exotic potted plants that looked like they enjoyed warmer climes. The guests were shown the ballroom before their sleeping quarters – the Duke understood their priorities.

But this brief tour did little to reassure Vivian.

'Did you see a deck of cards?' Vivian asked her husband when they were alone in their generous room.

'Which deck?'

'*Any* deck!'

'I wasn't looking for cards, dearest, you know I don't play. The shelves of spirits, on the other hand...'

'None of the tables I saw had a deck.' Vivian opened the wardrobe, where her evening dress had already been hung. 'We need to return home.'

'Home? But we just arrived.'

'I am serious, Roderick. No decks on the tables can mean only one thing.'

'The Duke ran out of cards?'

Vivian turned to her husband. 'It is a good thing I tell the Devotee how much I love you, idiot man; Blind or no, she would find it impossible to see! No, the most powerful man in Western Perlanse has not *run out of cards*. He does not intend for us to play cards. Any of us!'

'But then—'

'The Torn Game, Roderick!'

'Oh, that's a relief. I was worried we had travelled all this way for nought.'

Not knowing what else to do, Vivian threw her hands in the air.

The outburst embarrassed them both. Roderick crossed to the water basin and, removing his shirt, splashed his face. 'I am going to enjoy my evening at Westerly Strife. I suggest you find a way to do so too.'

She came to rest her head against his shoulder. 'But a new game, Roderick.'

'You're not so old as all that. You may even enjoy it.'

She looked at them both in the mirror and said, 'That's what has me so scared.'

They descended the wide stairs to the ballroom at a fashionably late hour. The tables were already full and, if her past experience was worth anything in this new-game world, there would be longstanding circles alongside the newly formed. Both had their interests and limitations. Vivian had thought to ease neatly back into an old grouping, perhaps for some Jilt, Hounding the Horses, or western-rules Wisherwell. Now she stood at the bottom of the stairs like a debutante – despite being unhelpfully encumbered by a husband. That encumbrance came to her aid in that moment.

'Would you join me for a drink before your game, dearest?' Roderick said.

She smiled at him. 'A small something, perhaps.'

The bars were just as full as the tables. The discarded wives and husbands of players made the best of their situation. That appeared to consist, when the disproportionate number of husbands made it possible, of outrageous flirtation. As Roderick ordered them both a decent eastern wine, she wondered if he spoke loosely with other women while she played. She wondered enough to ask him.

'Oh no, that always looked like a lot of effort. I prefer to watch people.'

'Watch people? As they do what?'

'Sometimes I watch the players. Or I watch the rest of us talk and drink and be at ease.' Roderick gave a lazy shrug. 'I find it quite edifying.'

'Then you can help me,' Vivian said. They had, quite by chance, found themselves simultaneously at the bar and near one of the tables.

'Is that this *Torn Game* you're so worried about?' he said, nodding to the table.

'Shh, not so loud, Roderick! But yes, I believe so. At least, it's no game I've ever seen before.' She sipped her wine. 'What do you make of it?'

'Looks complicated.'

'So I'm told.'

'What are all those symbols?' Roderick said.

'Silence take me, I wish I knew.'

A man beside her grunted. He looked and smelled as if he'd been at the bar since daybreak.

'Excuse me?' Vivian said, not entirely hoping for a response.

With some effort the man slumped round, sprawling with his back resting on the bar.

'See,' Roderick whispered, 'edifying.'

Vivian recognised this inebriate as Georges Stanubins, though he had finally done away with that dreadful moustache.

'Learners' tables,' Georges blurted, raising his empty glass in a nondescript direction.

'You appear to be on the wrong side of the room, Georges.'

'Not my game, Bouncing Bones. Not my—' He swayed drastically, and would have fallen if not for Vivian's intervention. Mere inches from his face, she could smell the bitterness of lost fortunes on his breath. 'Stay clear of it, W'oventrout. It feeds on the likes of you and I.'

'It is just a game,' Vivian said.

'Ha!'

'Georges.'

'Ha, ha, ha!' He was lost to his own hysteria.

She and Roderick shared a look. 'Thank you for... the drink,' she said.

'I will be here until you're ready to retire, dearest.'

She left him to his watching of people. After a few discreet enquiries, she found one of the learner tables nestled in a corner of the bustling ballroom-turned-games room. She was grateful there appeared to be no demarcation or seclusion for those learning, no apparent stigma, at least at first glance. As she took one of the empty seats, she realised the only indicator necessary to mark this table out from the others was the look of confusion on each face. One or two of them smiled weakly at her, but the others were too occupied by the game.

The table was led by a liveried woman, the only one standing. Vivian was relieved to find that she and the woman were of an age – she could not abide being taught by anyone younger than herself. She watched the final throes of a demonstration and was perturbed to find no one left their seat when it finished. This did not bother the tutor, however, who simply began the demonstration once more.

'Bouncing bones, or the Torn Game, as it is often referred to outside the Tear, is a fairly complex tile-based blocking game. Sets are typically fifty or seventy-five pieces, depending on the number of players. Unlike similar games, the Torn Game does not use numbers or recognised suits, but a long and changeable series of markings that—'

'Pardon me,' Vivian said, 'did you say "changeable"?'

'That's correct. Tiles can and will change their markings over the course of the game.'

'I don't understand. It sounds as if you're suggesting the tiles have a life of their own.' She laughed, looking to the rest of the table, but no one joined her.

'Yes, indeed. Many "conditions" can cause a power to build in a bone, until it has no choice but to bounce – quite literally – and reveal a new set of markings.'

'But how does—'

'Please,' the tutor said, 'the demonstration will explain everything.'

It did, and it did not.

Perhaps the Torn Game has also confused you? At least, those of you who have not played it. Perhaps you are not interested in the workings of games? And why should you be? You have been promised a story. Stories are the haunt of heroes, villains, great loves and great rivalries, not little polished pieces and complicated rules questions.

Your storyteller asks your indulgence: those with an interest in games, pay close attention and you may just understand the Torn Game as the story concludes; those who have no such interest, do not let such trivial things concern you – there is more than enough suffering and foolishness here for your entertainment.

Returning to poor, confused Vivian. Like the others before her, she stayed in her seat once the demonstration had finished. And again. And again. And with each time round, what started as a bemused smile edged ever closer to a grin.

A grin that, had she not been so absorbed in learning this new game from a distant land, she may have recognised as the same grin splitting the face of one Georges Stanubins.

Vivian watched, learned, and then played the Torn Game until the early hours of the morning. She eventually returned to her room in an excited daze, of a kind she recognised but had not felt in many years. Despite the hour, the dark room, and the slumbering form of Roderick beside her, she struggled to find sleep. So instead she told the Child stories of a game that she was only beginning to know, and that he was too innocent to understand. Stories of positions, of placements, and of possibilities. Stories that may have been overheard by the likes of the Wit, the Partner, or the Professional. When sleep did come, it was brief and it was all that she required.

The following morning, with little care for her dress, the

setting of her hair, or the bowl of fruit her husband was picking through, Vivian made for the door. Roderick looked up from the sinta he was slicing.

'You are abroad earlier than the robin this morning, dearest.'

Vivian made a grunt-like noise, surprising them both.

'Will there be players so early?' Roderick said.

'More than there are birds in the sky.'

'Well, do enjoy yourself.' There was a note of concern in his voice that she did not appreciate. But it was soon forgotten.

Entering the ducal ballroom, Vivian found she was correct in her assumption. However, unlike the early rising birds, the animals at the gaming tables had not in fact risen early. They had not risen at all.

She passed tables of haggard men and women with sunken cheeks and eyes glazed a watery red. Knowing that she and Roderick were due to return to Truss House later that day, she forwent the learning tables in favour of a seat at a lower stakes game. Her joining was acknowledged, though barely. She was pleased to find she knew none of the other players – her more egregious errors would not become the week's gossip at home. So absorbed in their game, these westerners forgot to offer the usual fare of barbed pleasantries to their eastern better. She watched the game in its final throes; a three-point Invasion marker bouncing to Diplomacy at a significant moment deciding the entire affair in favour of a woman who smoked bindleleaf in the modern fashion. She accepted her victory with little fanfare, and the next game began.

Stakes were set at a modest five hundred marks, with the opportunity to adjust during the 'spring' and 'autumn' of the game, depending on one's position. A portion of the game tiles was allotted to Vivian. Like most, she could not help but constantly handle the rectangular stones which, despite the lines carved into their surface, had a smoothness to them. The stones felt good to touch, with a satisfying weight, and were not made of bone despite the game's common name. However, she did not yet conform to the belief that such a handling bonded player and stone in a way the Latecomer might reward.

The opening placement of tiles followed a predictable pattern that Vivian recognised from her hours at the learning table. Early connections – referred to as bridges – were made between players whose settings were close. One connection was severed by the aggressive play of the bindle-smoking woman, perhaps emboldened by her previous win. But once bridges were down, the real game began.

As the jarringly geometric lines of the tiles formed or broke bridges, the game flowered outward in ever complicated patterns. To Vivian's understanding, it was these connections that charged the stones with their mysterious, foreign life.

When the first bone bounced, she had been looking at another part of the table. She cursed. What had been a Trade tile between two players to her right leapt a foot into the air and span at a dizzying speed. All watched, holding their breath – no amount of play or experience lessened the excitement of a bounce. Especially the first of a game. The tile crashed neatly into place with a reassuring thud, its face changing to a four-pronged Negotiation.

The ripples were felt all along the table.

Another bounce was immediately sparked: a Border Dispute was settled by an Assassination. Bridges were broken and formed. Vivian's position shifted dramatically. It was a foundation on which she was able to build a respectable third-place finish among the eight players. She retained most of her stake but, more importantly, she had correctly anticipated a crucial bounce. Because, as she later explained to a napping Roderick, each bone had only a finite number of outcomes that depended on the surrounding circumstances. The *conditions*. Read the table correctly and you could read the future.

'And there lies the game's wonder, you see?' Vivian said as their coach drove out of the ducal grounds. The last thing she had done during their visit was to buy a set of tiles. She clutched them now, in their heavy bone case, and would not let go the entire journey home.

'Were they expensive?' Roderick asked, not opening his eyes.

'What a question! We could not very well be the only house in Eastern Perlanse without a set.'

'Quite.'

'I am embarrassed to think how long that has already been the case. No wonder the Lock'ambs declined a match between our Cecil and their daughter.'

'I thought the girl was already with child?'

'That's what they *said*, but where is the child?' Vivian said.

'Hmm. And how much did you win under the Duke's roof this time?'

'No, I was fool enough for the Drunkard in refusing the Torn Game until now. The W'oventrout name will no longer raise smirks in eastern games rooms.'

Not smirks, no. But grave faces and the soft shaking of heads.

Vivian had no winnings from that first trip to Westerly Strife. She did not lose a large amount either, but she *did* lose. That in itself would have been no trouble for the W'oventrout family

– a thousand marks here or there would barely be noticed – were it not for the manner in which she lost: it was the start of an addiction. An addiction that she continued to feed every week without fail. And that is how a fortune the size of the W'oventrouts' is lost.

The passing of the years, and the passing of Roderick, were no help to Vivian's obsession. Though she grew in skill at the Torn Game, it was not a game where such skill might be leveraged into financial gains. It lacked the fluidity and ease of many card games, and required an unhelpful degree of concentration and sobriety. It was too challenging to teach a new player with an eye to lightening that player's purse. Though she was never short of company at her table – Judith Mon'butter continued to extoll the game's virtues – for most it was a pleasant distraction. To Vivian, other games were an unwelcome one.

And so it was that an unmarried and middle-aged Cecil W'oventrout was called into his mother's room. She was sitting at her dressing table and dabbing her eyes with a handkerchief. Her skin was thin and stretched too tight.

'I'm sorry, Cecil.'

He flinched. First she had been crying, and now she apologised, and Cecil had never known her to do either.

'Would you fasten my dress?'

'Where is...?' The question died on his lips – he had seen his mother's maid dismissed earlier that week, though he did not know what she had done. He crossed to his mother and began with the lower clasps.

'Ask me, Cecil.'

'Ask you what, Mother?'

'You know.'

He took a deep breath and recalled that which he wished he

could forget. 'A bone that showed Diplomacy is bouncing, last round you played a two-point stone beside it.'

'The *conditions*, Cecil. What else is happening around the Diplomacy? The *conditions*, you know that.'

Looking at her in the mirror, he said, 'Invasion. On all sides.'

She reached for his hand. 'It is not so hopeless as that,' she said. 'Do you see my flowers on the windowsill, Cecil?'

'Yes, Mother.'

'Pretty, aren't they? Fetch them for me.'

Cecil touched the small white petals. 'They are all over the lower gardens this time of year.'

'My father's passion. Phineas, he brought them to Truss House.'

'I assumed they had always been here.'

'Sit with me, Cecil, while we still have time for a story. I will tell you of their invasion.'

My father was a shy, softly spoken man. He was made so by his overbearing father and his absent mother. She preferred to spend her days and nights abroad in the far reaches of East Perlanse, where hunting was very different from Horse and Hound... but that is a story for another to tell. This is Phineas's tale. Shy, softly spoken Phineas.

He enjoyed the grounds of Truss House more than its interior. Under a paper parasol, he wandered the craggy paths, stopping often to sit on warm rocks and admire the hard-living shrubs and heather. He favoured loose-fitting linens over the layers of silk or velvet that you or I might wear. I have heard, though I did not see it myself, that he was known to walk barefoot on the paths of Truss House, his feet dirty as a Fenestiran street urchin. And yet he was a fastidious man in other respects. His beard was trimmed in the East Perlish style, decently oiled, and though he had the family's tendency towards baldness, he wore it fashionably. So when his marriage was announced, it came with no sense of surprise or scandal amongst the eastern social circles.

The surprise was Phineas's alone.

He had not met his wife-to-be. She was from the southern slopes of the duchy; not so far as the crow flew, but too far for respectable coaches and polite visitations. When his father told him he was to marry – days after Father had announced the match to his games table – Phineas was given a small portrait of the woman in question.

'She is... pretty?' Phineas said.

Bertram guffawed, a loud noise from a loud man. 'Don't sound so scared, boy! Of course Lucinda Knotting'oot is a beauty. We can't have the heir to Truss House trussed up with some cart mule, now, can we?'

'No.' Phineas looked at the portrait again. He wanted very much to drop it to the study's carpeted floor, but could not bring himself to do so.

'Now, your brother Henry, *be* we can sacrifice to a mulish type that carries heavy coffers on her back.'

Henry, Phineas's younger by five years, laughed dutifully from across the study. He was bent over one of his many maps. That was his passion, as he often told the Student: where one part of the world ended and another began. He longed to be the one who finally sketched the true extent of the Northern Steppes, or Break Deep, or what lay beyond the southern deserts. Impossible, as all good dreams should be.

'Mother's last letter placed her here,' Henry said, his finger a safe inch above the faded scroll.

'What's there?' Phineas said, staring at the empty region his brother was pointing to.

'Mother.'

'But why?'

They both turned to their rosy-cheeked father.

'Pah!' was all the old man said.

'This,' Phineas said, pointing much further south, 'this is where my...' He could not bring himself to say it, not yet. 'This is Knotting'oot Castle.'

'So it says.'

The map marked it in just the same manner as Truss House. Perhaps the Knotting'oots were not so different? They simply lived a little further south, in sight of the River Stave, halfway between Fenest and Break Deep.

'You look a little pale, Phineas. Are you quite all right?'

'I think I will take a turn in the lower gardens before lunch.'

'Silence take you, wear some boots this time,' his father shouted from across the room. 'If there's one thing a Perlish wife cannot abide, it is dirt under the nails.'

Only in Phineas's case did this well-known Perlish proverb apply to toe nails. Not knowing what to do with the small portrait of Lucinda Knotting'oot, he took it with him.

The lower garden was his favourite of all the walks around Truss House. The thin, gravelled paths wound between rock-lined flower beds that burst with colours and scents. There, on the south-facing sheer slopes, the pine and heather were kept at bay by the diligence of Head Gardener Mertins and his boy, Dorothy – born on Drunkard's Day, the unfortunate soul.

Dot, as he liked to be called, was amongst the Sweet Dandies, pulling up weeds. Phineas gave him a half-hearted wave, as the other half of his heart was rather burdened by the day's tidings.

So much so, he had forgotten his parasol; like the lizards in his brother's stories, he basked on a rocky seat in the mid-morning sun.

A wife.

What a notion. There was such inevitability, such finality to it. Like death. Except death did not scare Phineas.

He would not admit the source of this fear. Not to his brother, not to his friends – the few he had – and certainly not to himself. But in this story you and I know more than those who lived it. So it is our secret to share.

In all his twenty-two years Phineas had never seen a woman naked. Is that hard to believe? Impossible, you say? What of sisters? He had none. His mother? Rarely at home longer than a handful of days at once. He had no obliging cousins. Servants, surely? A maid or housekeeper who, driven by their lonely station or by mischief, knew no better than to tempt the young master? Evidently not. The Audience, in their infinite wisdom, saw fit to keep the female body that most frightening of unknowns to Phineas. A cruel jest, perhaps. But a young Perlish nobleman not driven by lust, not consumed by visions of bouncing bosoms nor the tantalising promise of shapely hips, was taken as a rare blessing by all who worked at, or visited, Truss House.

And what of Lucinda Knotting'oot? Would she count such a thing amongst the many blessings life saw fit to bestow upon her?

Phineas leaned the portrait of Lucinda against the low border of Rock Roses. He stared at her face. She had soft features, small eyes, and an all-too-knowing smile. Though he saw the plunging neckline of her dress, he did not follow it. Could not. He broke out in a sweat, despite feeling a chill against his skin. He looked beyond the portrait, beyond the roses, and far to the south. Somewhere, on a road nestled between hills that another man might call comely, his wife was coming for him.

But her gift arrived first.

The bell in Phineas's room rang just after dawn the next morning. He was already awake, already washed and shaved, being by nature an early riser. The bell caught him deciding whether the day to come might hold enough spring freshness for socks. He decided it did.

They met in the entrance hall, though all customary greetings were silenced by the large crate at the bottom of the stairs. Both he and his father watched as Henry eased his way around the obstruction, as they themselves had just done, and offered no aid. The crate was shoulder height but narrow. Though none of the W'oventrout men had any significant sense for such things, they would have said the wood was fresh and clean, which gave a favourable impression.

Staff loitered nearby, principal among them the butler and the young porter, Perkins – those responsible for the crate's entry into the house.

Bertram, the great W'oventrout patriarch, could take no more. His curiosity sizzled inexplicably to ire. 'What have you boys been up to *now*?'

Neither boy had a response, each searching their own memories and souls for a possible answer. What *had* they been up to that might explain such a crate arriving at Truss House through the front door?

'Well, Phineas, it's addressed to you.'

'Father, I have no idea—'

'Let's open the blasted thing then!' Bertram said, waving the staff forward.

Phineas took a step back. 'Is that wise, Father?'

'Open it!'

The porter, with help from some of the kitchen staff, prised the side of the crate free. It fell to the floor with a solid slap and a cloud of dust. Coughing and spluttering, waving ineffectually at his face, Bertram peered inside, blocking Phineas's view.

'Phineas? What is this? What have you done now?'

The staff glanced at each other. The brothers W'oventrout pointedly did not.

'Nothing, Father,' Phineas said.

'Then— Oh, I see. Here.' Father plucked a rolled scroll from somewhere inside the crate and thrust it at Phineas.

The scroll was of fine parchment sealed with a family insignia: a plant whose roots knotted their way all around the edge of the red wax. There would be no escape from such knots.

'Are you going to read it, or just stare at it?' Father said. He rubbed at his loose chin. 'Strange lot, sending a crate, but then they do live quite far south.'

Phineas cracked the seal, a sound which echoed around the entrance hall like the cracking of stone. He was not the only one to shiver at the sound. He read the contents of the scroll and then swiftly rolled it back up.

'Well?' Father said.

'Phineas, are you blushing?'

'No, Henry, I am not. The Knotting'oots sent me— That is to say, sent us a gift in advance of her— I mean, their, arrival.'

'Get a hold of yourself, boy, and get it out then!'

Someone giggled at the back of the hall.

'Father, please.'

'Now,' Bertram roared.

Phineas entered the gloom of the crate and, with no little effort, pulled out a large potted plant. Hundreds, perhaps thousands, of white flowers clung to a cleverly wrought trellis that grew from the pot's base. The trellis was a striking V shape, the flowers arranged to cascade inwards, towards its centre. To an innocent eye it was quite beautiful.

The giggler was not so innocent.

In fact, the entire kitchen staff were far from innocent. They saw immediately what Phineas and Henry did not, could not – because the brothers had never seen its like before. And, try as they might, the staff could not contain their laughter.

'Just what has got into you?' Bertram said, turning to where shadows and staff huddled at the edge of the entrance hall shaking with their mirth. Bertram did not see it either, though not even the Audience could say what *his* excuse might be.

'What did the scroll say?' Henry asked.

Phineas was too distracted to lie. 'It said, "A Hook of flowers, ready for the right member..."'

'The Audience? Which member?'

That proved too much even for the kitchen staff. Chef shooed them back to the bowels of Truss House, though their laughter lingered in the eyes and tight faces of the butler and the head housekeeper.

'Someone told the Knotting'oots you favour the Dandy with your stories, boy.' Father started towards his study. 'At least this Lucinda knows what she is in for.'

'But do I?' Phineas said under his breath.

Some might say Lucinda had made that as clear as possible, with her womanhood in white flowers.

***

Phineas ordered the pot carried to the lower garden. Though it filled him with a degree of dread, he recognised beauty when he saw it.

'We'll leave the lady's display as it stands, Dot.'

The gardener's boy nodded as he wrestled the pot into place, having cleared space in one of the beds. 'Right you are, Master Phineas. We'll leave the lady's display.'

'Maybe after the... after they have arrived we might take a few cuttings?'

They stared at the shapely plant. 'Can't say I know what this is, nor if it'll grow in these parts.'

'It's Caskanese Plotseed,' Phineas said.

'Caskanese?'

'Certainly rare this far north. I believe it prefers the warmer reaches of Bordair, though we do get some sun on these slopes, don't we?'

'I'd say.' Dot whistled. 'Bordair.'

'I think it says much about Lady Knotting'oot, sending an exotic gift such as this.'

'Says much how, Master Phineas?'

'That she's not averse to the foreign, not averse to things from the other realms. In their correct place, of course,' Phineas added, noting a growing discomfort in Dot.

Dot handled the plant with more care after that, as he might have handled crystal.

Phineas stayed with the Plotseed well after Dot excused himself on account of the east woodland path needing edging. He stared long and hard at the gift – what Lucinda called her

'Hook'. He was educated enough to know that a Hook was a teaser of the story to come.

As with most educations, it was wasted on him.

The wait is the hardest part. The Audience know it. They are patient, experienced, they know that the wait is the making or the breaking of someone's story. Phineas's fear – known to us, but still not admitted to himself – took hold in his stomach. All sangas and stitchers know *that* is where strong feelings affect the strong and weak alike. Every day Phineas experienced cramps, dull aches, and his mornings were spent, more often than not, on his chamber pot. Worse still were the stabbing pains brought on by the sound of horses' hooves, of wheels on gravel, of voices muffled so they were foreign to his ear.

He avoided windows. That was not so easy as it might sound; Truss House was blessed with many windows. Like all great Eastern Perlanse houses it was built to offer a view of every angle and every aspect of the surrounding lands. Lands owned by the house's occupants, of course. Rather than the huge boxes the wealthy of Fenest favoured, which were born from a lack of imagination, an old Perlish house was as faceted as a diamond. Phineas hurried through corridors with his gaze fixed on his feet. Where possible he used servant stairways, which rarely had anything but a slit for a window. He avoided all but the dining room and his own bedroom. He avoided windows.

And still he found himself staring out of them.

Every day his guard would drop once, maybe twice, and he lost an hour to gazing at the Perlish countryside, wishing he was anywhere else. If it was a window angled in some way to the north, he did his best to keep the path to Truss House in his periphery. He looked beyond to the wooded hills that rolled down and away into the distance, until they rose again on the horizon. More easterly views were shorter thanks to the Moral Mountains. Westerlies much longer, despite the crenelated towers and walls of that side of the house. Long views full of fields and farms and the happy workers of Perlanse.

The south showed only heat and horror for Phineas.

Heat, horror, and the lower gardens. Because, like most horrors, Phineas's was a heavy mixture of fear and fascination. He continued to find solace in his lower garden, despite how it, too, was changed by what was to come.

'Dot,' he called from where he sat in the sun. The boy ambled over, wiping the sweat from his brow. Dot tied his hair back when he worked and, as spring turned to summer, that hair turned to gold. An unusual colour for a Perlish lad. 'Dot, what do you suppose Lady Knotting'oot would make of her gift here?'

'Make of it, Master Phineas?'

'How we have situated it, here in the lower garden.'

Dot glanced at the flowers on their suggestive trellis. 'It's a fine spot,' he said. 'Plenty of sun, none too windy. What more could a foreign flower want?'

'To put down roots?'

'You want it out of the pot,' Dot said.

'I worry Lady Knotting'oot would see her gift placed here as a kind of unwelcome addition, to be tolerated until its inevitable demise. To die in the pot, without a chance in Perlish soil.'

'That has a ring of the Poet to it.'

'No doubt he would enjoy such a story. But could you plant the gift without ruining the arrangement?'

The boy tested the trellis in a few places and appeared to find it solid. 'No telling how it might grow, but she should be able to recognise it.'

'I would like to try,' Phineas said.

The two of them worked together that afternoon to ease Lady Knotting'oot's gift from its pot. Despite Dot's claims that he did not need the help, that Phineas should not dirty his hands with such work – he even brought forth the same proverb as his father, about dirt and nails – they worked well together. Phineas was no wool-headed son of a noble when it came to the gardens. He knew how to tease roots, how deep annuals like Sweet Dandies liked to be planted, and how soil should be looked after for the perennials. He would be no good to a Seeder crop field, but a flower bed was his favourite bed.

As the sun set over the other duchy, Phineas ordered ale brought to the lower garden. They drank with little conversation and enjoyed how the last warmth of the day mingled with the warmth of well-used muscles. The Caskanese Plotseed was also enjoying the warmth of fresh soil. Enjoying it very much, in fact.

The next morning, Phineas came down to breakfast to find Dot at the bottom of the stairs. The boy was wringing his cap in his hands, but looked relieved to see him.

'Thank the Audience, Master Phineas, you have to come quick. But quiet.'

Phineas looked the boy up and down. 'Dot, how long have you been waiting here?'

'Since dawn.' He would not sully the second floor of Truss House with his presence; a boy acutely aware of his place in the world.

'Whatever is the matter?' Phineas said.

'Come see. But we mustn't tell Father.'

'Yours or mine?'

'Both,' Dot whispered harshly.

All thoughts of breakfast were banished as Phineas followed the boy. The heir to Truss House snuck about his own house, through the linen stores, past where the game birds hung, and out the coachmen's entrance. Dot moved as a thief in a tale for the Bailiff: hunched, careful with his footfall, and yet doing his best to make haste. Phineas had little choice but to follow his example. Much as they tried, they did not pass unseen – what did, in a Perlish house? Mute maids stared doe-eyed as Phineas hurried after Dot. Everyone would know of that unusual start to the day before long. They might even risk telling the master of the house, but Phineas doubted it. What good was gossip if everyone knew it?

When they finally finished their illicit journey and made the lower gardens, Phineas was almost out of breath from the tension.

'What has happened?' he said, his hands resting on his knees. 'Is it the Caskanese? Is it all right?'

'In a manner of speaking.'

'Could that manner be plain?'

'It's a thing better seen,' Dot said, and he set off through the winding gravel paths to where they had planted the Caskanese Plotseed. And then Phineas saw that Dot was right; had he tried to describe it, Phineas would not have believed him.

Phineas's first concern, when Dot had led him through the house, was that the Caskanese had died. A rapid death it would have been, but perhaps here the Perlish soil was toxic to the foreign plant? For a moment he had entertained the thought of a dead plant, a supreme insult, and a marriage called off.

His relief was short-lived, unlike the Caskanese, which stood healthy and happy in the early morning sunlight.

Dot climbed into the bed, but not by the Caskanese. Instead, he was a good five feet further down the slope. 'Look.' He parted the long stems of the Student's arnica, which were already starting to flower that year.

Phineas squinted from the edge of the bed but could not see. He climbed into the bed alongside the boy, pushing more of the arnica aside, and knelt. A handful of green shoots greeted him, each no longer than a finger.

'That's not arnica,' Dot said.

'Well, what is it?'

Dot looked up the slope to the newly planted Lady Knotting'oot's display.

'Impossible,' Phineas said. 'We only planted it yesterday.'

'It's all over the bed. All over.'

Rather than air his disbelief – the boy seemed in a fragile state – Phineas inspected the bed for himself. Whether it was with the arnica, or genteelana, or even the low-growing plants, wherever he looked he saw the same short green shoots.

'How extraordinary.'

'Promise you won't tell my father,' Dot said.

'Why ever not?'

'We...' Dot squirmed. 'We didn't ask him before planting.'

Phineas could not help but laugh at the earnestness of the boy. 'Do not fret. I decided we should plant the Caskanese – and for good reason.'

'But—'

'I even helped with the planting. No, I recall that I planted it by myself. Do I need to tell a tale of tying you up? Of bribing you to secrecy? Hmm?'

'No, Master Phineas.' The boy looked suitably chastised, but still crestfallen.

Phineas knew what it was to fear a father's wrath. 'I'm sure the Knotting'oots will be delighted to see their gift flourishing here. And *my* father will see it as a good omen, I am sure.'

'If you're sure.'

In truth, he doubted Bertram would care to hear what had happened to the Knotting'oots' gift. That was, unless it caused him trouble.

That trouble came in the shape of an irate head gardener.

Phineas was summoned to his father's study later that day. It had not taken Mr Mertins long to notice what his son had spotted; after all, the display of Caskanese *was* rather conspicuous. Mr Mertins held a healthy scepticism for things foreign. He had seen Plotseed in the more exotic greenhouses of the Union – as a younger man he had travelled to broaden his horticultural knowledge, something he wished his son would also do. But he had never seen it planted in the open soil. He supposed it must occur in its native Bordair, but nowhere else.

All this knowledge and experience gave weight to the man's scowl as he stood beside Bertram.

'Phineas, tell me why my afternoon is being ruined by talk of plants?' Bertram said.

'A plant was the gift from the wife you chose for me.'

Bertram grumbled. The study was thick with cigar smoke, and for once Henry was not there pouring over his maps. 'Mertins is angry. Why is he *angry*?'

'I planted the gift, in the lower—'

'Yes, yes, but *why*? Tell me that, Silence take you!'

Phineas took a deep breath – as much as the smoky room would allow. 'I did not want to risk insult to the Knotting'oots by leaving the plant potted, separate from our own gardens.'

'Do plants not live in pots?' Father asked his gardener.

Mertins nodded.

'Then what insult?'

'Of not being welcome,' Phineas said, unable to keep his true feelings from his voice.

Bertram waved this away. 'She is coming here to marry you, of course she is welcome.'

'There's also the issue of the shape of it, Master W'oventrout,' Mertins said.

'Shape? What does the shape of leaves and the like matter to me?'

Mertins leaned forward and whispered into his master's ear.

Bertram's eyes grew rapidly wider. 'It looks like *what*?' he roared.

Mertins only nodded.

'It must come down! Now!'

'But Father—'

'Do *not* talk to me, Phineas. Not now, not today, not until long after your wedding day. How *could* you? In our gardens, for all of Perlanse to see?'

In this, Phineas was as innocent as the Child. He had no answer for his father, who would not have wanted one even if he had. Bertram W'oventrout did not make proclamations lightly. Not a word would pass between the two until long after his wedding to Lucinda Knotting'oot.

And so he silently followed his father and Mr Mertins out to the lower gardens. Dot was nowhere to be seen, which Phineas hoped was a good sign. He would not entertain any darker thoughts on that matter. Bertram made hard work of the narrow paths, stumbling more than once and loudly refusing Mertins' offer of help. When he reached the point below the Caskanese and looked back up the slope, he turned such a deep crimson that Mertins took a step back as if his master might explode. In a way, he did.

'*Down.*'

The sheer force of the word sent the birds from the nearby trees. Bertram tore his way through the flower bed towards the Caskanese. He left destruction in his wake, and wrought even more as he reached the trellis. He ripped it apart with his bare hands. The air filled with white petals. Strips of wood and stem were tossed aside.

Phineas and Mertins looked on, utterly stunned. Though combined they had known this man for over fifty years, neither had ever seen him in such a fury. Bertram did not stop until the whole display was destroyed. But not being a man of plants, he did not think to pull up the roots of the Caskanese; and he would have struggled to do so, even in his rage. Instead, he stood panting at the epicentre of his own carnage and felt the task was done.

He was right, and he was wrong.

In the days that followed, Phineas made every effort to avoid his father. He ate at unusual times or ordered food be brought to his chamber. He wasted hours in dusty rooms at the far reaches of Truss House – rooms he had explored as a child, and then forgotten as an adult. He played cards on his own. He made plans to whittle wood, something ornamental, but the tools lay unused on a side table. During those long days he did not visit the lower garden.

He went by cover of night instead.

The clouded sky helped him sneak out but did not help him locate the Caskanese. Lady Knotting'oot's display was gone. Utterly gone – not just by his father's hand, but also by the careful work of Mr Mertins, which had removed all sign the display was ever there. It took Phineas almost an hour groping in the dark to be sure he was even looking in the right bed of arnica. But then he found it: shoots of Caskanese, only measurable in inches, but there nonetheless. He wondered if Mertins was ignorant of the plant's spread, or if he knew but was unable to stop it. Or perhaps leaving the shoots was the compromise he and Father had settled upon. Either way, Phineas was glad to find the plant still a resident of Truss House.

He came out every night to check progress: impressive, that was the word that struck him. Other people might have struck Phineas with something stronger. And yet the Audience, in their great wisdom, took an interest in him. The Widow, the Luminary, and the Dandy all whispered together in the back row, conspiring towards a gift for Phineas on his last night as a fearful innocent. They conspired, until the Child shushed them.

When Phineas left the house on said night, it was once again under the cloak of cloud. But as he reached the ordained flower bed that cloak opened. Naked light, as pearly white as a milkmaid's thigh, bathed his face – and his face alone, at first. He could not move nor speak for the beauty of the Audience, though he would speak of it many times in the life to come.

Then that light spread to the bed and he found beauty there too. Where there had been arnica and growing shoots just the night before, now the Caskanese Plotseed flowered. But those flowers had been white by day. In the moonlight they glowed such a range of deep blues as to make the night sky envious. Still more wondrous, the centre of each flower still burned a strong white. Walking the bed was like wandering amongst the stars. Amongst the Audience themselves.

When he reached the edge of the bed he made to turn back, but realised he did not need to. The Caskanese was in *every* bed in the lower garden. He had not even thought to look beyond the stone-walled enclosure in which he and Dot had planted the display. Dot, who he had not seen since Father tore that display down.

They are everywhere, Dot, he thought.

He felt dizzy, felt as if he might weep and laugh all at once. He did neither; too awed to risk a sound. Such a moment was so fragile.

They're everywhere.

'They're here!' Henry said, bursting into Phineas's room.

Phineas was not yet dressed, having slept uncharacteristically late. 'Who is here?'

'*Who?* The Knotting'oots, of course!'

Phineas dropped his bar of soap in his wash basin, splashing the carpet. 'Here? Now?'

'No, not now. They sent a rider ahead – their coach is starting up the path to Truss House. But they'll— brother, are you quite all right?'

'Yes, yes, of course.' He hurried to ready himself. At least, ready in all outward appearances. Henry helped him pick something to wear that was more appropriate than his usual loose linens. He did not like the way everything pinched at his neck and under his arm, but he knew enough to know such things were socially expected. He powdered his face, righted his wig, and permitted Henry to rouge his lips.

'I look ridiculous,' Phineas said.

'You look Perlish, for once in your life. Now, shall we go down?'

'Together?'

'I've been ordered to deliver you to the entrance hall.'

Father was waiting for them. As were the heads of the household staff. A great welcoming party for his new wife, all lined up in a row. Phineas felt sick to the stomach, but that was nothing new.

'Do *not* mention the... Lady Knotting'oot's display,' Father said.

'The flowers are growing all over the lower garden.'

'Well that's a rare mercy; at least we won't have to explain what happened to them. You look,' Bertram paused, still staring out of the open double doors, 'suitable.'

'Thank you, Father.'

Phineas took deep breaths until he felt he might drown, like a trout tossed onto a river bank. Not the effect he was hoping for.

His brother took pity on him and, leaning close, said, 'Did Mother ever tell you the story of her arrival at Truss House?'

'Yes. But tell me again, Henry.'

'She was not appropriately dressed as far as Father was concerned.'

Father grumbled something in the affirmative, an obvious blessing for Henry to continue.

'If there ever was a more inappropriate W'oventrout,' Henry said, 'only the stories would know it.'

***

Our mother married younger than you, dear brother; she was only nineteen when her coach brought her to Truss House. She did not travel so far as your bride – the Col'bolos being a suitably *local* family. She has always claimed it was a sunny day, much like today, but Father says it rained enough to please the Painter. Does either condition excuse what she was wearing?

No. Adeline Col'bolo arrived at Truss House in full hunting gear: a hunting shirt bearing the Col'bolo family moto, *The Audience attends our churn*, embroidered in irony as Adeline wanted nothing to do with the family's ancestral business of cheese; shabby breeches over spatterdashes that lived up to their purpose; and boots that looked more loved than Father ever has. As she stepped out of the coach she made quite the sight when framed by its polished black lacquer. She donned a short-brimmed hat that would have looked unfashionable on any Perlish gentleman, and strode forward to shake Father's hand.

Bertram had not the wits, Jittery or otherwise, to do anything but respond with a firm handshake.

'Trout!' Adeline said to Bertram's mouth-flapping silence. He was all of two years her senior but that counted for nought. The basis of their marriage was established in those first moments. In many respects – all respects that matter – we are fortunate to be here at all, Brother.

Adeline slapped her bridegroom about the shoulder and said, 'Where's your stables?'

Father was accompanied, as we are today, by his dearest family so he looked to them for aid. But his parents were busily opening negotiations with the Col'bolo matriarch, who at least travelled in a respectable and well-fitted dress.

'Stables?' Adeline said once more.

Bertram waved in a westerly direction. 'New,' he spluttered. 'They are new. Newly built, I mean. My father—'

'Oh, I know that. Why else would I agree to our marriage?' Adeline started towards the stables. 'Trout!' she called back.

Bertram was left there, in front of the house, bride-less and alone as the staff returned to their stations, and the parents withdrew to wherever it is old people go to talk in private. If that day *was* truly blessed with sunshine, he squinted in all directions and softly sweated into his coat and shirt. If it was raining, he stood under the Painter's downpour for longer than he should. Either way, his confusion was total. He was unmoored, his home already irrevocably changed and different to him, his life oddly not his to steer; so disorientated, he reached for Casker metaphors, this man who had never seen a barge. You will know the feeling soon enough.

But Mother is where this story's heart lies. At that very hour she was sheltering from the hot sun, or hard rain, in the W'oventrouts' recently completed stable. She entered through the grand coachway, watched by all fifty members of the Audience accounted for in stone. Some appeared more interested than others. She gathered herself in the covered courtyard, admiring the fountain with the statue of the Rogue at its centre. He stood handsomely with horse, hound, bow and quiver captured in exquisite... exquisite...

'You there, what stone is that?'

'Rustan travertine, Miss,' a stable boy said.

'Rustan?'

'Expensive, they say.'

Adeline let the boy get on with his work. Stalls lined every side of the courtyard and most of them were occupied. The

W'oventrouts could have mounted a whole troop, though these horses were used to chasing foxes not westerners. Adeline had never chased a westerner herself. She assumed it would be just as exhilarating.

She splashed her face and neck at the fountain. The cool spring water cleared the day's sweat and grime, coaches being such a stuffy way to travel – yes, Father, sweat and grime because it was hot and sunny. And then she sat herself down at the feet of the Rogue and told him a story. If this was to be her home, her stables, it was right and proper she honoured the Audience with a tale.

That was how Adeline Col'bolo arrived at Truss House, and shared more words with the Rogue than her intended.

Now, I lean closer and lower my voice, dear Brother, because her story for the Rogue is not one for Father's ears. He may have heard it – perhaps from Mother's own lips – but I cannot, will not, tell it as it needs to be told in his hearing. You're surprised? Then you have forgotten much of our mother's tale and it is good that I am here to remind you.

She began in the middle, like any proper storyteller should.

'On my eighteenth birthday I saw two things for the first time: what lies between a man's legs, and what lies in the eye of the dying stag.'

'He was from the far north, and I don't mean the outer-most reaches of Perlanse. Born and raised on the Steppes, he bore all the marks of a hard life: scars dotted his neck and legs like lines on a map; parts of him were loose where they had once been tight; and the way he looked at me made me remember I was young and knew little of the world.

'What was he doing so far south? I didn't think to ask at the time, but I have wondered many times since.

'I found him at his lowest. I felt like apologising for that, but he would not have listened. He was wasted. He was majestic.

'On my eighteenth birthday I went hunting. It was what I had done on my birthday for as long as I could ride. Before I could ride, but after I learned to walk, I would stumble-run after the horses and the hounds as if I could keep pace by sheer will alone. Then I joined the foot followers. Before even that I was known to howl from my crib, perfectly in tune with the dogs. What could I do, being born under a Rogue's Moon? Birthdays meant hunting. When I realised this was not the case for everyone – my mother and father's birthdays were far more stoic affairs – I felt deeply sorry for them, and deeply pleased for myself.

'But my eighteenth was different. That year father had hired a new whip, a Wayward man looking for a season's worth of wages before he wandered again. I had seen him about the stables and while his appointment was still gossip amongst the staff I was vaguely aware of the man, nothing more. Father said he did his job adequately enough, and did not shirk duties when not in the field – what more could be asked of him? All that is to say, I did not seek him out. I did not even know his name. I just knew him as the Wayward.

'Mother woke me before dawn. She was still dressed in her nightclothes and carried just a small candle against the last of the dark.

'"Quiet, now," she whispered. "Best not wake the house."

'I rubbed my eyes. "What is the matter?"

'"The matter is your birthday. Come, we best not keep him waiting."

"'Keep *who* waiting?" I said, growing worried by my mother's secrecy. I knew marriage awaited me, that I had been fortunate to be unencumbered by a husband for so long, but what little I understood of the sorry business did not include much of the clandestine. Perhaps if it had, I would have been more disposed to it; the pomp and pageantry of marriage was not to my tastes. Even so, thoughts of a demanding husband who lived in a demanding house consumed me in that moment.

'My fears were not eased when Mother assured me I need not dress, that my nightshift would be sufficient.

'She opened the door to my room as if readying a tale to the Bailiff, who would have enjoyed hearing of a Perlish noble-woman creeping about her own house. Barefoot, we moved softly along the carpeted halls by the light of her single candle. Mother stopped at the top of the sweeping staircase: perhaps to catch her breath, I wondered. Yes, and no; Mother had been *holding* her breath the whole way. By which time I was utterly confused.

'This did not escape her. "Your father," she whispered with a weak smile, as if that were explanation enough. It explained that Father knew nothing of this... whatever this was and, more importantly, would not have approved. My interest was piqued.

'We eased our way down the stairs and past a sleeping porter, whose snores would have covered a galloping horse. But rather than make for the front entrance, Mother led me through the winding corridors and backways of Col Wedge House. Many times I guessed at our destination, briefly certain, until we took an unexpected turn and I was once more in the dark. We saw no one in that part of the house, except for the house baker up early to roll his dough. He glanced up from his table to see his mistress and her daughter, still attired for bed, tip-toeing their way through his kitchen. Though a look passed between him and my mother, he said nothing. And then we were into the maze of passages once more until finally we descended into the cellars.

'I wished for boots, or at least slippers, as the flagstones were cold. Here, Mother's candle cast all kinds of unexpected shadows. The cellars ran the whole length of Col Wedge; one long, wide, high-ceilinged chamber that seemed to elevate a simple draught to a wind-filled story for the Bore. One length was taken up by shelves of great casks of drinks I had no taste for. Huge blocks of ice sat wrapped in paper just waiting to be attacked with chisels for Father's preference for chilled water. The soft sound of our footsteps was echoed by the scuttling of much smaller feet. I had the feeling we were being watched, and followed, by rodent sentries... my imagination was set loose by the strangeness of that night or, should I say, that early morning. But even at my most imaginative, I would not have dreamt up what was waiting for me at the end of the cellar.

'"Mistress Col'bolo. Mistress Adeline." The Wayward whip greeted us from a distance, just a voice in the dark. I jumped at the sound, as did my mother.

'As we approached, the candle peeled back the darkness and, I initially thought, the Wayward's clothes. He stood there naked as the day he started his story, though considerably bigger, and casually leaning on an enormous bow. I had never seen one as large as that, and haven't since. I worry even as I tell this story that I may cause the Rogue no little envy in this regard; what man isn't struck by the greener emotion when seeing another is blessed with a greater weapon?

'"Yes, well, I... Well," my mother said, struggling. "Here we are then. I hope in the years to come you'll look back on this night fondly. And not a word to your father." With that she turned and left me there, taking her candle with her.

'Difficult as it may be for a member of the Audience, try to imagine what that moment was like for an eighteen year old woman who knew men only as father, staff, servant, or huntsman. There I was, in just my nightshift, plunged into darkness mere feet away from a well-armed stranger from another realm. Delivered to this man by my own mother, no less.

'And then he said, "Remove your shift."

'"Pardon me?"

'"Or I will."

'With no small tremble in my hands I pulled the nightshift over my head and dropped it to the floor. My eyes were beginning to adjust to the dark of the cellar, aided a little by an open trapdoor beyond the Wayward.

'He held the bow out for me to take. It was surprisingly light. He knelt and retrieved a quiver that was also for me. From the darkness he conjured another bow and quiver for himself.

'"You like to hunt," he said.

'"Yes, but—"

'"Then keep up, and keep silent." He moved off towards the trapdoor, through which large inanimate objects entered Col Wedge House. This night a very large, very animate object exited up a ladder, and I did my best to follow without staring. Having never seen a fully naked man before, my best proved a poor effort. How pale his buttocks were! How dark what lay between.

'I did not imagine a man to be so hairy.

'He led me from the house but not towards the stables. That we weren't attired for riding was obvious enough, and I didn't think even the Wayward rode naked; the horses may have been so lacking on the Steppes, but surely not the riders. Instead, I wondered why we hunted without hounds. When I asked the Wayward he grunted and said so softly that I almost didn't hear him, "Too loud."

'We looped below the house, crossing one of the long formal vistas. I hunched low, as if that might help escape notice as the only moving thing in such a wide open space. The Wayward strode ahead as if nothing were amiss. Perhaps he spent most nights wandering the grounds without a scrap of clothing? Perhaps many men did? I had never thought to look for them.

'I was relieved when we finally made the cover of the forest. Col Wedge had large, well-stocked woodlands on the estate. Deer, foxes, game birds: all were available without leaving the grounds. And yet there was something in the Wayward's manner, in the way he moved, that made me think we were going farther afield. He was quiet, silent almost, but not... ready. Not alert to what might be waiting amongst the trees.

'My attention was largely on where I trod next, unused to so much as traversing my room barefoot let alone a forest. It was uncomfortable and cold and I had never been more awake in all my eighteen years.

'We walked and walked and I did not know how long had passed. I entertained the idea I was being taken to some Wayward camp. In those dark hours I entertained a great many other ideas that involved more handsome Wayward men with long hair and unreadable eyes.

'Those unfulfilled stories were dispelled by a flash of colour in the gloom. The Wayward hadn't noticed, being a good few yards ahead of me. I slowed, then stopped, and waited. Another flash, closer, an unmistakable russet with splashes of white. I crept forward with more care than I'd ever shown when hunting a fox before.

'I found them lying between the roots of a huge tree. They were panting, their tongues slips of bright pink. I eased my bow up, from my hiding place beside a tree, but as I did so they came alive. At first I thought they were fleeing – a familiar sight to me. Instead, they frolicked amongst the roots, nipping each other and yelping.

'I'm not soft hearted, if that is what you're wondering. My arrow was ready and I just needed a clear shot.

'But the Wayward stopped me.

'I hadn't heard him. I hadn't smelled him either. He lowered my bow with a gentle hand. Without a word we watched until the foxes grew bored of each other and parted ways.

'"This is not a night for foxes," he said eventually. "As a girl you hunted foxes."

'Perhaps it was the strangeness of that night's events, or I was wool-headed from a rudely interrupted sleep, but it took me longer than it should to ask my Wayward guide the obvious.

'"Why are we naked?"

'"Your clothes stink," he whispered.

'"I beg your pardon?"

'He shushed me harshly. "Soaps. Perfumes. Powders. You are bad enough, clothes are worse. Stags catch your stink."

'I sniffed. "And sweat?"

'"Better," he said. "Belongs more in the forest. When the time comes, take your time. Only one arrow. Any more questions?"

'I had many, but they seemed small and petty under his gaze and under the canopy. I shook my head, indicating I was finished with any unnecessary chatter. We started off again, and I worked hard to imitate my guide. Not just his crouching, his nocked arrow, and his way of searching the surroundings, but the manner in which he used his muscles. How he took each step. When he tensed, or didn't. His body was slick with sweat, and it was difficult to tell what marks were dirt and what was hair. But the body beneath was as clear as horseflesh; nothing could hide the power held there.

'I may have been remiss in my storytelling so far, and forgotten to express just how much I was enjoying myself. My audience must forgive me on this account. I am only a Perlish noblewoman after all. I have focused on the unusual circumstances and neglected my excitement.

'I was alive with it. The hunt, not necessarily as I knew it, but the hunt nonetheless. The crackle of anticipation was building within me, as lightning builds in a cloud. I would be tested. My strength against the life of another. And whatever the outcome, a tale for the Rogue, who revels in our defeats as well as our victories.

'And so there I was, my bones bouncing under my skin when the Wayward brought us to a stop. I did not know why. I could not see what he had spotted. But he was as rigid as a scent hound the moment before they bolt.

'We were at the top of a gentle slope that ran towards a trickle of a stream. I heard the water as much as I saw it; the forest was dense, old, and wary here. Centuries may have passed since the last human trod on that ground. The deer tracks, however, were clear even to my ignorant eye. With the tip of his bow he indicated down, beyond the stream, to a tangle of bushes. I stared with such an intensity, I believed myself capable of willing a deer into existence. But I saw nothing.

'My guide indicated I should draw my bow.

'I opened my mouth to complain and only just caught myself before I ruined everything. Instead, I did as he bid.

'I sighted along the arrow, the huge bow now bearing all my earlier excitement and tension. I breathed slow and soft and waited, though my arms could only take so much.

'Sweat slid down my temple, circled my eyes, and dropped from my nose. My gaze blurred at the edges. I was cold and hot at the same time, but on different parts of me. I breathed but it felt like smoke and fire. I was so far from home.

'Then the top of a bush moved.

'Amongst the thicket and bramble the shape of a stag came into being, like a constellation found for the first time.

'I loosed my arrow straight to his heart.

'He was majestic. He was wasted.

'I felt like apologising for that, but he would not have listened. I found him at his lowest.

'I didn't think to ask at the time, but I have wondered many times since: what was he doing so far south?

'And the way he looked at me made me remember I was young and knew little of the world. Parts of him were loose where they had once been tight. Scars dotted his neck and legs like lines on a map. Born and raised on the Steppes, he bore all the marks of a hard life. He was from the far north, and I don't mean the outer-most reaches of Perlanse.'

Adeline cupped her hands and drank from the Rogue's fountain; reward for the story offered. She stood and stretched. Back from her own story, she enjoyed the sounds and smells of the stables.

'I don't have so much hair on me,' the stable boy said from the other side of the fountain.

Adeline laughed. 'I should suppose not.'

'But I know what lies between everyone's legs.'

She went to where the boy was sitting, where he'd sat for her story with his pitch fork forgotten by his feet. She lifted his chin. His face was not unattractive, and might improve with age. 'If that hair starts appearing, come to the main house and show me.'

Despite his gawping, she took a slow circle of the stables, admiring the stock of field hunters. The W'oventrouts at least knew their horseflesh, or knew others who did. There were few Gaters, which suited her; now she was here, she'd lead every hunt from the very front. Or she'd wander the forests with just her bow. The seasons were warmer this far south.

Father was waiting for her at the entrance to the stables. It is hard to imagine, I know, that he was once shy and bashful and would fit into one of your shirts, Phineas. But there he stood, hands clasped behind his back and unable to meet the eye of his bride-to-be.

'I hope you found our accommodations to your liking,' he said to his boots.

'Very fine. You know your horses,' Adeline said.

Father wrestled with the idea of lying to her. The thought of rising in her esteem was an alluring one. But he had ever been a pragmatic man, and saw the trap of that lie stretching out into his future. 'Not I,' he said. 'My father.'

She shrugged. Her indifference was like a dagger to him. He desperately wanted to impress her. She fell in beside him with an ease he envied. They walked down the wide path towards the house.

'I chose the ornamentation,' he said. 'The stone work and such.'

'The Rogue's statue?'

Bertram stood a little straighter. 'The sculptor tried to get away with a simpler design. But I insisted. On the bow, and such. Your father said you hunted in every manner imaginable.'

'And why Rustan stone?'

'That is a long story,' he said.

'Perfect. I find gardens so very dull without a good story.' She sat on a bench overlooking the lower gardens of Truss House.

Father had evidently avoided the trap of one fabrication, only to stumble into the jaws of another. It was the pattern of their relationship from the beginning; even when telling the truth he would be wrong-footed into something far from it. He blinked at the space on the bench beside her. He very much wanted to run in the opposite direction, but instead sat and stared at the sun arcing its way across the western sky. His audience was waiting.

'It is no great family secret that my father married a Rustan woman,' Bertram said. 'It was, however, quite the story at the time.'

Despite the splendour of Truss House, my parent's marriage was not one of silver or gold, but of tin. I cannot speak for the Col'bolos, but most of the eastern families have some degree of stake in the eastern tin mines. You could not say either? No, I imagine your father preferred not to burden you with such crudities as business. Perhaps I will ask him of it after dinner. Regardless, not so long ago the W'oventrouts and other families faced a significant downturn in their tin mining concerns. For my family in particular this meant a problem further along the supply chain. You see, we did not just own stakes in mines but also much of the surrounding industry – smelters, craftsmen, traders, and such. Sadly, most people do not appreciate the complex web that is industry, especially here in Perlanse. The noble families consider it a subject beneath them, for the commoners it is too challenging to conceive, and for others—

What is that? Boring? Yes, I suppose you have the right of it. For most people, regardless of station, it is simply too boring. So I will return to that eternally fascinating subject: marriage.

Before she was my mother, Watcher Darmst was the youngest daughter of the Great Watcher of the Rusting Mountains. More exciting? I thought so. As did many of the eastern families at the time. The marriage was arranged by my grandfather, who spent much of his final years in the Rusting Mountains and the southern parts of the Lowlands in pursuit of tin. My father never left Truss House. The bride and groom had never met. Until she arrived here with nothing more than a hardy leather sack slung over one shoulder.

Watcher Darmst had not walked the entire length of the Union, though few would have doubted her capable of doing just that. She had, with her father's blessing, taken a somewhat circuitous route north on a Casker barge she boarded at Bordair. What occurred on that barge, and the day's layover in Fenest, is a story for another time. But Darmst parted ways with the barge due south of Truss House. Typical Rustan logic; she did not consider what lay between the house and the River Stave. Were there roads? How safe was the countryside? How would a lone Rustan woman be treated so far from home?

You may know little of the Rustan people – few this far north do. But they are a very *direct* realm. Not just in their conversation or their opinions, but in their *thinking*. Darmst truly believed she should be able to travel the straight line from the banks of the Stave to Truss House because in the Rusting Mountains she would have been able to do just that. The concept of a bend in the road simply does not occur to a Rustan. What is the need of a corner when one can simply go higher?

But I see I have lost my audience.

All that is to say, Watcher Darmst arrived at Truss House with even less pageantry than yourself. No coach, no gig, no family, not even attendants, only one leather sack and the heavy Rustan clothes she wore. She had been expected for weeks. My father was beside himself with worry. She did not understand why.

On that very first day, my father was summoned from his room to find his bride standing in the entrance hall. She was... striking. He stood on the terrace, unbeknownst to her, and tried to order his thoughts. She was attractive, he felt that much, but not in a way he understood immediately. She was far from a typical Perlish beauty. She had a strong jawline, a serious set to her face, and her skin was darkened by what he assumed were days in the southern sun. Her hair was tied back into a single, thick braid.

He had expected all manner of metal parts sprouting from her. He'd feared his wife would embrace him with metal arms, that when they kissed he would taste iron, that when she spoke he would hear the grinding of gears. As with most fears it was intertwined with excitement; he found himself disappointed when he saw little metal on his wife-to-be. From where he stood she looked different, out of place, but not terrifyingly so. He found his courage and descended the sweeping staircase.

'Samuel W'oventrout,' she said, before he had a chance to properly introduce himself. 'I know you from the portrait your father carried. You are to be my husband.' She spoke as if she was talking of the weather or the weeding of a garden.

'Yes,' Samuel said.

She offered her hand, which in his confusion he shook rather than kissed. She appeared satisfied.

'Welcome,' he said. 'Welcome to Truss House.'

'It is a big house.' Her tone suggested this was not necessarily a good thing.

'Would you like to see it?'

'I can see it.'

'I meant the rest of the house,' Samuel said.

She turned a full circle, her gaze lifting to the marbled terrace, until she came to look at him again. 'You polish your stone,' she said.

'Someone does, I suppose.'

'Someone.'

'The staff, perhaps?' He felt his cheeks warming, though he wasn't entirely sure why.

'The staff.'

'You must be tired, from your journey,' he said, trying to regain some kind of control of the situation. 'Would you care to accompany me to your chamber?'

She stared at him.

'I mean, that is to say, I did not mean—' He took a breath. 'I'll have someone show you to your rooms.'

'I would like *you* to show me.'

'Of course. Why not. I know where they are, after all,' he said, laughing at his own jest until he realised she wasn't. 'May I take your bag?'

'No,' she said.

'I meant, not to *take*, but— never mind. This way.' Samuel

was glad to be walking ahead of his bride, his burning cheeks hidden at least. He felt he had not comported himself well in their first meeting. She must think him a buffoon, he thought, stumbling over his words and making unsophisticated attempts at humour. A tale to share with the Drunkard and the Amateur. He could picture them laughing as they listened, as the Devotee just shook her head. Such musings made him hurry down the carpeted halls, past his own rooms, beyond the main terrace and along to the east wing. She kept pace easily. When he opened the door to the next corridor, he advised her to take care with the step down as it surprised many guests.

'Whose house are we in now?' she said.

'Whose? Mine, still. I mean Truss House. This is still Truss House.'

She eyed him suspiciously. 'How many families live in this house?'

'One.'

'But it is so big!'

'Of course,' he said, not trying to hide his pride.

She shook her head. 'Such waste.'

She was similarly confused by the size of her quarters. She paced the main room, looked at the bed as if it were the size of a Seeder field, and was downright perturbed by the adjoining bathroom.

'A whole family would live in less in the Rusting Mountains.'

'But you're not in the Rusting Mountains,' he said softly.

She dropped her bag on the floor. 'No. I have a lot to become accustomed to.' She crossed to where he stood by the door. 'These are nice,' she said, touching his dark ringlets.

In an instant he was blushing again. 'They run in the family.' She had rather lovely dark brown eyes.

Then he noticed her fingers. Two of them, on her left hand, the two smallest, were well-worn metal. He flinched, causing his hair to snag in the metal joints. They stumbled over each other to apologise first.

'I suppose I also have a lot to become accustomed to,' he said.

'Not so much,' she said. She hid her hand behind her back. 'Now, I would like to see your trees.'

'My trees?'

'Yes, trees. Please.'

Samuel decided against showing his bride-to-be any more of Truss House, for fear of her disapproving glances and tuts. They left by the main entrance, under a bright early summer sky, and walked without conversation towards the treeline. There were a number of modest woods and copses on the W'oventrout estate. Being part of the Morals chain, they did grow some fairly sizable pines and cedars on the slopes of their hills but nothing particularly specialist. Darmst, however, seemed impressed.

She knocked one trunk, then another, sizing each tree up as she passed it.

'You have an interest in trees?' Samuel said.

'Our marriage does.'

'Pardon me?' he said. 'Our marriage?'

'Yes. We are to be married.' She knocked another pine, then nodded.

'I know, but what do trees have to do with that?'

'My father needs wood,' she said. 'Your father needs tin. I need a husband, and you need a wife.'

'I see.' Samuel steadied himself as he followed her down

the pine-covered slope. 'I suppose love can sometimes be that simple.'

'Love?' she said, looking up at him with a small smile. 'Do Perlish men believe everything they hear in the stories?'

'Is it so hard to believe? Compared to stories of death and destruction and worse still?'

She turned back to the darkened woods. 'Perhaps in Perlanse there is time for such stories.'

Samuel reached the plateau on which she stood. He kept his distance, turning pine cones idly with his boot. 'You've only just arrived, but you *have* arrived here,' he said. 'In Perlanse. It's—'

'Shh.'

Darmst stood still as a statue, staring into the tree's gloom. He moved next to her as quietly as he could.

'What is it?' he whispered, struggling to see anything.

'I've never seen one. Just heard the stories.'

'Oh, a doe,' he said, finally seeing it for himself. 'We have plenty on the estate.' The doe was making her way down a slope opposite, stopping every so often to nuzzle amongst the fallen pine needles and such. He had the impression there were more deer further into the shade, but could not make them out fully.

They stood and watched the deer for some time. He felt a great deal of peace in that quiet. His worries, the work that had occupied him in the days previous, the thought of becoming a married man, all those worries drifted away. So soft was the light, so silent the world, it was like a waking-dream.

And when he woke, he found her hand holding his.

Samuel W'oventrout liked to draw. Like most, he began by

drawing what was close at hand for a young boy: his family, his home, the gardens. His mother encouraged this creativity whenever she could, though his father was more sceptical. He was unfashionably pragmatic for a Perlish noble and worried that his only son would waste his hours filling scrolls with flowers and sunsets and other useless things. But Samuel had no affinity for the growing of flowers. Nor did he position bowls of fruit on tables, just so. He found people and animals frustrating. They moved so swiftly and though he understood the mechanics of that – understood, for example, how a horse's leg extended from rump to hoof and each played its own part in the motion – he was unable to transfer that knowledge from head to hand.

Samuel's talent extended almost solely to the drawing of buildings. And in this, at least, his father approved.

He sketched every one of the many aspects of Truss House. He came to understand perspective from looking back at the house from the undulating lower gardens. He learned to capture sunlight on glass from the many windows. He made the flat scroll appear round when he sketched the towers and their conical roofs. Scroll after scroll he dedicated to single, isolated elements. In others he gave a grand, sweeping view of Truss House.

And then his gaze turned inwards, but not necessarily in the manner his mother had been expecting when she asked him to draw her favoured sitting rooms. He gave her a three-room floor plan that was exactly to scale but devoid of any of the furnishings. His father was delighted.

Which brings us back to his first days with Watcher Darmst, his wife-to-be.

'You drew this?' she said, looking at the scroll stretched out across the table. They were in the upper study. Samuel preferred to work there – the main study was too much his father's room.

'It's not finished,' he said.

She leaned closer, her face only a few inches from the parchment. 'All this for horses?'

'And the hounds.' He hadn't meant to sound defensive; he wasn't ashamed of his family's position. But he wanted to impress, not offend her. 'There's more,' he said. He circled the table and pointed to one edge of the scroll, which was largely blank. 'Something for you.'

'Me? I can't even ride a horse.'

'What do you mean?' he said, momentarily distracted.

'I've never ridden a horse before. We don't have them in the Rusting Mountains.'

'No horses,' he said. It was beyond him to imagine such a thing.

'The mountains are too sheer, the air too bad. And what use is a galloping horse when clinging to a cliff face?'

'But—' He waved away his own questions. 'I wasn't thinking horses and hounds anyway. This part of the stables.' He tapped the blank space. 'Here, once the ground has been cleared, this will be the highest point over the valley below.'

She peered at the off-white empty parchment as if it would show such a thing.

'A good forty, fifty feet sheer drop,' he said. 'Before the slope even begins again. Then, who knows how far before the ground levels out. Would that be enough?'

'Enough for what?'

'For you to fly.'

Once again, Samuel found himself walking beneath the pine

canopy with Darmst. This time, they set off hand-in-hand. Her metal fingers were cool against the back of his hand. She seemed excited, though Samuel did find her hard to judge in those early months. Her smiles were small, her laughter short, and her bluntness caught him off-guard more often than not. In the same vein, the few times he saw her anger it was a short-lived flare and though her patience was often tested it rarely broke. His mother said she would make an excellent player of games, but Darmst had little interest in such frivolities.

That morning, she walked quickly. Not so much that she was dragging him along but enough for him to notice.

'Does it get much warmer here?' she asked, weaving between the trees.

'Late summer can become quite uncomfortably hot and muggy.'

'Muggy?'

'Humid.'

She stopped and stared blankly at him.

'When the air feels heavy, like it wants to rain but it's too hot and sunny.'

'It rains or it doesn't.'

'Yes, but...' He struggled to explain something he barely understood himself. 'You'll feel it soon enough.'

'Muggy,' she said, trying the word. 'Heavy air does not sound good for flying.'

'No, I imagine nothing heavy is good for flying. And yet.' He held up her hand, indicating the metal there.

She shrugged. 'No lockports, no flying.'

She had offered to show him her lockport on her first night at Truss House. The subject of Rustan hidesails had inevitably come up at dinner, despite the W'oventrouts being at their most polite.

Darmst explained the sails attached to their wearer between the shoulder blades through a large, circular locking mechanism – known commonly as a lockport. When met with the table's incredulity, she began to slide her dress from her shoulder. Mother's cries of surprise were enough to stay her hand.

Samuel would be lying if he said he'd thought of much else since seeing the curve of that shoulder. They had yet to lie together, though his bride-to-be had been at Truss House now for some weeks.

He cleared his throat. 'I had thought it was as simple as jumping off something very tall.'

'Your Morals Mountains are tall. Do you see Rustans flying there?'

'No, but—'

'And the Spires of Fenest, Rustans do not fly there either.'

'Why not?'

'Too cold,' she said, 'and too dangerous. Come, show me the place.'

They continued through the copse for another hundred feet or so before the trees abruptly stopped and the ground disappeared. Beyond, the valleys and peaks of the Morals stretched out to the horizon. A warm gust of wind met them as they stepped out from the tree-line, as if the Bore had heard Darmst's earlier question regarding the warmth of Perlanse. They stood together on the narrow clifftop, but could not have stood more differently: Samuel was leaning back towards the trees, his knees bent as if he were ready to crawl to safety if need be; Darmst was as steady on her feet as a mountain goat. She let his hand go as she walked up and down, looking over the edge to the sloping ground below.

'There is a good wind up the valley here,' she said.

'That's promising,' Samuel said. He had retreated to the safety of the trees.

'Not enough for flying.'

'Oh.'

'But gliding, perhaps.'

'Gliding?'

Darmst spat over the edge and counted until she reached eleven. 'Gliding. A person with a hidesail is not a bird. We can't flap. Only air hot enough pushes a hidesail upwards, creates flight.'

'As hot as the Tear.'

'Hot as the Tear,' she said.

'I'm sorry.'

'Why?'

'To take you away from that. To fly must be...'

'My father needs wood, your father needs—'

'I know what our fathers need,' he said.

She smiled. 'Flying through the Rusting Mountains is glorious. But, for a Rustan, it is like the Perlish riding a fast horse – glorious, yes, but something people do every day.'

'You can't ride a horse.'

'Then you shall teach me.'

'And you can teach me to glide?' he said.

Darmst walked back under the shade of the trees until she stood right in front of him. He was a good foot taller than she was. Though he'd never considered himself as willowy or spindly – he'd not really considered his body much at all – that was how she made him feel. She was solid, strong, and he might be blown over by a stiff breeze. Fortunately, the Bore's winds were not so strong in East Perlanse. She looked up at him with a sadness he didn't understand.

'You can never glide,' she said. And before he could say anything, she turned her back to him and released the top clasp of her dress.

His first thoughts were to stop her, that they weren't married yet, that someone might see them. Those thoughts were soon forgotten.

Her neck was less sun-marked the further it tapered towards her shoulders. She released another clasp and the dress parted to reveal something more than skin. From behind the lace and cloth rose a silvery moon. A wedge at first, but then she pulled back the dress and rolled her shoulders and the lockport was free.

To his shame, he gasped.

Between the blades of her shoulders was a deeply set hole lined in pristine metal; a hole the size of a side plate. Where skin met iron was seamless, and then the hole plunged deeper until... until he saw bone.

But it wasn't bone, not as he knew it from shanks of meat or from the carcasses of game. That bone had a natural colour – a complicated beige.

This was the dull colour of iron.

The bone consisted of interlocking segments that were more intricate than anything he'd seen from an animal, yet solid despite that intricacy. These metal bones bounced and buzzed as Darmst turned her head to look round at him.

'Does it hurt?' he said, and immediately regretted the question. It was foolish – a childish reaction to something he did not understand.

'When I was a girl, yes. Sleeping was agony. It's as big as it needs to be, right from the start, and you grow into it.'

'Is it... were you... I mean to say, was it your choice?'

'Of course!' she said, re-fastening her dress. 'Who would not choose to fly?'

'I for one.' Samuel could still picture the metal spine embedded in a hole of iron – something he knew would stay with him for a long time. To one not offered the choice, to one who only wore metal that could be removed before getting into bed, the answer appeared obvious. She just shook her head.

'This cliff, this valley, pretty as it is – it is nothing. Your Moral Mountains would be little hills in the Tear, not worthy of naming.'

'Well,' Samuel said, not trying to keep the indignation from his voice, 'we're quite fond of our little hills.'

She put her hand on his arm. The hand with two metal fingers. 'That's not what I meant. It is hard to explain, but once you're among the Rusting Mountains the choice to have a lockport is no choice at all.'

'And yet you chose to come here, to me.'

'I did.'

'Wood and tin?' he said.

'I *chose*.'

He offered her his arm. But that day had quite the effect on Samuel W'oventrout; a changed man that made for a changed family.

That Samuel had been somewhat of a romantic before the arrival of Watcher Darmst was a well-known fact at Truss House. Who could spend their days drawing and *not* have a romantic way of telling their stories to the Audience? So, it was perhaps no great surprise that the arrival of his bride-to-be did nothing to lessen that side of his character.

His parents were surprised, however, when Samuel demanded the wedding be postponed until Darmst could fly from the grounds of Truss House.

His father was a well-travelled man. He had seen the Rusting Mountains, the spindles of red earth that stretched higher than the clouds, and seen the Rustans make good use of their hidesails. His objections were therefore grounded in some personal experience. As he understood it, Truss House was neither high nor hot enough. That was the logic he wielded in defence of the trade arrangement with the Great Watcher.

To his mother, he had to explain the whole idea – his father did not have the patience. She quailed at Samuel's tale of the lockport, her handkerchief to her mouth and a steadying hand on the study's modest games table. Hard as she might try, she was unable to picture the solid little Rustan soaring through the air like a hawk or a buzzard, or even the ungainly gull.

'But what if she falls?' Mother said.

'Silence take you, Caroline, she's a Rustan – she won't fall.' Father rounded on Samuel. 'How long?'

'How long?'

'Yes, boy, how *long* will this delay the wedding?'

Samuel did his best to estimate the amount of work needed to complete the stables and Darmst's platform above the cliffs of Truss House. Then he estimated a little lower.

'Impossible!' His father's face blazed almost purple. 'You would have hundreds, nay *thousands*, lose their livelihoods for your foolish fancy?'

Samuel was crestfallen. He had forgotten that his father's trade arrangements might impact anyone other than the W'oventrouts and the Great Watcher. But he was determined not to marry a Rustan who could not fly. Or glide.

A compromise was reached. The grounds for the stables would be cleared, the trees stripped and readied for the journey south to the Great Watcher, and then work on the platform started. It would be finished before a single brick was laid for the stables. Three somewhat troubled W'oventrouts left the study that day.

Watcher Darmst had not been present for the conversation that in no small way would decide her tale for the Audience. Has it not ever been thus for brides?

Samuel began work immediately. Darmst explained the various types of flying platforms that could be found in the Rusting Mountains. As Samuel had tried to explain to his mother, there was more to flying than simply jumping from a cliff edge. From such a position, over such a drop, and with little warmth to the wind, a very particular kind of platform would be needed. Samuel drew many designs, each trying to translate Darmst's descriptions of her home into something he could have built. Her patience for such work was only so great – she was a Watcher, after all, not a Builder. She used flying platforms, and there ended her engagement with them.

Eventually a simple design for the platform was chosen, with none of Samuel's decorative flourishes of kenna birds or Audience members. A well-braced platform that extended both before and after the cliff edge long enough for Darmst to achieve some speed.

As labourers toiled to bring down the great pines to the west of Truss House, Darmst stitched. Among her meagre belongings she had not brought a hidesail with her from the Tear. In fact, she had only brought a single piece of clothing made from slipdog hide, which was the best hide for sails; a dress that, in Perlish terms, left her ankles scandalously displayed. Even if it had been floor-length it would have been little more than a patch for the giant sail. But rather than tear the dress, she took it to a tanners two villages over from Truss House. The bewildered old man scratched his head and said,

'We 'ave some unsplit leathers tha' strong.'

'Leathers?'

'From the cows by 'ere.'

Darmst narrowed her eyes. 'Cows.'

The tanner turned to Samuel, who until then had been waiting in the doorway and trying not to laugh.

'Do they not have stories of cows in the Rusting Mountains?' Samuel said.

'Ah, the milk makers?' she said.

'That's them.'

'They have strong hides too?'

The tanner cleared his throat. 'Strong 'nuff. Little heavier than your... hide there.'

They left him with an order for leather that made his eyes bulge and had him calling for his sons before they'd even left his shop.

So, as many men felled many trees, Darmst stitched the hides of many felled cows. More and more hides came. So many, she had to move from the upper study where Samuel worked and into the long top gallery. She stretched the enormous hidesail along the carpeted corridor. She found the soft Perlish faces disconcerting, so worked with her back to the portraits. When Samuel found her working there one afternoon, she made him promise that her face would never be on that wall. He looked along the gallery, smiled, and made his promise. Then, he knelt and kissed her.

It was their first kiss. A fleeting kiss, little more than a brushing of lips. A thing to be cherished, but more often than not forgotten. But not by the Audience.

The work to clear the ground dragged on. Samuel's father bemoaned his son's stubborn nature, his meticulous eye for detail, and his romantic notions – all of which he apparently gained from his mother. A mother who just shook her head, knowing that her husband might as well have been describing himself rather than their son. The only thing that mollified his father somewhat was the increasing stream of stripped lumber that made its way down the mountain track from the house.

Darmst's work was similarly proving taxing. Once the hide for the sail was in hand, she had to call upon a number of blacksmiths to work the iron for the locking mechanism and the sail's frame. Samuel said she should summon them to Truss House rather than trudge across the Perlish countryside in the summer heat. But Darmst insisted she wanted to see each smithy at their forge. It was, after all, quite specialist work she was commissioning. Like the tanner, the blacksmiths were somewhat bemused by the little Rustan woman who came into their workshops demanding finer work than most had the skills for. But a combination of the W'oventrout purse and a willingness to show those metal-men her iron fingers and even her lockport, discreetly of course, soon won them over.

By the last days of summer, the grounds west of Truss House had been cleared of all trees, the platform had been installed to Samuel's specifications, and Darmst had her cow-hidesail.

It was time for her to fly.

***

'Glide!' Darmst said, for perhaps the tenth time that morning. She was on the terrace with the whole family as they watched members of the household staff wrestle the hidesail down the main staircase. They didn't need to be told to be careful.

'Yes, dear, I know you'll be gliding,' Samuel said. 'But allow everyone else their stories. Today they see someone *fly*.'

'Everyone' was the right of it. There was a long corridor of people all the way from the house to the platform: the entire staff, from coachmen to scullery maids to the butler; the many teams of lumber men; the tanner and his sons; the blacksmiths and their families; and many more beside who had heard tale of the flying soon-to-be W'oventrout. As Darmst appeared in the wake of her hidesail there were cheers and cries of 'huzzah!' as if the whole of Eastern Perlanse had taken her for their hero. A little girl broke from the lines and brought Darmst a handful of wild flowers. It was quite the spectacle.

The crowd fell in behind Darmst and her husband-to-be. Much was made, then *and* after, of what she wore: strong boots, tight men's trousers, and an equally fitted waistcoat that had something shiny on its back. That was the most common story – the Perlish imagination was not quite ready for the truth of the lockport.

For Samuel, the short walk to the platform felt like crossing the whole Union. He ran over the design of the platform again and again in his head. He desperately wanted to ask Darmst of the hidesail. Had she tested each part of the frame? Was she sure of each of her stitches? Was cow's hide too heavy after all? But he had put these questions, and more, to her in the days previous and she was happy. She would glide across the Moral Mountains valley and wait for her horse-riding husband wherever she might land.

He helped her with the hidesail. It was his hands, not those of the household staff, that locked the sail to her. The metallic snap was almost sickening.

'Did I hurt you?' he hurried to ask.

'No, dear. That sound is a good sign.' She rolled her shoulders and stretched her neck, trying her new sail. She shook her right arm, and the right side of the sail shook also. She raised her left arm and the left side of the sail rose. The crowd oohed and ahhed. She clenched her two metal fingers to her palm and the sail turned and banked. 'It feels good,' she said.

Samuel came to stand before her. 'Wood and tin,' he said. 'Those things seem very small now.'

'They are.'

'Would you allow me to say I love you, Watcher Darmst?'

'I might.'

'This is something you have to do, something important, I know that. But now we're here, I wish you didn't.'

'Would you allow me to say I love you too, Samuel W'oventrout?'

'Tell me once you're back on the ground.'

She pulled him close to kiss him then. The crowd roared.

He joined his parents just a little way behind the platform.

'You two look pale as western milkmaids,' his father said.

'I hope you know what you're doing, dear,' Mother said. 'I've become quite attached to our little Rustan.'

'As have I, Mother.'

Darmst stood alone on the platform, her hidesail locked between her shoulders and sprawled out behind like an enormous, heavy veil. The crowd quietened to a silence that was almost torturous. One heartbeat. Two. He told quick stories to every member of the Audience he could think of. Stories of a happy marriage, of children, of a legend that would give them so many more stories if she just lived beyond that day. A third heartbeat, and she was off.

Adeline waited, half-turned on the bench and gazing at the profile of her husband-to-be. The sun had nearly dropped behind the stables of Truss House.

'And?' she said.

'And what?' Bertram said.

'Damn you to Silence, Trout! Did she fly?'

'Silence? But if so damned, how could I tell you?'

Adeline crossed her arms and huffed. 'It is good that I'm marrying you for your stables and not your stories.'

'Perhaps, as time goes on, it will be both,' he said, failing to keep the hope from his voice. 'I would have thought the ending of my story was obvious. I am here, am I not? My parents are discussing our marriage with your parents right now, are they not? *Both* my parents.'

A grin spread across Adeline's face. She punched Bertram's arm, none too gently. 'You're a crafty thing, Bertram W'oventrout. Maybe this won't be the most boring marriage in the history of East Perlanse.'

'Oh, I have no fear of that,' Father said.

In front of the carriageway of Truss House, Bertram gave one of his *harrumphs* that his two sons knew so well.

'She was right,' Henry said. 'It hasn't been boring, has it?'

'No,' Bertram admitted. 'I dare say what's driving up that track of ours won't be boring, either.' The three of them squinted under a hot Eastern Perlish sun. 'Trust a southerner to keep us waiting.'

Phineas turned to his father. 'Did Mother really kill her first stag in the... Wayward fashion?'

'So the story goes.'

He then turned to his brother. 'Another thing, didn't Grandfather break his promise? We have a portrait of Grandmother Darmst in the top gallery.'

'Well, now, that is another story entirely.'

'Henry, really!'

'Quite scandalous, actually.'

'That's enough of that, boys,' Bertram said. 'Try to look presentable now, Phineas. Here comes your flower girl.'

Henry burst out giggling. Amongst all Father's bellowing and blustering, it was easy to forget he had quite the wit to him.

For his part, Phineas was in no mood for wit as he watched two white horses cresting the rise of the track, and the carriage behind. He felt a churning in his stomach that threatened fire in his throat. The horses were foaming at the mouth and their flanks were sleek with their efforts. Pomp and tassels hung limply from their leathers and the carriage, all wilted by the hot journey.

'It won't be boring,' Phineas said to himself, as if that might in anyway reassure him. But the truth was, he wasn't frightened of boredom. Quite the opposite. It was the excitement that was coming up the track that scared him.

Vivian gestured to her son to join her at the dressing table. He had been listening to her story perched on the end of her bed, as he had done when he was much younger. She had forgone her full routine of powders and liners and rouge to tell him of the family. As far as he was concerned, she looked all the more beautiful for it.

She took her son's hand in hers once more. 'You see, Cecil, it is *excitement* that is the W'oventrout's undoing. It always has been. From your great great grandfather to this very day.'

'I don't understand, Mother.'

'I know, dear boy, but you will. I'm so sorry, but you will.'

'But I don't like Rustans or hunting or flowers or games or anything else.' Cecil paused. Then, in a very small voice, he said, 'I don't like anything that comes from far away.'

Vivian kissed his hand. She was fighting the tears in her eyes. 'I wish you did. I wish you did. At least then you could play some part in your own misery, rather than suffer consequences not of your making.'

He helped her from her stool and attended her as she adjusted her wig.

'You look wonderful, Mother.'

'Thank you, Cecil. I know you will stay gallant to the last. Devoid of excitement, but gallant to the last.'

Cecil drained the last of his wine, his throat hoarse from his tale. He still stood in front of the drawing room's hearth, which had burned down to embers, and was weary beyond his own understanding. His audience were similarly encumbered. Little Florence lay curled at the end of a window settle, snoring like a Casker bargeman. Gideon and Rosamund dozed together on one of the softer sofas, their secret obvious to anyone who cared to look. But poor Edwin Adlesworth, merchant of Fenest, husband to his second wife, poor Edwin was fast asleep with an empty brandy glass fallen at his feet.

Cecil righted the glass on his way to the slumbering form of Gideon. Even in his sleep the boy was handsome. Cecil moved as quietly as he could and, holding his breath, reached down; he eased the fish knife from the boy's pocket.

The Adlesworth family slumbered on in their new drawing room, oblivious to the fading glory all around them. Truss House was once the ancestral home to a great Perlish dynasty. Now it was a Fenestiran's investment. But as Cecil's mother had tried to warn him, so long ago, the W'oventrouts had no one but themselves to blame. Each one of them could have stopped the rot, stopped the decay, and saved their way of life.

It was in their power to stop the forces of change.

We all have the power to stop the forces of change.

Instead, as dawn broke over East Perlanse, Cecil W'oventrout found himself closing the door of his rightful home behind him, with a southern family in his place. He picked up his modest holdall, but in doing so noticed something small and glowing beside the main doors. He bent to get a closer look.

A little white flower greeted him like he were the sun itself.

'Hello there,' Cecil said. 'You're a long way from the lower gardens, aren't you?'

Lo and behold, over the many years the Caskanese Plotseed had made its way from the lower gardens, through the foundations of Truss House, right to the front entrance. It had undermined the whole place, even the stables.

Cecil plucked the flower and tucked it into the lapel of his coat.

'We'll be all right,' he told the Plotseed. 'It's the rest of them I worry about.'

Eight

The two Perlish storytellers bowed to each other, bowed to the Audience, then turned and disappeared under the balconies of Z'anderzi's Kantina.

At once, the public gallery was a roar of noise as people started to discuss the Perlish story with their neighbour. *Stories*, Cora reminded herself. The pennysheets hadn't been wrong with all their different ideas about what the Perlish election story would be. In fact, they'd all been right.

'It was clever, wasn't it, how the 'tellers passed the story back and forth between them?' Jenkins said, and Cora had to agree.

With the appearance of each new relation of the W'oventrout who began the story, as the tale moved backwards in time, the 'teller gave way to their partner. The effect had been like following a river upstream to the source, every so often taking a new branch.

'They did a good job of it,' Cora said. 'The way they told the story together – it was smoother than I thought it would be.'

'They must have practised.'

'So they *can* work together.' Cora shook her head. 'Why that realm can't find a way to unify, I will never know.'

Those in the public gallery began to move towards the staircases, but the number of people in the tight space meant progress was slow.

Jenkins leaned against the balcony rail. 'Perlish unification is one thing; they don't seem keen on anyone outside the realm, either, do they? All that talk of foreigns.'

'They've never been a subtle realm.' Cora took out her bindle tin and started to roll a smoke. 'What a message to voters: don't let strangers in because they'll ruin everything. Such an awful—'

'I thought it was an excellent story,' said the woman who'd been seated next to Cora. A thin woman whose mouth was so pursed, she looked like she was trying to suck her lips inside herself.

'Did you now?' Cora muttered.

'All those southerners coming here, bringing their plague, begging in the streets. It's disgusting.' The woman bristled with her own indignation, clutching her handbag to her chest as if Cora or Jenkins might try to rip it from her grasp. 'The Perlish are right – we must keep them out. It would be a black stone from me.'

'Well,' Cora said, 'it's a good job you're not in the voting pool.'

'Fine Fenestiran you are,' the woman spat, pushing past Cora. 'Don't you read the pennysheets?' was her parting shot.

'Unfortunately, yes,' Cora said, and sighed. She put the bindle tin back into her pocket. 'Come on, Jenkins. Time to get back to the station.'

'I would say that's a very good idea indeed, Detective Gorderheim,' said a voice from the shadowy gallery.

Cora peered into the gloom. Someone needed to light more lamps. 'Is that you, Chief Inspector?'

Hearing that, Jenkins scuttled down the stairs. Cora couldn't blame her.

'How did you find the Perlish story? So soon after your visit to Perlanse?' Chief Inspector Sillian said, and stepped free of the shadows.

The chief of Bernswick Division police station was a few years over fifty – Cora had never been quite sure of her superior's age. Sillian was slim and sharp – her cheekbones as well as her tongue. She regarded Cora with a look that Cora knew only too well: scepticism blended with disappointment.

She found herself pushed towards Sillian by the press of people wanting to leave. 'You've seen my report on the prisoner transport, on their deaths, I take it,' Cora said.

'And the local stitcher's. It confirmed everyone involved in the transport was poisoned.'

'I left these out.' Cora reached into her coat pocket and pulled out the feathers found on Finnuc's corpse. 'A black feather and a white one, both left on the Casker's body. Another warning about the election.'

'The poisoner killed himself,' Sillian said, and flicked a speck of dirt from her pristine black jacket. 'Anyone would be forgiven for thinking there was no case here.'

'You know what this is really about, ma'am,' Cora said, hastily. 'You've known all along. *Someone* is responsible for these deaths – not just the person doing the killing. And it won't stop. Not yet.'

Sillian's gaze dropped to the floor. Cora caught a glimpse of the white scalp that seemed to burn a neat parting line through the chief inspector's dark hair. 'It has to be discreet.'

'It will be.'

'And keep your team small.'

'Yes, ma'am.' Cora hesitated. She could leave it at that: implicit permission to pursue the case – wherever it led. But the time for chancing her luck was well behind her, and the Latecomer knew it. 'I can only put it off so long, ma'am.'

'Put what off, Detective?'

'I have to speak to the Chambers.'

'From what I saw this morning, right here in Z'anderzi's, you're already speaking to them.'

So that feeling of being watched earlier, before the Perlish story started – Cora had been right. She wouldn't have guessed it was one of her own doing it.

'I can't help it if *the Chambers* come to *me*,' Cora said.

Sillian stepped forward. Cora could smell her perfume: surprisingly floral. 'From a distance only, Gorderheim. I don't want them involved.'

'They *are* involved. And there's nothing to be done about it.'

'You're right: I can't stop the Chambers seeking you out. But if I hear you even so much as step foot in the Assembly building of your own accord, it'll be your badge, Detective. I'll have no choice. Is that clear?'

'No choice?'

'Is that *clear*?'

'Yes, ma'am.'

Cora waited until Chief Inspector Sillian was well out of sight before she made her own way out of Z'anderzi's

Kantina. There still seemed to be people everywhere, many not in a hurry to leave, despite the stuffiness of the air that now had a distinct smell of sweat to it. As she elbowed her way towards the door, she found herself knocking into Wayward, Caskers, and Rustans as well as too many chattering Fenestirans. All of them chewing over the message of the Perlish election story: keep the foreigns out.

The next morning, Marcus, the gruff-voiced pennysheet girl, brought the early editions of the 'sheets to Bernswick and stayed long enough to eat a whole bag of pastries before heading back to the streets.

'Exit poll in *The Spoke* has the Perlish behind the Seeders,' Jenkins said.

They were in Cora's office, the door wedged open with a stack of old reports. It was the only way to get some air moving. The day was unbearably hot.

'Good,' Cora said. 'I was hoping the voters weren't all like that woman we were stuck next to. The one with the awful lips.'

Jenkins smiled, then carried on her perusal of *The Spoke*. 'Those questioned said they liked the different parts of the Perlish tale but felt it lacked "emotional gravitas".'

'Butterman must have some new writers in,' Cora said, thinking of the hack who edited *The Spoke*. '"Gravitas" isn't in his vocabulary. Or "emotional" for that matter. What about *The Fenestiran Times*?'

Jenkins leafed through the 'sheets laid out on Cora's desk, knocking over an empty cup as she did so. 'The *Times* poll puts the Perlish ahead of the Caskers but behind the

Seeders. The Wayward are still favourites to win, if they can find a new storyteller in time, after Ento…'

'Well that's something,' Cora said, trying to chase away the memory of Nicholas Ento's corpse. 'Maybe the Seeders will see to Fenest's potholes.' She stood and stretched. Sitting for so long yesterday had played havoc with her back. 'And *The Daily Tales*?'

'Really, Detective?'

'What?'

'*The Tales*? I thought you were more… discerning.'

'Just read me the headline, Constable.' Cora pulled her coat from the hook. She was fairly sure she'd left her bindleleaf tin in her pocket.

'"Perlish Petals: How to Grow Your Own Womanly Display".'

Cora stopped. 'That's not funny, Jenkins.'

'No, it's not.' Jenkins held up the 'sheet.

'Audience take them, I don't know why we bother. You never get any sense from something written down.'

'Tell that to the Commission and their forms.'

Cora resumed her search of her own pockets. 'Aha!' She pulled out the tin, only to find it wrapped up in paper. 'Is this your doing?'

Jenkins shook her head.

Cora untied the string and unwrapped her tin. From under the paper, a black voting stone fell onto the desk. A black stone for yes. But there was more; on the paper was an address. And below it:

Madame Vendler, how can this be a just system of government?

Madame Vendler – her old Seminary teacher. Why had someone given Cora Madam Vendler's address? Cora hadn't seen her in years. Hadn't even *thought* about her in years. Vendler had been an old woman when Cora and her sister Ruth were studying; she'd surely joined the Audience long ago. The note was a mistake. Wrong pocket, and no surprise in the crowds at the Perlish story. Hadn't she bumped into a whole load of people after her encounter with Sillian? She'd had the bindle tin in her hands before then. No note. So it must have found its way into her pocket as she left the Kantina. Now, in her office, she weighed the stone that had been wrapped against her tin, imagined putting it into a voting chest. A black stone for yes. A white for no. Two stones for one choice.

But what if the address *wasn't* that of the old seminary teacher? What if the two parts of the note were separated? The address was one thing, Madame Vendler's name another. A message, for Cora, as the black and white feathers found on Finnuc's body had been a message, and likewise the black and white laces threaded through the mouth of Nicholas Ento, the murdered Wayward storyteller. Because Madame Vendler's name was shared, by Cora *and* Ruth. Those times Ruth had answered back in the seminary – so many of them. *How can this be a just system of government?* In Cora's memory, it was always Madame Vendler's lined and liver-spotted face glaring back at Ruth.

Ruth… Was this message, this address, really from Ruth? After all these years? Perhaps Cora truly *had* seen her in Fenest. Now she was letting herself think it through, she recognised the handwriting. Ruth still dotted her i with a dash and looped her g.

'Detective, are you all right?'

'No— Yes. I'm fine.'

'You don't look—'

'I'm *fine*, Constable.' She screwed up the paper and stuffed it back in her pocket. The question, the address, could wait. Audience knew, Cora had been waiting to hear news of her sister for long enough. 'I need to be doing something. Reading 'sheets won't find us Tennworth. Where are we up to with that?'

'Well, of the three female Chambers, we don't yet have enough to whittle down the list as to which might be Tennworth.'

Cora kicked a couple of old pastry wrappers across the floor. 'Casker Chambers Kranna certainly has something to hide.'

'I saw you speaking with her before the Perlish story,' Jenkins said hopefully.

'Much good it did me,' Cora said. 'Kranna didn't tell me much, but it was clear she *is* involved in moving that unlisted cargo south via the River Cask. But why, or who it's for, we're none the wiser. There seemed no obvious link between her and the Captain Tennworth who rescued Finnuc Dawson as a child, and who owns a winery in Fenest.'

Jenkins started to collect the rubbish from the floor, looking deep in thought as she scooped up the pastry wrappers and forgotten coffee mugs.

'There's not much point bothering with all that, Jenkins. Place will soon be in a mess again.'

But the constable wasn't listening.

'We could go back to dock forty-nine, Detective, couldn't we? Maybe some of the Caskers there knew Dawson?'

'They might, but that other bargehand, the one at the Perlish Hook, he said Dawson was a private man. Kept to himself.'

'He could have had a sweetheart.'

Cora swallowed. There was nothing in Jenkins' voice to suggest this was anything other than an innocent suggestion.

Cora handed the constable a teaspoon that had been hanging round far too long. 'What are you talking about, Jenkins?'

'You know, someone he cared for? Someone he told things?'

'No, Constable,' Cora said. 'I don't.' She didn't want them pulling at that thread. She knew how it ended. 'I think we're done with Caskers for a time. What do you know about the Rustan Chambers?'

'Latinum?'

'Well, you know that much at least,' Cora said.

'And that's about the end of it; there's a private person for you. I do know she's not been the Rustan Chambers long.' Jenkins dumped the rubbish she'd collected in a bin outside Cora's office.

'So not been in Fenest long?'

'A few years at most,' Jenkins said.

'Well, she seemed to know who I was.' Cora told Jenkins about the unsettling moment when the Rustan had mouthed 'Detective' across Z'anderzi's Kantina, just before the Perlish story had begun.

'It felt like there was something personal about it,' Cora said, her skin crawling at the memory.

'Personal how?' Jenkins said, frowning.

The note in Cora's pocket, the one with Madame Vendler's address, seemed to grow heavy. Was it something to do with Ruth? It was frustrating, the way her sister kept snaking into her thoughts.

'Doesn't matter,' Cora said. 'Rustan Chambers Latinum. What did she do before she was a Chambers?'

'Do?' Jenkins said, as if Cora were telling a tale to the Drunkard.

'As in, earning a living.'

'I don't know.'

'Who *would* know?'

'The Rustans, I suppose.'

'As much as I'd like to go out and collar a Rustan, don't we have more official means than that?'

'Of course, the Commission keeps everything,' Jenkins said, starting to sound excited. 'All business records for the Union are kept in the archives in Uppercroft.'

'Uppercroft? I thought that kind of thing was kept by the Commission in the Wheelhouse? Beans for the bean-counters, and the like.'

'The Wheelhouse only stores the records pertaining to Fenest,' Jenkins said. 'Everything for the Trading Halls, Electoral Affairs, Wheeled Conveyances Bureau, The—'

'All right, Constable, I get the idea. So you're telling me that the records covering the realms, they're held separately. In Uppercroft. But the building would need to be huge. There's nothing like that in that part of the city.'

'That's because it's underground,' Jenkins said.

Cora pinched between her eyes. 'Underground. Wait now, Constable. When we checked records for Tennworth, did we check the records in Uppercroft?'

Jenkins paled. 'No,' she said. 'What with the winery being in the city…'

'Right, I need to get out of this office anyway, or you'll put *me* out with the rubbish next. Come on. If Tennworth did any business in the wider Union, any at all, we need to find a record of it.' Cora grabbed her coat and stuffed her bindleleaf tin in the pocket. The same pocket as the note with the address. That would have to wait.

As they made to leave, Jenkins was in a rush.

'What's got you so excited, Constable?'

'Uppercroft is also where all the old election Hooks go! Once they've finished being displayed – there's *thousands* of them there.'

'Fine. Just don't be grinning like that the whole time.'

On the way out of the station they met Sergeant Hearst. Judging by his empty paper bag and the crumbs speckling his boots, he'd been up on the roof again. 'Where are you two going in such a hurry?' he said.

'Commission archives,' Cora said.

'What, the ones in Uppercroft?'

'The very same,' Cora said over her shoulder.

'Keep an eye on the archive walls!'

'Why?' Cora called back. 'What's wrong with them?'

'You'll find out.'

Nine

They caught a Clotham's gig to Uppercroft; Commission funds wouldn't cover the more expensive, and comfortable, Garnuck's. But even a bone-shaking Clotham's gig was better than walking. Cora's foot was still playing up and, by the looks of her bandied legs, Jenkins was still feeling the effects of her time in the saddle from the trip to Perlanse.

The address of the archives, according to Jenkins, was 4a Mutton Fold. The gig driver had never heard of the place, which wasn't a good start. The woman knew the street it was meant to be on, at least, and said she'd drop Cora and Jenkins there. The gig lumbered off with the customary Clotham's rattle. Jenkins fished a pennysheet from the floor, left by the previous occupant.

'Today's?' Cora asked.

'No, it's from yesterday. The main story is... Oh.' Jenkins folded the page and seemed to have difficulty meeting Cora's eye.

'Oh?'

'You're not going to want to read it, Detective.'

'Let me guess,' Cora said, and settled back in her seat.

'Finnuc Dawson was killed by bandits in Perlanse. Wrong time, wrong place, but one fewer mouth to feed on the Steppes.'

'How can they print such rubbish?'

'Don't tell me you're surprised?'

'Less so by the day.' Jenkins' gaze was straying to the folded pennysheet.

'Go on, read it. It's election time; who needs to worry about truth?'

Jenkins opened the 'sheet and was drawn in at once. Cora reached into her coat pocket for the slip of paper there. The paper that had been folded around her bindleleaf tin. Someone had managed to give her that note as she left the Perlish story venue. It couldn't have been Ruth amongst the people pushing to leave the building. Could it? Cora would have noticed her. Unless she was so changed after thirty years that she was unrecognisable. These were mad thoughts – that her sister was back, after all this time, slipping notes into Cora's pockets at election venues. It couldn't be from her. But if not Ruth, then who?

When the gig stopped they were on a wide thoroughfare. She and Jenkins stepped down onto well-maintained cobbles. No cracks deep enough to turn an ankle, no stinking water caught between them. Tubs of flowers were set out on the pavements and curly metalwork graced the streetlamps. People ambled to and fro, not in a hurry, not getting into fights over coach queues or the price of bread. A nice part of town. But no obvious archive in which to hunt for Tennworth's name.

'Best see if these folks can help us find this 4a Mutton Fold,' Cora said, glancing about. 'What kind of address is that anyway?'

'A small one,' Jenkins said.

'That's actually quite a good joke from you for once, Constable.'

Jenkins looked thrilled, her prominent teeth bared in a grin.

'But it makes no sense,' Cora added. 'How can the archive be a *small* place? It holds the records of all the realms!'

'Sergeant Hearst did say there was something funny about the walls,' Jenkins said. 'What if they're—'

'We have to find the walls before we can worry about them.'

They set about asking for directions. No one seemed to have a firm answer.

'Behind the cobbler's, but you have to go back and then back *again*.'

'Go down the alley there and cut through by the carving of the wheel, but don't go so far as the old well. Then when you see the sandstone, go back three paces.'

'Isn't it near the fountain? No, that can't be right. Commission moved the pipes.'

Cora stopped outside a butcher's. 'Doesn't this seem strange to you, Constable?'

'I don't know – the Commission probably moves all kinds of pipes.'

'I *meant* it's strange that a Commission department – usually one of the busiest places in Fenest – isn't known to those who live near it.' Cora threw up her hands. 'I don't think this place even exists.'

'My mother used to talk about it so it must be here somewhere.' Jenkins looked up and down the street as if the building might suddenly appear in front of her.

'But she never took you there?' Cora asked.

'Said it was too dangerous.'

'First Hearst talking about the walls, now your mother. What kind of place is this archive?'

'Archives you're wanting, is it?' someone said.

A woman was standing in the doorway to the butcher's. She wore a blood-stained apron that put Cora in mind of a stitcher, if it weren't for the neat cuts of meat gleaming in the window.

'I recognise that lost look,' the butcher said.

'You know where they are?' Cora said, taking out her badge.

But the woman didn't seem bothered to see it. She'd turned back into the shop. 'This way. Watch out for the bones. I was about to take them out the back anyway.'

The shop smelled only faintly of blood, and was spotless: the metal trays winked in the sun streaming through the window, and the knives were bare of mottled marks. The butcher led them behind the counter, picking up a neat pile of bones as she went, some with scraps of flesh still clinging to them.

'The archive is behind the shop?' Cora said to the woman's back, which bore early signs of a hump though she moved freely enough.

'In a manner of speaking. There's another way to get to the archives than through here. I couldn't have everyone traipsing through every time there was a new bit of paperwork to file. Wouldn't be sanitary, would it? I'd fail my Commission inspection.'

The butcher pushed open a door and hanging from the

ceiling were the skinned carcasses of pigs. There was a soft gasp behind Cora.

'Eyes on your feet, Constable. Deep breath now.'

The butcher wove between the pigs, heading for another door on the other side. 'Just through here.'

They emerged into a narrow alley that curved out of sight in either direction. The buildings on the other side were no more than three feet away, and none of them had doors. The butcher opened a tall wooden box that stood by the back entrance to her shop, and dumped the bones inside. She wiped her hands on her apron, then pointed right.

'Down that way, there's another alley opening on the left-hand side. Take that, then it's the first door you come to. If you reach the courtyard with the fountain, you've gone too far. That's the best way back to the main road, when you're done there. The archivist will show you. That's if you can find him.'

'That door in the second alley, *that's* the sheep fold in the address?' Cora said.

'It was once.' The woman craned her head to look at the strip of blue sky visible between the two sets of walls. 'All this was fields once, before the city grew.'

'People kept sheep here, in *Fenest*?' Jenkins said.

The butcher shrugged. 'They had the space then. Now we need Seeder farms to send us meat. Only the old names survive.'

'The archive building must be old then,' Cora said.

'One of the oldest parts of the city, after Burlington Palace and First Wall. They say that's why it's the way it is. Built from tornstone.'

***

Now they knew what they were looking for, they found the second alley easily enough. It was even narrower than the one that led from the butcher's shop, and lower, too. As she headed down it, the walls felt too close to Cora's face for comfort. This was something to tell the Partner, who liked journeys – the more difficult, the better.

'Who builds anything out of tornstone?' Cora said.

'The Torn,' came Jenkins' no-nonsense reply.

Cora rolled her eyes. 'Yes, Constable, the Torn use the rock they basically live in. But only a damn fool would use it outside the Tear. It's unstable.'

'Maybe it has other properties,' Jenkins said. 'Watertight? It's partly lava, after all. That would make sense for keeping paperwork dry.'

'I think that butcher has spent too long with only dead pigs for company. Tornstone walls aside, we're looking for any mention of Tennworth in the archives.'

'Don't worry, Detective. If Latinum had a business before she became a Chambers for her realm, this is where we'll find it.'

'I hope you're right,' Cora said, trying to fight off the feeling of being trapped in the narrow alley, 'and I hope that business is a winery, because if not— Wait, was that it?'

Cora had passed a door on her left. An ordinary door, old-looking with its flaking black paint that was easy to miss in the gloom of the alley, but the white of the Spoked Wheel in its centre burned bright: the black and white of the Commission. The colours of the election too, and of the chequers: the men and women who took bets. Black and white were the colours of counting.

There was a small brass plaque next to the door. Jenkins read it,

'*Commission Archives. Open Tuesday and Friday, 3.30pm – 5pm, and some Mondays by prior arrangement. No admittance without appointment.* That could be a problem.'

'This place is a Commission operation,' Cora said, 'and we *are* the Commission.' She raised the knocker and banged loudly.

They waited. Nothing happened. Cora put her ear to the door. Not a sound behind it. The place could be deserted. She knocked again, then thumped the door.

'I haven't got time for this. Try the handle, Constable.'

But there was no handle. No keyhole either. How did this door even open? Brute force was needed. She lifted her foot to kick it but Jenkins stopped her.

'Detective – listen.'

On the other side of the door, metal was grinding. Bolts sliding back. There had to be plenty of them, the noise they made. The archivist must favour the Bailiff.

And then the door opened. A young man stood there, blinking. He carried a lamp and thrust it at Cora as if not realising that she and Jenkins were standing in daylight. There was a wall of darkness behind him, from which a cool draught blew.

'You don't have an appointment,' the man said.

His voice was reedy, thin, like his waist – the man needed a few more meals inside him. He wore a heap of scarves piled around his neck, over his shoulders. Even one round his middle. Was this what counted for fashion in Fenest these days? Or perhaps it had been, the last time this young man left the archive. Commission probably made him live here as part of the job.

'We don't need an appointment,' Cora said, and went to hand him her badge.

The man gave a shrill gasp and swiftly stepped back. 'Let me see your hands and feet, both of you. Now. Don't come any closer until I've checked.'

'Black Jefferey's eased off,' Cora said. 'No new cases. Don't you read the pennysheets?'

'The archives are about the past, not the present. News doesn't concern me.'

'Well, you're obviously concerned about some of it,' Cora muttered. 'Guessing you don't get out much to see what's actually happening in the city though.'

'Why would I need to leave? Everything important is here. Now, wrists.'

There was no budging him. She and Jenkins held out their arms for inspection, then each took off their boots and socks to show there were no black marks on their ankles. These were the signs of Black Jefferey, the plague from the Casker election story, which had then become very real in Fenest. And which had supposedly devastated the Casker homeland of Bordair, if the pennysheets were to be believed. The scarf-decked man peered at Cora and Jenkins all the while from the safety of the doorstep, as if it were an island and the alley was dweller-infested water.

'Satisfied?' Cora said, shoving her boots back on and doing her best to ignore the sudden stabbing pain from her scarred foot.

'One can't be too careful,' the man said. 'Now, why should I let you in without an appointment? It's against Commission rules, and the Commission—'

Cora shoved her badge at him. He put it close to his face to read it.

'You're working a case?' he said.

'We wouldn't be calling otherwise. Not the easiest place to find, is it? Not keen on visitors.'

'No,' he said.

'What's your name?'

'Hoyer Dray.'

'Well, Mr Dray,' Cora said, putting her badge back inside her coat. 'You going to let us in?'

Dray seemed to consider this, as if he had a choice, then moved back inside the darkness. 'Mind the first step, Detective Gorderheim. It's easy to miss.' He almost sounded hopeful.

The light from Dray's lamp immediately started to descend and was almost lost. Cora hurried to follow it and found she was going down a narrow winding staircase, barely wide enough for her shoulders. Jenkins was close behind. There was a loud bang from above, then the same metal grinding noise as before. The door had shut and locked itself.

'Even if we find what we're looking for,' Cora muttered to Jenkins, 'we might not get out with it.'

'And what *are* you looking for?' Dray called back. His eyesight might not be good but his hearing was.

'A name.'

'We've plenty of those.'

'We need to check the records kept for businesses,' Cora said.

'Just the two of you?'

'Yes...'

The man laughed.

They went down and down, the staircase never seeming to alter. Dray was quick and Cora had to go faster than she liked just to keep the lamp in sight as it swept round the next bend. Her chest rasped and her foot throbbed but she couldn't slow down. No light on those stairs was not a good idea. The air was cool, and getting colder with every step. No wonder Dray was wearing his own weight in scarves. As the temperature dropped further, the darkness began to lift; wherever they were going, there were more lamps there. More lamps, and people, Cora hoped. She never thought she'd find herself hoping for a noisy office of Commission employees.

When she reached the last step, she stumbled, her feet having forgotten what a flat surface was. Once she was upright again, she saw that they had reached an open space – a hall was the best way to describe it. The ceiling was low, but the space went on as far as she could see. Jenkins had been right: the archives were under the city. From here, it looked as if they ran *all* the way under it. Fenest stood on the Union's history. Every dull mile of it.

Wall lamps were lit at regular intervals, lighting the rows and rows and rows of shelves that stretched into the distance. Each shelf was crammed with ledgers, scrolls, stacks of loose paper, boxes of it. If it happened in the Union, the Commission made a note of it. At least here, in archives that focused on the Union's history and ignored that of Fenest, Cora could escape her family's own past. Her parents' embezzlement, Ruth's betrayal to the pennysheets, even her parents' reaction to Cora joining the police force – it was all recorded somewhere, just not here. And that was some small relief. Everyone else in the Union – all non-Fenestirans – would be here in the archives, one way or another.

And Tennworth?

Where they stood at the front of the hall – or maybe it was the back? – there was a large desk that held only a ledger, opened on a clean page, an ink well, and a candle in a plain metal holder. Each of the things on the desk was positioned the same distance from the other, and at such sharp right angles that Cora felt compelled to move away from it. She suspected Dray was the kind of person who wouldn't take kindly to things being knocked out of order.

Even though she'd stopped walking, Cora found she couldn't catch her breath, and Jenkins looked to be struggling likewise, which wasn't usual.

'It's the dust,' Dray said, hearing them wheeze. 'Perlish Assembly cut the budget for cleaners. Audience send us a Torn victory this time. They know the value of the past.'

'Makes sense when your people were massacred,' Jenkins said.

'And the Perlish want people to forget,' Dray said in reply, 'given they were the ones doing the massacring.'

'We're here for more recent history than the War of the Feathers,' Cora said. 'I need to see—'

But Dray was in his stride, his voice quickening now that he had people to talk to. 'The Perlish Assembly has halved the Commission's budget for maintaining the archives. Halved it! I've had to ration the lamp oil.' That explained the death-trap staircase. 'The binders can only be replaced every ten years rather than the recommended four. And don't get me started on the mice.'

Cora wasn't about to, but there seemed no shutting him up.

'They'll have digested the last six months of Bordair barge inventories by now,' Dray went on, 'what with there being no money to fund the Office for the Removal of Pests Winged and Footed.'

'The Office for *what*?' Cora said.

'Is that what happened to the others?' Jenkins said. 'Lost their jobs when the Perlish cut the money?'

Dray looked puzzled. 'Others?'

'Other staff,' Jenkins said. 'From the Commission.'

He rearranged his scarves. Cora saw she'd have to talk plain with this one. And firm.

'I need to talk to the archivist,' Cora said.

Dray gave a short laugh. 'People tend to make that mistake.'

'*You're* the archivist?'

'You sound disappointed, Detective. That tends to happen too.'

'Do you work here by yourself?' Jenkins said.

'If you mean are there other *people* here, the answer is no. But if you mean, am I alone, the answer is also no, because the past—'

'We didn't come for riddles,' Cora snapped. 'We came for a history of business.'

'As you wish, Detective.' Dray walked past the desk. Cora and Jenkins followed, but he seemed to be further ahead of them than he had a moment before. 'You might find the task more onerous than you imagine.' He turned into the maze of shelving.

And then he disappeared.

Ten

'What— what just happened?' Cora said.

Jenkins ran into the space where the archivist had been before he... vanished. If that was even possible. But he was very definitely gone.

'Do you think it's like the butcher said?' Jenkins peered between the shelves. 'There's tornstone in the walls, making the place shift about? Maybe the whole place can move around the city! That would explain why the gig driver didn't know the address.'

'I think some kind of hidden passageway is more likely.' Cora spun round. 'But where—'

'I thought you said you were in a hurry, Detective.' Dray's mocking came faintly from further down the hall.

Cora gritted her teeth and strode to where the voice seemed to be coming from. After more than a few minutes of walking through identical stretches of filed paper, she and Jenkins came upon the archivist leaning against a glass cabinet and picking his nails.

There were scores of cabinets, each one taller than Cora. Scattered amongst them, free-standing, were the larger items that wouldn't fit into a cabinet. Cora caught sight of what looked to be the prow of a boat in the distance. The hall had changed here, like crossing the border from the Seeder lands to the Perlish duchies. Paper had given way to... things. Objects. Items. The Hooks of the previous elections. Jenkins gasped and pressed her nose against the nearest cabinet.

'How did you do that?' Cora asked Dray.

'Do what?'

Cora flapped an arm as if that would somehow demonstrate. 'Leave,' she said eventually.

'There are many ways to move around here, more than even the Partner can keep up with. When the archives extend so far, such shortcuts are necessary. I'm sure you'll understand, Detective, why I can't share them with you. Commission rules.' Dray smiled. 'We have much that is valuable here.'

Cora looked around at the dust-covered records. 'You're not talking about the mice.'

'This is the firecat skull from the hundred and third election,' Jenkins said. 'The year the Rustans won with the story about the baby raised by cats on the edge of the Tear. And *this*,' she tapped another of the glass panes, beneath which gleamed a large, round mirror, 'this is the Lowlander Hook the year they lost control of the Assembly after four terms in a row. A story about loyalty, when the 'sheets were telling a different story all through the election: that their Chambers was sleeping with his brother's wife.'

'Impressive knowledge,' Dray said, and sounded like he meant it.

'You were a better Seminary student than I was, Jenkins,' Cora said.

Despite herself, Cora was drawn to the nearest cabinet

and she walked around it to better see inside. Hooks of elections past. Glimpses of stories. Though their tales were long since told, the elections lost and won, the Chambers who gained power likely long dead, the Hooks were still doing their job: hinting at the stories behind them.

There were model houses and carts on cabinet shelves, and beyond them a real cart in a central clearing of the cabinets, each of its wooden boards wrapped in a ribbon of a different colour. Dolls of varying sizes wearing clothes from all corners of the Union. Heaps of shells and oddly shaped rocks. A sinta, looking perfectly preserved. A cask painted blue with a spiral burnt into the wood. A snakeskin, long as a barge, running across the floor. Attached to every offering was a twist of paper. Cora tried to read the faded scrawl: each label gave the name of a realm, the election number, and the name of a storyteller.

Jenkins was flitting between the cabinets and the larger objects that sat beside them, chattering excitedly to Dray, who was at her heels. Their voices grew distant.

Cora found the cabinet with the firecat skull. The skull was huge; good thing those creatures stayed in the Tear. Below one of its eye sockets there was a hole the size of Cora's fist. Someone had brought this thing down. She found herself picturing the moments just before the firecat's death, working backwards. The weapon in a hand. A spear? Javelin? A sweaty grip, readying it to throw. And before that, the choice to pick it up, to fight. Why? Was someone else in danger? She was telling herself the story, just as the Hook wanted.

Something moved in the mirror next to the skull.

Cora turned, expecting to see Jenkins and Dray, but they

were nowhere to be seen. Cora was alone amongst the cabinets.

There it was again – a flash of brown hair in the mirror. Then gone.

She spun round. Nothing. Was this one of Dray's tricks? Her chest felt tight. The dust must be worse here, that was all. She wasn't afraid. Why would she be? This was ridiculous. Cora stood in front of the mirror, separated from one kind of glass, highly polished, by another – a dusty cabinet pane. She looked into the mirror.

Ruth's face stared back at her.

Cora stumbled from the cabinet, and straight into Dray. She cursed, loudly.

'Careful, Detective,' Dray said. 'It doesn't do to be crashing around in here.'

Breath was hard to come by. Her palms were slick with sweat, even in the cool air of the archive hall. She risked a glance at the mirror and saw only herself – hair in need of a wash and bags under her eyes. Herself. Not Ruth. It was the close air down here, making her see things. Time to get what they needed and get out. Any longer and she and Jenkins would become as foolish as the archivist now smiling at her.

'Where's the constable?' Cora said, and grabbed one of Dray's scarves. That made his smile fade quick enough.

'No need for that, Detective. We're all part of the Commission, and our job is to—'

'Jenkins. *Now.*' Cora tightened her grip on the scarf.

'She's... in the Room of Business Interests.'

'Let's go. And no more of your disappearing acts, Dray,

or instead of a bindleleaf I'll be lighting one shelf at a time until you give me what I've asked for.'

Dray nodded furiously. 'Of course, of course! This way.'

He led her on a winding route through the many cabinets of former Hooks, and those Hooks too big to be kept behind glass. When they got to the far wall, there was an arch and Dray gestured that she should walk through. Was she about to vanish? She peered through to the other side and caught a glimpse of Jenkins' blue coat weaving between more towers of paper that reached from floor to ceiling. Seemed safe enough, though the dust here was worse.

Dray stayed in the archway.

'This is what you wanted. Now, you will have to excuse me. I have work to do.' He turned to go.

'Not so fast,' Cora said. 'Where are the business interests?'

Dray frowned. 'You're standing in them.'

'All *this* is the same archive?' Jenkins said. 'Everything in this room?'

'It is a record of the whole Union, since we began keeping records,' Dray said. 'What did you expect?'

'Something manageable,' Cora growled.

'I don't know why visitors keep making that mistake. It's as if no one in the Commission understands what we do here.'

'Wait,' Cora said. 'Visitors? Who else from the Commission has come here lately?'

'Well,' Dray said, adjusting his scarf. 'Rustan Chambers Latinum paid us an unofficial visit. She was very *polite*.'

'Was she now,' Cora muttered. 'And what was she *politely* looking at?'

'Business Interests, just like you.'

'Could you be more specific?' Jenkins said.

'I'm afraid I didn't ask. Just as I won't ask you two.' Dray stepped back, into the main hall. 'I only lead people to the records – I don't pry.'

'Pity,' Cora said.

So, Latinum had been here recently – had beaten them to it, in a manner of speaking. Interesting.

'What now, Detective?' Jenkins said.

'We do what we can.' She turned to Dray. 'Show me the section for the last twenty-five years.' Finnuc wasn't much older than that – *hadn't been* much older. If Tennworth was part of his life growing up, as in his stories, that span of years should do it.

'My pleasure,' Dray said. The archivist went to the stacks of paper in the middle of the room. These weren't so tall as some of the other towers threatening to topple, but he still needed a ladder. He rested it against another stack of papers, which didn't look safe, but Dray hared up it quick enough. He checked the top few layers of paper and called down, 'This should be the right range. These are the Perlish records. The other realms are... let me see.' Dray leaned over and began rifling through the other stacks near him. 'These five here.'

'*All* those pages are the ones we need to check?'

Dray blinked, still at the top of the ladder. 'Yes. Is there a problem?'

'Only my advancing years,' Cora said. 'It'll take... I don't even *know* how long it'll take to read all these.'

Dray climbed down. 'That's not my problem, Detective. The archivist's job is to tend the records, not to read them for you. I have much more pressing concerns.'

Jenkins mumbled something about the mice.

'*Actually*, Constable, the Wheelhouse has recently

delivered the minutes from the last eleven years' meetings of the subcommittee of the working group for the Prevention of—'

'We'll take it from here,' Cora said.

'You can let yourself out when you've finished.'

'Audience knows when that will be,' Cora said. She looked up at the nearest stack. 'Jenkins, we'll start with the Rustans. I want any mention of Tennworth, but I don't want to be down here all week. Perhaps if we skim read we can get through it more quickly.'

But they couldn't, and they didn't. Each new company record was a fulsome and pedantic form: the Commission in its element. They had to check the name of the business, the names of the directors, major shareholders, any interested parties, addresses for all of them, job titles, salaries, conflicts of interests...

After four hours, they'd barely made their way through the first foot of the Rustan stack, which was only the last six months of records. Cora called a halt. Her bones were frozen and Jenkins' sneezing in the dust had become so bad she considered stuffing the records into the constable's mouth. But another murder wouldn't help anyone.

'Make sure you take plenty of breaks, Jenkins,' Cora said.

'What? Where are you going?'

'To get you some help. The election keeps going, the spoked wheel keeps turning. I need to be there to see it.' And the note in her pocket was working like a summons. 'If that archivist tries any more tricks, arrest him for obstructing a murder enquiry.'

Eleven

Back at street level, Cora headed in the opposite direction to the butcher's shop. The alley was narrow and twisty, but the fresh air and weak daylight flowing through it were a welcome relief after the archives.

A footfall behind her. Close.

Cora turned, but there was no one there. No one in the twists of the alley. She waited a breath, two, but there were no more footsteps.

She pressed on, a little quicker now. There it was again – a footfall, scattering the thin gravel of the alleyway. And another. She spun around. No one. But the gloom at the far end of the alley seemed to reach towards her. Didn't feel like a cutpurse, didn't feel like a story for the Bailiff. But someone *was* following her.

She thought about going back, running to find whoever was there and confront them. But she kept pressing forward instead. Now wasn't the time to be chasing shadows in alleyways – she had enough of that elsewhere.

When she reached the courtyard with the fountain, as the butcher had said she would, the sky opened again, and there was air. Cora realised she'd been holding her breath.

Tall, well-maintained houses backed onto the courtyard. People were sitting on the lip of the fountain, chatting, chewing on what smelled like roast gresta bird. Children raced about, pushed each other over, cried, and were picked up. It was good to be back with people again – something she didn't often find herself thinking.

Cora joined those sitting at the fountain and watched the alley opening she'd just left. But no one else came out. People continued eating their sandwiches. The day rolled on. Had she imagined it? Too much time in the dusty, lightless vaults of the archives; her mind was playing tricks on her. And Jenkins was still down there – Jenkins. She was meant to be getting the constable some help and here she was rattled by a few loose stones scattering in an alley. This case was getting to her.

A man in the washed-out purple of a Commission underling was fishing in the fountain with one hand, gloved to his elbow. In his other hand was a sack. As Cora watched, he pulled out fistfuls of thick, greasy-looking weed, caught in which were food wrappers and a glass bottle. He dumped them into his sack and put his arm in to fish again. Cora nodded to him as she passed – Commission seeing Commission. In his nodded return was a world of weariness. The smell from the weed was foul.

'Perlish Assembly finds money to keep a fountain running, but they won't mend the roads,' the man said.

'Won't help their chances this year.'

'Heard their story was a strange one. All those different parts.' He shook a clump of weed from his glove.

'Just like life, eh, friend?'

Cora took her leave, and, as she carried on across the

courtyard, thought about why Rustan Chambers Latinum might have visited the archives. Did she go to remove all mentions of Tennworth, to cover her own tracks? Or was she, like Cora, trying to find Tennworth's trail herself? Or, perhaps most likely of all, was she simply looking for old business records?

Cora went through an archway. Partner knew how she'd get back to the station from—

She'd emerged onto a busy thoroughfare that, surprisingly, Cora recognised: there was Yammers, a very good bakery, and she knew the gig stop, too, with its distinctly worked metal hitching post twisted to look like a tree growing out of the pavement. And towering over them, the back of the Commission Wheelhouse. This couldn't be right. She could have sworn the archives were in a different part of the city altogether. The archives must be closer to the centre than she'd thought.

'Or it's the tornstone in the walls,' she muttered to herself.

She ducked across the street, dodging the many carts and gigs, the drivers shouting, and came to the alley that cut through to the street beyond. She glanced behind her before she set off down it. There was no one following her. She pressed on, to the Wheelhouse. Jenkins would have to wait.

At the end of the alley, Cora looked up at the hulking building now just a stone's throw away, its many thin windows staring back at her. Behind each one, a bean-counter, and behind that bean-counter, twenty-five more of them, fifty behind each of those, and on it went.

But she hadn't come for that today. She'd come for the Wheelhouse's near neighbour. There it was, the place Chief Inspector Sillian didn't want her poking her nose in.

The Assembly building. Where the Chambers met.

No matter who won the election, there was always enough money for the potted sinta trees forced to grow into fancy shapes and flanking the grand entranceway, money for the gardeners whose job it was to bend those branches around wire. Money for the men and women who stood at the entrance night and day, for the batons tucked in their belts, ready to be pulled out to keep the unwanted from going in.

Chief Inspector Sillian had said Cora couldn't step foot inside, but Sillian hadn't said anything about being *outside*. So Cora sat herself down on a bench opposite the main entrance, tried to get as comfortable as possible, and waited. And watched. And by the end of the day, she had what she needed to talk to Rustan Chambers Latinum.

The following afternoon she was back on the very same bench outside the Assembly. She had finished her lunch – a greasy pie with an unknown kind of meat in the middle – just about the same time as the Chambers came back from *their* lunch. How was that for coincidence?

A coincidence, too, that a Commission coach carrying Rustan Chambers Latinum and her dining partners was rattling down the cobbled street at that very moment.

The coach was huge, as all Commission coaches were, needing two pairs of horses to draw it. It was painted glossy black, the Spoked Wheel in white. There were two drivers in purple uniform, and for a second Cora let herself think about Finnuc. Finnuc before he was poisoned and his lips blistered away, his eyes forced from their sockets by choking.

As the coach pulled up outside the Assembly building, a purple-liveried figure jumped from the back of the coach to open the door. Chambers didn't open their own coaches, that was something Cora had quickly learned during her time on the bench the day before. She'd learned a few other things too. Like just who was going to be in that coach with Latinum. As she saw the first flash of a brown robe, Cora started towards the Assembly.

The first Chambers to emerge from the coach was the Seeder, her grey hair cut close to her head. Cora hadn't learned her name yet, but as a woman she was one of the three Chambers who could be Tennworth. She liked to be first, far as Cora could tell. Liked to make the others wait as she came down the coach's steps. Then came the Torn Chambers, glass mouthpiece in place to allow him to breathe in Fenest – the air so different here than in the Tear. The Torn Chambers wasn't first, nor last, but had the safety of the middle of the pack. He must have said something funny, because the Seeder Chambers turned and laughed. Cora was halfway across the street now. She made the pavement at the same time Latinum emerged, the Rustan's metal hand winking in the sun. What were the odds of such a coincidence?

Like any game, the numbers didn't matter, not really – it was rigged. So when the three Chambers started towards the Assembly building, Cora raised her hand to the pennysheet boy standing nearby; a friend of Marcus, and just as loud. He headed for the Assembly's door too. Made quite a sight, he did, swinging his stack of 'sheets, his brow furrowed in concentration.

And then precisely as the Seeder Chambers was almost at the door, the boy tripped and sent his 'sheets to the wind.

The Seeder Chambers cried out in surprise, the security at the door struggled through the white whirlwind to catch the boy, and then Cora stepped quickly beside Rustan Chambers Latinum and said, 'A word, your honour?'

The Rustan turned, her surprise evident.

It was an expensive way to get a Chambers' attention. But it worked.

'Detective Gorderheim?'

'That's right, your honour. Could we?' Cora said, angling away from the chaos of the pennysheets and the other Chambers there.

'Of course,' Latinum said.

Cora was aware of the woman's gaze on her as they moved towards the bench, and thought of the look Latinum had given her at the Perlish story, mouthing the word 'detective'. Latinum had wanted Cora to know she was known. And now, Cora was doing the same to this Chambers. Chief Inspector Sillian would not be happy.

Latinum was short and looked sturdily built beneath her robe, though how much of that was down to her own bones and flesh, Cora couldn't be sure. The way these Rustans liked to re-make themselves, just like Fire Investigator Serus and his metal cheekbones. Latinum shared Serus's colouring – ruddy skin, her auburn hair knotted the same way Serus wore.

'I will wet my throat,' Latinum said as she sat down on the bench. 'Unless that is a problem. We Chambers spend so much time talking – the mouth, the dryness. One must take steps. Do you drink, Detective?'

'I don't.'

'Few of the Audience appreciate moderation.' Latinum

produced a small metal flask of the Rustan kind from within her robe: a flask that had two metal teeth attached to the lip. These she locked into her mouth with a clang.

Cora couldn't help but flinch.

'Apologies, Detective. It is easy to forget not everyone is used to Rustans.' The flask hung from Latinum's jaw, even while she wasn't drinking. Unsettling *and* practical.

'I do my best not to stare,' Cora admitted. She lit a rolled bindleleaf. The Rustan's drink was the stronger smell, an expensive smell. No real surprise there. Something from Seeder blenders, if Cora had to guess.

'Like so many Fenestirans,' Latinum said, 'but then it is as if you ignore us. Do I flatter myself when I expect you to know my name, as I know yours?'

'No, your honour, I have a very well-informed constable helping me.'

'Good. That is good. It can be hard to find reliable help.' There didn't seem to be any guile in the woman's words. Like their neighbours, the Torn, Rustans had a reputation for plain-talking.

'I imagine as a Chambers you've your pick of competent aides,' Cora said. 'From across the Union.'

'We do. We are lucky, I think.'

'Sometimes I wonder if my constable and me are from different realms, not just different parts of Fenest. The things she says!' Cora didn't have to fake laughter, thinking about Jenkins. 'Have you had an aide that wasn't a Rustan?'

Latinum tipped back her head and drank from the flask still attached to her jaw. 'My first aide, not that long ago,' she said when she had finished. 'A Casker.'

Cora felt a tremor in the hand holding her bindle. A

Casker – was Latinum referring to Finnuc Dawson?

'Oh?' Cora said, trying to sound relaxed. 'What was she like?'

'*He*, Detective. He was a big man. Very helpful in certain… situations. But I did not always trust his discretion.'

Cora took a long drag on her smoke. She didn't want to rush this. 'Caskers do a lot of talking, must be something to do with life on a barge.'

'Perhaps. This man did not grow up on a barge.'

Just like Finnuc. Cora felt she was edging closer to Tennworth with every word the Rustan uttered.

'I thought they were all born on the water?' Cora said.

Latinum shook her head, apparently missing Cora's jest. 'Most are born in Bordair, Detective. On land.'

'Of course. So what happened to him – your Casker aide?'

The Rustan unhooked her flask. The metal teeth were white with spittle and the smell of spirits swam from them. 'Happened to him, Detective?'

'Well, you made it sound like he's not your aide anymore.'

'No. He is not.'

'So? How did he join the Audience?'

'Who said anything about the Audience?' Latinum smiled. It took Cora a moment to understand, to realise she had been gulled like an eager, precocious child. 'His name is Rinan,' Latinum said. 'He works in the Wheelhouse now.'

At least Latinum hadn't drawn out the game too long. Of course, whoever Tennworth was, she wasn't going to admit directly to having Finnuc as an aide. But there was something to be taken from the Rustan toying with her: it meant Latinum *knew* about Finnuc. Knew enough to see through Cora's questioning. And two could play such games.

'I recently found myself amongst Commission records,' Cora said. 'Not the Wheelhouse, but in Uppercroft. All *kinds* of interesting information to be found there.'

'I could not agree more,' Latinum said, and wiped the metal teeth of her flask. 'Hoyer Dray is very helpful, is he not?'

'Very.'

'You want to know why I was there,' Latinum said, looking hard at Cora. 'Like you, I was hoping to find a name.'

'Find it, or erase it?'

'Come now, Detective. You have seen the Commission's great archives, how extensive they are. How could I alone erase something from such a body of knowledge?'

'So how could you alone find it?'

Latinum shrugged. 'I couldn't. My grandfather once owned a mining interest in the Rusting Mountains, until it was cheated from him. I hoped to find something in the archives that would prove such treachery. My father... he has never forgotten, never forgiven. But that is a long story, and one for another day.'

'A story for an election?' Cora said.

The Rustan smiled. 'If it please the Audience. But don't look so disappointed, Detective. We have a mutual friend, you and I. One that will show you the way, when you're ready.'

'What way?'

'It is all in the telling,' Latinum said. 'Our friend will make that clear. And when the time comes, I trust our cause can count on you.'

'I don't know what—'

'You will, Detective. I'll make sure of it.' She tucked her flask back inside her robe, then strode towards the Assembly Building.

At the main entrance, the ground was littered with pennysheets but the boy was nowhere to be seen. Cora hoped he'd got away.

A mutual friend. The way Latinum talked, that friend was alive and still telling stories. And that last thing Latinum had said: *I'll make sure of it*. Was that a threat?

Cora finished her bindleleaf, but before she could head back to the station another coach pulled up – this time not at the main entrance but right in front of her bench.

The door was opening before the coach had even stopped, with no liveried staff to help this time. Whoever was inside had to do for themselves.

A Torn woman stepped quickly out of the coach. She was wearing a baggy dress made of coarse, blue fabric and stout boots. A glass mouthpiece too, like all of her kind. After generations of living in the ash-rich atmosphere of the Tear, living with stinging rain that turned the air against you, the Torn had changed to survive their homeland. But it made leaving difficult. There were ways. A mouthpiece, like the one this woman wore, fitted with burning lumps of tornstone, kept them alive when they made the trip north, but few came. The woman's eyes met Cora's.

The woman's face was familiar, as was something in her scarring. Not that Cora had met many Torn in her life, and not that any of the people of the Tear were without the scars caused by the rain of their homeland. But the long scar that divided this woman's forehead, *that* Cora had seen before, at the Opening Ceremony of the election, back when Cora only had one body on her hands, that of Nicholas Ento. The Torn woman was Sorrensdattir, advisor to the Torn Chambers, and the person who had first given

Cora a glimpse of what the Wayward election story was about. A story that had got its 'teller killed.

Sorrensdattir came towards her. 'Is something for the Latecomer, this, Detective. To find you here.'

'Why? Were you going to come and see me?'

'My intention, yes, but...'

Cora held out her hand for the Torn greeting she'd first experienced at the Opening Ceremony: her hand taken in both of the Torn's and each knuckle quickly pressed. But instead, Sorrensdattir glanced behind her, at the Assembly building.

'I saw your Chambers go in,' Cora said.

'Could be yours too, if our story is for the black stones.'

'Fancy your chances?'

Sorrensdattir laughed and the tornstone in her mouthpiece flared orange. The air around Cora was at once smoky, and not in a bindleleaf kind of way. This smoke was sulphurous and somehow hotter than bindle ever produced.

'In Fenest, everything is numbers,' Sorrensdattir said. 'For the chequers, yes?'

'It's all one long gamble. Pennysheets say the Torn Hook will be made of tornstone. That one worth a mark to the chequers?'

'You must wait, Detective, like others.'

'Like I'm still waiting to hear about the Wayward story.' Cora started forward. 'You know more than you told me at the Opening Ceremony. What's—'

Sorrensdattir held up her hand. 'Not here,' she said more quietly. 'We meet elsewhere. I have something for you. That you will need.'

'What is it? Surely you can just tell—'

'The Hook Barge,' Sorrensdattir said. 'Not this night. Not the night of tomorrow. The third night, you come. Late. I will be there for the changing of the Hooks.'

Cora nodded, and the Torn woman made her way to the main entrance. Cora was once more left alone in front of the great Assembly building of Fenest. She waited a moment longer than she needed to, just in case the Audience sent her another coach carrying someone to talk to. But then it started to rain, the Painter as subtle as ever.

Twelve

It was close to dawn when Cora arrived at Beulah's games house near Tithe Hall. Marcus was none too pleased to be woken by the secret doorbell, rung by pulling the rusty lamp beside a boarded door. The girl glowered at Cora, looking short of sleep. Fortunately, Marcus didn't have to look healthy for what Cora needed – in truth what she was about to ask wouldn't help the girl's pallor one bit.

'I need a quick word,' Cora said.

'With Beulah? She's not—'

'With you.'

'Oh...'

Marcus led her down a carpeted corridor, her feet tripping over the hem of the long shirt she was wearing. The cloth was a lurid mess of red and yellow birds. Some Perlish design, likely left behind by someone whose losses took them down to their underwear.

The carpet was thick, the wallpaper's print as headache-inducing as Marcus' nightshirt. Cora felt as if her ears were jammed with wool, the games house muffled.

They passed doors onto rooms where cards were dealt, risks were taken, threats made. There was no sound from the games, but Cora could feel the hum of excitement through the doors.

Up ahead, there was a prone figure lying on the floor. Without breaking her stride, Marcus stepped over him. It was a Perlish man, snoring. Stale beer wafted from his stained clothes.

'This one been with you a while?' Cora said.

'Long as he's got money left to bet, Beulah says he can stay.'

Marcus stopped between two doors. She put her hand on the wall and pushed, and the paper seemed to fall inward: there was a door here, invisible until a knowing hand touched it in just the right place. Marcus stepped through and Cora followed. She'd seen plenty of this games house, as a detective and as a guest, but she'd never seen behind this wall.

They were in a narrow passage, well-lit and plain, thank the Audience. Marcus kicked the door shut and led Cora into a small sitting room where the remains of a fire glowed, casting warm light onto the comfortable-looking chairs and decent rug, a scrawny cat gently snoring. A clock on the mantle ticked out the night. It was as if she'd stepped into another world.

'I can see why you put up with late hours,' Cora said, looking around the room. On the chair nearest the fire, a boy was curled in sleep. A blanket was pulled up to his nose, but Cora recognised him.

'How's he doing?' she asked Marcus.

'Tam? He's a quick learner. Clears the tables fast as you like. Gets out the way quick too.' Marcus yawned and took the chair next to the sleeping boy. 'Beulah says you can bring her more like him.'

'Hoping I won't have to.'

Tam was a Seeder boy Cora had found living in an abandoned stone works, just as she was closing in on Finnuc. He'd come north from his home only to find hunger and cold alleys to bed down in. Why he travelled all the way to Fenest, she hadn't found out. She wasn't going to tonight, either: Tam was sound asleep. Marcus yawned again, this time louder, and Cora got the hint.

'I won't keep you long,' Cora said.

'What you needing? Can't wait for *The Spoke*?'

'That 'sheet arrives too often for my liking. You been keeping up with the city school?'

'Those stiff-shirt teachers,' Marcus growled. 'They don't know *nothing* about this city. I keep telling 'em—'

'Have you been going?'

A muttered *yes*, which Cora hoped meant the girl's learning had improved. It was a sad irony of Fenest that the kids who sold the pennysheets could rarely read them. The bosses told the sellers the headlines and the sellers shouted them. Counting was more important in that line of work.

'Good,' Cora said. 'I need you and some of your mates from school, those you can trust, to go to the archives in Uppercroft and look for something.'

'How many of these *mates* am I supposed to have?'

'Just bring as many as you can.'

'And how long for?'

'That depends how quick you get the work done, doesn't it?' Cora said. 'Can you get them out of school?'

'If you're paying, they'll come. But what do I tell my 'sheet boss?' Marcus said.

'That you're ill. That Beulah needs you here. Choice is yours.'

Marcus rolled her eyes. 'Thanks…'

'Jenkins is already there. She'll tell you all what you need to do.'

'The toothy constable? She'll be no good with these kids.' Marcus' raised voice made the boy Tam stir in his sleep. Cora waited, but he soon settled. The cat was awake now though and rubbed itself against Cora's boot.

'Constable Jenkins might surprise you,' Cora told Marcus. 'And go easy on her – amount of pennysheets I've had off you since the election started, you owe me.'

Even Marcus couldn't argue with that.

'Any more on the new Wayward storyteller?' Cora asked, scratching behind the cat's ear. 'This person who married into the realm?'

'Nothing. I think maybe that story I told you wasn't so good after all.'

'You just keep telling me what you hear.' Cora nodded to the still-sleeping Tam. 'If he can read and needs the work, take him too.'

Marcus saw her back to the main door.

'I want you and the others at the archives as soon as you can get your boots on,' Cora said. 'Speaking of which…'

'I bought 'em.'

'Good to hear you haven't started throwing your money away in here.'

'You're an example to avoid, Beulah says.' Marcus grinned.

'She's not wrong.' Cora stepped out into the street.

'Where you going, Detective?'

'Going?'

Marcus considered Cora in that cutting, all-seeing way of hers. 'You got a look on your face. I know that look. And you're making *me* go to the archives, with *Constable Jenkins*. You got to be going somewhere.'

'Somewhere I shouldn't.' Cora headed down the street. 'Be nice to Jenkins, and take a coat – you'll need it.'

The address wrapped around her bindleleaf tin had to be wrong. She was looking at a row of stables.

Eight doors, the split kind they used for horses. The top of each was open. Some of the beasts looked out, and swung their thick necks to and fro. In other stalls, the inhabitants were just shadows and noise. People were milling about with pitchforks and barrows, opening and closing the doors, murmuring to the horses. The air was sweet with hay. All the early business of the new day.

Cora was in an alley across from the stables. She'd made the time to come here, so she felt she should stay a few minutes. Time for a smoke and to give her aching foot a rest. It hadn't taken her long to find the stables after she left Marcus at the games house. The place was only a few streets over from the station. Did that make it more or less likely that Ruth was here, near Cora? It didn't matter. She wasn't going to see her sister. Ruth wasn't here.

Some part of Cora was pleased the address was wrong. A large part, if she were honest. Now Cora didn't have to find out if Ruth really was back. She didn't even know why she'd tried.

Because of Nicholas Ento, the murdered Wayward storyteller. Because of Finnuc. People were dying, the election was facing problem after problem. And Ruth was back. If she had anything to tell Cora about the Wayward story, about why Tennworth didn't want it told, then Cora had to see her. But it was pointless. She'd done what she could, and now she was going back to work.

She tossed the end of her bindle to the ground then turned into the street.

'You came then.'

That voice. It was familiar, but it wasn't her sister's. Cora looked back at the stables. A small woman in a cowl was coming towards her. Inked designs stole up her wrists.

Nullan, the Casker storyteller. And Nicholas Ento's lover.

Cora had last seen Nullan in the grounds of Burlington Palace tending the victims of Black Jefferey, a plague many in Fenest believed the Casker story had brought to the city. Nullan was the last person Cora had expected to see here, but it couldn't be coincidence.

'I thought you'd gone back to Bordair,' Cora said.

'Wish I could,' Nullan said.

'What's keeping you in Fenest then?'

'The same thing that's brought you here this morning, Detective. She's been waiting for you.'

'I don't—'

But Nullan turned on her heel and walked back towards the stables. Cora had no choice but to follow.

The stablehands paid no mind to her and Nullan, didn't look up from their work or stop their chatter. Several wore cloaks of stiffened animal skin: Wayward clothes. There was an alcove halfway between the stalls that Cora hadn't noticed before. As she followed Nullan she saw the alcove had a short staircase, which led to a loft space.

'Nullan, what's going on? Do you—'

'It's not me you need to speak to, Detective.'

Is it Ruth? Cora wanted to ask but her mouth was dry. Is it Ruth up here? Her heart was hammering in her chest. It was anger but it was love too. How could it not be? Anger's fire could only exist if there was love to stoke it.

The stairs ended in a tiny landing and a low door. Nullan knocked, twice quickly, then a pause, then two more knocks, slow this time.

From behind the door, a floorboard creaked. Then a voice said, 'Come'. A voice Cora knew, even after all this time. She had to lean against the wall, fearing she'd fall over. She wanted to get out, back down the stairs and out into the open air. Back to the station, to her world. But her legs wouldn't move. Her lungs wouldn't fill. Nullan opened the door, then did her best to stand aside in the narrow space to let Cora pass. Cora took a deep breath, feeling her chest rattle with all her years of smoking, and was surprised to find herself thinking: how much bindleleaf have I smoked since Ruth left? She stepped into the loft space.

She had to duck immediately to avoid hitting her head on the beams, but at the apex she could almost stand upright. The door closed behind her. Nullan was gone. The loft was long and narrow, the low beams running the length of it. At the far end was a table, and seated behind it, staring straight at Cora, was a woman in a dark dress. The same woman Cora had seen outside the station the other day, amid the chaos of the street. The same woman who had been in the winery carriageway when Cora had arrested Finnuc. Her sister.

Ruth stood and came towards Cora. 'It's been a long time.'

'More than thirty years.'

Ruth's steps were slow, deliberate. She was just as thin as Cora remembered, but the years looked to have been hard on her. Her face was pinched. Grey hair peppered her temples but the rest was still deep brown. There were only five years between the two of them but the gap seemed to have widened. Ruth looked worn out. She picked her way through the trunks and cases scattered about, and the saddles – so many saddles. What looked like bedding was squashed into the far corner amid spider webs and old straw. And, hanging from a hook, a Wayward cloak.

'You must have thought I'd joined the Audience,' Ruth said, closer now, and Cora wanted to stop her. Couldn't bear to have her within reach because she feared she'd grab her, hurt her, or forgive her. And too much had happened for that.

'I hoped you *had* died,' Cora said.

Ruth's step faltered and she stayed where she was, ten or so feet from Cora, but it might as well have been the length of the Union.

'I told the story to the Widow every night until I could finally leave that house. Every night,' Cora spat. 'The story of your death.'

Ruth blinked several times but she didn't look away, Cora would give her that.

'It was bad then,' Ruth said, 'after I…'

'After you sold our parents to the pennysheets and fled the city? Yes, Ruth, it was *bad*. It was the end of the world. And you left me to deal with it. You left me—'

Cora turned away. This wasn't how she wanted this to go, and what did it matter anyway? The past was a story with an ending, one that couldn't be changed.

'I had no choice, Cora. What I found in the files at home, I couldn't ignore it.'

'Yes, you could. It was only money. Half the trading halls were on the take, not just our parents.'

'Only money?' Ruth said, incredulous. 'It's corruption. It's rot. How can you blind yourself to it?'

'Because I *live* in Fenest, Ruth. It's easy to take the high ground when you don't stick around to see what it's really like being here.' Cora shook her head. 'You're just the same as back then, so ready to tell everyone else what's wrong with their lives when you can't see the truth about yourself.'

'Which is *what*?' Ruth said, her voice hardened now.

'That you... it doesn't matter.'

'What, Cora? Now's your chance to say it. After all these years.'

'You love a cause more than you love people.'

'Cora—'

'That's why you've come back now, isn't it? All these years and no word to me, and now here you are. Tell me I'm wrong.'

'That you should think that way about me...' Ruth looked away. She was surely too thin, too brittle, this woman who was and was not her older sister. But she was strong, too. Ruth seemed to burn with strength. 'It's *because* I care about people. I care about their lives – their cause, if you want to put it that way, Cora. It wasn't just about the money. The files in the study – there was so much more going on. I only saw a glimpse that night, our family's part, but I was right about the injustice.'

'So you decided you were going to change the Union,' Cora said flatly.

'I decided to try! I had to, Cora. And I'm glad I did. Everything I've learned since— The north has always had power over the south, Cora, and Fenest has helped them to keep it.'

'Well if it's always been so terrible, why come back now? What's changed?'

'Everything.' Ruth looked her dead in the eye.

'You did go to the Steppes, didn't you?' Cora said.

Ruth seemed uncertain. 'What? That's not important. What matters—'

'The last Mother heard was that you'd joined a caravan going to the far north. You joined the Wayward. Is that where you've been all these years, with them?'

Ruth looked like she was weighing up what to say, then she nodded. 'I don't think I was meant to stay in one place all my life,' she said softly. 'When I joined the caravan, I realised how much I needed to move around. To see life from all angles, not just the Fenest way.'

Cora looked around at the chaos of the stable loft. 'So I can see. This is how you live?'

'I don't need the trappings we had as children, the things Fenest values. It's worthless. I don't know how you stand it.'

'Stand what?'

'This place.' Ruth swept her arm around the loft and the city beyond the roof tiles. 'The Wayward people helped me understand a different way of living. And in return I helped them.'

'Helped them how?'

'That's a story for another day,' Ruth said. 'What you have to know, Cora, if it's going to work between us—'

'If *what's* going to work?'

'—is that I didn't plan any of this, how my life has turned out. What happened at home. The people who asked me to get the files, they offered to take me with them. I knew I had to get out of Fenest, but I always meant to come back. For you, Cora.'

'But you didn't.'

Ruth's shoulders slumped. Her thin, black-clad shoulders. When had her sister got so old, so tired? 'There wasn't time that night to explain everything,' Ruth said, a world of weariness in her voice. 'I asked you to come with me.'

'I was twelve! How could I have understood what was happening?'

Ruth sat down on a trunk and didn't look at Cora. 'You should have trusted me.'

'Like I should trust you now? I saw you with Finnuc Dawson, the man who killed the Wayward storyteller!'

Ruth flinched. 'As a prisoner.'

'You expect me to believe that?'

'I do.' Ruth turned to face her again. 'Because of your actions in the winery that day I was able to escape, and I'm grateful for that, believe me. Without you I'd have gone the same way as... as Nicholas once the Casker had finished with me.' She gripped the trunk with both hands, her knuckles whitening. 'But I wondered about that, what brought you to Tennworth's place.'

That Ruth should mention that name. What did she know of Tennworth?

'Wondered why you were so keen to see Finnuc, too,' Ruth said.

'I...'

'And I'm still wondering about that, Cora. If I can trust you.'

'If you can trust *me*? I—'

Nullan burst into the stable loft. 'Word's just come – it's not safe here.'

Ruth paled. 'Make ready.'

Then Nullan was away down the stairs. A moment of silence. Of stillness. Then, without looking at Cora, Ruth started rifling through one of the trunks.

'Why are you living here, like this, Ruth? Why the secret knock, Nullan keeping watch?'

'There are plenty of people – powerful people – who would like to find me. People like Finnuc Dawson.'

'But the embezzlement story was all so long ago,' Cora said, having to raise her voice over the noise of Ruth's furious packing. 'No one ever found the money. No one's bothered about it anymore.'

Ruth glanced up at Cora and there was a world of withering in that look. Cora recognised it only too well from seventeen-year-old Ruth, and recognised her own burn of shame, too.

Ruth went back to rummaging in the trunk and pulled out some clothes that looked to Cora like riding britches. She put them on under her dress, which had large slits up the side. A Wayward riding habit that looked like a Fenestiran dress. Clever.

'Cora, this is more important than our parents. I was right then, when I took the files, and I'm right now. It's all connected but it's bigger than us.'

'Who's "us"? You and Nullan?'

'Oh, Cora. You're still thinking too narrow, when the truth is widening all the time.'

Cora wanted to push her sister's face into the pile of clothes and papers she was now stuffing into a smaller bag. 'Why don't you just tell me why you've come back?' Cora said. 'What do you know about the Wayward story?'

'The best way is to see for yourself. You need to go south, Cora. Once you've seen it with your own eyes, it'll all make sense.'

'Go south? With you?'

'Cora, you don't understand. Nicholas' story, it...'

'You're right, I don't understand! But I'm beginning to put things together. Someone doesn't want the Wayward story told. Is it you, Ruth? Are you helping Tennworth?'

'I can help you find her, Cora, but you have to trust me.'

Before Cora could speak, the door flew open and Nullan was back. 'Time to go.'

It was too quick, all of this – Ruth leaving her again.

'You're going now, to the south?' Cora said.

'When you're ready, we'll go south together. Until then, I'll be in the city.' Ruth threw a bag to Nullan who raced back down the stairs. Then Ruth grabbed her cloak and a saddle.

'Goodbye, Cora.'

It was like the past had reared up and was happening all over again and there was nothing Cora could do about it. 'Ruth – wait!'

But her sister was through the door, down the stairs. 'I can't stay here now, it's not safe.'

'Why? Where are you going?'

She hurried after Ruth but her foot was too painful.

Ruth seemed further and further away. When Cora reached the bottom of the stairs, Ruth and Nullan were already on horseback.

'The south, Cora. Think about it. It's important for everything. For Nicholas, his story.'

'But—'

'I'll send word. This time I promise.'

And with that, her sister disappeared into the streets.

Thirteen

At the door to the Oak, the niche dedicated to the Latecomer was stuffed with pennies and string, rolled betting slips, even what looked like a clutch of apple seeds. This member of the Audience was always popular near a ring. Cora asked for good fortune herself, to be able to forget, even for a little while, what had just happened at the stables, seeing Ruth again after all this time. For payment she murmured a few words to the Latecomer about her trip to Perlanse. She wasn't ready to talk about her sister yet. She needed the Oak to distract her, and from the case, too. Three election stories told and she was still no closer to finding Tennworth. Her chief inspector was hardly helping, and now she couldn't shake the feeling she was being followed. As she stood at the Latecomer's niche outside the Dancing Oak, the night air seemed to thicken around her and in the growing silence she heard it: the scuff of a boot. A low cough.

Then the door to the Oak swung open and a man staggered towards her, his hand fumbling for his fly. The night resettled to its usual gig wheels and pennysheet seller calls, and Cora went inside.

The front bar was full, as it had been every night since the election started. Tonight's customers looked like they were mostly Seeders. The small groups spoke softly to one another over thin glasses. A pair of young Casker women roared with laughter in the corner, back-slapping and spilling their beer as one told the other a story.

'... then the bargehand, she took off her clothes and pissed all over the deck.'

'And the captain?' the younger one spluttered.

'Joined in!'

As she went through the bar, Cora caught the Seeders sending disapproving glances at the Caskers. Drunkard take them, did the people of the Lowlands *ever* smile? No wonder the Seeder election story had been so miserable. But then, the Caskers' tale hadn't been much to laugh about. For all their faults, at least the Perlish tried for a funny amid all the tragedies.

She nodded to the barman, then turned down the passage that led to the back room. She thumped the door three times.

'Who wants to know?' came a bored-sounding voice.

'Jittery Wit,' Cora gave for the password.

The door creaked open just enough for her to squeeze into the back room.

'Good timing, Detective,' said the big man on door duty. All he wore was some kind of skirt that barely covered his backside, and greasepaint on his other cheeks that made his dark skin gleam.

'Beulah at one of her other houses, is she?' Cora said.

'Beetles still in their pens. Chance to see the form before the action starts.'

Ash beetles. Brought all the way from the Tear because Fenestirans loved to see them fight; so much so, people lost the little sense they had ringside and bet big. The beetles were impressive to watch, Cora had to admit that – much bigger than the cockerels, yet the insects were swifter and their pincers were more vicious than any beak. In short, they were exotic, and Fenestirans liked a bit of that come election time.

Or some in the city did. Others believed what the pennysheets told them, that anything from the south – person or beetle – wasn't to be welcomed in the capital. But Cora had been hearing so much about the south recently, what with Casker Chambers Kranna's undocumented supply lines and Ruth's insistence that Cora should go down there, that the Audience seemed keen for a southern tale. She might as well make the most of the opportunity offered tonight.

'Remind me,' Cora said to the whore, 'it is the Rustans who bring the beetles up to Fenest, isn't it?'

'Right you are, Detective. Torn raised, Rustan transported.'

'Good. I've been wondering how the Rusting Mountains were getting on.' She found herself thinking of Fire Investigator Serus again – another Rustan.

She let the whore take her coat. Only place she would. If she kept it on, she'd sweat to death before she had a chance to see the night's numbers, and the patrons of the Oak knew better than to thieve from her pockets.

There weren't many here yet, but that was no surprise: it was early for the fights. A few Fenestirans waited in the booths, idly checking betting slips, the clouds of bindle thin above their heads. For once, Cora could smell the perfume of the whores who milled about – some looking for early customers, some lighting more lamps. That good air wouldn't last long. Soon the smoke and sweat would run thick in the back room of the Oak.

The ring was empty but ready for the sport to come: the sawdust fresh, free of the blood and carapaces from last night's fighters, raked all neat. The huge numbers-board that hung over the ring had been wiped clean. A man and woman, each looking as old as the Oak itself, were lounging at the back of the tiered booths, next to the numbers-board. Their chequers coats of black and white were cast beside them. Cora felt her blood begin to thrum.

'Back to settle your debts, Detective?' someone called from the far side of the ring. It was Beulah: ringmaster of the Oak and plenty of other gaming houses across Fenest. Most of them, some pennysheets claimed.

Cora said, walking round the ring to meet her, 'Might have to wait until payday.'

'Some things never change.' Beulah pulled a handful of crumpled slips from her pocket and waved them at Cora. 'All noted.'

Cora tried to ignore just how many slips had her name on; such a thing wouldn't help her night.

'Getting too old for the job?' Beulah said.

'Never too old for a bet.'

'Who have you been chasing, Detective?' Beulah gestured to Cora's boots. 'You're limping.'

'No more than usual,' Cora said, but the truth was

Beulah was right. Her scarred foot *was* more painful than usual. She reached where Beulah was waiting.

'I heard you caught him,' Beulah said, her worn face squinting up at Cora who was almost twice her height. 'The one who killed the Wayward storyteller, did the nasty stuff to the poor man's face.'

Cora grunted.

'Heard he didn't make it to the Steppes though,' Beulah said. 'Seeders got him, so the 'sheets are saying. A hold-up.'

'You know better than to believe the pennysheets, Beulah. Not much truth crosses those pages.'

'If enough people believe it, it becomes the truth.' Beulah turned towards the dark recesses of the Oak. 'Come and see what the election brings us, *if* you can manage the walk.'

'You got a storyteller back there? The Wayward need a replacement.'

'Something almost as good.'

Cora followed her to a pair of doors marked 'Private' along with a list of threats if that was ignored. Some of the threats, Cora had to admit, were quite imaginative. She'd never thought of *that* use for story glasses.

Beulah pushed open the doors and Cora stepped into a large room she'd not been in before, but had guessed must exist somewhere in the Oak. The smell confirmed the contents: ash.

Once she'd swatted the flies from her face, she saw that each side of the room was divided into pens, a wide central space left between them. It made her think of a Seat, with the benches and the aisle laid out the same. But instead of people quietly telling stories to the Audience, the pens were full of movement and sound: clicks and buzzes, shiny carapaces twitching.

Here were the Ash beetles, brought up from the Tear for the election.

People hurried between the pens, carrying buckets and brushes. One of them banged into Cora, and when the woman offered a muttered apology, Cora caught a glimpse of metal winking in the lamp light. A metal hand. The same modification as Rustan Chambers Latinum.

There was a good reason for the Rustans bringing the beetles up from the Tear, rather than the Torn who bred them: Fenest's air was too clean for Torn lungs. The glass mouthpieces they wore helped, but the experience of leaving the Tear was still unpleasant, so Cora remembered from her Seminary lessons. There weren't any Torn in the Oak tonight, by the looks of things.

The Rustan handlers were eyeing each other's beetles and there were mutters of weights and title fights. Cora stopped beside one of the handlers.

'Looks like a real scrapper,' she said. 'Bit on the small side, though.'

The Rustan took the jibe calmly. 'Size is not so important in the ring,' he said. 'Only the Drunkard places his bet on size alone.'

'The detective here should know better than that,' Beulah said. The beetle clicked a kind of agreement.

'They all look a little small this year,' Cora said. 'Something the matter down there?'

'Down where?' the handler said.

'How's things in the Rusting Mountains?'

'As hard as ever. The Great Watchman does what he can, but the Skarni ranges to the west are struggling.'

'I had a friend who said the whole south was struggling. You came from there recently?' Cora said.

'A month before the election.'

'Thank the Audience for the election,' Cora said. 'If you Rustans win, maybe your Chambers can do something to help. She seems the sort to get things done.'

'Maybe.'

'You don't sound so sure.'

'She can be... a little rash,' the handler said.

Cora thought back to her conversation with Rustan Chambers Latinum, outside the Assembly, and struggled to imagine Latinum as 'rash'. For all their volcanic homeland, the Rustans were colder than a Wayward winter.

'Rash?' Beulah said. She was now following the conversation almost as keenly as Cora.

The beetle handler glanced about him, clearly making sure none of his fellow Rustans were listening. 'There are stories.'

'There always are,' Cora said.

'Stories of a temper. Let us just say her advisors tread carefully.'

'Wasn't there something in the pennysheets about that?' Beulah said.

'One of them lost an ear. Apparently by accident.' The handler shook his head, suggesting it was anything but. 'If you will excuse me, I must ready Bjaren.' He turned back to his ash beetle, and taking a dead rat from a hanging bag tossed it into the pen. The sound of small bones crunching was surprisingly loud.

'If you're quite finished, Detective?' Beulah said.

'Just curious.'

'Don't take me for a fool. But your business is your own, until it's mine. Speaking of which.'

Beulah made for a pen at the end of the room, where a dark blue beetle the size of a large dog was stamping the ground.

Beulah leaned over and patted the beetle's back. 'Not long now, my dear.'

Cora wasn't going to get that close. There were too many moving parts – plates that seemed to slide over one another, revealing a fuzzy emptiness beneath, not to mention the cruel-looking pincers curling from the beetle's mouth.

'Impressive, wouldn't you say, Detective?'

'I wouldn't want to meet it in a dark alleyway.'

'Pay your debts in good time and you won't have to.' Beulah let the beetle sniff her hand. 'Unbeaten in four bouts. If you have any marks left, this is where you should put them.'

'I don't suppose you'd consider an advance on—'

'You know the rules, Detective. No special favours, even for the Commission. Unless…'

The beetle gave an especially loud clack and reared up on its back legs. Its neighbours either side answered with angry-sounding noises of their own. There was no doubt about it: tonight was going to be a good night at the Oak.

'Unless?' Cora said.

Beulah leaned against the pen. 'I'm having trouble with suppliers. Of the refreshment kind.'

'I don't work in trade, Beulah. I find murderers, not beer barrels.'

'Your pay comes from the Wheelhouse, doesn't it?'

'Yes but—'

'Then you're Commission, and it's you who've been holding up my beer deliveries.'

A bell rang at the front of the room and one of the chequers shouted, 'First match, ten minutes!'

Beulah walked towards the doors that led back to the ring. Cora took one last look at the blue beetle and reluctantly followed her.

'What's the problem with the beer?' Cora said, resigned to this next twist of the tale.

'If I knew that, I wouldn't be asking, would I?' Beulah snapped. 'Something to do with permits. I had to change supplier – Seeder I've used for years has stopped trading. Can't get hold of them. Found a new one, but the Commission won't authorise them to sell. Provenance uncertain, they're saying.'

'You mean they can't trace it? Commission won't like that.'

'You don't have to tell me! They think my new supply is stolen. A lot of that down there these days. That's what people are telling me.'

Theft in the Seeder lands. Caskers drowning themselves in Bordair. A Chambers sending undocumented food supplies. The south sounded in a bad way...

Beulah was looking at Cora expectantly.

'So find another supplier,' Cora said.

They were back at the ring now, the booths filling up. It was hot and smoky. The whores were out in force.

Beulah's old lined face was set in a scowl. 'Don't you think I've tried that? There's an election on, Detective. If I don't have enough beer in the pipes, people will go elsewhere. I've enough for two weeks but that's it, and there are still three stories to be told.'

The doors behind them opened and the blue beetle appeared, dragging its Rustan handler as it strained against its harness.

'If you could see your way to smoothing the wheels…' Beulah was saying.

The way the light caught the beetle's wings, it was almost too much. A gasp went up from the booths. The chequers were shouting numbers.

'… I'm sure I could see *my* way to advancing a line of credit.'

The blue beetle's opponent was close behind it – Bjaren the beetle, with the handler she'd spoken to. Bjaren was the smaller of the two beetles, and red coloured, but its pincers were larger. A good match.

'… and besides, you owe me a favour, Detective.'

The beetles went by and entered the ring. Cheers went up from the booths, a hundred paper slips waving. With difficulty, Cora turned her attention back to Beulah.

'A favour?' Cora said.

'For giving you a way to get behind Tithe Hall – a story venue, closed to everyone apart from election staff, which I'm fairly certain you *aren't*, Detective Gorderheim.'

'I'll see what I can do about the beer. No promises though, Beulah. The Commission is more of a maze than the passageways under Tithe Hall.'

The chequers smiled. 'You'll find your way.' She wrote out a fresh slip and then gave a sharp whistle. A whore jogged over for the paper, took one look at it and headed for the numbers-board above the ring. Turning to Cora, Beulah said, 'Enjoy yourself, Detective.'

Behind her, the beetles were facing each other, straining against their harnesses. The Rustan handlers each had their fingers on the buckles, waiting for the signal to let the beetles have at one another. The air was gritty with sawdust. The booths were loud with cheering. Somewhere, a glass shattered and a man's voice cried out about the numbers, the numbers.

And then the Rustans let their beetles go.

This time, size did matter in the ring.

After an evening of small, poorly calculated bets, Cora returned to her boarding house with far fewer pennies in her pocket than she started with. As she made her way along the quiet corridor and up the stairs to her room, she saw no one, for which she was grateful. She unlocked her door quickly, but stopped on the threshold.

There was a slip of paper on the floor. Someone had pushed it under the door.

Cora knew she was late with the rent again, though notes weren't usually her landlord's way of chasing payment. He preferred ambushing her on the stairs, but he'd not had much chance recently; she'd been spending more time at the station than ever. Cora was at once overwhelmed by a wave of tiredness.

She realised she was still standing in the doorway. The folded sheet of paper somehow throbbed with white light on the dark floor. She knew it wouldn't be from her landlord, and that meant someone else had been in her building, had climbed the stairs to her room. And in the last couple of days she'd been followed – she was almost sure of it. Sweat began to prick her armpits, the back of her neck. Cora quickly shut the door and made herself pick up the paper.

The note was in Ruth's handwriting. Cora let out a breath she hadn't realised she'd been holding.

When you're ready to travel, come to the coaching inn, South Gate.

At the back door, ask for the Washerwoman.

Come alone. Tell no one.

Ready to travel? As if all Cora needed was time to pack a saddle bag and she'd be off to the south of the Union with a sister she hadn't seen in decades. Ruth had been travelling the Union for too long; she didn't know how things worked in Fenest, what Cora's job was. And she hadn't even bothered to find out. That was what annoyed Cora most of all.

Cora lay down on her bed. Her thoughts were moving faster than her body could these days. The note meant several things.

First, Ruth knew where Cora lived.

Second, Ruth had a web of informants. Cora had suspected as much when Nullan had raced down the stables' stairs, only to then reappear shortly afterwards with news that it was safe for Ruth to move. That there was a place for Ruth to go.

Third, Ruth chose not to leave the note at the station. She didn't trust the police. That made sense, given that she'd made clear she didn't trust Cora. But then, Cora wasn't too sure about Chief Inspector Sillian these days either.

There was a fourth thing too, coming clear: Ruth's pain when Cora had mentioned the death of Nicholas Ento. Ento was Wayward, Ruth had joined that realm. Her sister seemed to have more than a professional interest in the case.

But then, the same was true of Cora.

Ruth wanted her to go to the south. It was just like her sister – the seventeen-year-old version of her, at any rate – to turn up and expect Cora to drop everything, for Ruth's desires to be more important.

She realised she was still holding the note and hobbled down to the kitchen where the embers of the fire glowed, never allowed to go out completely. Cora held the note over the grate. She wasn't going south with Ruth. She wasn't doing whatever Ruth told her to do. Too many years had passed. The note was still in her hand. Why couldn't she let it fall into the embers and be rid of it? Be rid of Ruth again.

Because of the south. There'd been a lot of talk about it recently. Too much to ignore.

Cora stuffed the note into her pocket, then took a heel of bread from the box on the table and climbed slowly back to her room.

Beulah claimed she was having trouble with beer supplies in the Lowlands. That was a hard one to believe. The old chequer was one of the most well-connected people in Fenest – she had a finger in every pie going. She *baked* the pies, for Audience sake. For her to ask Cora for help, things must be bad. Cora wasn't sure what she was going to be able to do about it. The amount she owed Beulah, she wouldn't be calling at the Oak any time soon. Beulah's troubles were part of some trouble in the Lowlands. And that stitcher in Perlanse. She'd left home because of it. Was this what Finnuc meant when he'd said the south was falling apart?

She fell asleep before any answers came to her.

Fourteen

The next afternoon, Cora caught a gig to Uppercroft. She was due to meet the Torn woman, Sorrensdattir, at the Hook barge that night. The hours beforehand could be put to good use seeing how the search for Tennworth in the archives was going. No word had come to the station to say Jenkins and the pennysheet children had found anything yet, but there was no harm in reminding them she was waiting for news. No harm checking the archivist wasn't getting in the way either.

This time, her knock was answered quickly. Hoyer Dray stood gasping from breath in the doorway.

'Oh, thank the Audience.'

'Run up all those stairs, did you?' Cora said as she ground out her bindleleaf.

He leaned against the door jamb. 'I'll have some peace at last.'

'Peace?'

'Haven't you come to take them away, all those nuisances in the Room of Business Interests?'

'Only if they've found what I need.' She pushed by

him and headed down the staircase, followed by Dray's whining about noisy children.

'At least the mice will have scarpered, hearing them,' Cora said.

'I'd take the mice of Fenest over its children, Detective.'

The trip down the narrow staircase sharpened the pain in her already-aching foot. That piece of glass that had been tucked inside it all these years was on the move – she was certain of it.

When she reached the bottom, she followed the sound of Marcus' booming voice to the room where she'd left Jenkins amid the towering piles of paper. The air seemed to grow cooler with each step. By the time Cora reached the Room of Business Interests, she had to jam her hands in her pockets.

Jenkins was sitting on the ladder, wrapped in some kind of… sack, that was the word that came to mind. A small boy was hanging upside down from the top rung, reading something. Well, as long as they were reading…

'Interesting new fashion you're starting there, Constable.'

Jenkins looked up from the papers in her lap and peered at Cora. It seemed to take her a moment to focus. 'Detective, I…' A yawn took her words.

'He said the bags was all he could find,' Marcus said, and cursed. She was buttoned up to the chin in what looked like someone else's coat, it was so huge on her, and had made a hat out of similar sacking to what Jenkins was wearing. 'It's what the records come in. Musty old rubbish.' Marcus kicked a pile of papers and Jenkins shook her head.

A girl dressed head-to-toe in sacking came round a stack of papers, a sheet rolled up like a kind of trumpet at her mouth. She tootled away as she led a kind of procession of children, all following in a line and all with their noses an inch from an archive record.

'It's how they're keeping warm,' Marcus said. 'Care for a turn?'

'Here.' Cora handed a big parcel of sandwiches to Marcus. 'Share them round.'

'And there was me thinking you'd forgot about us.' Marcus opened the parcel and pressed a sandwich into Jenkins' hands. 'You should eat that, Jenkins. You're looking a bit pale.'

Cora would have to agree. She'd never seen *those* kinds of shadows beneath Jenkins' eyes. She glanced behind her. Dray had disappeared. 'Have you found anything on Tennworth?' she asked.

'Yes,' Marcus said.

'And no,' Jenkins added.

'Yes and no,' chimed in the boy hanging from the ladder. He kept saying that, over and over, until Marcus shushed him.

'Tell me,' Cora said.

From somewhere within the sack she was clad in, Jenkins produced a scrap of paper. 'This is a list of money paid to a Tennworth. At least, we think that's what it is...'

Cora took the paper – now they were getting somewhere. 'Good work,' she said, but for some reason neither Jenkins nor Marcus would meet Cora's eye.

There were five names on the list: Robinsons, Fimmons, Summerleaze, The Larkhouse, Salter. Each had a number written beside it, but there were no dates, no other identifying marks. Just the words 'Tennworth' and 'Monies due' across the top in slightly larger letters. The bottom of the page was torn. She turned it over. Nothing on the back except a boot print. The trumpet-led reading parade went round the stacks once more.

'Which of the records was it in?' Cora asked quickly, looking around. 'Dray had them in different piles for different realms.'

Jenkins glanced at Marcus, then said, 'Well, you see, Detective, the thing is—'

'It wasn't my fault!' Marcus boomed.

From somewhere in the hall behind her, Cora heard a distant groan from Hoyer Dray.

'What happened?' Cora said wearily.

'There's too much paper,' Marcus said. 'It got in the way. Jumped out at me.'

'We experienced some… re-ordering,' Jenkins said, 'but we tried—'

'So you don't know *where* in the Union this Tennworth is operating?' Cora said.

Jenkins shook her head.

'Or whether she's a Wayward fence-builder, a Casker barge captain, or a Rustan beetle-handler. This Tennworth could be anywhere.'

'Could be with the Audience,' Marcus said, munching on the sandwich. She headed for the archway that led back to the main hall. 'I'll be glad to get out of here. Right you lot, come on!'

Cora grabbed the pennysheet girl by her hood and pulled her back into the paper-strewn room. 'No one's going anywhere.'

'But we found you Tennworth!'

'You found *a* Tennworth but not much more than that. I need more information. Stay here until you find it.'

Jenkins huddled deeper into her sack and sighed.

'Don't worry, Constable. I'll send more sandwiches.' Cora stuffed the paper with the names in her pocket.

'Where you going?' Marcus said.

'To see a woman about a barge.'

The approach to the Hook barge was quiet, the usual daytime crowds gone, as Fenest slumbered in the warm night and waited for the next Hook – that of the Torn. For all that slumbering, the barge was a well-lit hump out on the River Stave. Sorrensdattir had said that tonight was the night they changed over the Hook, the story teaser of the Perlish replaced with that of the Torn realm. As best as Cora could tell in the darkness, the giant Perlish picture frame was gone and someone was already inside the barge: a shadow crossed a lit window. The last thing she needed was to worsen her aching foot so she made no effort to hurry down the street.

Until she smelled smoke.

Musty, heavy smoke. Not acrid like she'd smelled before, when she met the Torn. This was hearty, damp, and wooden – much more familiar.

She hurried towards the barge, knowing she was likely already too late.

'Sorrensdattir?' she shouted from the quayside.

No response came.

Smoke poured from the barge's windows and hatches

– a stronger black against the kind dulled by city lamps. The light from those windows spluttered and gushed, rolling like the waves of the river. Waves of fire, sloshing about the barge room where she'd seen the election Hooks.

She made the gangway before the heat pushed back against her. Her eyes started to sting. Despite the crackle and spitting of the fire, she heard bells far off, somewhere in the city. Queller-bells. If Cora was too late then the fire-quellers would be right on time to poke around in the ashes of the barge – or whatever the river left of them.

'Sorrensdattir, are you in there?' she called once more, hoping for no answer now.

Shielding her eyes against the glare and the heat, Cora tried to understand what she was seeing. This was the Hook barge. One of the busiest places in all of Fenest, and for these weeks of the election, one of the most important. Such a place didn't catch fire, didn't burn down. It just couldn't happen anywhere except in the stories. But it was happening right in front of her, as if it was a story for her and the Audience alone. More queller-bells sounded, but closer now.

And following their chimes, a scream.

Cora cowered from the growing flames, hoping the noise was her imagination.

Another scream. Cora moved without thinking, pushing past the wall of heat and along the gangway. The flames ran all along the roof of the barge now, licking upwards like serpent tongues, having scorched the windows and their surroundings black. The main doors were closed, but not locked as they had been for the Perlish Hook. Cora braced herself to haul the huge doors aside, having the sense to wrap her hands in the sleeves of her coat first. But when she tried them, the door slid back, light as a summer breeze. Inside, it was a summer's furnace that greeted her.

The walls were fire: yellow, orange, red, black, white. There was nothing else. Rivers of flame snaked their way along the floor. Above, nothing but the same. The barge was consumed, the Brawler's fire making for a story only he would want.

In the far corner, the shape of someone. Someone curled in on themselves against the heat.

'Sorrensdattir!'

The Torn woman looked up. 'No, you must not,' she shouted back.

'Get up, now! You have to come now.'

'Did I— Did I tell enough stories?'

Cora picked her way closer, testing each step carefully, feeling the heat press against her calves, her ankles, her toes.

'No use,' Sorrensdattir said. She pulled her heavy robe back to show a roof beam, and the mess it had made of her legs. The blood nearby bubbled as it boiled.

'We—' A wracking cough shook Cora. 'I can help.'

'There!' The Torn pointed to the other side of the barge. 'Not me. Help the Torn.'

Despite herself, Cora looked. More of the roof fell, undone by the fire. But in the other corner she saw... something. A dark shape that wouldn't stay still, it seemed to dance even, but not as if it were avoiding the flames. As if it were at home with them.

'No, I won't,' Cora said.

'You will,' Sorrensdattir said, soft and almost unheard.

Cora tried again to reach her. The path to the Torn was there, somewhere, amongst the fire and the darkness it left behind. That darkness, she realised just before she stepped into it, was the river below. They were laughing at her, the Audience, laughing at her struggles. At her petty little life that would end here, on the Hook barge. *Did I tell enough stories?* she thought, echoing the Torn. Would there be a place for them both among the Audience? Widow welcome them.

The coughing shook her. A sharp pain in her chest – a pain that reminded her of the life left there. Something worth the struggle.

'I'm coming,' she spluttered.

'No! The Hook!'

But Cora had made her choice. She risked hurried steps, heard the crack and the rumble too late. The floor under one foot went and then she was falling. A different kind of heat, closer, from inside not out, gripped her leg. She fell forward onto the hot floorboards, burning her hands. As she pulled herself up blood ran down her leg. Cora could see the deep cut there, but she had no time. The roof was collapsing about them, and the timbers engulfed one end of the barge. It was sinking, ready to give way to the river.

Gritting her teeth against the pain, against the scorching, bitter heat, she hobbled on.

'Cora, you must—'

With a strangled cry the Torn started to slip into a jagged hole where the floor had been.

Cora caught her arm. She felt the rough cloth, made hard and heavy by life in the Tear. With her vision blurred, her head pounding, she remembered there were firecats in the Tear. And there was one in the archives too – the skull. Did firecats feel rough, like a Torn robe? Were their stripes really scars? Sorrensdattir would know.

'Do they…' Cora shook her head. She tried to pull the Torn up, but her grip was weak. She was so weak now, and warm, and ready for sleep. She needed a sleep deep enough for the Audience.

'Cora. Listen to me. South. South for the hottest season. The *hottest*!'

'What?'

And then Sorrensdattir was gone. Falling amongst the broken, burning beams. Her mouthpiece a small light in the river's black beyond. Cora's grasping hand was so tiny, so useless in that black.

But other hands had Cora now. They hauled her back from the edge like she was a child, back from the Widow, the Brawler, and the others. Out of the barge and into the night's air that wasn't all smoke. They too had words for her. These strong-handed people, in their special red jackets and helmets. They asked her things, shouted at her to listen, and they were angry with her.

But all she could say was, 'South for the hottest season.' She said it with a smile.

The fire-quellers dragged her a safe distance and left her propped against a wall. A closed warehouse, one of those renovated for the coming of the Hook barge – warehouses that until recently had been alive with people eating, drinking, and placing bets with the chequers. Now that barge was going. And so was she. Only the coughing fits kept her awake. She was vaguely aware of the quellers hurrying to and fro. Sounds drifted in and out of her hearing with no way to see their cause in the thick, black air: creaks and splinters, the odd clang, an unsettling crackle, and, far away, a final fire warning bell tolled.

Cora moaned at the pain in her leg. She turned it, the little she was able, trying to find what was hurting so much. It was hard to see through the blood and tattered cloth of her trousers. And then suddenly she wasn't alone: a stitcher knelt on one side of her leg, and a constable she didn't recognise on the other. Where had they come from? Cora wondered hazily.

'Bring me a lamp,' the stitcher said.

The constable shook his head. 'Investigator says they're not allowed.'

'Why not?'

'Something about the barge, something dangerous. You'll have to ask…' The constable looked up as someone called a name, and then slipped into the smoke.

The stitcher began their work on Cora – the poking, prodding, tutting work of a stitcher. As they did so, Cora kept one eye on the red jackets running in and out of the smoke, carrying buckets of water and thick hessian mats to beat out the flames. Their shouts were muffled then all at once loud as the dense smoke played its tricks. A thin breeze shifted the black coils and for the first time the deck came clear, and then the gangway. Or what was left of them. It all looked too low in the water, and then she saw why: one end of the barge was sinking. The barge would soon be at the bottom of the River Stave. Sorrensdattir…

Something moved in the smoke. There was a figure

stumbling about the tilted deck. Tall, thin, a mane of copper-coloured hair safely tied in a knot on his crown – he'd lost his helmet. No red jacket like the quellers, but a long coat of shiny slipdog hide. She tried to call out, but there was little breath in her lungs – they were full of something else. The stitcher shushed her.

'Stay still, Audience take you.'

'Serus,' Cora managed to croak.

'What?' The stitcher turned to look for themselves. 'Oh.'

Two fire-quellers were carrying Investigator Serus between them. The stitcher motioned for them to lay him down next to Cora.

Cora held up a hand in greeting. She didn't think he would recognise her. In his state he likely wouldn't have recognised his own mother. As the stitcher turned their attention to Serus, Cora took the Rustan's soot-smeared hand in her own. His face, too, was streaked with dirt, including the metal plates in his cheeks.

With a cough, Serus came to. The stitcher helped him to sit, and Cora let his hand go. He spat smoke. 'Drunkard have you,' he said, 'what were you doing?'

'Me?' she said.

'On the barge. It was me who dragged you out.'

The stitcher pulled down on his cheek, despite the metal there, and stared into his eye. The Rustan didn't even flinch.

'I owe you,' Cora said. 'I— I went in to help someone. I heard screams.'

'Who?'

'They're gone.'

'It'll all be gone before morning,' Serus said through his coughing.

The stitcher stood. 'You'll both be fine. Eventually. Investigator, why can't I have lamps to work with?'

'The fint,' he said.

'What are you talking about?'

'The speed of it. The heat. It ripped through the barge. I didn't understand at first.' He grimaced, his metal cheeks slipping over one another with a smooth mechanism. 'The stuff all over the barge… the dust.'

'Fint?' Cora said. 'From the Seeders' mostins?'

'Highly flammable. I'd not come across it before, not in all my training, but we'll be retelling the story now.'

'We all will,' the stitcher said. They moved off into the smoke, to find more prone bodies to prod into waking.

Serus tried to speak again but could only cough. A shout went up from the now still-burning barge. Serus struggled to his feet and lurched over towards the water. Cora limped after him as quickly as she could. Her leg seemed to be more painful.

What was left of the barge was sinking rapidly, one end completely lost. The wood groaned as it went under, but there were quellers frantically stabbing at it with long poles. To push it down? But that made no sense. Then she saw that one of them had lain on the quayside and was stretching an arm towards something in the water, something near the poles. A sack. No. Not a sack. A dress. Made of a dark-blue cloth Cora recognised. But it might not be a dress, it could be anything; it didn't have to be what she feared.

She made herself step closer to the water, beside Serus. Those quellers with poles steered the cloth towards the quay. The queller there was at last able to grab it. He pulled it towards him, and as he did the shape seemed to turn. The light from the dying flames caught the glass mouthpiece. Half the woman's face had been burnt away and the mouthpiece hung loose around her neck. The tornstone once inside it was likely at the bottom of the river, as Sorrensdattir was hauled onto the quayside.

Fifteen

'Hawker take you!' Cora shouted. 'I thought stitchers were meant to make their patients *more* comfortable, not less!'

Pruett, the stitcher of Bernswick Station, poked his needle back into Cora's leg and dragged through the thread. It felt thick as a boot lace.

'The people who usually receive my attentions are a lot quieter,' he said. He pulled the thread tight and Cora winced.

'They're usually dead,' she said.

'Makes for a quicker job.'

She was lying on a stone examining table in the station's cold room. The room was living up to its name: her shoulders seemed to be rattling against the table with chills. Pruett had said that might be from the shock. Either way, her teeth were chattering as if a story were trying to force its way out of her. On the tables next to her were sheet-covered forms. But not Sorrensdattir. Cora didn't know where the Torn had been taken, had barely managed to get herself back to Bernswick, leaving Serus to oversee the investigation. Serus. She hoped he was all right.

She kept her gaze on the ceiling, or as much of it as she could make out in the gloom above her. Pruett had all the lamps pulled close to him to work on her leg.

A hot stab jolted through her. 'You said you'd make it go numb.'

'Trust me, without this salve, it would be worse,' Pruett said. 'You'd likely pass out again.'

'That might be better.'

'Stop moving, Gorderheim.'

'Stop stabbing me!'

Pruett ignored her and the needle went back in. 'I'd like to see how far you'd get with *this* hanging open.'

Cora pushed herself to sitting and risked a glance at the bloody split in her calf, then looked away again. Pruett had sewn half the flesh back together but there was still too much of her insides on show. At least the wound was in the same leg as her bad foot. The pain of the glass would surely be eclipsed now that her leg was so badly ripped. That was a funny for the Audience.

'It's a miracle you made it out of that barge without joining the Audience,' Pruett said, 'the blood you've lost.'

'They want a few more stories from me yet.'

'As flattered as I am that you decided to come all the way back to Bernswick,' in the needle went again, 'why didn't you see someone local to the Hook barge?'

'They were busy enough,' she said. 'And because I don't have to pay you.'

'And yet your pockets are full of betting slips. One last stitch; this is going to hurt, Gorderheim.'

'Just get it done.'

She felt the needle go in and then the thread pulled all the way down the sewn wound as Pruett tied it off. It felt like he'd used a burning lance, as if her skin had been ripped open again, and then there was a strange, hot tightness.

Pruett stepped away to wash his hands. 'I would say this is going to stop you running down cut-purses,' he said, 'but with all that bindle-smoke in your chest, you weren't doing much of that anyway.'

'That's what constables are for,' she muttered.

The stitcher put his palms on the table, either side of her boots. 'You were lucky tonight, Gorderheim.'

'Lucky? That's one way of looking at it.'

'Now, don't—'

'I owe you, Pruett.' She dragged what was left of her trouser leg, torn and stiff with dried blood, over the stitched wound.

He looked like he would say more, then decided against it.

Cora swung her legs over the side of the table and let her good leg take her weight on the floor. When she put the bad leg down, the jolt it sent through the rest of her nearly made her fall over.

Pruett was at her elbow. 'When the salve wears off, you'll know about it, so you'd better plan on sitting down in the next few days. The pain will be bad.'

'I've had worse.'

It seemed to take her an age to climb the stairs from the cold room, and when she reached her office she found the door open. Someone was leafing through the pennysheets on her desk. Someone in a shiny slipdog hide coat. His long auburn hair was loose about his shoulders.

'You won't find a fire in here, Serus,' she said. 'Just a lot of rubbish.'

'But I've found you,' he said softly.

'Not joining the Audience just yet.' She shut the door behind her. 'And you?'

'I'll live.' But the words sent him coughing. Cora barked into the corridor for some water. A constable came and went, and Serus drank slowly between coughs. She waited.

He set the glass down. 'That was thoughtless of me, to say I'd live. Your friend wasn't so lucky.'

'You mean the Torn woman? She asked if she'd told enough stories, there at the last.'

'The Torn always have enough stories,' he said. 'A blessing, and a curse.'

'I could do with fewer to tell,' she admitted.

'Yes, well, I... I did hope you might have time for one more.'

'I'm on a case. But if you need help, I could recommend a constable or two. Is that why you're here?'

'It's not—' His fingers fretted at the corner of her desk. 'That is to say, it's not an official matter.'

'Serus, are you blushing? I can't tell with those metal things in your cheeks.'

That did set him blushing. 'I'm not very good at this sort of thing.'

'What sort of thing?' she said, trying to sound kind, and warm, and other things that didn't come easy.

He cleared his throat. 'I know we haven't seen each other in some time. But, with last night at the barge, it reminded me... I never said anything, before, because of the work. I would like to see more of you, Cora, *not* because of work.'

Cora went to say something, then stopped, her mouth

flapping open and closed. A distant memory of the Perlish story shouted, 'Trout!'

'Not work?' she said eventually. But what else was there, really, except for brief visits to the Oak? And even that felt more like work of late. She looked at the Rustan, looked beyond the shiny metal plates that held a kind of reflection of herself, at the strong jawline, the warm brown eyes, and the full head of hair. And she found she liked what she saw. 'Not work,' she said again. 'I want more of that.'

'You do?' He looked down, as if afraid of her answer, as if she might change her mind. This man who pulled people from fires, who grew up on the Rusting Mountains. This man – afraid?

'I make no promises,' she said. 'I've no time, not really. But I'd like that, Serus, I'd like to see you more.'

He glanced up, doubt still writ large on his face. She moved towards him, reached for him to pull him closer, but her feet knocked something on the floor. She stumbled, then Serus was fussing with a small sack near her boots. The moment was gone.

'Thought you might like to see it,' he said, 'before I take it to the Wheelhouse.'

'See what?'

From the sack he drew out a large lump of stone. But a special kind of stone, one that was veined with red. From the Tear. Tornstone.

The lump had been fashioned to look like a face. It was dominated by the crudely worked features of eyes and a nose, and ears formed a handle on each side. The mouth was wide open, the ends turned down as if grimacing. Inside the mouth, in place of a tongue, was a little dish with a short wick and the gleam of the last of its oil. Serus placed it on her desk. It was a stumpy, ugly thing.

'The Torn Hook,' she said. 'Looks like Fenest didn't miss much.'

'On the contrary. Watch now, Detective.'

Cora looked from Serus to the lamp and back again. 'You're sure it's safe?'

'Trust me. I'm the investigator here, remember?' He managed a smile. He took out a little flint set and worked to find a spark. The lamp's wick was soon burning down. Soft light spilled from the lamp's eyes, nose, and mouth. For a moment nothing more happened. Then the surface of the lamp changed, growing darker, and then it started to fracture. Pulsating red veins appeared in the cracks. Cora leaned back. The lamp was spitting and sizzling and making all kinds of strange sounds. Through the deep crimson of the veins, the lamp was changing.

Where there had been one squat face there were now many faces stretching up the sides of a tall, much more graceful shape. And those faces were in constant, silent motion: talking, laughing, crying, sneezing. They didn't stop twisting themselves into new expressions. From their eyes, mouths, and nostrils came a pure, sharp light – so different from the barge fire. She made the sign of the Tear before she even realised her hands were moving. Something she'd not done in years.

The light pulsed more brightly for a moment, then began to dull. The faces pulled back into the stone and the tall sides slumped into the squat shape of before. Then there was only one face, the first one. But it was changed. The original, miserable face was now grinning.

'That's the oil spent.' Serus moved to pick up the lamp and Cora put her own hand in the way without thinking.

'Careful – it'll be hot!'

'You've not had much to do with tornstone, Detective.' Serus touched the cheek of the face in the lamp, which at that moment looked more real than his own. 'It cools as soon as the light fails, like us when the Widow decides our stories are over.' He bent to put the lamp back in the sack, and when he straightened again his face was close to hers. 'I'm told the Torn planned to hold paper shapes up to the light and make a story of the shadows. That was their Hook, how the lamp was to be used.' He shook his head. 'With the barge gone, who knows?'

'The Commission will make it happen,' she said. 'Somewhere... Somewhere without the flammable fint from Seeder mostins. The fint was left on the barge by the Seeder Hook. I'll have to look into it.'

'Cora, be care—'

She kissed his words away. The shock of it made him slow to respond. Cora tried to ignore the slight metallic tang to him. Maybe she'd grow to like it.

Sixteen

Sergeant Hearst had no stories for the Nodding Child yet; Cora found him still in the briefing room, despite how late it was. He was explaining the mating habits of gresta birds to a wide-eyed constable who looked like he'd rather be anywhere else in the Union.

When the sergeant saw Cora, he gave a start. 'Brawler take me, did you roll around in that fire, Gorderheim?'

She had no idea what he was talking about until he steered her to the mirror in the privy. Her face was streaked with smoke and one of her eyebrows looked to be thinner than when she'd last looked at herself in the mirror. That was at the archives. How long ago that seemed. And Serus hadn't even mentioned the dirt. Had kissed her through it. She laughed, which seemed to unsettle Hearst. He shouted for the constable to find him a towel, and, when it appeared, he wetted the corner and handed it to Cora.

'There's nothing left of the barge,' she said as she wiped the fire's marks away. It wouldn't be so easy to rid herself of the memory of Sorrensdattir's ruined face.

'And the cause?' Hearst said.

'We need to go somewhere private.'

'More private than the privy?' he joked, but the smile soon left his face when he saw that Cora wasn't laughing.

She led the way to her office, closed the door, then slumped in her chair. Her leg felt as if a flame from the barge had settled beneath her skin, and every time she breathed in, she tasted smoke.

'Investigator Serus said the fire was caused by the fint.'

Hearst looked puzzled.

'The stuff left behind by the mostins,' she explained.

'Mostins…' Hearst scratched his cheek. 'You mean those funny flying insects the Seeders – sorry, *Lowlanders*.' Hearst checked himself for using the slur. 'The insects the Lowlanders used for their Hook? I didn't make it to the Hook barge to see them, but I heard they were flying around the place, getting in people's hair.'

'I heard the same,' Cora said. 'The *Lowlander* election story was all about them. Well, the mostins and other things. Mostins leave a sticky kind of dust wherever they go – fint. It makes your eyes itch. Until tonight, I thought that was the worst of it.'

'And now?' Hearst said, the dread clear in his voice.

'It turns out, fint is highly flammable. I got that from authority – Investigator Serus was there tonight, at the Hook barge.'

Hearst whistled. 'Doesn't sound too safe for Torn to be near this fint stuff then, what with—'

'Live flames strapped to their faces? You're not wrong there, Sergeant.'

'That what happened then?' Hearst said. 'The Torn who died, her mouthpiece set the fint alight?'

'Seems so.' Cora coughed.

'Could be an accident.'

'Could be.'

They were both silent then.

'It must be an accident, surely?' Hearst said quickly. 'Why would anyone kill a Torn woman?'

'She was an advisor to the Torn Chambers.'

'Oh.' Hearst sighed.

'An advisor who asked me to meet her at the barge, alone, at night. A Torn who had a message.'

Hearst glanced to the door as if he'd forgotten it was shut. 'A message?' he said softly.

'*South for the hottest season,*' Cora said.

'What does that mean?'

'Couldn't say. Not yet. But it was the last thing the Torn said to me before... before she went into the river.' Cora shook away the memory. 'It *has* to be important.'

'Did the Torn know you were looking for Tennworth?'

'She never said so, but she knew what the Wayward story was about. I can't believe her last words have nothing to do with Tennworth.'

Hearst shook his head. 'Another body. What a mess.'

'I have to go, sir. I don't have any choice.' Cora stood up but winced as the flame in her leg flared again.

'Go where?'

'I know Sillian said not to. But with the fint being a Seeder thing, Sorrensdattir being an advisor to the—'

'Cora...'

'I have to. I have to speak to the Seeder Chambers. What Jenkins and Marcus found in the archives, what Sorrensdattir told me before she died – it's not enough. We're missing something, and Tennworth is still out there.'

'If Sillian hears of it... our chief *inspector* has that job title for a reason. She tends to find things out.'

Cora stretched her leg. 'I'm just doing my job. Have you ever wondered why Sillian doesn't want me to talk to any of the Chambers? Can we trust her?'

Hearst became very still. 'She's our commanding officer, Gorderheim. We don't have a choice.'

'That's where you're wrong, sir. We all have a choice in this story.' She pulled on her coat. 'And my choice is to go to the Assembly building and talk to the Seeder Chambers. What I should have done from the start.'

'After all that's happened, you're going to ask her about the fint?'

'And grapes,' Cora said.

'*Grapes?*'

'Apart from in Finnuc Dawson's stories, the only other place we've come across Tennworth's name is the winery. And you can't have wine without grapes.'

Cora had never been inside the Assembly building before. Not because she wasn't allowed in. It was more that she didn't feel invited, even as someone who worked for the Commission, which in turn worked for the Assembly, carrying out the leader's bidding. But whatever the leader decided beneath the glass dome, everyone on the outside would soon know about it. Cora felt the Assembly's presence in all parts of her life. But today was different. She was going to the heart of business with business of her own. As long as she could get inside, that was.

Cora's badge was studied long and hard by one of the

burly individuals guarding the main door, while the woman's partner made a show of keeping her baton handy. At last the woman handed Cora's badge back and grunted for her to 'go on through'. Cora didn't hang around and went into a huge vaulted space, the walls of which were round. She was standing in a giant circle, with so much light it was as if she was outside, the sky open above her.

It was a trick of the light. The domed glass roof was there, and it was impressive, even she would admit it. From the roof of the station, which had a good view of the Assembly building, the dome had always looked filthy. But inside, looking up, the glass gleamed. Did that mean something? She could imagine a storyteller making something of it. Or Ruth. 'From the outside, power looked grubby, but those on the inside thought it was glorious.'

The dome was made up of many large panes, held together by thick solder. Fifty panes of glass in the Assembly's dome, one for each Fenestiran voter per election story. In reality, no realm ever got – or needed – all fifty votes for yes. The dome's panes were an aspiration.

'Can I ask your business at the Assembly this morning?' a voice called, echoey and all but lost in the huge space.

There was a long desk to Cora's left, behind which was a young man in a pristine purple jacket. The lines of his shoulders and lapels looked sharp enough to draw blood.

Cora went over to him, to save shouting. 'I'm here to see the Seeder— I mean, the Lowlander Chambers.' She handed over her badge.

'Your appointment time?'

'I don't have one.'

The young man frowned. He couldn't be long out of the

Seminary, being *so* young, and yet he'd gone straight into a job like this. That meant a good name. If Cora asked it, it would no doubt be familiar. Her mother had been prone to listing off the 'great' families of Fenest as if just the sounds of the names were a story for the Audience.

'I'm afraid Lowlander Chambers Morton is very busy,' the young man said, without much trace of apology. 'She won't be able to talk to you today, but if you'd like to come back next week, I'm sure—'

'Tell her it's about the Hook barge,' Cora said.

'I'm sorry, but—'

'And the death of the Torn advisor.'

That shut him up. He disappeared behind a white screen she hadn't noticed was there, it blended into the white walls so well. It was only once he'd gone that she realised he'd taken her badge with him.

The walls of the large entrance hall were all white, but few were actually as they appeared. People in the clothes of all the realms, and in purple too, of course, were moving through the space, carrying papers, murmuring to one another. Every so often, someone seemed to vanish into a white wall, thanks to the trick of the screens. There was something of the archives here, but without the magic of tornstone. Solid things that weren't as they appeared. At the far end of the hall was a wide staircase that led deeper into the building, to the Chambers' main debating space.

The young man was a long time coming back with her badge. She half wondered if Chief Inspector Sillian had left some kind of message here: Detective Cora Gorderheim wasn't to be admitted to speak to a Chambers. Perhaps the chief inspector herself would appear on the stairs to catch

Cora in the act of rebellion. Cora sat on one of the little black sofas dotted about the hall to give her aching leg a rest. She'd be old enough to interest the Reveller by the time she got anywhere today.

All the other black sofas were occupied by pairs of people deep in conversation, going through files, making notes. Cora recognised one or two from the nearby Wheelhouse. White walls and black sofas; election colours for the place where the result of the election took on a life of its own. There was sense in that, but it made for a stark impression. The splashes of colour that ran around the far wall were a relief, though Cora hadn't expected to see *them* here: the masks of the Audience, worn by the election voters.

Fifty different faces, over-sized and each its own bright colour. The leer of the Drunkard, the bearded Liar, the Weaver frowning as he cast his plots. Every day the elected Chambers had to see reminders of those who had voted for them.

She looked back to the desk. Still no sign of the young man. Was someone sending a message to Bernswick, informing Sillian? Well, Cora was here now, she'd made her choice. No turning back. Might as well wait it out.

One of the masks on the wall opposite her was gold, flashing in the sun that streamed through the dome's glass. She made her way over and looked at the small plaque beside it, which read: 'The Gilded Keeper, Audience member for justice, fairness, cages'. His Seat wasn't far from her boarding house but she couldn't remember the last time she'd gone to share her stories with him. There was an irony. Something in the mask's upturned mouth, the way the face enquired, seemed to say the Keeper knew this already. She tapped his cheek. Whatever the mask was made of – light wood? Some kind of hardened paste? – it gave a dull sound in response. She wouldn't want to have to wear this for the duration of an election story, and, thank the Audience, she never would: Commission employees weren't permitted to vote.

Seeing the Keeper, she felt the words of a story on her lips. 'There was a Torn woman who wanted to help me, and now she's dead. Will there be justice for her, Keeper? For a Casker, too, who died, for a story? Though whether Finnuc deserves justice… But then, it's not only stories about justice you like, is it, Keeper?' She gave a low laugh. The gold mask seemed to shift and slide in the sun, like the Tornstone lamp and its many faces. 'You're one for cages, too. And I'm in one now. How's that for—'

'Detective.'

It wasn't the young man from the desk. Cora knew this voice, and she didn't want to turn to see its owner. His grey eyes, that flat stare. She remembered it from the station's cold room, back at the start of this case. She hadn't had answers for this man then, and she didn't now. Now there were only more questions.

She turned to face the Wayward Chambers. He was in his brown robe; could hardly be otherwise in the Assembly building. An aide hovered a respectful distance away, a cloak over his arm.

'They did not tell me you were here,' the Chambers said.

She licked her lips and fumbled for his name. Arrani?

'You have come to see me about the death of the prisoner,'

Wayward Chambers Arrani said, 'the Casker who murdered Nicholas Ento?'

'I— I haven't, your honour.'

Arrani was broad, a strong man who looked to move through the world as if he was always seated tall in the saddle. His aide stepped forward with his cloak. The Wayward waved him away.

'The Wayward realm deserves justice,' Arrani said in a low voice, and nodded towards the gilded mask on the wall behind Cora. 'The Keeper knows this is right. The pennysheets too. The whole Union knows it. And yet, the man who killed the Wayward storyteller will not face the punishment for his crime.'

Cora took a deep breath. 'Finnuc Dawson faces The Mute and Silence. But I will find the person responsible, that I swear to you, your honour.'

Arrani didn't move, didn't blink. Cora thought he'd stopped breathing, then at last he said, 'See that you do.'

He turned to leave.

'Your honour – I've heard a rumour, about the new Wayward storyteller.'

Was he smiling? Or as close to a smile as the weathered face of the Wayward could manage.

'You have, have you, Detective Gorderheim? And what is this *rumour*?'

'That the new 'teller is from outside the realm.'

After a pause he said, 'Nothing else?'

'I'm sorry?'

'You have heard nothing else about this storyteller.'

Was that a question or an instruction? Before she could

answer, there was a polite cough, somewhere near her elbow. The young man from the desk was back.

'Lowlander Chambers Morton will see you now,' he said, deferentially averting his gaze from that of Arrani.

'Morton?' Arrani said. If the smile had ever been, it was gone now. 'You are here to see the Lowlander Chambers?'

'I am,' Cora said. 'The Hook barge caught fire last night. I'm investigating the cause.' Not strictly true as that would be Serus's job, but it sounded plausible.

'I heard about the death of the Torn advisor,' Arrani said. 'It is a great loss.' He caught Cora's eye. 'To us all. Good day to you, Detective.'

He strode to the main doors and his aide hurried in his wake.

'If you'll follow me, Detective?' the young man said, and gestured towards the stairs.

'Not before you give me back my badge,' Cora said. 'I want to be able to get out of here again.'

Seventeen

'Keep up, Detective,' the young man said, in the haughty tones Cora's mother would have approved of. 'Lowlander Chambers Morton has granted a special dispensation to see you today when normally an appointment—'

'I know, I know. Appointments. Where would the Commission be without them, eh?'

Audience forbid anyone decided to do something on a whim, or do something that didn't lend itself to prior arrangement. Like solve a murder.

At the top of the stairs was a long corridor, which had other long-looking corridors branching off it, and tall double doors every so often. The young man set off down the corridor and Cora followed. The place had a buzz of noise about it, people beset with papers, the sense they were busy at something.

As she passed one of the open doors, she caught a glimpse of a broad brown robe and red hair. It was Casker Chambers Kranna. Cora had time to see Kranna was looking at her, and then the door shut quickly. Voices behind it, but she couldn't catch the words. The wood was as gold as the mask of the Gilded Keeper downstairs. But unlike the Keeper's smooth skin, the door was carved with a design of barrels.

Another cough. The young man was waiting for her, his hands tucked beneath his ridiculous lapels. She'd happily give him some creases to worry about.

A little further down the corridor and he stopped at another closed door, this one marked by the crossed spades of the Seeders. Lowlanders. She'd have to get that right, today of all days, or this would be the first and last time she got to talk to this Chambers.

'The office of Lowlander Chambers Morton,' he said, with the seriousness of the Master of Ceremonies announcing a story.

She waited for him to knock, but he didn't move. Was she meant to tip him, as if he were a Clotham's gig driver? Just as she'd decided enough was enough and moved to knock herself, he threw the doors open and invited Cora to step inside.

The room was large, and filled with large furniture. An enormous desk took up most of the middle, with chairs scattered about it. The walls were lined with shelves, themselves lined with papers and ledgers. It was like a smaller version of the archives, but less organised. Here, papers had escaped to the floor where they mixed with an untidy collection of shoes and boots that looked to be responsible for the mud traipsed across the thick carpet. There were empty fruit crates holding plant pots overflowing with glistening leaves. Trailing plants cascaded down the shelves, the rich scent of their flowers mixing with something else, something Cora was pleased to smell.

Bindleleaf.

'Come in, come in,' called a cheery voice from the other side of the room.

A small figure was all but lost in a huge old armchair, her stockinged feet propped on the window ledge. She was surrounded by a cloud of bindlesmoke, through which Cora caught sight of what looked to be a pipe, and a wink of gold: manacles on each wrist.

'You must forgive this,' Morton said, waving away the smoke, which only made it drift further into the room. 'I wasn't expecting anyone this afternoon.'

The young man gave Cora a pointed look, then withdrew, closing the doors as he went.

'Thank you for seeing me, your honour,' Cora called over, unsure if she should wait to be asked to join the woman. The office wasn't what she'd expected, but a Chambers was still a Chambers.

Morton pointed to the chair opposite her: a saggy thing made of cane that didn't look as if it would last too much longer. Cora sat down carefully.

'Can one refuse a visit from the police?' Morton said.

Another question that might not be a question at all. It was a day for them.

The smell of the bindle was too much to bear, and Cora's face must have betrayed her. Morton offered her a smoke.

'I'll have one of my own, if that's all right with you.' Cora took out her tin.

'Perfectly. It's banned in the building, you know.' Morton sucked on her pipe and blew out the smoke.

She was close to the age Cora's mother would have been, had she lived: around seventy. Her hair was grey but cut short in a way that made her look younger, as did her impishness.

'You're here about the fire at the Hook barge?' Morton said.

'It's usually me that asks the questions.'

Morton looked out of the window and gave a deep sigh. 'A tragic event to make the Brawler weep. The thoughts of the entire Lowlands are with the Torn delegation. I hadn't had much to do with the aide. I forget her name...'

'Sorrensdattir. She was an advisor.'

'That's it. All those funny sounds! No wonder their names never stick with us.' Morton smiled at Cora.

'Given you're a Lowlander,' Cora said, 'I'd have thought you'd find it easier to remember Torn names.'

'And why is that, Detective?'

'The Lowlands run much closer to the Tear than Fenest.'

'Ah, but I have spent much of my life in the capital lobbying the Assembly for the Lowland realm, fighting elections.'

Cora flicked through her notebook. 'You've been Chambers for the Lowlands for... twenty years, is that right?'

'Goodness! As long as that?' Morton looked out the window again. 'How the time flies when in public office.'

'I'm sure it does. About the fire—'

'It's Gorderheim, isn't it?' Morton set her pipe on an ashy saucer on a side table then folded her hands in her lap. The gold manacles on her wrists were almost close enough to lock together. A tiny pair of crossed spades hung from each manacle. Morton smiled.

Cora's mouth was dry and she regretted the smoke.

'I knew your parents,' Morton said.

'Oh?'

'A wonderful couple. Such parties!'

Had Morton come to the house when Cora was a child,

before she took office? Cora's memories of what her mother liked to call 'soirees' were hazy: doors closing, laughter, always glasses clinking. Once, a woman had stumbled into Cora's room in the middle of the night, her breath fiery with spirits as she'd leant over Cora and said, take them, take them, quick. Her cupped hands were full of billiard balls. Cora hadn't thought about that night in years. But that drunk woman wasn't this woman sitting opposite her now. It wasn't Lowlander Chambers Morton.

'I was so sorry when it all went so wrong,' Morton said. 'The scandal...'

Cora felt she was being eyed keenly, that this was some kind of test. She thought of what her mother would bark at her: sit up straight, remember you're a Gorderheim. Remember what that means, Cora.

'The mostins,' Cora said, and stubbed out her bindleleaf. 'They left the Hook barge covered in fint. I'm told it's highly flammable.'

'And who told you this?' Morton asked quickly.

'The fire investigator assigned the case.'

'Their name?' Morton said.

'Does it matter? The Commission assigned him to the job so—'

'It was Serus, wasn't it?'

After a moment, Cora nodded, knowing what was coming.

'A Rustan,' Morton said, and gave a short laugh. 'That makes sense. They are such *precious* creatures.'

'Rustans?'

'Mostins, Detective. I find it comforting to have them around me, as a reminder of my home, though I'm rarely there.' She glanced at something behind Cora.

It was a glass tank with a branch inside. Perched on it were huge brownish winged creatures, each one in a different pose, each one strangely still.

'You've not seen mostins before?' Morton said.

Cora got up and peered in the tank. 'Only dead ones, like these.'

'They've been coated in a special treatment to keep them preserved,' Morton said, 'and pliable, too. That's how they can be arranged in such pleasing tableaus.'

'On the barge for your Hook they were... sadder.'

'They're a wonder in the wild,' Morton said, as if Cora hadn't spoken. 'But too useful to be left alone.'

'Like those children in your election story – selling mostins to a Wayward woman.'

'You heard our story.' Morton sounded pleased.

'Your numbers aren't—'

Morton waved such ideas away. 'The story, Detective.'

Cora stood with her hands on the back of the spindly cane chair. 'Did you know the fint the mostins leave behind is flammable?'

'I swear to you, I did not.' Morton spoke slowly and kept her gaze on Cora. 'If I had known, I would never have approved the use of mostins for the Lowlanders' Hook in this election. It was, as I have said, a tragic incident for which I grieve. If you'll take my advice—'

'I'd be glad to hear it.'

'—then you'll speak to my colleague, Torn Chambers Raadansutter, about this. About the Torn's part in the accident. If it *was* an accident, of course.'

'What are you implying, your honour?'

'Who can know the inner workings of such people?' Morton raised her hands in a gesture of futility. 'Life in the Tear, it can do strange things to the mind. Just what was the Torn aide doing on the barge at that time of night?'

'Preparing the Torn Hook. The Torn election story *is* about to be told.'

'It's possible,' Morton said. 'But so is a deliberate fire that puts blame on another realm.'

Cora struggled to speak for a moment, and when she did find her voice she could barely keep her tone even. 'Are you seriously suggesting that the Torn set fire to the Hook barge so that the Lowlanders would be blamed for leaving the fint?'

'Events have brought you here today, to my office, have they not? And can you prove otherwise, Detective?' Morton's tone was reasonable, and so was her expression. But there was something beneath it. Something hard and forceful.

'Not yet,' Cora said.

'Then I wish you well with your enquiries.'

'You could help me with that.'

'Oh?'

'Why would the Torn want to frame the Seed—'

Morton's face was at once livid. It was a useful 'slip'.

'Forgive me, your honour,' Cora said. 'I understand such language is disliked by the Lowlander community.'

'It is indeed, Detective.' Morton re-filled her pipe but her earlier languor was gone.

'Why would the Torn want to frame the people of the Lowlands?' Cora asked.

Morton sparked a match, drew deep on her pipe, and

when she spoke again her tone was back to being measured. 'Because the Caskers wish to disrupt the election.'

'The *Caskers*? Why?'

'Because their chances this year are no better than any other year, and yet the realm is in dire need of controlling the Assembly. You will have seen the stories in the pennysheets, Detective, about the Caskers drowning themselves in what's left of Bordair.'

'I thought that was just the usual pennysheet rubbish.'

'Would that it were,' Morton said. 'There is a crisis among the Casker people, I have heard. Poverty, illness. The despair takes such people very hard. They haven't the reserves of courage that we tend to see in the north, such that you and I would share, Detective.'

'Not sure I see how the Torn fit into this... theory.'

'Well, they're in cahoots, aren't they?' Morton said, as if Cora was an ignorant child. 'Bordair is practically in the Tear. I've been arguing for years that we should stop thinking of them as separate realms – the Rusting Mountains too. Just one Chambers for all three southern realms, one election story. It would be more efficient, don't you think?'

'Then I'm assuming you've argued the same thing about the Perlish too.'

'Ah, now that's different. The duchies of Perlanse are clearly separate realms. Their socio-cultural and economic structures can hardly be compared.'

'Can't say I've noticed much difference between them,' Cora said dryly, and then, before Morton could chime in with more about the nuances of Perlish identity, she added: 'The Hook barge. You were claiming that the Torn set fire to it deliberately.'

'*Could* have done, Detective. If the Torn did commit this act, and I'm not saying I believe that—'

'Of course,' Cora said, as flatly as she could manage.

'But if they did, it would have been at the request of their Casker allies. The same is true of Black Jefferey. Those southern realms do stick together.'

'You share the view of some of the pennysheets then, that the Caskers deliberately brought plague to Fenest.'

Morton lifted her palms in another gesture of resignation. 'If it's in the pennysheets…'

'I wanted to ask you about grapes, your honour.'

'Grapes?' Morton looked wrongfooted, which was something. Cora felt she might be able to take back control of the conversation.

'Do you grow many of them in the Lowlands?'

Morton stubbed out her bindleleaf. 'Grapes are a Perlish crop, Detective, as I'm sure you know. Their soils better support the vines. In the Lowlands we—'

'What about you personally?'

'Do *I* grow grapes *personally*? I'm not sure you've fully grasped the commitment of being a Chambers, Detective. Perhaps some instruction from your chief inspector, now, what's her name—'

A knock at the door meant Morton stopped short of invoking Sillian.

Morton stood. 'You must forgive me, Detective. The debating chamber awaits.'

'I would have thought you'd have time off, given we're in the middle of the election.'

Morton laughed. 'Would you believe me if I told you this is our busiest period? The Perlish Chambers are trying to rush through as much legislation as they can before the end of their term, and of course with two of them they seem to have twice the energy for it.'

She made her way to the door and Cora followed.

Morton held out her hand. 'A pleasure to see you, Detective Gorderheim. May the rest of the election be quieter for you.'

'For us all,' Cora said.

Eighteen

As Cora went down the stairs to the Assembly building's entrance hall – slowly, the pain flaring in her injured leg again – she chewed over what Lowlander Chambers Morton had said. Morton's theory was far-fetched, but was it plausible? Morton had certainly tied all the threads together. Tight as the stitches in Nicholas Ento's mouth had been. As bloody as them too. A conspiracy by the southern realms to aid the Caskers at a time of crisis. Was that what Ruth was working towards? She seemed to be part of the Wayward now. If Morton was right, then Ruth could be leading the Wayward effort in this story. That would mean that Ruth and Finnuc *had* been allies, Ruth's claim that Finnuc had kidnapped her a lie to cover her own part in the plot.

Ruth: was she still in the city? How long would she wait for Cora to change her mind before she set off for the south, and whatever it was that took her there?

Cora was so lost in thought that she was halfway down the stairs before she noticed the large, brown-robed figure waiting for her at the bottom: Casker Chambers

Kranna. The same person who had watched her from the doorway earlier.

Cora stopped. Casker Chambers Kranna didn't climb the remaining stairs to meet her, but nor did she move away from her position. She didn't call up to Cora either. This was a woman who waited for people to come to her. Being a Chambers, she wouldn't ever have to do otherwise. Cora carried on down the stairs, all too aware of her limp.

When she reached Kranna, the woman offered Cora her hand. As she shook it, the tiny gold barrel attached to each of the Chambers' manacles made a tinkling sound that was a strange contrast to the firmness of the big woman's grip.

'Pleased to see you again, Detective Gorderheim.'

Kranna regarded her, and though the Casker didn't turn to look behind her, didn't glance over her shoulder, Cora had the feeling the woman knew exactly who else was in the entrance hall and might see them together. It was cool in the hall, but Kranna still seemed to need her large purple handkerchief and mopped her face as she stepped closer to Cora.

'You're here about the fire, I understand. On the Hook barge.'

'Among other things,' Cora said.

'I hope my... friend Lowlander Chambers Morton was able to help with your enquiries?'

Cora nodded. She wouldn't give this woman any more than that. Not when she was still wrestling with Morton's theory herself.

'You've had much to keep you busy this election,' Kranna said.

'There's been plenty to tell the Audience.'

'It's a dangerous job you've got, Detective.'

Was it her imagination or did Kranna glance at her injured leg?

'Some days are more dangerous than others,' Cora said.

Kranna said nothing for a moment, then swept by her up the stairs. 'Stay safe, Detective.'

'Ah – there you are, Detective,' Lester called from the front desk as Cora made her way inside. The desk sergeant had shaved for once. She wondered at the occasion. Audience help her if it was inspection day.

'Needing me for something, Lester?'

'Not me. Pruett. Told me to send you down to the cold room soon as you appeared.'

'Don't tell me the body count of my case has gone up again.'

Lester grinned. 'It's your body he's muttering about today, Detective.'

'What?' She took the opportunity to lean against the front desk and take the weight off her leg.

Lester peered over the desk at Cora. 'Seems the stitcher's right to be worrying, the state you're in.'

Cora pushed herself to standing and swallowed the flare of pain. 'Thanks.'

'He says he needs to take your stitches out. I'm to ignore the screams.'

'Wonderful...' With great reluctance, she went down to the cold room.

The smell of blood grew stronger with each step, and when she reached the bottom of the stairs, it was clear why. Beneath one of the stone examining tables was a large puddle of something she was certain had been inside someone until recently. Pruett was sluicing the floor with water while his assistant, Bowen, mopped. To Cora, all they seemed to be doing was spreading the blood across the rest of the cold room.

'Cut the wrong vein again, Pruett?' she said, stepping round the spreading patch.

'Our latest visitor had twenty-three stab wounds and was still breathing when she arrived.' He set his pail down with a loud clank. 'Lasted long enough to empty her veins over the floor, then breathed her last. Wasn't much point trying to save her' – Pruett turned to glare at his assistant – 'but soft-hearted Bowen here insisted.'

'We could hardly leave her in the street!' Bowen said.

'Tell me if you feel the same once you've spent the rest of the afternoon cleaning that up.' Pruett turned to Cora and pointed to a chair with a box upturned next to it. 'Come on, Gorderheim. Let's have a look at my handiwork.'

She sat down and lowered her leg onto the box.

'Here, read this.' The stitcher handed her a copy of *The Fenestiran Times*.

'Trying to depress me, Pruett?'

'It's to distract you. If you move as much as you did last time, we'll be here all afternoon. I've got the uncomplaining dead waiting for me.'

She'd already spotted the sheet-covered forms on the far tables of the cold room. Cora rolled up her trouser leg. The wound looked grim to her, but Pruett seemed pleased. He poked it with a worryingly sharp tool and pronounced the flesh healthy.

'Tell me all the news, Gorderheim. And best hold that 'sheet close to your face.'

She gritted her teeth as she felt him start to pick at the thread that had held her flesh together.

'Says here, the Torn story is tomorrow,' she told the stitcher. 'The Office of Electoral Affairs have refused the Torn petition to have the story delayed so that their Hook can be displayed. Torn Chambers Raadansutter claims his realm is being unfairly disadvantaged.'

'He's right,' Pruett said. 'To not have a Hook...'

'And yet here we are, talking about the Torn story anyway. Partner hear me, that's sharp!'

'Keep going!' Pruett said from behind the pennysheet.

Cora forced herself to focus on the print. 'With the unfortunate destruction of the Hook barge, the Hooks of the Rustan and Wayward stories will be displayed at the Seat of the Stalled Commoner.'

'Hooks in a Seat. That's unusual.'

'Commoner will enjoy all that Hook speculation,' she said, and sucked in her breath. This was even worse than when Pruett put the stitches in, which didn't seem possible. 'Easy site for security too.'

'This will hurt, Gorderheim.'

Pruett pulled and Cora cursed him.

'I think I've got some spirits down here somewhere,' he said. 'Medicinal, of course. Bowen – get the detective a draught.'

'You know I don't drink,' she said. 'I'd take more of that salve.'

'Too messy,' he said. 'It'll get in the way of the stitches. Hold still. I read *The Spoke* just before you came in.

Editorial agreed with the Torn, that the Commission aren't playing fair.'

'At least the Torn have the venue they want.'

'First Wall this year, if I remember right,' Pruett said.

'That's what it says here.'

'Cosy.'

'Means the Torn storyteller will be able to breathe easier,' Cora said, struggling to breathe herself. 'Being down there.'

'Unlike those listening to the story,' Pruett said. 'I'll have a wagonload of the asphyxiated before it's over.'

'Have to keep you out of trouble.'

'This is the last bit. You've been very brave.'

'Silence take you, Pruett! If it wasn't for those scissors you've got in my leg right now—'

'What about that woman who died on the Hook barge? A Torn woman, one constable told me.'

'They were right,' Cora said quietly. '*Times* says it was a tragic accident.'

'That true? You were down there.' Pruett got to his feet and stretched his back, which popped with an alarming noise.

'I was. And I don't know. We done here?'

The stitcher nodded. 'I wouldn't go telling the Beholder, but the flesh is healing well.'

Cora looked down at the purplish, lumpen strip in her leg and quickly looked away again. 'I'd better leave you to the dead then. Enjoy a quiet afternoon.'

'I will, and Gorderheim, try not to—'

The door at the top of the stairs opened and Hearst leaned over the banister. There was a hum of noise drifting in from the corridor: a loud voice Cora knew only too well

– Marcus, shouting – and the shriller tones of Jenkins trying to get a word in.

'You'd better get yourself up here, Detective,' Hearst said. 'The archive hunt is over.'

'You saw them?' Hearst said in a low voice as they walked down the corridor to Cora's office. 'The Lowlander Chambers?'

'Not just that one. Three of the brown robes.'

She filled Hearst in. When she told him Lowlander Chambers Morton's theory, that the southern realms were working together to ensure the Caskers won the election, Hearst took a huge, sudden slurp of coffee then cursed the Brawler for its heat.

'But how would that work?'

Cora shrugged. 'Maybe we're not seeing the whole story yet. But I hope we're about to.'

'Morton is right about the stories in the pennysheets,' Hearst said, 'about Caskers doing away with themselves. Things might be bad down there.'

'They're bad in the Lowlands too,' Cora said, 'what I've been hearing. Brawler take me, Beulah!'

Hearst glanced around as if he expected to see the old chequers.

'She asked me to do something,' Cora said, 'and I forgot.'

'Don't tell me Beulah's got you over a barrel?' Hearst said, eyebrows raised. 'Now, what could that be about, I wonder?'

Cora was just wondering how to dodge that particular question when they arrived at her office, where the noise from inside gave the distraction she needed.

There wasn't much space in Cora's office once she, Hearst, Jenkins, and Marcus were all inside with the door shut. Marcus seemed to have as much energy as usual, despite not having seen any natural light for days, but Jenkins' eyes were ringed with shadows. She seemed to be only just keeping those eyes open. That didn't bode well for good news.

'Well?' Cora said.

'We went through all the records that the archivist directed us to,' Jenkins said through a yawn. 'There were no other references to Tennworth.'

Cora sat heavily on the corner of her desk, knocking a full ashtray to the floor – but she didn't care. She kicked at a pastry wrapper for good measure.

'What about the names on the list you gave me?' she said.

'No records of them neither,' Marcus said.

From her coat, Cora pulled out the scrap of paper with the five names: Robinsons, Fimmons, Summerleaze, The Larkhouse, Salter. Something was tugging at her thoughts, but Marcus' booming voice put an end to any ideas.

'So we come to tell you, Detective, that me and my friends are finished. I'm going back to selling 'sheets. That's the kind of paper people want. The kind they pay for.'

Hearst leaped out of the way as Marcus made for the door.

'Tell Beulah I haven't forgotten what she asked me to do,' Cora called after the pennysheet girl. 'Tell her I—'

'Tell her yourself, Detective!' The door slammed shut behind Marcus.

'So where does this leave us?' Hearst said.

Cora looked at Jenkins in the chair, nodding. Her stories were only for the Child.

'Well,' Cora said. 'We know Tennworth exists. Or existed. And that she's connected to the names on this list, whatever they might be.'

'"Wherever" would seem to be the important word,' Hearst said, taking the list from Cora. 'We still don't know where in the Union to look for her.'

'Look… look,' Jenkins mumbled to herself, and lolled towards the desk. 'Marcus, look again. We have to…'

Cora coughed loudly and Jenkins jerked awake.

'Sorry, I was just…'

'I've now spoken to all three of the female Chambers,' Cora said, 'and we're still no clearer which of them might be Tennworth.'

'From what you've told me,' Hearst said, 'each of them seems to have something to hide. Casker Chambers Kranna's unregistered barges going south. Rustan Chambers Latinum's own trip to the archives.'

'Latinum might be telling the truth about that,' Jenkins said. 'She might not have been looking for traces of Tennworth there.'

'But we can't be certain,' Cora said, 'and the same is true of Morton and the fint on the Hook barge – did she know it was flammable? Did she want to destroy the barge? Kill the Torn advisor?'

'Motive would seem to be an important question there, Detective,' Hearst said, and handed her back the list of names from the archive. 'Why would anyone want to kill the Torn?'

Cora sighed. 'I don't know. The fire could genuinely have been an accident, but the words Sorrensdattir shouted to me just before she died meant something: south for the hottest season. There's a message there. I just can't work out what it is.'

Jenkins was nodding off again. Cora gently shook the constable's shoulder.

'Get some rest,' Cora told her. 'Tomorrow's going to be a long day.'

'Tomorrow is… What day is tomorrow?'

'The day of the Torn story. I'll meet you at First Wall.'

At the name of the Torn's story venue, Jenkins shivered. 'Why did it have to be there?'

'I thought you'd be used to being without daylight now, Constable.'

'I—'

The door opened. No knock. And it was soon clear why.

'Detective Gorderheim. I will have a moment with you.' It was Chief Inspector Sillian.

Jenkins was all at once awake and out of the office as quick as you like. Hearst mumbled 'Ma'am' in the general direction of Sillian's feet, and then he, too was gone. Sillian shut the door firmly enough to rattle the handle.

Cora had known this would happen. As soon as she'd shown her badge to the security at the door of the Assembly building, this moment had been coming.

Sillian began to pace, even though the cramped office didn't leave much room for that – it wasn't a habit Cora kept. The chief inspector made good use of the space, striding around and shoving aside anything that got in her way.

'What did I tell you about contacting the Chambers, Gorderheim?'

'That I shouldn't.'

'Correct, but what was the exact phrase I used, just days ago?'

'Ma'am, I—'

'Don't tell me you've forgotten,' Sillian snapped. 'You're a police detective. The kind of person expected to remember details like this.'

Cora swallowed. 'You said I could only involve the Chambers from a distance, ma'am.'

'Correct.' The word was sharp as a cutlass tip. 'And what part of you interviewing Lowlander Chambers Morton fits that description?'

'None whatsoever, ma'am.'

Sillian stopped pacing and glared at Cora. Her colour was up. First time Cora had ever seen that.

'I was warned about making you detective, Gorderheim, given your family history. There were some in the Wheelhouse who thought you were a risk, who told the promotion committee your application should be denied. But I defended you, advocated for you.'

'I've made good on that promotion. How many unsolved cases do I have against my name?' Cora said, surprised by the passion in her voice. 'And when you give me a murdered storyteller, first of his kind, I solved that too!'

'Cases are only part of the job, Gorderheim.' Sillian grabbed a fistful of papers from a stuffed shelf. 'I can cope with gossip about chequer debts. Likewise your... less than savoury habits.' A glance at the contents of the ashtray spread across the floor. 'But involving the Chambers in a murder enquiry.' Sillian dropped the papers, which were soon lost amongst the mess once more.

'I had no choice, ma'am!'

'That's a lie and you know it. You've been aiming for the Chambers since this wretched case started.'

'You said yourself, ma'am, the Chambers were the only ones who could have known that Nicholas Ento was a storyteller. The Casker, Finnuc Dawson, he as good as told me that the person who instructed him to kill Ento was a Chambers, and a female one at that.'

Sillian looked like she would speak but Cora ploughed on. She'd gone this far.

'Those facts alone were enough to warrant a visit to the Assembly building, and then the Hook barge blew up, caused by the fint it was practically painted in. Fint from the Lowlands. I had to speak to Lowlander Chambers Morton.'

'You could have put this request to me, Detective, and I would have made the relevant enquiries. But you didn't.'

Unspoken at the end of that sentence was another word. One Cora hoped Sillian wouldn't say: why? The answer was: Cora didn't trust her. And Sillian knew it. But now, Sillian didn't trust Cora either.

'What's done is done,' Sillian said coldly, 'but it must not happen again. Make no mistake, Gorderheim, this is your last chance. If I hear you've so much as wished good morning to one of the Chambers – any of them – before this election is over, I'll have your badge. Is that understood?'

Cora nodded. It was all she could do in that moment. She felt her blood was burning hot as the Hook barge.

'Good,' Sillian said. 'I think we can say you've done all you can to find the killer of the Casker prisoner. It looks like it was those bandits, after all.'

'I suppose it does, ma'am. And the death of the Torn on the Hook barge?'

'An accident.'

'Of course,' Cora said. 'If it's in the pennysheets...'

Nineteen

It was chaos at First Wall.

Huge crowds had massed at the narrow entrance in the sandstone expanse. The constables looked to be struggling to control the surge, Commission staff in purple tunics cowering behind the blue jackets. Having just arrived at the venue for the Torn story, Cora was close to telling the driver to take her back to Bernswick station. She'd wait for the pennysheets to tell her what the story was about, rather than get caught up in all this, especially after the night she'd had.

Cora had been unable to sleep, unable to stop herself going over everything: Nicholas Ento with his lips sewn shut. Finnuc Dawson's ruined eyes. The Torn aide Sorrensdattir floating in the River Stave. Three bodies, and three female Chambers. That was a symmetry the Audience would enjoy. Alongside which was a pair of people Cora didn't know what to make of: Ruth, back in touch after all these years and talking of problems in the south, and Chief Inspector Sillian, threatening to take Cora's badge just for trying to do her job. When Cora had finally fallen asleep, some time near dawn, her dreams trapped her in alleyways, with an unknown figure always at her back.

'You'll have to pay extra if you want to stay in the gig,' Cora's driver said. 'Day's hire, that'll be.'

'Don't tempt me.'

She saw Jenkins waving from the crowded entranceway. Maybe Cora's badge would get her through the throng. As long as she didn't get crushed doing so.

She pushed her way towards Jenkins, helped by her height and her free-swinging elbows.

'What's the problem here?' she asked the constable, having to shout over the crowd.

'The public gallery. First Wall's got fewer seats than other venues.'

Cora wiped the sweat from her face. 'What's the Commission thinking, using First Wall?' Jenkins made to answer but Cora held up her hand. 'I know, I know. Enclosed spaces – good for Torn breathing. Good for telling a long story.'

'And an important one!' Jenkins added.

'There'll be a crush at this rate, then no one will get to vote. We'd better get down there.'

To Cora's relief, Jenkins asked a purple tunic for a lamp before stepping inside the stone giant that was First Wall. Cora shook away the memory of her dreams, of the unseen figure following her. She had a job to do.

At once the air became close, with a kind of cold mugginess. She and Jenkins were in a narrow yet staggeringly tall passage that ran through the middle of the wall. The structure was hollow but strong, each side several feet deep.

The whole thing had stood for as long as Fenest had existed. Only Burlington Palace was older. Cora followed Jenkins' back, the lamp the constable carried sending shadows up the stones on either side. Those shadows reminded her of what Fire Investigator Serus had said, that the Torn Hook had been designed to tell a story with paper shapes in the light from their changing tornstone lamp. And her own story with Serus, what might that be?

Ahead, other lights danced and there was a hum of voices. Every so often her injured leg twinged but it wasn't too bad, and was getting better. She had to admit, for all the ugliness of Pruett's work, the stitcher had done a good job in keeping her walking.

'You ever been here before?' she asked Jenkins.

'No, I don't think it was used as a venue while my mother was at Electoral Affairs. Pennysheets say people are excited the Wall's being used again. Say it might help the Torn's chances. What about you, Detective?'

'Only once, long time ago. Seminary trip.' She touched the side of the passage, as she had done then, and felt the same light coating of sandstone on her fingers that she remembered. How many other Fenestirans had done the same since First Wall went up?

It was part of Fenest's early construction, the original perimeter wall of the city, before the city outgrew it. '*The wall was a ring, Burlington Palace the ring's jewel*' – she remembered Madame Vendler, her old Seminary teacher, saying that. Vendler had always wanted to be a storyteller. Teaching the sons and daughters of the wealthiest and most powerful of Fenest, the future Commission staff, often needed the same talents as a storyteller, Cora realised now. What was Seminary teaching but stories? What was anything in life?

'Always struck me as funny,' Cora said to Jenkins' back, 'that defences like this were built *after* the War of the Feathers.'

'No one knew how long peace would last,' Jenkins said.

'What you're really saying, Constable, is that no one trusted the Perlish dukes to keep from killing each other and dragging the rest of the Union back into the bloody mess.'

'I guess I am.'

'Shame so little of it is left now though,' Cora said. 'Only this section.'

'No need to keep the Perlish out anymore.'

'We let them all in, both duchies, all the way into the Assembly building.'

'Do you smell that?' Jenkins said.

Cora sniffed the dry air and felt a prickling burn in her nose and the back of her throat. 'Tornstone.'

The noise ahead grew louder, the hum shifting into voices, words. The passage turned and then the space opened into a huge square filled with people, and with shadows. Lamps were high on the walls, the flames jumping in a breeze that swirled in from somewhere. Despite that breeze, and the extra space around them, the air seemed even thicker here than in the closeness of the passage. It was being so deep into First Wall, so far from fresh air, or as fresh as Fenest ever got.

Directly ahead were the rows of voters' seats, which faced an enormous sandstone rock that looked to have fallen out of the wall in the distant past. At the far end of the cavernous space was a white tent: the garbing pavilion. Inside it, the voters would be getting on their robes, taking one white stone, one black to weigh their pockets, and their consciences. And then would come the masks of the Audience, like those Cora had seen in the Assembly building.

It looked to be nearly time. The public gallery was to one side of the voters' seats. Jenkins had been right: the gallery was far smaller here than at the other venues used so far in this election. But just the same, it was filled with excitable-looking souls leaning over one another to jabber and make their predictions.

On the other side of the voters' chairs the Commission box looked as comfortable as ever. The finery of those lucky few, the glasses in soft hands, and the jewellery at their throats, on their fingers, at their wrists, it all caught the flickering lights from the wall sconces. First Wall was dancing with gold and darkness, loud and excited.

Cora caught sight of Casker Chambers Kranna. She was dabbing her broad face with her purple handkerchief, and she was watching Cora. And then another face in the crowded Commission box came clear behind Kranna. It was Chief Inspector Sillian. Cora quickly steered Jenkins in the opposite direction, towards the public gallery.

'Let's see if these purple tunics can find us a seat.'

They showed their badges to the nearest tunic and then the lad leaned into Jenkins to say something Cora didn't catch. The tunic was pointing towards the front of the public gallery, near the huge sandstone rock that stood alone in the space, and Jenkins was asking Cora a question but she couldn't hear. First Wall did something strange to sound. But then there was a noise she *could* hear: a bell rang. Everyone in the Commission box and the public gallery stood and the chatter grew louder. Purple tunics rushed by. Jenkins was waving her towards the huge rock that faced the chairs. Commoner take her, were they going to sit right at the—

Investigator Serus was there, in the Commission box. He was talking to someone – Rustan Chambers Latinum. Their heads were bent close together, Latinum's dark hair all but touching Serus's auburn knot. Cora stumbled into a chair and cursed, and then Serus saw her, and the gap between him and Latinum widened. He nodded to Cora. Cora nodded back. It was enough.

She and Jenkins were in the last two seats of the front row. There was a surge of voices as the side of the garbing pavilion was raised, and then silence sharp enough to interest the Mute.

The Swaying Audience were here. Fifty black-robed voters, each masked, each carrying two stones – one white, one black. And with them, the Master of Ceremonies, ready to call the story into being.

'Audience, welcome,' the Master called out, his voice clear and deep. 'In this, the two hundred and ninth election of our realms, we give you a 'teller who gives you a tale.'

'The Audience is listening,' came the response from the masked voters.

The Master bowed to them, then turned to face the sandstone rock, which towered over him. Beyond the rock was darkness, the deep recesses of First Wall where no lamps had been lit. But a light was coming out of the shadows. A small orange glow weaved towards the gathered listeners, getting brighter. With it came the deepening sulphur burn of tornstone.

The Torn storyteller was coming.

Jenkins clasped her hands and seemed to shake with excitement. But for Cora, a feeling of dread made her heavy in her seat, made her curl in on herself. A Torn story would be a story of the south, and recently she'd heard nothing but bad things about that part of the Union. A story of the south, and Sorrensdattir had died telling Cora about that place. A story of the south, and Cora knew, knew well enough to tell the Whisperer, that the south, Tennworth and the election were all somehow connected.

Cora saw the glass mouthpiece first, then the scarred face wearing it. If she'd thought Sorrensdattir had been badly marked by her life in the Tear, this Torn looked to have been regularly battered by burning rocks. His skin was a patchwork of scars that put Cora in mind of the Assembly building's dome, the glass plates held together by thick lines of solder.

The storyteller's head was hairless, like all the Torn she'd ever seen – which wasn't many, she had to admit. He wore a loose-fitting white coat which was made of different swathes of cloth. The same was true for the trousers that bagged around his waist and hips, then tapered at his ankles.

He came to the huge sandstone rock, and there he stood for a few moments, looking out over his listeners. Not just the masked Audience who would cast their votes on his tale, but everyone at First Wall. Still there was no noise. Still the Mute was with them. Then the Storyteller turned to face the rock, reached up and found handholds, and then he began to crawl up the rock at speed, to gasps from everyone. In seconds, the storyteller had scaled the rock and stood on its highest point, far above the seated listeners. He put his hands to his face and pressed the mouthpiece that sat across the lower part of his face, where the burning tornstone kept his lungs working in Fenest's thin air. And then, he lifted the mouthpiece away. The gasps of those in First Wall came again, but louder.

A Torn risking the air of Fenest, air so different to that of the Tear it could kill him, all to tell his realm's story.

This election wasn't like any other Cora could remember.

The storyteller took a deep breath, and then he began, his voice crackling – a voice like tornstone. Warm, lit, burning through the words.

'Aris watched Mattina lay her eggs.'

The Torn Story

Aris watched Mattina lay her eggs. This was something Aris had seen hundreds of times; Mattina was not a young ash beetle. She had been in the family a long time. How long, Aris did not know. She might ask her father, if she remembered to, or she would not trouble him. But the question of who came first, Aris or Mattina, brought a smile to Aris's face – as it would to his. He needed more smiles in the hot nights.

Aris was a breeder of ash beetles; a lucrative yet dangerous trade looked down on by many of the Torn. Aris, who bred beetles but had still to try coupling with her own kind – the Audience were waiting. Her father was a breeder of ash beetles, as was his mother before him. To understand the story of that family is to understand the breeding of ash beetles.

An ash beetle lays eggs meticulously. It knows the dimensions of its enclosure. It has prepared the ground. Like Mattina, it puts its mate to work to clear rocks, hardened ash-fall, fossilising bones, and all the scattered offerings of a year in the Tear. Offerings from the sky, offerings from the earth. An ash beetle has much to tell the Affable Old Hand.

This ash beetle shuffled a precise distance and then speared the ground with her foreleg, exactly so. Quick, otherwise the hole would fill once more with ash, she turned and squatted. An undignified beginning. She walked herself upright – all three feet of her length – balanced, and then burst with light. A light she had deep within herself, burning only as an ember until her laying ignited the flame. Then it flared, not the colour of fire, but the green of Seeder grass. Green, in a place that only knew black and orange. Beautiful and bizarre. Aris had seen the light many times, and often wondered what it meant. Was it a warning, telling the Tear these were guarded eggs? Or a firing of joy at a new life? Or something Aris had not thought of yet.

This was why Aris watched. That, and it was her work.

The ash beetle matriarch fell forward and was off to dance the dance another twenty-five times. There was half a grid of egg holes behind her, half ahead. Fifty eggs in total – no more, no less, and all registered with the Commission – every year since Mattina had come to her maturity as an imago. The beetle made no complaints, but Aris did. To register them was something better done by her father.

Aris ran her tongue over her teeth and spat black. The ash clouds were heavy, and they spoke of cinders and clasts to come. But she knew enough to trust her ash beetles: Mattina would not have started her laying if there was not time. Aris's task was to check the tarred fences and be vigilant against tatterwing bats, which would dig in their limbless way and make off with eggs. She kicked each fence post with her heavy boots. If it did not jar her leg, from toe to hip, she stopped and asked it why. At the corner of Mattina's enclosure one post told a story of heavy skyfall, not struck directly, but a gouge from the ash-layered earth undermined it, and allowed for a wavering.

She fetched her shovel. A glance for Mattina, still occupied.

'You are digging holes. I fill in others,' Aris said to the beetle. A flash of green, another egg in the ground.

Aris bent to her work. Her shovel was worn and pitted, but reliable. After clearing some of the loose ash, she stopped. For a choking moment Aris thought she saw a thin line of Wit's Blood – lava – under her shovel, beneath the fence post. Wit's Blood this close to the breeding grounds would be beyond catastrophe. But her eyes played tricks on her, did they not? One shaking breath later she looked again. There was nothing there, except hot soil turning to deadened grey. She helped it on its way. With the hole filled, she stamped it solid and found the post improved. Elsewhere, she repaired one of the lower beams. A protest from Mattina's mate, Mir. They did not always get along. What lovers did?

Mir, now in a separate pen, waited with all the impotent patience of a new father. He scraped and jabbered when Aris approached.

'You should know better, old man,' she said.

He tensed, low, and then thrust his horn at her. She forgave this.

'Leave the fence out of your arguments.'

She would walk him back to Mattina when the matriarch's grid was complete. There, beginning his sentry duty, Mir would not rest nor eat nor attend his mate until the eggs hatched. In this he would be insufferable. She threw him a dead rat from the pouch she carried at her hip. Her inspection finished to the tune of crunching bones.

Nine rows of neat black holes, and Mattina starting on her last. Was her climb to the vertical slower now? Her flash any dimmer? Not that Aris could tell. But it would come, one day, and they would stop breeding her. Aris would have no say in this. That was how time worked.

This time was passed by watching the ash clouds, or else gazing at home. Aris did not want to go back, not yet. But there was no escaping it. Nowhere to go but to her ailing father and fussing mother. She could feel them, lurking behind the pitted balconies and walkways and tunnels of Hadun-Har. So far away from here, at the breeding fields, only the shadows of the tunnel mouths made any impression on the cliffside. It was called many things: warren, burrow, survival. Everything in the Tear did what it had to, or the Widow welcomed it.

And so Mattina struggled her way to the corner of her enclosure, where Aris waited. The matriarch's plated legs shook as she pushed her way upwards one last time. Aris was too slow in closing her eyes. Brilliant green blinded her, but in that blindness she saw a transformation. The Tear blanketed by grass, not ash. Rocks that didn't burn to touch but had cooled over countless years. Rain that was not black, no colour at all. A vision of Mount Hadun no longer telling jittery stories to the Wit, but slumbering deeply enough to please the Child.

The call of the exhausted matriarch cut through her silliness. There was only the grey ash fields. The orange glare of Hadun. The darkening clouds.

'All right then, Mattina, I will fetch him.' She stepped off the fence. 'You are sure you want him back?'

The call continued by way of an answer. Aris envied another woman's certainty. She imitated it when she could.

Mir was just as determined as his mate. He scraped his horn against the fence as he followed Aris's progress. She did not waste breath on telling him to stop. There would be no explaining that his display was lost on her, that it only created more work, not intimidation nor admiration. At least the old bull knew not to charge when she opened the gate. The younger males learned that lesson eventually, flailing at their mate's enclosure until they had no choice but to drag themselves back to where Aris waited with the lead. Mir did not test her.

She knelt and affixed the lead around his dull elytra, the straps firm but not too tight. He would pull – he had to show willing, even as old as he was. She walked him from one enclosure to the other. Such a separation was essential; he would only have fussed and worried during the laying, been no help at all. She could feel his whole body vibrating through the lead. She smiled and said nice things to him.

As they drew close, Mattina's call turned to clicking. Mir matched her, as if their separation had lasted years, not hours. He strained those last few paces and bashed the gate as Aris unwound its ties. When he could squeeze through, she knew enough to drop the lead. She would recover it when he had settled into his duty. Mir rushed to his mate along a path of right angles, not once disturbing an egg hole. The pair, reunited, stood side-by-side and pulsed. That they did so, in time, reaffirmed their bond.

After a while Mir's responsibilities pulled him from his mate. His ritual began. First, he checked each and every egg hole. At every one he looked back at Mattina: acknowledging its existence, that he would guard it, and – Aris always felt – that he was awestruck by what Mattina had achieved. Another! And another! And so on. It was not swiftly done. For her part, Mattina began to burrow into the ash until only the top of her wing-cover could be seen.

'Rest. Keep safe,' Aris said.

It had been a long day. An important day. This was her

family's livelihood. Ash beetles were the only beetle bred and then sold for fighting in the whole of the Union. Pits from the Tear to the Northern Steppes paid good money for ash beetles. Though their grubs were edible, each grub in the frying pan was one fewer champion for the chequers. And not every beetle made it to adulthood. Even for feisty knee-high beetles, the Tear was a dangerous place.

She was packing her things when Natalia Geirsdattir hailed her. It was customary to do so from a distance on the breeding fields – not a place for sneaking nor for snooping. Natalia was a long friend of Aris's father. As friendly a rival as the Tear could know. She bred good ash beetle.

'Look at this old horn,' Natalia said, resting her huge frame on the enclosure's fence. Beetle breeders spent their days on a fence, the beetles inside one. The years had made it so – Aris wondered if she could go dawn to dusk without leaning on something. 'Have children, Aris. See Mir? It makes you young again. You are looking too much your age.'

'You are not,' Aris said. She pulled up her heavy cloak's hood. The Painter would let loose the sky soon and it would burn anything soft.

'Little Sturri runs me to ruin,' Natalia said. 'What could be better?'

'How are your pairs this year?'

Natalia cleared her throat as a panogar roars, and spat. Mir braced himself to defend his unhatched brood. 'None so fierce as these two.'

'You sound worried.'

'Worried was last year.' She shrugged. 'This is worse.'

'And yet the north still buys our beetles,' Aris said.

'What do they know of good beetles? As long as it fights to live – not too well, not too poorly, and looks different from the feathers.' She waved dismissively.

Mir stabbed his horn at the giant of a woman, fearless, reliving his ringside glory. He had cost Aris's father half a year's earnings to buy. In his prime he was the Brawler's favourite. He missed those days, that was obvious.

'Looks like rain,' Aris said.

'As if life was not bitter enough.' Natalia raised her hood. 'Tell your father he is a villain for having you out here. Seeing to beetle broods when it should be your own.'

'I will own it, too soon I think.'

'That is not what—'

'When you tickle little Sturri's feet, tell him I told you to. Aris told you.'

Natalia clapped a huge hand on her shoulder and then lumbered away, watched by Mir.

Aris collected her shovel and satchel. Needlessly, she checked the gate ties again. Then looked to the two other breeding pairs her family owned. Kraki and Kata, their youngest pair, were still days from ready. Father cursed them from his bed for being shy; told the Fishwife of the misfortune she had brought them in beetles that refused to mate. He looked right at Aris when he told those stories. Doari and Dyrley were ready. But where Mattina had worked all day to lay before the rains, Dyrley preferred to wait, full of eggs as she was. Doari was impatient, but what male was not? He marked their enclosure as she burrowed in for the night.

It was a little over an hour's walk from the breeding fields to Hadun-Har. It was not an easy hour. Though the path was well-worn, there were many steep climbs. At points she had to haul herself up large, black rock ledges, and up the sides of gullies carved by streams of Wit's Blood. Some streams still ran hot and that heat pressed her against the cliffs, dried out her mouth and nose and eyes and made her skin tight. They were her favourite parts of the walk home. They at least defied the rain.

When it came, the ground steamed. The top-ash turned to mud and her boots were soon covered. Another chore – if left overnight, the mud would eat through the soles. Left long enough it would eat through everything. Against the rain, her cloak and gloves, so thick and thickly treated – heavy beyond the Union's understanding – were fair protection. Better to have a shell like her ash beetles, but the Audience had not seen fit to give her one.

She hurried to the relative shelter of a cliff. She searched her satchel, twice, slow and thorough. But she could not find her rain-veil: a heavy treated cloth that attached to the inside of her hood and protected her face. It was not in her satchel, where it was supposed to be. She cursed the Latecomer for her misfortune in losing it.

She could wait out the rain, but the Painter was lazy not just in name – in what stories was the rain ever in any hurry? And night was not so distant. The worst kind of fool was out of their har at night, in the Tear. A mistake only made once.

No, better to risk a scar. She had her fair share already. She pressed on. Somewhere distant, a firecat howled, a chilling sound amongst the fire-blooded mountains. Aris listened hard – the echoes would tell her just how distant. The sound died quickly. Perhaps it was howling from the mouth of its cave, as frustrated by the rain as she was?

Mir, Mattina, and the others would be fine, of course. Adult ash beetles were so poisonous to eat that everything in the Tear avoided them. Their eggs and larvae, however... Aris preferred trumpet beetle larvae, fried with dried holen. Mir guarded the eggs now, and in a matter of days the pair of beetles would guard the grubs together. Her father might demand some for the table, or he might say they could not be spared, risking her mother's disappointment. Such small uncertainties kept the year interesting.

An old blood flow, now hardened and smoothed, forced her to turn back on herself briefly. The breeding fields stretched out below her along the relatively smooth slopes of Hadun-Valley. There were a handful of ash beetle breeding families in the western Tear. Talk was of eastern families doing well these last years; that it was cooler there and the pairs had managed the change even better than their breeders.

'Too big, too slow, they will not last,' her father said to any who brought eastern beetles to a conversation. Hadun-Valley had lasted longer than many thought it should. Generations longer. And it would still be there tomorrow.

She turned back towards home and slipped. Some of the valley was smooth underfoot, and she had forgotten the rain. She did not forget to catch herself before falling. But she clung to an outcrop of blood flow, too close, and the Painter took her chance. A fat drop bounced from stone to Aris's cheek.

The burning came quick.

A reflex nearly ruined her: she raised her wet glove to wipe the drop away, but that would only smear more scarring across her face. Instead, she leaned forward and willed the water to fall from her as it did the sky. Nothing to do but grit her teeth as it made up its mind; the black earth proved irresistible. Finally, she dabbed at her cheek with the inside of her hood. Quick and light or she risked taking skin instead of water. There was no stopping the stinging, nor the scar to come, but it could have been worse. An eye. Lips and nose blistered in a bad way. A burn on the tongue made eating a cruel thing.

How had she misplaced her rain-veil? She called herself all manner of names. That helped the frustration and the pain, but then there was nothing to be done. She would tell her stories to the Painter, or perhaps the Bore – thanking him for not sending his winds that day. They both had Seats in Hadun-Har, though neither close to her family's rooms.

Merciless Audience, the rain eased as she reached home.

She presented herself at the main gate of Hadun-Har. Preparations were being made to close it, but she had made good time – less than an hour, even with the rain. The huge, solid metal gates were ponderous but well-oiled in their closing. As black and pitted as anything in the Tear, they kept many troubles out and many troubles in. A bored sentry nodded her through.

'Rain today,' he said.

With her cheek still stinging, she did not waste breath on a reply.

All of Hadun-Har was carved into the black rock of the cliffside. While not directly below the volcano Hadun, it was impossible to tell where one stopped and the other began; perhaps the bats, the flies, or the Rustans could see – looking down when the ash clouds broke. But nothing earth-bound could. When Hadun grumbled and the Wit bled, the har felt everything – even as it was safe from the bloodtrails. Last week a shake had thrown the salt jar from the shelf; Mother flew to her knees and saved half of it. She wept at her dusted fingertips.

At the modest gatehouse she approached the Commission clerks sitting at their desks. Aris had heard stories, dull stories, that said the Commission was so situated all across the Union. She only knew Hadun-Har, and Hadun-Har had its share of northerners who counted and recorded the necessary and unnecessary alike. Not even the Tear was safe from them. And, like a beetle lived in its shell, a clerk lived in its desk – and never did so alone. The first, a woman with a dangerous amount of grey hair on her head, squinted at Aris in the lowlight. The Commission was not generous with its candles.

'Name?' the woman said. Her tone made for an accusation, but it was deadened by her mouthpiece. Northerners wore them in the Tear – weak-lunged, none of them could breathe there without coughing and spluttering until they brought up blood. The mouthpieces were made of delicate northern layers of cotton and some Seeder plant's leaves; they were so big they covered mouth and nose and chin. They looked ridiculous.

'Aris Rafnarsdattir.'

The clerk checked her ledger. 'No. No Harris.'

'Aris. A. R. I. S.'

'Ah.' The woman turned to her colleague and shouted Aris's name as if it were a great discovery. Aris shuffled along the desk to the next clerk.

'Aris Rafnarsdattir,' she said once more.

'*Dattir*?' the clerk said.

Aris struggled for calm. 'Yes. Rafnarsdattir.' Commission-paid northerners relied so heavily on appearances. A woman without hair was not a woman in their eyes. A woman with scars was not a woman in their eyes. And yet, here she was.

The clerk stamped his ledger and announced her one more time.

'How is your father?' the last clerk asked.

'He is dying,' Aris said.

The clerk shifted in her seat as if she had mites. She did not look at Aris again as she signed and stamped the third ledger to bear the name Aris Rafnarsdattir for the day. The clerk had asked a question and Aris had answered. What was her trouble?

So logged and accounted for, Aris entered the har proper.

Lower Hadun-Har was busy by its own standards. Three market stalls still offered their wares, even as two others packed up. A handful of people meandered through the wide walkway. Aris joined them, remembering her mother had asked her to buy... something on her way home. Was it for Father? He favoured sintas, when the markets had any, but Mother disapproved. Exotic foods did not agree with him, she said. He would call her the Bore incarnate, and so it would go. But no, it was bread and flour her mother wanted.

Cracks in the rock were a permanent feature of the lower market's ceiling. Just as permanent was discussion of whether they were bigger or smaller that day, that month, that year. The simple act of looking, as Aris was looking now, invited the conversation.

'Never been that big,' one man said as he joined her. 'Never.'

An older woman dragging a child in her wake stopped. 'What do you young ones know of "never"?'

Aris shared a look with the man, and they both went on their way. She stopped at Holger Falkisutter's food stall. He smiled at her incessantly. She chose a small bag of flour and a small loaf of bread. Holger undercharged her, though the wink he gave her had its own cost. He had some unfortunate ideas regarding Aris and his son, Palmi. She mumbled her thanks.

The market chamber extended far beyond the stalls, and then tapered off to a junction of tunnels. So many that, in her childhood, Aris had enjoyed nothing more than exploring a different one each day. A young imagination could not believe she would ever know them all, but as an adult she did. They were less exciting for it. Her step did not falter as she took the tunnel sixth from the right. She lit her lamp – at least she had not misplaced *that* – and idly followed the cracks in the floor, up the wall, over the ceiling and back again. She was alone in the tunnel's twists and turns. Miles and miles of them, empty. It had not always been so. That was what the old ones said – they all said it, though their stories did vary.

The old couple that lived nearest to her family – the only others on their floor – insisted they remembered a time when Hadun-Har was half full. Half! Aris could not imagine that many people; all of them tripping, talking, worrying over one another. The noise must have been unbearable. There were others who said there had been more people than that. They claimed Hadun-Har had once been the home of the entire Torn realm. The first har ever built; the others came later when the brave and foolhardy ventured out together for more than a day's walk. How could anyone remember such a time? No one could, but there were stories. These were the things that occupied Aris in the lonely tunnel home.

Her mother was waiting for her – Mother, a small box of a woman who kept her hair short but not short enough for outside the har. She had scars of her own from seasons since forgotten. Her nose was flat, and she sneezed once when she woke and once again before bed.

Mother waved her on, frantic, as if a firecat were chasing her. Aris almost turned back.

'Where have you been?' Mother said.

'The breed—'

'Shh, no matter. But look at you! What have you been doing?'

'The—'

'No matter. We have a guest. Come in, come in.'

Aris did not want guests. She wanted food, water to splash her face, and her bed. None of which needed guests. She took off her cloak and dirty boots; surely her exhaustion was evident? But Mother was not to be stopped. Had she a lead, she would have fixed the straps to Aris and made a beetle of her. As it was, Mother took her arm and the effect was much the same.

'Look who is home,' Mother announced, as if it was a great occasion, not a thing that happened once every day.

Home was as big as it needed to be, and theirs was a modest family. The three of them had their own rooms. A kitchen and a room for sitting comfortably. A store for the ash beetle workings, all of which Mother could not abide. She should have married a weaver – the whole family knew it. She had an unhealthy regard for rugs.

'Look who it is,' Mother called once more. With every step Aris succumbed to the inevitable. She was being led to the sitting room, which meant only one thing.

'Hello, Palmi,' Aris said.

He was tall, close to brushing his bald head against the ceiling as he stood. He smiled easily at her – no skin on his face was pulled or pinched by scars. He had good teeth. Broad in the shoulder and muscular – though through no effort of his own – Palmi was what most considered *beautiful*.

'Aris.' Even in his greetings he was lazy.

'Finally!' Father said. He was sitting up in a chair, a blanket over his legs. 'How are they?'

'Rafnar, please,' Mother said, 'we have guests.'

'Guests?' Father looked about. 'Oh. The boy has bored me enough. You take him. There is business to speak of.'

Mother bristled. But Palmi was not offended. What could offend a man without a care under the Audience? He followed Mother into the kitchen where she prattled on about this and that.

'Well?' Father said.

'Mattina is fine – she laid her fifty.'

'Good, good.'

'She is tired though, Father.'

'We all are.'

Aris glanced to the kitchen, but held her tongue. She doubted their guest knew what it was to be tired. 'This may be Mattina's last year.'

'And the others?'

'Not ready. Dyrley tomorrow, if the rain holds off.'

'I have talked the ear from the Fishwife with those pairs. Come, sit with your father.'

Aris did as she was bid. She felt heavy next to him, his legs thin under the blanket. 'You look—'

'Do not tell me,' he said. 'I told your mother I would smash the next looking glass I see. She wants you married, you know.'

'I know.'

'Do not choose that scar-less dandy.'

She grinned. 'No, Father.'

'But be good tonight. That much for her, at least.' He took Aris's hand in his. His palm was damp. His face spoke of how sorry he was for that, and more. She helped him from the seat. He weighed less than her satchel, or so it felt. 'We both demand more of you than we should,' he said.

'Aris, did you forget the sintas?' her mother called from across the kitchen. She was rifling through Aris's satchel.

'You asked me to bring home flour and bread.'

'And *sintas*,' Mother said. 'We can afford little luxuries, you know that.' She was speaking to Aris, but looking at Palmi.

Aris was sure her mother had not asked for sintas; she was playing a foolish game. 'I got a good price,' Aris said.

'Of course you did – Holger is most generous.' Mother touched Palmi on the arm, both so pleased with each other. *They* could marry, for all Aris cared, and leave Father and her to the business of business.

'Here,' Father said, pouring them all a glass of mutters. 'If we are to eat all your mother has made, I need a drink.'

Aris and Father knocked back the hard spirit and slammed the glass on the table – the ending of any good toast in the Tear. Palmi and Mother sipped theirs. For the Torn, mutters was more than a method to muddle the mind or lose inhibitions. It allowed them, however briefly, to know a throat clear of ash and cinder. It was shared as a sign of respect between business partners, neighbours, friends. And it cleaned metal more efficiently than water.

'Drunkard save me from slow drinkers,' Father said, easing himself down to the table.

'Rafnar, please!'

As the evening began, so it continued. Father grumbled, Mother wittered, and Palmi was softly smug. Aris left them to it. Her cheek was still stinging and it took all her concentration to simply load her fork. Mother had cooked too much food, to Aris's embarrassment. They were two dishes shy of a wedding feast. Palmi picked at everything available. Politely not favouring the roast holen over the meat stew, nor the black bread over the medlar cake. Even that was irksome. What man did not have favourites at a dinner table?

'... another reason the match makes such sense,' Mother said. 'Aris loves to work.'

Aris had not been paying attention.

'You are talking nonsense,' Father said. 'What time does she have that is not in the ash fields?'

'It is such dangerous work, and so dirty.'

'Pah! Anything else is not *real* work.'

Aris tried to make some sense of their words. 'What are you—'

But they would not be stopped. 'Holger is a successful merchant. I will not have that taken lightly.' Mother stabbed a finger at the table. 'Not when we enjoy his wares at this very table.'

'Nine generations of breeders. Would you dishonour them all?'

Palmi, at least, seemed to notice her confusion. He leaned across the table, from where he sat next to Mother, and said, 'It is good news, I think. My father will retire when I marry.' He glanced to her parents. 'When we marry.'

'What?'

'I said to your mother that you would make excellent work of the market stall.'

That was why Palmi was here, at her home, eating at their table: he wanted a working wife. A wife to do the work. A wife to work the market stall so he did not have to. So he could keep doing... whatever it was he did with his days. He clearly had no real feelings for her. In that, at least, they shared something mutual. And what of her mother? With such a match she would have Aris safely inside the har, no longer doing the kind of work most Torn thought low, poor. Aris's work.

Aris stood up. 'I have to clean my boots.'

That set them all to fluster.

'The Relative forgive—'

'You see? The girl is dedicated to the ash—'

'Will there be dessert?'

Aris collected her boots and a stiff brush and left. She had no care for where she went, as long as it was away from the kitchen. She followed the tunnels of their home, until the tunnels were not theirs anymore. There was no door, no gate, no line drawn on the rough rock walls. Objects they owned simply petered out. As did the light. But her eyes managed the dark well enough. So she walked until she found light again.

The tunnels came to a hewn balcony, below which was a wide square that may have once been busy but was now empty. A trickle of Wit's Blood ran along the far wall, casting a welcome glow. Aris sat, her legs over the edge, and brushed the dried mud from her boots. She did this methodically, in no hurry. The Wayward leather was strong, worth the price she had paid, and held up well under the thin tar she had treated it with. The boots were more than an excuse to leave the table. Without them, she could not go to the ash fields. And that would bring ruin in so many ways.

She stopped her brushing when someone emerged from a tunnel below. She recognised Palmi's sauntering as much as his big bald head. He did not notice her. Perhaps he was returning home to his doting father. Perhaps he was going to... she could not imagine where else such a man might go. She knew nothing of him except that he was lazy.

Her boots finished, she placed them by her side and sat for a while. She considered sleeping right there and then, but tomorrow would bring complaints from every joint and bone. As much as she might wish otherwise she had no choice but to return home. There was no use putting it off, not really; her mother would wait up.

When she returned, Mother was wiping the plates in the sink, a puddle of water in its bottom. In the unguarded moment, Aris saw the strain – the bags under her mother's eyes, her sallow cheeks, the prominent veins. These things that her mother normally hid through sheer force of will.

'It is my fault,' her mother said, without looking up from the sink.

Such a thing to say. How could Aris escape to bed now?

'What is, Mother?'

Her mother carried a stack of plates to the shelf. Had Aris offered help she would have refused. When growing up, such a thing would have been demanded of Aris. But help offered is a different creature – an insult, even, from one adult to another.

'I should have had more children,' Mother said flatly. 'But you cried too much.'

'I see.' Aris put her clean boots by the door, next to her satchel. Her rain-veil was still missing. Silence take her, where was it?

'Too much crying for Adar Aronsutter, remember?'

'No.'

'Yes you do. Adar had a tornstone lamp – loved that lamp more than his wife. Though it was a beauty, and she was... Well, you must remember? As a baby you stared at that lamp, at the twisting faces. Only time you were quiet.'

'I don't remember. I was a baby.'

'You do! Then Adar moved his family to the other side of the har. Other families went too. You cleared the tunnels with your crying. Your father was proud.'

'You were embarrassed,' Aris said.

Her mother shrugged. 'I was tired. I said, "never again".'

'Now we're both tired.'

'I should have had more children. Kiss your father before you go to bed.'

She kissed her mother's cheek first.

Her father was sitting up in bed, staring at the shadows cast by his candle. They did not dance, and they told no stories. They only stared back.

'Goodnight, Father.' Aris bent to kiss him.

He blinked, slowly, as if waking. 'Mir and Mattina today,' he said.

'More tomorrow, maybe.'

'Registered?'

'I...'

She did not want to register the egg laying. It was a job her father had done last breeding season, though he had insisted she go with him. The Commission's Office for Trade, Livestock, and Realm Affairs was as officious and airless as its name suggested. Masked northerners, too many to count, sitting behind desks and making marks on parchment. All of them gathering dust as if it were part of the job. Nothing was done in a hurry. And the man overseeing it all? She did not like the way he looked at her.

She did not like the way her father was looking at her now. To see him reduced to this. He had built and tarred the fences that had become her job to mend. Bred more ash beetles than she had ever seen. And now he grew breathless crossing his kitchen. To lose him to his bed meant facing the risk of losing their business. Of the family's ruin. Without her efforts, starvation.

'I will register the laying before going to the fields.'

'Good girl.' He patted her leg. 'Ignore your mother. Where is our need of more children?'

Everywhere, Aris thought bitterly. The need walked the empty tunnels and corridors of the har. It had more stalls than anyone in the lower market. It filled their rooms with its silence. The need was everywhere, except where it should be.

Aris kissed her father on the forehead and left him to his shadows.

Before she went to bed herself, she checked her room over twice. It was too large for her, really. She had too few possessions, and those she did have looked marooned – like rocky outcrops in a river of Wit's Blood. There were few drawers to open – wood was expensive. Few clothes to move, though the heavy cotton was bulky. Few things to look under. Her rain-veil was not there.

Getting into bed, she told the Painter of her newest scar – how her luck had run as bad as his rain. She told him it had to be dry tomorrow.

The Office for Trade, Livestock, and Realm Affairs was deep within Hadun-Har. Why they chose such a place confused Aris – typically those from outside the Tear grew more nervous the closer they were to a volcano. They would sweat a lot, not all from the heat. They preferred the edges of the har, as if five hundred paces would be such a difference were Hadun to wake.

The Office was empty this side of the desks, full on the other. The only sound was the scratch of nib on paper – a horrible sound. To hope for a crowd to hide in was to hope for gold marks buried in ash. But at least registering a laying would be as swift as anything the Commission managed. She approached the closest clerk. So chosen, panic tugged at his eyebrows. She cleared her throat.

'I come to register my ash beetle laying,' she said, slowly. Northerners often struggled to understand her. Father said they had bad hearing due to too much bathing as children.

Behind his mouthpiece, the clerk's relief was obvious. 'Two desks along and three back, for registering Livestock.'

She had to turn sideways to pass between the rows of desks. She had a vague memory of doing the same, trailing behind her father. She did not remember the woman who looked up from a parchment covered in lines and numbers.

'Good morning,' the woman said.

Aris glanced about her. What good was here?

'I come to register ash beetle laying,' she said.

'I'm sorry, but—'

'What seems to be the trouble here, Marie?' said a short man with hair that curled down to his shoulders.

'Well, Mr Pemberton, I was just about to explain to this young woman that we don't register layings until the afternoon sessions.'

Mr Pemberton looked at Aris. His gaze was as greasy a thing as his hair.

'Oh, I think we can manage a laying in the morning, just this once, don't you? It's a great thing, to breed the beetles. A fine job.'

Aris glanced at one northerner, then the other. Even if she had any idea what to say, she had the better idea to be quiet. To the northerners, beetle-breeding was a job that deserved respect. Why, Aris was not sure. Perhaps because the work created so much for the Commission to record.

'But I—'

'Don't worry, Marie, I'll take it from here. Why don't you have an early break?'

'Yes, Mr Pemberton.'

The man slid into her vacated seat. 'Now then, ash beetles. How delightful!'

Aris frowned. 'They are a champion pair. Killed many northern birds.'

'Would you sit, Miss...?'

She had been towering over the man and his desk. She liked that. The chair was too narrow, her robe ballooned uncomfortably. And this man liked to look directly at her eyes. It was not good. But this was not a thing to fight, not here in a Commission office.

'My name is Aris Rafnarsdattir.'

He consulted his parchments. 'I see your father has been in the business a long time. He must be so proud to have his daughter following in his footsteps.'

'I do not follow my father.'

'Quite. We forge our own path, don't we?'

'I do not work at a for—'

'So, who is the lucky couple?'

She did not understand what he was asking, so did not reply.

'What are the names of the two beetles you have mated?'

'Mattina and Mir,' she said.

He noted down their names alongside her own. 'And the number of eggs?'

'Fifty.'

'I know it's always the same,' he said, 'but we have to ask. It's on the form, you see?'

She did not see. She could not read anything in such small letters, and upside down. She did not want to read it. That this man, Mr Pemberton, had her name written on a parchment made her wish for ash clouds overhead and more miles between her and this office than the Tear had to offer. But here she was. And he had more questions. She answered as if words were clean water, not wishing to spill a drop. He drank them all with his parchment. He knew where she lived. How old she was. How many breeding seasons she had seen.

Had she travelled? No. Not even Bordair, or the southern Seeder border? The border, once. The Rusting Mountains? No. Was she married? No. Living with a partner? No, her parents. Were her boots her own? Yes. Her cloak? Yes. Satchel? Yes. Were any of her working items owned by her father's business? No. How far did she walk to work? Three miles. Every day? Yes. How— What— When— If— Had—

On and on. He filled pages with her. Morning turned into afternoon. The faces at the desks changed, all except for Mr Pemberton.

Someone else entered the Commission's labyrinth. A tailor, so Aris overheard. She and the man shared a look of shared suffering. The tailor had stopped using an imported red dye, instead favouring a flower found on the far side of Hadun that produced a paler red. Small change, customers unaffected, entirely new business license. Status changed from import-trade to export-sole-trader, couldn't he see? An afternoon lost.

Mr Pemberton scattered sand on the parchment and smiled as they waited. She could see he was smiling behind his mouthpiece because his eyes became very small. 'Used to be three departments: Trade, Livestock, Realm Affairs. There were three of me, perish the thought!'

'Three.'

'Now I have to look after it all. Such different concerns, but all utterly fascinating.'

Fascinating. She tasted the word and found it bitter in such a place.

'What can we simple Commission staff do?' Mr Pemberton continued. 'There are always cuts.'

'Cuts.'

'Well, then, that should be everything. Congratulations on your latest brood.'

'And when other pairs lay?' Aris said, dreading the inevitable.

'You'll need to register them, of course, but we did some important groundwork today. Next time we'll have a chance to become *properly* acquainted.'

Aris left Hadun-Har and made her way to the breeding fields. She had lost the morning but there was still work to do, and light to do it. The ash clouds were pale today, so she walked with her hood down. On occasion the clouds even parted and the sky could be seen. She stopped then – not looking where you were going in the Tear was a mistake only made once – and stared upwards. The blue was unreal that day. She did not believe it. She stopped many times, expecting the deception to run its course and a grey sky – clouds lighter than ash, perhaps – to return.

But as she drew closer to the fields, the snatches of blue remained. This display was not for her alone; at first she thought the black specks in the sky were rocks, perhaps thrown into the air by a different part of the Tear. But they moved differently. Instead of falling they flew, like bats or the birds other realms were so proud of. She watched longer than she should. Envy had four fingers, a thumb, and a grip like no other.

The specks were Rustans.

She had seen them before, flying on their hidesails, but rarely so clear as today. They were up there, she and the rest of the Torn were down here. Somehow both realms found a way to live in the Tear. That was something they shared. Perhaps that was enough? Aris could not imagine sharing much else with a Rustan. She also rarely saw them fly beyond the spires of their mountains. Those journeys told a tale of necessity. Today, the Rustans flew for the sheer joy of it, that much was clear. Aris looked away, back to the path that lay in front of her, and the rocks of the valley. Solid, certain things. She carried on to the breeding fields. There was contentment in this. The ground beneath her boots.

A smell. That was the first sign.

New smells were ill tidings in the Tear; anything strong enough to cut through the sulphur and ash was cause for concern. This had a lively edge to it, something burned, but freshly so – not just recent, but the fuel, whatever it was, it couldn't be an old thing.

Then she heard the keening.

The nearest enclosure was Kraki and Kata's. The young pair were clearly agitated by the noise. Kraki butted the fence when he saw Aris. She hurried on. Doari and Dyrley were unsettlingly still. Aris's breath caught to see them so. But then Dyrley fluttered her wings briefly and what Aris had taken for death transformed to a sense of waiting. They were waiting, as still as possible, for calamity to pass.

Aris did not want to know. In that moment she was weak. She wanted to hide from what was to come. It could not be faced, not alone as she was. To walk those hundred paces and see the last enclosure was too much. The smell was causing her eyes to water and her nostrils felt singed and raw. And then she saw.

Mir was chaos, Mattina broken.

That was unmistakable as she looked into the enclosure. Mir did not know which way to go, where he was needed, where he might make any difference. He skittered from hole to hole in fits and starts, sometimes returning to the same one – as if part of him hoped to find that singular constant: change.

Mattina had backed herself into a corner. She was the one keening. How she made the sound, Aris did not know. It was not the right sound for an ash beetle. But it was right for a grieving mother, which was why it was impossibly foreign to Aris. That scared her as much as anything else. In the years the pair had been in the family, they had lost eggs before. Tatterwings had taken their share. Some eggs simply did not hatch. A boulder had crushed one corner of their enclosure. They had seen loss, but not been so totally lost themselves.

Aris touched the gatepost, but opening the gate was beyond her. She looked to Hadun-Har, so far back along the valley. No Wit's Blood there to see. She had to trust that her parents were safe. Her father would know what to do, he might have seen such a thing before. Too terrible to speak of, too terrible to give air to a warning or suggestions of what to do. Too terrible—

A sob burst from her.

Tears staggered down her face. They burned as if sent from the Painter. She had failed the pair, her father, the family. Somehow, she had failed.

Mir hit the gate. Post and beam shook under his desperation. Aris felt it all through her body. She should not go into the enclosure. She knew this. But the knowing did not stop her. If Mir hurt her... She owed them that much.

He moved aside, then escorted her to the first hole. Aris felt heat through the soles of her boots and she trod carefully, aware of how much more she weighed than an adult ash beetle. But the layers of ash and grit and sand, however many hundreds of years in the making, held firm beneath her. She looked down and saw the blood. Impenetrably orange, burdened by its own heat, uncertain of itself when it was not moving. The hole was full of Wit's Blood. So was the next. And the next. The entire row, column, all fifty holes in the enclosure. Like Mir, she could not believe at first. She went from hole to hole in hope. There was none.

The eggs were gone.

She stood before Mattina. The matriarch screeched again, a sound sharp with hysteria. Aris felt as if she were hearing it for the first time, but part of her knew Mattina had not stopped screaming her question. Aris did not have an answer.

'I am sorry,' she said. It was all she could say. It was true, and it was worthless.

At her feet, a hole that was made for an egg now only held the blood. To fill an enclosure, there must have been a lake of it underneath. It was rising. It *is* rising, Aris. This was what she told herself. Enough times to make it real, to cut across the keening of Mattina and the worry of Mir.

She had to get away. They all had to get away. Only the Wit knew how far his blood stretched under their feet. All the enclosures, all the breeding fields, perhaps even the entire valley. But that could not be. The valley, and Hadun-Har at one end, had been their home for hundreds of years. Thousands, maybe. It could not end that day. Not in a time when people like Aris lived, she was sure of that. She was too ordinary for such things.

If not the valley, then, only this enclosure. One small square of the breeding fields. *That* she could comprehend. She could see the blood rising for herself, in Mattina's egg holes. All the eggs were gone. But she could save Mir and Mattina.

She reached for the matriarch. She gave it no thought; she had been picking up ash beetles since the day she learned to walk. But Mattina was not willing. She reared up on her hind legs and spread her wings, and then Aris felt a pull on her heavy robe from behind. Mir had hold of her. His only thought to protect his mate, even as he damned them both. Aris tried once more with Mattina, but the beetle was too determined to stay.

'Please!' she said.

Mir's pincers cut through Aris's robe. He latched on again and pulled. He could not topple Aris, but she risked injury in staying.

Though it broke her heart to do so, she left them.

Wit's Blood was only an inch or so from the surface. Smoke rose from every hole. Through it she saw, in the corner of the enclosure, Mir and Mattina huddled together.

***

Aris fetched the leads and harnesses from the small shack they used as storage at the fields; she would not be able to carry the other two pairs to safety on her own. Every step she took was tentative, expecting the ground to crack and blood and smoke to rise in her wake. But the shack was on higher ground, solid ground formed of blood flows long stilled and cooled. The wooden walls and ceiling were pitched and tarred, like the enclosure fences, to give them some chance against the Painter's rain and the occasional grumble from Hadun.

The inside was dark and cramped. Aris did not have time, or the spare hands, for lamps. She left the door wedged open behind her, though it was little help. The harnesses and leads hung from nails on the far wall. She also found a body sling, which would help her carry one of the matriarchs if necessary. As she left the shack with the harnesses for four beetles, she looked to the sky and told the Painter a quick tale of a tragedy that did not need rain.

Was a part of her broken already, a part that caused her to avoid Mir and Mattina's smoke-clouded enclosure? Or was it a hardened pragmatism? Something else, perhaps? She did not know, could not admit to any possibility – none of them sat well. If her desire was to spare herself, the Audience offered her no such mercy.

The path from the shack to Doari and Dyrley's enclosure was the steeper of the routes, hewn into the rocks with dark banks on either side of her. Encased so, the fields were silenced. She only heard her own breathing. No keening, screeching, and no dull thuds of a male's useless frustration. The quiet made her go

333

faster. She could not run, so burdened by old, trusted leather, but she hurried.

As she emerged from the path there was a flash of green light. She dropped the harnesses.

She did not move, did not breathe, and did not blink. The light could have been a tale for the Child, a dream in the day, an imagining of the unthinkable.

Another flash, and she screamed.

It was not a noise that came readily for Aris. Hers was a guttural noise, and one she did not recognise as her own. But it came nonetheless when she saw Dyrley lay an egg.

Aris rushed to the enclosure. Dyrley stabbed the ground with her foreleg, then withdrew it quickly. There was a hiss from either the beetle or the released Wit's Blood, perhaps both. The matriarch pushed herself up on her hind legs, smoke billowing about her, and with a flash sent her egg into the blood.

If Dyrley knew what she was doing, she gave no sign. She moved on to the next point on her grid.

When Aris opened the gate, it was evident that Doari was relieved to see her. This was not how it was supposed to be, none of it. He clicked at Aris as if to say, 'I am not supposed to be here, what can I do?' Though the males fought her when she separated them from their mates, it was just a story they told themselves; they did not really want to be present for the laying of eggs. That was not their part of life. And now, when it was going wrong, Doari wanted none of it. He left a stunned Aris there, scuttled out of the gate, and waited beside the pile of leads and harnesses.

'Why now?' Aris shouted at the matriarch. But she was ignored.

The ground was higher in Dyrley's enclosure than in

Mattina's. Tougher layers of ash and sand and rock, hardened over many more centuries, made for a worse breeding ground. Worse in a normal season. Mattina had pride of place, and now she was dying in it. But there was still time for Dyrley, the blood still inches from the surface.

But, unusually, time was not the problem.

It was a different unassailable force facing Aris.

For the second time that day she reached towards a determined mother. Not only did Dyrley open her wings, she lashed out at Aris with her small pincers. She caught Aris's hand, cutting the skin from the knuckle of her little finger all the way down to her wrist. Aris gasped, and held the cut quickly, but still her blood fell to the ground and met that of the Wit's. Dyrley returned to her hopeless laying.

Aris carried bandages in her satchel. It was an easy thing to cut yourself on an ash beetle. Less common was for them to cut you, but the bandages worked the same. She wrapped her hand, the off-white turning red, and tried to comprehend what she was seeing. More flashes of light, more eggs dropped into molten rock, more death than the Widow needed to hear. And Aris would have to tell them all. She would have to tell Father. Tell him there was nothing she could do. This was Dyrley's choice.

Doari was frantically pawing at the pile of harnesses. He had made *his* choice: he wanted to be away. He was not so wrong in that.

Using her bandaged hand carefully, Aris attached a harness and lead to him. He did not pull or tug in any particular direction. The security was what mattered; that he was no longer responsible for himself; and who had not wished for the same at some time in their life? She led him to the last enclosure.

Aris had been called stubborn many times. Accused of being slow to learn lessons. Not so that day. She opened the gate to Kraki and Kata's enclosure and waited. She would not risk another hand on a lost cause, no matter how important the beetles were to her family. These were animals they bred to fight, and fight they did. It was *they* who were stubborn. Stupid, stubborn, set in their ways. Laying eggs while the world around them burned. What use were eggs then? What use were eggs—

Aris choked back a sob. Her tears had not stopped the whole time she had been at the breeding fields; she had just forgotten them.

Kraki and Kata walked out of their enclosure and stood before her. Kraki's earlier agitation was gone. A flicker of his wing-casing was all he gave Doari; for once two males too sensibly occupied to posture. And here was the youngest breeding pair, Kraki and Kata, full of the wisdom of youth, open to the sense of change. Here was hope, standing still as she lashed a harness to it and led it away from disaster.

Aris looked back often. She should not have, and she told herself this every time she did. But she had to know, if she were to tell her father, had to see it happen. And it did. The whole of the family's breeding grounds were destroyed. A lake of Wit's Blood, newly formed, perhaps no deeper than a puddle, perhaps as deep as any well, glowed in the fading sunlight.

Everything was gone.

Aris took the higher paths back to Hadun-Har. But even so she had to change course more than once as new seams of Wit's Blood hiccoughed and gurgled their way over unsuspecting ground. The two male beetles kept to their leads well, neither straining nor dawdling. Kata lay still in the sling, pressed close to Aris's chest, and gently pulsed. They were all quiet too; shocked to silence. As was Aris.

The har was safe from the blood. Her parents were safe. That much managed to cut through her shock. Her family's breeding fields were gone, perhaps other breeding grounds also, but Hadun-Har stood high and proud and ignorant. The sentry nodded her through without a word.

She entered at the lower gate and, with little conscious thought, made her way to the Commission gatehouse. At the sight of three beetles, the clerks clucked like the northern birds they were. Unplanned livestock. Separate forms. Most irregular. Different ink stamp, do we have one? Not here, dattir, that gentleman over there. Names? No, dattir, of the ash beetles.

It all blew past Aris as hot air. She sat as mute as her beetles and waited until the Commission was satisfied. She left with pages of parchment that shared the clerks' disapproval. None of which made any difference to what had happened, what was happening now, or what would happen next.

Leaving the gatehouse she wandered through the lower market. All the stalls had packed up for the day or were in the process of doing so. One cloth merchant was stacking his rolls on the back of an enormous beetle. She knew trumpet beetles could grow big, but this one was the size of a small cart – hence its current occupation. She felt the tug on the leads just in time, and gripped hard against Doari and Kraki's return to life. They tried to charge the great beast, slicing the air with their pincers and clicking a rapid war cry. The trumpet ignored them. Its owner was concerned enough, though. He shooed Aris and her little fighting beetles.

'People conduct *business* here,' he said.

She backed away, all the while looking at the trumpet. She backed herself right into the market barroom. A thin place carved out of the rock, it was little more than a bar with a line of stools in front, most of which were empty.

The owner saw her, and saw what she was leading. 'Not in—'

Aris's expression silenced his protest. She tied the ash beetles to one of the stools and sat on it. Checking her satchel, she found her coin purse but nothing for the beetles. She had left it all in the shack. 'You have any fruit?' she said.

'It is yesterday's.'

'Perfect,' she said.

The owner gave her a metal bowl with some sorry fruit, which she put on the floor for the beetles. Kata pushed her way to the fruit first and the males made do with what was left.

Aris wiped at her cheeks, finally tired of the feel of dry tears. 'And a line of mutters.'

He filled three small glasses with the hard spirit. The sharp, thin taste did its best to cut through the ash and smoke and pain that coated her throat. The second glass made a better job of it. She sipped the third and muttered her troubles to it, should the Drunkard be interested. There were more troubles than there were spirits.

'That is the truth,' she said, to no one.

'They fighters?' the owner said from halfway across the bar. The two other drinkers in the barroom did not raise themselves from their own muttering. In a barroom, the Torn offer a glass of mutters to the Drunkard in the hope he will mistake their whinging for a story; no one but the Audience listen to your troubles in the Tear, where everyone else has too many of their own.

'Were fighters,' she said. 'They breed now.'

He laughed bitterly. 'It is the way we go.'

'Not yet.'

'What can we do?' he said with a shrug.

'Not yet,' she said again.

She paid for the drinks and put the empty bowl on the bar. A younger Aris, an Aris from the year before even, might have stayed there and muttered the night through. But horrors had not tested that Aris. Now, she found herself more settled and more alive to what had happened. She was ready to tell her parents, and the Audience.

When she left the barroom, the market was empty, the cloth merchant and his trumpet beetle long gone. She walked home through the twisting tunnels of Hadun-Har, leading the last three beetles her family owned. That night there would be stories, tomorrow would be problems. And the day after, who could say. But it would come. It would come.

When she arrived home, her news had arrived before her. Mother and Father were sitting at the kitchen table with Natalia Geirsdattir, sharing their own mutters. Mother embraced Aris in the doorway, kissing both her cheeks and thanking every member of the Audience she could think of. Father stared at the beetles.

'Just three,' he said.

Aris could only nod.

'The others wouldn't leave,' he said.

'Dyrley started laying, just as...' Aris swallowed. She did not want to cry, not then.

'Rafnar, our daughter is safe!' Mother said, as a kind of admonishment.

'Of course she is safe, I can see her.'

'I should leave,' Natalia said, starting to rise. But Father's hand, small as it was, stopped the woman.

'No. Tell Aris of your fields,' he said. 'She will want to hear it.'

Natalia said, 'See to yours, then I will speak of mine.'

Aris led the beetles through the kitchen to a chorus of her mother's tuts and fussing. Beyond the bedrooms was a small set of pens. She could not remember a time when they had been used but, when she was a child, cleaning them was part of her chores. All those years ago she had marvelled at how empty and unused things grew dusty and filled with dirt. Now, she understood the lack of use *was* the cause. It was the cause of many things.

She put Kraki and Kata in the same pen, even though it was a little cramped – there would be no end to the noise otherwise. Doari she sat with for a moment. With a flutter he shook himself clear of the feel of the harness. He paced the small room.

'She is not here,' Aris said, though it pained her to give the thought to the air.

Doari settled by her outstretched legs and pulsed in time with her own heartbeat. Despite knowing otherwise, Aris thought the beetle was trembling.

She stayed with him longer than she should have. Natalia and her story were still waiting in the kitchen.

Father poured Aris a glass of the mutters. Her mother's

initial disapproving look turned when Aris did not drink straight away.

'Tell the girl,' Father said. 'I should have been in bed hours ago.'

Natalia cleared her throat. Though it clearly pained her, she spoke of her part of the valley – closer to Hadun-Har than Aris's. Natalia, too, had seen the blood rising in her enclosures. But her pairs had bred earlier. The eggs had hatched already and she had pens of larvae eating their way through a small fortune. So far she hadn't lost a single egg or larvae; a good season.

But because everything in the Tear likes to eat juicy beetle larvae, early or no, Natalia had hired in to make sure they were watched. Her hands had poled a number of tatterwing bats and seen off a skinny, desperate firecat. She nearly lost one man to the cat. He was alive, but wouldn't walk well again.

'Your father never believes me when I say a firecat is made of ropes of stone,' Natalia said. 'Your fields are too low for them, so what does he know?'

Father made a noise, but Natalia continued her tale. With each enclosure holding fifty or so larvae and the only kind of forest the Tear will ever know, it was hard to see what was happening. One moment the larvae were busy doing what they do, the next they were busy doing what they *do not* do: they were trying to climb. The fences, the potted fruit trees, the edge of a bowl, anything. But they are not climbers. Seeing them try would have been funny, the kind of story that would have the Drunkard rolling on his sides, if Aris were not seeing death.

The larvae fell, plump and gorged, into the blood. Little flames burst upwards when they did, like brief candles. Though she knew the numbers, it felt like hundreds of candles. And then none. She lost an entire enclosure that way. The men too slow, too ignorant, to be of any use. She chivvied them to the other enclosures. There she saved as many as they could carry – first, in their shock, they carried each wriggling mess in their arms, then sense took hold and they brought buckets. That way they cleared five enclosures. In the end, only three were lost to Wit's Blood. How many larvae, she did not know, not yet.

She was the largest ash beetle breeder in the western Tear. Perhaps she still was, but she was not so large now. She drained her glass and muttered a thanks. Aris did the same.

Father stood, gave a curt nod, and then shuffled away from the table.

'Rafnar, where are you going?' Mother said, though it was obvious.

'Calamity will still be here in the morning,' he said.

'I will not sleep tonight.'

'I should have been long home,' Natalia said. 'When the shock has gone, and you wonder what next, come see me, Aris. Come see me.'

Then it was just Aris and her mother at the table. Though she was bone-tired, her head heavy, she could not think of sleep either. To her surprise, her mother had nothing to say. Between them they finished the bottle.

The following morning she found Father sitting with the beetles. He did not see her, not at first, so she watched from the doorway. He was smiling, talking softly, and looked ten years younger.

'I have missed them,' he said when he noticed her.

'They missed you.'

'She has no eggs.' He gestured towards Kata, who was still in her pen, unlike the more adventurous males that busied themselves about him.

'No,' Aris said, steeling herself against her father's anger. Or, worse, his disappointment.

'That is good,' he said. 'We will not have that rush when we look for another breeding field.'

'They are gone, Father.'

'What is that?' His smile slipped.

'The fields.'

'Nonsense.'

'I saw them. What wasn't blood may as well have been, the use it would be to an ash beetle. The higher fields, Natalia's, perhaps. But not ours. Not anyone else's.'

'Then... then the other side of Hadun.'

'There are no fields there, Father.'

'Then the eastern Tear, Silence take you!'

She had thought he understood. But he had not been there, so how could he? He still had hope. Perhaps he thought she was exaggerating, a little girl telling tall stories. But they had both listened to Natalia.

'I am sorry, Aris,' he said. 'What will we do?'

It was too much, the desolation in his voice.

But he asked again, the question following her down the corridor and out into the har.

She walked for a while. She knew that she should be thinking, but what good would that be? Thinking would not stem the flow of Wit's Blood. It would not change the many faces of Hadun from rock to ash and sand. But it might change her mind. And, when she was honest with herself – something that happened only in the dark, empty tunnels – she was avoiding that the most. So, instead she wandered without purpose or thought. That way she found herself in Upper Hadun-Har.

How long had it been? she wondered. Months, years? No, not years, surely. She used to have friends up here. Friends to share drink with, to idle away hours, to gossip and dream. What had happened to them?

She emerged into a small, well-kept square and looked from one house to another, as if those friends would be waiting there in the window. But as she looked closer, many of those houses were abandoned. In good order, tidy, but with a staleness and lack of life that she recognised from other parts of the har.

She was bothered by the idea of friends. She could not remember names. But some faces: a girl with a long nose and thin lips, another whose cheeks were always red, and a boy with good teeth. Others, too, she could almost see, laughing and talking all at once. And then, one by one, they were gone. To the fields, like her? Or to market stalls, to cloth looms, to blacksmiths? Did some go east, west, north? She did not know where, just that they had gone. As she had gone too.

She walked until she found a home that was clearly occupied. She forgot herself, with these thoughts of lost friends, and she went as far as to knock on the door. An old man opened it immediately, as if he had been waiting for her. He nodded politely through her stumbling apologies.

'It is two streets over,' he said. He leaned beyond his

own threshold to squint down the terrace of homes carved into the rock-side. 'Impossible to miss it.'

'Miss what?'

'The bath house. That is all the young ones want up here.' He started to close the door. 'What is so interesting in being clean, I do not know,' he said to himself.

Aris stared at the door. She should have stayed at home, slept longer, cleared her head of the mutters. But a bath was a reasonable idea.

The man was right, the bath house entrance was not hard to find; as with bath houses in Lower Hadun-Har, it spilled green into the street. Aris found this a difficult thing to trust. The colour came from the algae growing all along the entrance arch. It grew inside, too, wherever was free from the tyranny of footfall and scraping nets. She stood at the arch, looking down at the reflected colour on her simple breeches and blouse. When had she last stopped, unwound, taken time for herself? Other than the moments before she fell into an exhausted sleep, when she gazed at the horizon of her pillow and just breathed?

'This is not the time,' she said. But it was.

At the desk she paid the two pennies, almost everything she had brought with her, and took the starch-rough towel. The transaction was managed with a total of four words. In the changing room she put her soft sandals and clothes in a wooden box, trying and failing to ignore its musty smell. The smell of countless sweat-lined shoes, years of unwashed clothes, the smell of people. Days and days in the breeding fields, scurrying home through empty tunnels – it was easy to forget that smell. If she had shared a bed... But she did not.

Her coin purse had long strings that she tied behind her neck. It was as light a necklace as any poor woman wore, but she could not afford to have pennies stolen. She could not afford a bath, either, but she put that thought behind her. Naked, she walked along damp corridors, grimacing at first at the wet feeling beneath her feet. And such a waste of water. At least the floor was clear of algae.

She was relieved to find herself alone in the first room. Candles and lamps, placed at discrete intervals, made sure she did not stumble in the dark. Even so, she stepped carefully into the pool of tepid water. Everything in the Tear was warm: the air, the ground, even the darkest parts of the har. But Aris did not really think of it as such, until she had cause to speak to someone from the Commission with their faces red and leaking, and their incessant fanning of themselves. That pompous one with the curls in his hair was particularly sweat-laden. It gathered in the folds of his face when he grinned – he had grinned a lot in those wasted hours when she registered the laying. Aris shuddered, despite the warm pool.

There was a shelf carved into the rock, so she sat and did her best to ease her shoulders and stop her racing thoughts. She had forgotten how much she enjoyed the feeling of water against her skin – water that the Painter had not sent to torment her. Water against the different parts of her body. The sore parts. The parts that felt older. Broken, or just neglected.

She rested her head back and stared up at the bath house ceiling, which was no ceiling at all. The rough, rocky, true face of Hadun-Har was bare to see – as bare as she was. A har was a glorified cave. All who lived in one knew it, but some had pretensions; markets, streets, houses. Though Aris did not know for certain, these things had the taste of the other realms to them. Her home was not a house, and they lived happily in rooms and tunnels. Not so happy now, but still.

She closed her eyes and dozed. Some of the tension leeched from her, she felt herself shrink from the loss of it. In some way that frightened her, though she understood it was a good thing. That tension, that purpose, propelled her from one day to the next. What if it never returned? What if it was lost to this tepid pool of water? What if—?

No, there it was.

She could not lose part of herself so easily. But there was the hot pool.

Unfortunately, there, she was not alone. A group of men lounged at the far end, some in the water and others sitting on the side. They looked up when she entered, but quickly dismissed her. What was she to them?

Except one man. He continued to watch her with a lazy smile. She recognised that smile as much as the man, and her heart sank faster than she did into the hot water and the steam. She should have known Palmi Holgersutter would spend his days in a bath house. How else would a man keep such soft skin? He and his friends talked easily. Laughed without being raucous. Men of leisure, to whom an unknown woman who walked without beauty was not even worthy of their curiosity. She wished she could reciprocate their indifference, but they made her too angry. So she was angry when Palmi eased his way through the water towards her, barely causing a ripple. His skin a uniform smoothness, where hers was blotchy with scars.

'Aris.'

'Hello, Palmi.'

His friends noticed his departure. She steeled herself for jeers and crudeness, but none came. She realised, seeing them properly for perhaps the first time, they were *men*, not boys. The rules were different, they had changed when Aris had not been looking.

'I have not seen you here before,' he said, his tone making his accusation clear: she had not been there before.

'Even beetle breeders need to wash.'

'More than most, I expect.' He sat beside her. 'It is hard work, is it not?'

'It is.'

'But you like it.'

'I do—'

'No, "like" is too small,' he said, resting his head back against the rock. 'My father is the same. His work is his *passion*. It is his despair that I do not share it.'

'*Do* you have a passion, Palmi?' she asked.

'Not that you would recognise. You, or my father.'

'Do they recognise it?' she said, nodding to his friends.

He looked at her then, right at her, with an intensity she had not thought him capable of. She did not know why, and it passed, leaving her confused as he said, 'Shadow dancing. That is my passion. That is what my friends recognise.'

'Dancing?'

'I tell my father not to worry. When time comes, I have plenty of stories to tell the Companion. And any others who care to listen.'

Aris had not thought of shadow dancing for a long time, not since she was a child. It was not an enjoyable thing. Shadows cast by a tornstone lamp that twisted and turned – a light that was as unpredictable as the Audience. How was she to know what to move, and when? The drum's rhythm was one thing, but the lamp's was a mystery. She was both unsurprised that

Palmi shadow danced – such a safe, frivolous way to spend his days – and a little impressed. She had not considered him able to do anything she could not.

She looked at his friends again. A group of young men, not a single woman amongst them. But women shadow danced too. A seed of an idea was sown in that moment. Except, seeds struggle in the Tear – they cannot do their work quickly.

'Our parents want us to marry.' Aris said this aloud because she wanted to hear how ridiculous it was – wanted him to hear it also.

Palmi shrugged. 'Not *your* father.'

'No.'

'But he will join the Audience eventually,' Palmi said without malice. A simple statement of fact. A statement that Palmi would wait if necessary. It was no flattery. He would wait for Aris, she knew, because until *his* father joined the Audience he was in no hurry. He would wait for his little worker-wife. He swam back to his shadow dancers – men with the same inclinations as Palmi. They waved to her in a friendly manner. It was perhaps the most embarrassing thing they could have done. She hurried from the pool.

Aris arrived home in time for lunch. Despite her conversation with Palmi, she did feel more at ease for her bath. She had even shifted some of the layers of ash and dirt under her nails and in the lines of her knuckles. The bath house was a habit she might acquire.

Her mother was waiting in the doorway once again. And once again Aris almost turned back; she still had a penny or two, she would not starve in avoiding whatever – or whoever

– was the cause of Mother's handwringing. But thoughts of her father made her press on. She owed him that much.

'We have *another* visitor,' Mother said. Her smile was forced.

'But I just saw P—'

The small Commission man was sitting at their kitchen table. His long curly hair was tied back but it still managed to both ooze and writhe in the candlelight. Father was sitting with him, evidently unhappy at being roused from his bed once again to make small talk with a man who was not there to see him.

'Mr Pemberton,' she said, surprised at how easily she recalled his name.

'Vernon, please. Hello, Aris.'

'Is there a problem?' She thought of the beetles in their pens. She glanced at her father, who gave a small shake of his head. That was all she needed – she had no desire to tell this man any more than she had to, concerning *anything*, and especially not in their home. Pemberton was not in his office now.

'I hope not,' Vernon said. 'I was worried, you see, when you did not return to me. Wounded, even.'

'Wounded,' she said.

Her mother shooed her towards the table. She had been lingering by the doorway, the hope of escape.

'We registered two other breeding pairs, didn't we, together? And then you did not come to see me about their laying. Why was that, Aris?'

The air in the kitchen tightened, as it did just before an eruption. And just as then, she had to tread carefully. 'Matriarchs can be fickle. They are ready when they are ready.' No good could come of telling this man, this northerner who oversaw Commission ledgers, what had happened to their breeding fields.

'Yes, I see.' He turned to Father. 'Even after all your years, there is no forcing these things, is there?'

'No,' Father said.

Vernon smiled. 'Well, I will leave you fine people to your luncheon.'

'You are not to stay?' Mother said. 'We have plenty.' Her lie was as sad as it was desperate.

The Commission man looked at their table. 'Thank you, but no.' He came to where Aris was sitting. Before she knew what was happening, he had taken her hand in his. 'But I will return for you, Aris. We have much to discuss.'

'Discuss?'

Pulling down his mouthpiece, he kissed her hand, and left three wide-eyed people in his wake.

No one said a word, nor did they move. Clearly each, in their own way, was trying to understand what had just happened – understand, and then move on from it. Aris most of all. But in truth it was beyond them. Aris held up the hand he had kissed, cleaner than it had been in months, and wished she could return to the baths. She would scour her fingers until the feel of his lips was gone, or there was no skin left, whichever came first.

Both her parents were staring at her. One in horror, one in horrified fascination. A Commission man was courting their daughter.

She broke the black bread and chewed, though her mouth was dry.

'I want to see the fields,' Father said. He was standing in the corridor wearing his heavy robe and boots. Aris thought those had gone long ago, when the illness first took him, but she should have known better. He was not a wasteful man.

'There is not much to see,' she said, stopping her sweeping. She was clearing out the beetles' pens, though they were not helping – they chittered and chattered about her, nipping at her broom.

'I want to see them now.'

Aris closed the little gate of Kraki and Kata's pen behind her. With only the three beetles there was little work to do, really, but their company was preferable to her other options. 'They will not mate this season,' she said. 'Not here, not now. But, they are still young – will it be a problem, do you think?'

'They are tough, they will be fine.'

'And us? Without beetles to sell this year?'

'We are tough,' he said.

'For as long as I could speak, I have told myself the same story: I would breed ash beetles, like my father.'

'You have. And you will.'

She wiped her eyes and turned to him. 'I will take you to see the fields. But only as far as Brawler's Bridge. From there, you will see everything.'

He took her arm as she led him back through their home. She had wondered if they might slip free without notice, but her mother had the hearing of a firecat. She fussed about them – her father staring stoically ahead – and tried to press provisions on them, as if the short walk would take weeks. When that failed, she asked each member of the Audience in turn why she was married to a stubborn mule who had given her a stubborn daughter. Mother had never seen a mule. Aris had once, at a distance. She would have said it was sad, not stubborn.

On their way out of the kitchen, her father stopped long

enough to pick up his walking stick; an old piece of polished Seeder wood. It was perhaps the most expensive thing he owned that was not a beetle. Yet he still leaned on Aris as they walked.

They made slow progress and stopped often, especially if there were steps. Whether it was up or down, he was happy to sit on a step and wait for his breath, which was quickly lost and difficult to find. They only saw one other person on such an occasion, whom Aris did not know but her father greeted. He was not embarrassed. Perhaps he had made similar short walks about the har while she was working the fields. She had assumed he spent his days in bed; that was where she left him in the morning and found him in the evening. But in truth she had given it little thought, beyond an underlying worry that her father was not a well man. That he, as Palmi had effortlessly said, would join the Audience soon.

'Do you think about death, Father?' she asked, as they stopped once more, this time at a bench carved into a tunnel wall. She had been arguing with herself whether to ask, and decided it was unfair to do so while he was so firmly focused on putting one foot in front of the other.

'Yes,' he said.

She waited for him to elaborate, but he did not. 'Does it frighten you?' she said.

'Not until recently.'

'Why?'

'Because I knew you would look after yourself and your mother. That I had given you that much, at least.'

'And now you are not so sure.'

'Now I am frightened,' he said, touching her hand.

'There are men who want to marry me, Father.'

'I know it! They keep plaguing my table.'

'If I marry one of them, you would not have to be frightened,' Aris said quietly.

'No, I would have to be angry.' He spat and then licked his teeth. 'Those are your mother's fancies, Aris, your mother's games. We let her have that much, do we not?'

She nodded.

'But we know they are no more than that. If I thought you were considering one of them...' He waved his walking stick, and the picture was clear.

'Natalia Geirsdattir says I should have children.'

'She is right, you should. We all should. There are too few of us – look at our har. Did your mother ever tell you why—'

'Yes, Father, because I cried too much.'

'No, although there was crying. We did not have a second child because your mother bedded another man,' he said.

'What?'

'Just once. So long ago now, you were only a child, all has been forgiven and mostly forgotten. But at the time it was different. I was stupid and I was furious and I was hurt. So we did not have another child, though we should have.'

Aris had many questions, some obvious and some not so obvious, but when she started to ask them she realised she did not want to know the answers. There was much she did not understand about her mother and father, and much she did not take the time to understand. That they were people who existed beyond their interactions with her was still an uncomfortably new idea.

Instead, she said, 'I wonder if all people speak about breeding the way we do.'

'We are breeders by profession, for generations.'

'Yes, but those in the markets? In the bath houses and the bars? Or even in the other realms?'

'The other realms have the other problem: there is too many of them. Do you remember when I took you with me to see a Seeder buyer?'

She said she did.

'Do you remember all those children in the barn? So many they were just a mess of eyes in the dark.'

She had not forgotten, though she had tried. 'There were more children there than in the whole har.'

'We Torn talk about breeding because we have to. But it is mostly talk.'

'People are happy to tell me I should have children,' Aris said. 'I think that is because I breed ash beetles, not just because I am Torn.'

'Could be,' he said. 'And it could be people are happy to tell others what to do.'

'Are you ready, Father?'

'To die?'

'No! To see the fields.'

'I suppose I am.'

Brawler's Bridge spanned one of the larger blood flows from Hadun. It was also the easiest way to cross from one side of the Hadun-Valley to the other, sitting as it did at the head of the valley. But few people had cause to cross the valley – their business, like Aris's, was on one side, not both. Such a wide, well-built bridge spoke of different times; of the laden carts of travelling merchants, skittish herds of Wayward animals, and those curious to see how the Torn lived. All counted and noted by the Commission, of course. It had never been so in her lifetime, but she had heard the stories and sometimes those were more powerful than memories. Now, they were alone on the black rock bridge.

Father was determined to have the best view. He would not go to the low wall until they reached the middle of the bridge's hump. When finally there, he stood at the parapet and looked out. Aris had never seen him so small.

Hadun-Valley was still there. Of course it was: the Tear had not swallowed it whole – she had not realised until that moment that, in her imagination, it had gone completely. Her part of it was, so the rest was too.

The valley was aglow. The colour of molten rock, as common in the Tear as candlelight, was as intense as she had ever seen it. The heat buffeted them. She felt her skin tighten, dry out, and it was not entirely unpleasant.

'Over there,' Father said, gesturing to a striped lake of blood half obscured by smoke.

'Yes.'

That was where their enclosures had been. The ground a perfect mix of ash and sand and grit for ash beetles to lay their eggs. The shack with their assorted tools and workings. Harnesses whose leather was older than she was. None of it expensive, just irreplaceable.

From the bridge it was possible to trace the river of blood from Hadun all along the valley. Thin, no more than a stream in places, as wide as the valley would allow in others. That was how Natalia Geirsdattir and a few others had been able to save some part of their lives.

'The Audience make him bleed for it,' Father said eventually. 'But it is never enough.'

'I saw it rise from the ground, where the beetles dug. If I had not...'

'The Caskers have rivers of water. So much water, too much for a well or a spring. Can you even picture such a thing?'

She could not, though she did not think her father was lying. There was too much awe, too much longing in his voice for a lie.

'You were right, Aris. There is no way back from this.'

'I will find a way.'

'Not here.'

'No. There will be change,' she said.

'Then it will make for a good story.'

The return journey was slow, her father having to stop more regularly. At such stops they did not speak; their agreement to make one stop at a barroom was a silent one. It overlooked the lower market, but was not the same barroom where she had taken three beetles and mended the shreds of her courage.

'I have been drinking more of late,' she said, as they both drained their glasses and poured another.

'You will. You are a good girl,' he said.

She looked down at the stalls. 'Life in a market is to always be packing things away.'

'If you choose that, if you choose Holger's boy, be sure.' They both drank. 'You can never be sure, but be sure.'

She remembered Palmi at the bath house, swimming back to his friends. The certainty of their waving. They knew she would not marry him.

'Those are big beetles,' Aris said. The cloth seller was loading his trumpet beetle again, for another day.

'Too big.'

'Perhaps.'

'What would it fight, a horse?' He laughed, but stopped

when he saw her face. Then he looked at the trumpet beetle again. 'Big does not fight well. Big does not have to, it is big.'

'Perhaps,' she said.

'Bears – from where the Steppes meets Perlanse. But with bears, the fight is slow.'

'And it requires more room.'

'Too much. In Fenest, maybe.'

'Here,' she said.

'Where "here"?'

She spread her arms like a tatterwing and turned in the empty barroom. 'There is room in Hadun-Har for anything.'

'No money here. Need to go north for the money.'

'Then who is paying for our mutters?' she said.

When they left the barroom, she glanced one last time to the market floor and the trumpet beetle.

'Aris?' Father said.

'This could help.'

'Help what?'

'Everything,' she said.

Outside their home, it was Father's turn to stop them. He embraced her and thanked her, without saying what for. 'Do speak to your mother of what I told you.'

She could not imagine ever doing so.

'It has been forgiven, and mostly forgotten.'

'So you said.'

'I say again, so it will be true for you.'

'It is not a thing for me to forgive,' Aris said. 'And I am busy enough to forget.'

'Good.'

But, even though Aris meant what she had said, she was surprised to find the knowledge did affect her. As they entered their home, she saw her mother differently. It was not that Mother herself had changed, had not done so for many years as far as Aris was concerned, except that she *was* changed. The fretting and the fussing took on a new shape; it was penance, of a kind. Mother hurried Father to bed, fetched him water and cooled a cloth for his head, made sure he was comfortable and then turned her attention to Aris. Had she eaten? No, of course not. She could not look after herself, not properly, not without her mother. Aris and Father needed her.

Aris let this wash over her, though it stung like the Painter's rain. There were things that could not be changed. And some that could.

That evening, Natalia Geirsdattir came. Aris was with the ash beetles, her chores long finished, but lingering for the company. The beetles chortled about her, clearly restless in this place where they did not belong. Kata would not let Kraki near, snapping at him if he strayed too close. For their part, the two males postured though would not come to blows – what was the point in such a place? That they were safe appeared to be small comfort to the beetles themselves, but it meant much to Aris as she sat with them.

That was where Natalia found her. The big woman filled the doorway. That she had neither Father nor Mother in her wake was not lost on Aris; the only way such a thing was possible was to come into their home through the tunnels. Natalia came in but did not sit. Instead, she stood at the little pen fence, its top not reaching her knees, and shook her head.

'I am sorry, Aris. I looked to your fields, but there is nothing to save.'

'Father says there is no way back.'

'And what do you say?'

'He is wrong.'

'He is.' Natalia turned to her. 'Do not mistake what I am about to offer as pity.'

'I should fetch Father.'

'No, this is not an offer for him. It is your business now – we all know it.'

Doari climbed onto Aris's lap and began to pulse. 'Father still meets with the northern buyers. If a hand needs shaking, he is the one to do it.'

'I am offering to buy your business, Aris. *Yours*.'

'What is there to buy? Three beetles – a young pair yet to breed, and a widower?'

'Yes three beetles. Yes whatever supplies and stores you have here. And yes, those northern buyers who like shaking your father's hand and not mine. They all have a price.'

'And what of me?' Aris said.

'Work for me, in the fields. It is what you do well.'

Even without talk of numbers, Aris knew this was not pity. It was not generosity, either. Natalia was a friend of her family, but more so she was a shrewd woman.

'I cannot sell,' Aris said. 'What a final tale my father would have for the Audience.'

'He said himself, that part of his tale is over.'

'It is. But I want what you have, Natalia: to breed beetles of my own. To work for someone else? I could marry Palmi and sell holens if I wanted that.'

Natalia smiled. Even her teeth were large. 'I understand. The offer will be there until you no longer need it. And Aris, some advice if you will hear it: this was Rafnar's—' she gestured to the beetles '— but that was before. Now it is yours, so make it that.'

Aris lifted Doari from her lap, stood in front of her big friend, and said, 'Who in Hadun-Har breeds trumpet beetles?'

It was not lost on Aris, as she made her way to the lowest levels of Lower Hadun-Har, that the Audience had presented her with possibilities. When she had fled the breeding fields with only three beetles she was unable to think beyond what had been, and what had been lost. Now, she had offers from two men and a competitor. Who, among the Audience, would be interested in such things? The Patron? The Glutton? The Companion, of course, but perhaps more so the Drunkard. What were marriages and business agreements for if not the entertainment of fools? Aris did not find these offers, these possibilities, reassuring. Each meant a failure of a kind. They were motivations for her to find a different story to tell whoever would listen.

Natalia had been surprised by her question of trumpet breeders. But the woman did know the only two people making a living in Hadun-Har that way: one was a charlatan, the other talked too much. The choice may have been obvious, but it was not necessarily easy. Had the charlatan been closer, Aris might have taken her chances. As it was, she found herself standing at the entrance to a cavern that smelled strongly of dung and dreading the approach of a slim woman.

Torfa Barasdattir introduced herself as if they had been friends as children and not seen each other since. She was old enough to be Aris's mother. Aris shook her hand and did her best to smile.

'Ash beetles? I could have guessed, could have guessed, to look at you,' Torfa said. 'Many scars, and easy to tell another breeder, is it not? We have a way about us, bringing so many things into the world.' Torfa had many scars of her own, though few on her face.

'Yes. You might—'

'Too much trouble, ash beetles. Are they not? Too much.'

'Well—'

'All beetles are fastidious, but ash? Too particular. Worse than my children. You have children?'

'No.'

'I could have guessed, could have. How could you have children with ash beetles?' Torfa closed her mouth for perhaps the first time since they had met and looked squarely at Aris.

'It would be difficult,' Aris said eventually, to fill the silence.

'What do you want?'

Aris was grateful to finally get to the point of her visit. 'First, to see the breeding of trumpet beetles. Then to buy one.'

'Buy *one*. Sensible,' Torfa said, her hands on her hips. 'No room in this enclosure for another trumpet breeder, is there? They live long, grow strong, person buys a trumpet beetle twice in their life, maybe.'

Torfa turned and walked through a metal gate, the bars of which were thicker than the woman's arm and ran right to the ceiling.

'Do your beetles try to escape?'

'What? Escape? No, why should they? This is easy life here: sleep, eat, mate, sleep again. No, once there were enough people in the har that some thought to steal trumpet beetles. Now, why bother?'

Bars and gates were common in the cavern; the equivalent,

Aris supposed, of pitched wooden fences in the breeding fields of the valley. But behind the first bars were not beetles, but horses. Two horses. Aris stopped and stared.

'Bored, lazy, keep them just for their dung, see? And they know it. Tried working them once.' Torfa spat on the straw that spilled from the enclosure.

Aris tried to remember stories from her childhood that involved horses. 'You do not... ride them?'

'Ha! Where? The tunnels, and hit my head with each step? Or outside the har? With their legs-like-pins we would both find our way to the Audience. I give them hay, they give me dung. Otherwise, we ignore each other.'

'Why d—'

'You know why,' Torfa said. 'Same reason your beetles need ash and sand and whatever else you give them: have to lay somewhere. Look here.'

The next barred enclosure held a large pile of horse dung. Dark, round layers like smoothed stones, like cooled Wit's Blood without the hot veins. The smell was heavy all about her, but sluggish, not a smell that was insistent. It was simply there. On the other side of the enclosure were two huge beetles, as big as the horses and entirely motionless.

'The eggs are in the dung?' Aris said.

'Pile it high and she is happy. Not as many as you might be used to, but do you see any tatterwings or firecats here?'

'They do not fuss over the eggs? Not even the male?'

'They sleep. That is what they do.' Torfa laughed. 'You are in the wrong business, I think, and starting to realise.'

In the low light of the enclosure's single torch, the trumpet beetles looked huge. If they could be roused, made fierce; what man or woman, drink burning a hole in their belly, would not roar and cheer and lose their money as two such creatures clashed? Just the noise of their wing-covers colliding would stir a crowd, let alone their pincers.

Torfa talked too much, but she clearly knew an eager customer when they were kind enough to walk themselves through her gate. She steered Aris to an enclosure on the other side of the cavern, away from the breeding pairs.

'Here, full grown and ready to work,' Torfa said. 'No trouble for you, these males, carry all you want through the Tear – even carry crates of your ash beetles.'

'I want a female.'

For the second time since they had met, Torfa was silent for longer than was comfortable. A male trumpet beetle flexed its casings, then settled once more.

'Why female?' Torfa said, narrowing her eyes.

'How many larval sheddings for a trumpet?'

'Twenty, sometimes more. Sometimes fewer. Fewer is bad, get you smaller beetle. Not your kind of small, but small.'

'They still breed when they are *your* kind of small?' Aris said, trying to sound curious but not interested.

'Not here, not for me.'

'But they could.'

'Yes, they could.'

'I want a small female,' Aris said. 'And, when she is ready, some dung.'

The wait was not as long as Torfa Barasdattir had warned, but it was long. Aris kept herself busy with the beetles she *did* have while thinking of those she did not. She also found a cavern in Lower Hadun-Har, not too close to Torfa and far smaller than her own, but big enough for Aris's needs. She could not keep trumpet beetles at home, nor could she be under the gaze of her parents as she tried what was new. She would rather keep the likely failure secret, so instead let her parents believe in the obvious failure in front of them. Her mother worried, her father compensated with an optimism he did not feel. Aris made sure she drank too much at home, and never elsewhere. But the wait was not without trial.

As discreetly as anything could be done in Hadun-Har, she discovered who owned the unused cavern: an old man whose only son had left for the eastern Tear. The man's voice hitched and buckled at the mention of his son. Aris did not speak of him again. Her request to rent the cavern was initially met with indifference.

'Use it with my blessing,' the man said.

'I intend to use it for business, and so require a formal arrangement. Otherwise the Commission...'

She need say no more. They lost much of the afternoon trading tales of Commission misery, though Aris omitted one in particular. The Audience punished her for that.

The man insisted on a mutters once the deal was struck and Aris had talked him up to a manageable, but believable rate. The bottle was old and better than the swill she bought cheaply for the tale she told her parents. So much better to just enjoy the taste and toast the old man. She did not see him again for many years.

She took his name, while she still remembered it, to the Commission.

Vernon Pemberton was upon her before she reached the first

desk in the office, as if he had been waiting by the door every minute of every day. He took her not to a spare desk, but to a private room. All the northerners stared as she walked past, and the older ones did so with pity. But what could she do?

The little room had a desk, two chairs, and a long soft seat of the kind the northerners liked. It was there he sat and told her to do the same. She perched on the edge, not fond of the sensation of sinking and very much aware of the closed door.

'I hoped you would be in to see me soon,' Vernon said.

'I have rented a cavern.'

'Congratulations! How wonderful. A cavern!'

She told him where and from whom and, though he clearly did not want to, he could not stop himself from writing the information down. But he did so sloppily and not in the appropriate ledger.

'We must celebrate,' he said, opening drawers in his desk.

'What is to celebrate?'

'Your new venture!'

She glanced at the door. 'But I did not tell you.'

'Why, then you *must*. No, wait. I do *love* guessing games.'

So often she did not understand what his words meant, and hid in the safety of her own silence. He did not seem to mind. He placed two glasses on the desk and poured something dark and red.

'Warehousing,' he said, passing her a glass.

She sipped out of politeness, but the taste was so strong and full and unnecessary she couldn't have drunk any more. He took her silence to mean her cavern was not a warehouse.

'Don't tell me, don't tell me. You need more breeding room for your ash beetles – it has been a good year!'

She shook her head, not trusting her own voice.

'Well, well.' He tapped the side of his face. 'You have acquired the business of a competitor.'

'No.'

'Seeking to export other goods to the north.'

He was excited. He stared into her eyes and his legs would not be still. Was it the game, or was he trying to catch her in a Commission trap?

'Yes,' she said, slowly, hoping a half-truth was the safer choice.

'Excellent!' he said. 'No, don't tell me yet. I want to save some surprises for next time.'

'Next—'

'Now, where did I jot your cavern's details?'

'There,' Aris said, pointing to the small scruffy ledger on his desk.

'I can be so forgetful sometimes, especially after a drink!' He had not sipped from his glass. 'But, do you know what always helps my memory?'

'It is right there,' she said again.

He came to sit next to her on the soft seat. 'A kiss from a pretty girl.' He lifted his mouthpiece and presented his cheek. 'Come now, we wouldn't want your new venture to have any problems with the Commission, would we?'

She looked at his sweat-sheened face.

Despite herself, she leaned forward. Despite keeping her eyes open, she was too slow.

He twisted at the last moment. Their lips touched and then she was up, and away, and across the room.

'Our first kiss!' he said.

She did not look at any of the northerners as she strode past their desks.

At home she scrubbed her face and her hands with sand

until she drew blood. She washed her teeth with mutters without swallowing. Mother was out, but Father could hear her cursing.

She filled the rest of her waiting days with the clearing of the cavern and the building of enclosures. There was no money for new wood, but she salvaged what she could from wherever she could. Among the detritus and dust in the cavern she found an old cart. It had one wheel missing and much of its bed was broken. She made twenty feet of fencing from it. She did not know if it would be high enough or strong enough, but fences could be mended, and they could be reinforced. She fashioned a gate-workings from parts of broken harnesses. It was good to be working again. Clear-headed and absorbed in a task that had a simple, obvious meaning. When she wasted a good few minutes wondering what she would do for pitch to save the fence from the Painter's rain, she was even able to laugh at herself. There would be many adjustments to come.

She did not have metal for a front gate. Instead, she made a small shrine to the Bailiff and told him stories of a beetle that did not exist yet, that would fight in pits no one had built yet, for an Audience that had never seen the like before. And this was just the beginning if he would keep the thieves from her cavern... once she had something to steal.

The moving of Doari, Kraki and Kata was soured by a lie. Aris had hoped to lead them out through the tunnels, not through the house. But she made too much noise. Or the beetles did.

'Where will you take them?' Father said, his blanket wrapped around his shoulders. Mother was looking on from behind him. Her being there made the lie all the worse. But Aris could not tell him, not yet.

'Natalia offered one of her enclosures. She has her larvae inside, so can spare it.'

'Really?' he said.

'I will be glad to be rid of their clicking and clacking,' Mother said.

Her father said nothing for a time. His disappointment filled the corridor like smoke and she found it hard to breathe.

'Nothing is more painful, more loved by the Audience, than change,' he said, and shuffled back to his room.

Her mother tried to smile for her. 'Aris, please, wait—'

But she would not. She led the beetles away. It was only when she was in Lower Hadun-Har that she realised what pain her father was speaking of. He thought she was selling their beetles.

She woke the next day on a bed of rags in the cavern. She tried to rid herself of the taste of yesterday's drink and sweat-stained cloth, but no amount of spitting helped.

Kraki and Kata were happy enough in their enclosure; Kata could have some peace without her mate stumbling all over her. Doari, however, was not so comfortable. He kept rushing from one side of the enclosure to the other as if to be sure it was as big as he first thought. When he butted the fences he was most upset with how they shook. He knew something was wrong. That something big was coming.

'You are right,' she told him.

And it arrived that morning, walking alongside Torfa

Barasdattir without a lead or a harness. When Torfa stopped, so did the trumpet beetle. The pair waited politely at what could have been described as the entrance.

Aris refused to run, as much as she wished to. But Torfa was smiling so she allowed herself that much.

'I should be worried,' Torfa said. 'You setting up down here, like me?'

'But small.'

'But small,' the woman agreed. 'I made sure you did not buy a male trumpet elsewhere.'

'She is all I need. She is perfect.'

The trumpet beetle was a deep red that shone when she caught the torchlight, but was black when she did not. She came up to Torfa's waist, and was an almost perfect dome. Her head was stubby and small, with short antennae.

'What is her name?' Aris asked.

'Name?' Torfa looked at the beetle as if seeing her for the first time. 'Why would I give a beetle a name?'

Aris knelt down beside the big beetle. 'Hello, Dalla.'

Torfa laughed, startling Aris and Dalla both. 'You ash breeders spend too long outside.'

'Not outside now.' Aris took her coin purse from around her neck and gave it to Torfa.

'You do not need to count it?' Torfa said.

'No.' She knew exactly how much was inside: everything she had.

Torfa left with the promise of regular deliveries of fresh dung. She said that helped her trumpet beetles. Would it help Aris's? Neither woman knew, and neither knew just what to call the results of the union Aris was working towards. Aris had thought on this, in idle hours before sleep or wandering poorly lit tunnels: what to call her new type of beetle. But she had shied away from a decision. It was too early for that. Too much could go wrong or simply not happen at all. A name invited a kind of tale that the Audience revelled in. Dashed hopes. The struggle to dream. Our own, personal failures.

The trumpet beetle Dalla had passed into Aris's ownership with a simple ritual. Under Torfa's guidance, Aris had knelt before the beetle and presented her hands, palms up. The beetle's antennae had stroked her dry palms and it was done. It needed to be done every morning, Torfa said, except on the day you wish to pass the beetle to another.

So it was that when Torfa turned to go, the beetle stayed with Aris. She did not need a lead. She walked Dalla over to the largest of her modest enclosures, where Doari was waiting. He was very still. Aris remembered him, back in the lower market, challenging a huge trumpet beetle. But that had been a male. She opened the gate and led Dalla inside.

The two beetles faced each other. Dalla was at least a foot larger in every direction. Her red colouring was too dull and her shape too round to think her aggressive. Grey, horned Doari, sleek so as to be nimble in the ring, could not have looked more different. As their antennae tested the air between them, Aris came to realise the enormity of what she was trying to achieve. She wanted something that had never happened before. But these were new times. If change could be made for the worse, perhaps there was room for her hopes.

Doari and Dalla stood there for a long time. At first Aris watched from inside the enclosure, then wondered if her presence was unwelcome. She closed the gate behind her and watched from outside and still they did not move. On occasion a leg twitched, or a wing-casing shifted, though that may have been her imagination. The longer this continued, the more certain she was that something was passing between them. Not words or ideas or promises, but something as important. A foundation, of a kind. Despite that feeling she could not leave them. She wanted to be ready if that foundation proved too weak. Doari was still proud, still a fighter.

Eventually, she sat on the hard rock floor. It was good to be at their height. An hour passed, maybe more. She lay on her back but ready, her breathing as quiet as she could make it. Her heart slowed. She felt close to them, felt that she understood.

Dalla broke her own spell. She left Doari standing there and wandered the extent of her new enclosure. Then, she settled in one corner.

What did it mean?

Aris was not the only one to ask that question, now and later and many times more. She took a deep breath and roused herself to feed the other beetles. She was also hungry, but that could wait. Doari took to his food as if the past few hours had been spent in the ring. Perhaps they had been.

She spent the rest of the day either watching Doari and Dalla or hurrying through chores to get back to them. When evening came and her hunger would not be denied, she permitted herself the black bread and small piece of cheese she had set aside for the day. It was, in its own way, a day worthy of celebration. A day anticipated for some time. And she was capable of waiting again. She collected her bed of rags and moved it beside the enclosure. She had time to pick through them and discard the worst, but that was done mostly to pass the time. Who was here to care how she smelled?

As she settled down to sleep she bid her beetles goodnight. Dalla was still in her corner. Doari was pretending to be busy among the rotten wood and rocks Aris had put in the enclosure to stop him becoming bored. He was fooling no one.

They might never mate. That was the thought that snagged at her, that refused to let her sleep. The first day was for nothing more than introductions; she had not even received any dung from Torfa yet. They might never mate. They had only just met. One very young, the other old enough to have lost a mate. One a champion, the other a runt. They might never mate. Doari understood clouded skies, burrowing against the Painter's rain, fifty holes in the ash. Dalla understood to carry whatever was put on her back, to follow her master, and to lay eggs in dung without ever having done so herself. They might never mate.

It was not lost on Aris that her fortunes, and the fortunes of her family, rested on a trumpet beetle doing what she herself would not: choosing an incompatible, unwanted mate.

For a moment she saw her mother's face, eager and false. Then sleep took her in a fitful, restless embrace. She woke often, and listened hard in case of movement from inside the enclosure. But the night was still and hot and hers was the only desire that stirred.

Torfa came the next day with dung. She led an enormous trumpet beetle to the entrance of the cavern, a basket on its back. Strange to have one animal carry the droppings of another. Though those droppings helped birth that animal, so... Aris pinched her brow to chase away unhelpful thoughts.

'Best not let the little girl see this one,' Torfa said. 'That would be a kind of cruel, I think. How was the night?'

'Quiet,' Aris said.

'Such things take time.' The skinny woman slapped the basket. 'And dung!'

Together they wrestled the dung from the trumpet beetle's back and carried it to the enclosure.

Doari was ready to meet them. He spread his wing-casing and showed them his full size. When they opened the gate he snapped the air with his pincers and made as if to charge.

'Is he always feisty?' Torfa said.

'No.'

'A good sign. I married my first husband because he was the only one in the barroom to throw something when I walked in. He was— Stop that!'

Doari had attacked the basket with a ferocity that Aris recognised. Torfa had clearly not been to a ring for some time; she dropped her end of the basket and hurried back. This only spurred Doari's efforts. Aris managed to upend most of the basket onto the ground before it was lost entirely. Shreds of woven reeds fell like ash. Then she retreated with Torfa and left the male beetle to his victory. If his companion was moved by this display at all, she did not show it.

Dalla was, however, stirred into movement by the dung. She shook herself, creating a cloud of dust, and came to inspect the heap.

'She will know what to do,' Torfa said. 'There is no escaping what we are.'

'That is what worries me.'

'I will bring fresh dung in a week. That can help. I sell the old on to the growers.'

'I have little—'

'Ah, you worry too much,' Torfa said. 'In a week. Check your heap each morning, tell the Matron a tale each night, and who knows?'

That is what Aris did. For the next four days she did not leave the cavern, except to find food and to empty her chamber pot. She did not go home. It was too far, she told herself. But the truth was she could not face her father. Not without something to show for her efforts. For food, she relied on Holger Falkisutter's misguided generosity. At first, she asked for the meagre bread and fruit to be put on her slate. They soon dispensed with that formality. She would have dearly liked a bottle of mutters to pass the quieter evening hours but that was one thing in the har that could not be bought on a promise.

Every morning she dragged herself from her rag bed and stretched, and then ventured into Doari and Dalla's enclosure. Neither beetle appeared to care. They kept to their separate sides – Dalla's included the dung – and barely moved until it was feeding time. Doari's fire and bluster had run its course. It had been wasted. They made a sad pair, Aris thought, as she knelt at the heap. And what did they make of her? Delicately lifting nuggets of horse dung, hands heavy with hope. She made sure not to look at Dalla after. She would *not* blame the beetle. This was her fault.

She tried other things after those first few mornings of disappointment. She did not feed them one night. That roused Doari to protest throughout the late hours, banging against the fence, until Aris could take no more. Her suggestion that his efforts could be put to better use fell on deaf ears. Deaf, too, was the Matron. Before Aris closed her eyes each night she told the Matron a tale of a beetle breeder, displaced, trying to find a new way to breed, may it please her. Did she not want such stories to continue?

Aris tried other things.

She collected a bucketful of ash from beyond the main gate. She ignored those that stared. With the bucket in hand she climbed where the fence was sturdy on Doari's side of the enclosure. Both beetles watched her.

'I will not fall,' she told them. She put one foot on the top rung, before her determination was tempered by her sense and she stood on the rung below. Steady, she threw the ash to the air. Before the bucket was empty she swung it back and forth in imitation of the Bore's best winds. For near a minute it rained ash in the cavern, and Doari danced in it. Danced as it fell, and danced when it littered the floor. Though the ash was for his benefit, his happiness hurt.

'I am sorry,' she said. She said it until her apologies drove her from the cavern, and back to the person most deserving of them.

She entered the kitchen as though nothing had changed: Aris returning from another day toiling at the family work. But she did not have boots that needed cleaning; her heavy cloak still hung from its hook, unnecessary; and her mother was not waiting for her, and yet was. Mother leapt up from the table and came to her. She kissed both of Aris's eyes and started to cry. Before Aris could say a word, it was her mother who was apologising. Though she would not say what for.

'Rafnar, look who has come to see us,' Mother called.

'How can I see from here?' he shouted back.

'Your father has missed you,' Mother said, and led Aris into his bedroom.

Father was lying with his back to them. She crossed the room and sat by the bed. 'Hello, Father.'

'Oh. You still live here I see.'

'Rafnar!'

'I did not sell Kraki or Kata or Doari,' she said.

'Oh.'

'I do not drink myself to a stupor each day.'

'What do you do?' he said.

'Not yet, Father, not yet.'

He closed his eyes. 'Then come back when yet is ready.'

'He is tired,' Mother whispered as they left him to sleep.

'He is dying.'

'Yes.' Mother poured them both a glass of mutters. 'Yes, you are beyond old enough to understand that.' They drank, and then together prepared a meal in near silence. Aris was grateful for the absence of curiosity, of questions. Of care. She was also grateful for a respectable meal.

'Fetch your father,' Mother said when the food was ready. 'Stubborn, he insists on eating at the table.'

Aris put down a plate of roasted medlars.

'Wait.' Mother brushed her hands against her apron. 'I have something for you. But you must know, I am sorry. It was wrong and I will never forgive myself.'

'I know.' Aris did not want to talk about *that*. She was tired and the smell of horse dung would not leave her alone. The time would never be right to discuss her mother's infidelity.

Mother nodded, but then she crossed the kitchen. From one of the many baskets she pulled Aris's rain-veil. The veil Aris had lost in those last days she worked the breeding fields.

'I did not take it,' Mother said. 'But I did not give it back. I wanted you to stop going out to the fields. I thought... I was foolish.'

Aris took the rain-veil from her. 'I had forgotten about this.'

'You do not need it?' Despite her apology, Mother could not hide the hope in her voice.

'No. Not anymore.'

She woke Father from his rest and helped him from the bed. He smelled stale and dry. When upright, he coughed until he bent double, though nothing came of it. He had nothing wet to spare. With her help, he shuffled to the kitchen table and picked at the food on his plate, his eyes down.

Aris ate with the hunger of many missed meals. This pleased her mother, as if the provision of food was recompense for her previous wrongs. To explain otherwise was beyond Aris – she was too tired and she was not that cruel. It was a simple meal with simple conversation. It was a shame to have such a thing interrupted.

But then Vernon Pemberton announced himself at the doorway to their kitchen.

Her father sighed and her mother was quickly up and welcoming the small northerner inside. She knew better this time than to offer him their food.

He also refused the offer of drink.

The shock of the insult left the room still and tense – Aris had felt nothing like it since she was a little girl and Hadun had murmured in its sleep.

Vernon continued to talk regardless. 'Official business I'm afraid, Mrs Domarsutter.'

Mrs – an aftershock.

'I'm aware of your... situation, very sorry indeed in fact,' Vernon said. He did not sound sorry. 'I assumed that was why you'd not been in to register this year's exports. Thought I'd save you the trouble.'

Aris glanced at her father. For a moment she entertained the hope that he might answer for them, that she would not have to even look at the vile creature standing at the head of their table. But Father was too angry to speak. He had a grip on his knife that worried Aris. She was trying to save their business from one disaster – she did not need another.

After a deep breath, she said, 'No, Vernon, we have no beetles for export this year.' Saying this thing before her parents, before a Commission man, before the Audience, was the most shaming moment of her life.

'None?' he said, surprised. Despite what he had said, he did not know what had happened to their family. That, or he had a cruelty in him that was as foreign to Aris as his long curls.

'But next year,' she said, desperate to salvage a scrap of pride, 'next year we will have a full slate again.'

They were all looking at her. None of them sure enough, brave enough, to call her a liar or worse.

'Well,' Vernon said. 'That *is* a relief. Because, you see, I am also here to invite you to a Commission dinner. We have the good fortune of entertaining the visiting Director of Trade, Livestock, and Realm Affairs. And I thought, who better to entertain him than my very own beetle breeder?'

'Anyone.'

'Pardon me, my dear?'

'Anyone would be better,' Aris said. She stood. 'I have work to do.'

'But— But—'

As she left the kitchen she thought she saw a small smile from her father. She walked quickly through tunnels, then stopped and listened. When she was sure Vernon was not following her, she continued on to her cavern and her work.

***

At the entrance she stopped at the shrine and told the Bailiff that, at least for another day, no one had stolen the little she had – and that she was grateful. Even she could not see how the ending for her tale would please the Audience. But that was their way, was it not? The twist. The surprise. Not the dagger carefully watched in front, but the blade plunged in the back.

Seeing her father take to his cutlery with intent had shaken her. More than Vernon and his foolish invitation. In an attempt to forget them all, she went straight to Doari and Dalla's enclosure. It was many hours until morning but she wanted to check the dung heap. She was so determined, she had rolled up her sleeves and almost opened the gate before she noticed what was happening. What Doari was doing.

He was dancing again. Not amongst the ash that lay scattered on the ground, not this time, but instead in front of Dalla. His wing-casing was open, but not just fluttering as was normal. Aris had the impression he was stretching. And amid his scuttling to and fro he pushed himself upwards, onto his back legs. Briefly, Aris was distracted by memories of his previous mate, Dyrley, doing the same to lay her eggs in the ash. Though he could not stay in such a position for long, he continued to try. Trying to... what? Impress his new mate? Seduce her? Intimidate her?

No, Aris realised. This was a simple thing.

He was trying to look bigger than he really was.

Aris moved for a better view of Dalla. The trumpet beetle was still in her corner, but Doari's dancing was not lost on her. Periodically she roused herself, as if readying to stand, but then stopped. Aris watched until she understood, then longer to be certain.

Dalla was almost fooled. But it was not his size that was failing the ash beetle. It was his sound.

He was making the wrong sounds. And doing so to a *trumpet* beetle.

It was a sharp form of tragedy, but Aris was hardened to that now. Had been made hard by Wit's Blood and northern men and a family's expectations.

What was it that Torfa had said? Best not let Dalla see a male trumpet beetle, that would be cruel? Perhaps it was time for Aris to find that in herself.

She ran the whole way to Torfa's cavern, through twisting pitch-black tunnels, fortunate that they were as empty as they were dark. Her haste was wasted somewhat as she arrived and could not speak for want of breath. Torfa crossed her arms and waited, for once at a loss for words.

'I need—' Aris struggled between gulps of air, her head between her knees '—need to. Borrow. A male trumpet.'

'What is this "borrow"?'

'Please, Torfa. I just need the noise of it.'

'Well, they are plenty noisy.'

Timed to please the Audience, the deep honk of a full grown male trumpet beetle all but shook the cavern.

'You have no money,' Torfa said. She did not make Aris say it. 'But there will be a time you do, correct?'

'Yes.'

'Remember this then.' Torfa led her to the nearest enclosure and opened the gate. 'Time to walk,' she said, slapping the wing-casing of a beetle taller than she was. It turned and followed her without complaint. Though it was not alone. 'No! Not you.' Torfa shooed another male back. 'Anything for some excitement. You will have as much excitement as a beetle needs when you are hauling rock all day.'

'Rock?'

'A boring story. Miners need beetles.'

They walked either side of the beetle, out of the cavern, until the tunnels narrowed. Torfa, unburdened by Aris's hurrying, remembered to bring a torch. Together, they led the docile beetle on his walk.

'I think it is long past time you tell me,' Torfa said, 'what you are doing with my trumpet beetles.'

'They are not all yours. And you know: trying to breed ash with trumpet.'

'Yes, but *why*?'

'To fight.'

Torfa stopped. Fortunately, so did the beetle behind them. 'Fight what?'

'Each other,' Aris said. 'Though, according to my father, northerners sometimes fight bears.'

'What is "bears"?'

'I do not know, but they are big.'

'Horse big?' Torfa shook her head. 'I did not ask this before because it is your story to tell, when and *if* you wanted.'

'You do not approve?'

'You do not need my approval. Do ash beetles like to fight?'

'Ask my fences,' Aris said, but it was clear Torfa did not understand her joke. 'Males fight whenever, and whatever, they can.'

'This will be dangerous.'

They both turned to look at the huge male trumpet beetle.

'I do not know which they will be more – ash or trumpet,' Aris said. 'But I hope for balance.'

'We all do.'

'I lost nearly everything in the ash fields. I will remember your help, Torfa.'

'If it ends badly, you can forget my help too.'

When they reached Aris's cavern they left the trumpet beetle near the entrance. By Aris's reckoning it was the sound, not the sight, that was missing. Doari was still dancing, though he was tiring. He no longer lifted himself upwards, and his wing-cases had to close often, but he was still dancing. Torfa watched it all and nodded. She returned to the trumpet beetle.

'Ready?' she said.

'I do not know,' Aris said.

Torfa leaned forward and scratched the trumpet beetle's front leg. It gave a shudder and then, pushing its horn towards the ceiling, made the sound that named its species. The call reverberated around the cavern. Even as Aris watched its source, it was as if it came from everywhere.

Dalla also shuddered. The little trumpet beetle stood and tested the air.

Another call.

Doari was no fool. He was old enough to see opportunity for what it was: rare and fleeting. He redoubled his efforts and, most importantly, made no noise as he did so.

The male trumpet apparently needed no more encouragement than a lack of admonishment. It called and called. Torfa came to the enclosure just as Dalla accepted her first coupling with an ash beetle.

It was not a graceful or pretty thing. Doari slipped and fell many times, the truth of his size now inescapable. Not graceful nor pretty, but it did not need to be.

'You have lied to that girl,' Torfa said when it was done. 'Manipulated like so many before, and so many after.'

'I had no choice.'

'Of course you did.'

'Of course I did,' Aris said, hardening herself against her own guilt.

Torfa took her male trumpet beetle back to her cavern, and Aris once more fell into the routine of looking into the dung heap in hope of eggs. To her surprise, she slept well every night on her rags. She returned home for some meals. Her parents asked no questions; she felt compelled to reassure them of next year's exports. But with every eggless morning her doubt began to grow. Had she really seen the pair mate? Even if she had, what if nothing could come of such a pairing? Perhaps someone had tried to mate ash with trumpet before, failed, and been too shamed to tell of it? She asked these questions and many more, until she found eggs.

Eggs the size of her fist nestled in the dung.

Aris remembered that the Commission had rules. Egg layings were registered in the afternoon. She waited, leaning against the enclosure fence, too excited to think of food, too worried to take her gaze from the dung heap. In weak moments she imagined Doari, confused and crazed, attacking the eggs. He was used to holes dug into the ash. Fifty holes to watch over and protect. Like Aris, he appeared to stare at the heap, but nothing more. She offered him an apology; she should trust an old hand like him to know better.

She waited until she could wait no more. She hurried to the Office for Trade, Livestock, and Realm Affairs. There were two dozen northerners in their masks, behind their desks, all sitting stiffly and staring straight ahead. Aris was the only Torn in the office. She quickly made her way between the rows of desks to where she thought she had sat last time: the time Vernon Pemberton wasted hours of her day.

'Beetle laying?' she said, barely above a whisper.

The Commission clerk leaned forward. 'Three desks over, dear. Livestock is Marie.'

Aris took the seat in front of Marie and shrank. 'I need...'

'Yes?'

'I need to register a beetle laying.'

'I see.' Marie hefted the ledgers on her desk. 'Ash, Blood, Darksing, Inkers, Jewel, Trumpet, or Young?'

'A—' Habit is a hard thing to break. 'None of those,' Aris said.

The Commission woman looked up from the page. 'Excuse me?'

'My beetles are not of those breeds.'

'Not of... I'm afraid I don't understand.'

'They are new.'

'New.'

This woman, this Marie, liked to repeat words. But that did not help her make sense of them even a second time.

'I have bred a new beetle,' Aris said, as slowly as she could, but wishing for haste. She could feel the piqued curiosity, the side-glances, of those sitting nearby.

'Well, I don't have a box for "new beetle".'

'A box.' Now Aris was doing it. 'They do not need a box yet, they are just eggs, not ready for export.'

'No. A box on my page. You see?' Marie held up her ledger. Ash, Blood, Darksing, all of them there and all of them with a little inked square beside them. A box.

'You write my new beetle,' Aris said, 'and draw a box.'

'I will *not*.' Marie reeled, as if Aris had demanded she jumped from Brawler's Bridge.

'Then I will.' She reached for the ledger but the northerner was quick, up, and away. Her chair crashed to the floor. The noise echoed in the airless office, loud as a trumpet beetle.

Marie opened her mouth.

'Please,' Aris said. 'Please do not do that.' But it was too late.

'Mr Pemberton!'

Vernon Pemberton slithered between the desks. The ripples of his passing could be seen in the Commission clerks. Somehow they sat straighter, stiller, like rocks hoping they might be ignored by the passing Wit's Blood.

'What is it *now*, Marie?' Vernon said. But then he saw her. 'Aris, what a wonderful surprise!' With a look from him, Marie righted her chair, gave him the ledger, and then wilted into the background.

'Hello, Mr Pemberton.'

'I wish you would have told me you were coming. I would have worn something special,' he said.

She had never seen him in anything but plain shirt and breeches. She did not want to.

Another Torn entered the Office or Trade, Livestock, and Realm Affairs. A man, carrying a tornstone lamp. Such craftsmen were rare in Hadun-Har, and like anything rare they were prized. Not even the stoic northerners of the office could contain their interest as he placed his lamp on the underserving desk. Vernon, however, did not look at the molten stone that twisted and turned to cast light and shadow in equal artistry. He only looked at her.

'I need to register a beetle laying,' Aris said.

'*Really?* Now that is wonderful news.' Vernon opened the ledger. 'Fifty ash beetles, I take it. Who was the lucky pair this—?'

'Not ash. Not fifty, but twelve.' She had counted more times than she had cared to count. Twelve eggs in the dung heap.

Vernon visibly thought on this. 'Very clever,' he said eventually. 'Very, very clever. You know beetle breeding. Your ash fields are swallowed up. I always thought there were too few darksing breeders. Half the trumpets are poorly raised. Blood, Young, really you could take your pick. *Very* clever.'

'I never understand what you say.'

'Isn't it so often that way? Words are such poor vessels for true feelings.'

The man and his tornstone lamp were moved to a desk near Aris. The clerk there looked most pleased. The lamp's light bubbled over Vernon's face.

'Twelve beetle eggs,' Aris said. 'Not of a breed in your ledger.'

'Not of a... Oh. Oh, I see. Well, that might be a problem.'

'Problem why?'

'If it's not in the ledger, it's not in the ledger, you see?'

'No, I do *not* see. It is not in the ledger *to* see. You write it, then I see.'

'My dear Aris,' Vernon said, smiling from behind his mask. 'That is not so easily done. This is the Commission. There are rules.'

'You make the rules here.'

'Well. I might be able to help. But the ledgers...'

'What of *that*,' Aris said, pointing to the tornstone lamp. 'Where is such a thing in your ledgers?'

'Really, there is no need for—'

'Show me, Vernon.'

He sighed like a child, and then picked up another ledger. He found the page with practised ease. Tornstone. Underneath, with their own boxes and written in box-like letters: curiosity, wonder, marvel.

She was lost for words – as if those three words had obliterated all others. She swallowed back the churning frustrations of uncertain days and anxious nights, of her father's disappointment and her mother's betrayals, of everyone who saw fit to tell her to marry, to have children. But it was too much to swallow.

The bile was thick in her mouth when she managed to say, 'Which?'

'It's obviously a marvel. Just look at it,' Vernon said.

Aris stood. She had to leave. It would not help to hurt this man. She damned the Commission to Silence, with its ledgers and boxes that had no room for her, but three ways of saying the same thing, three ways of recording 'tornstone lamp'. She had to leave. She deliberately did not walk past the tornstone craftsman and his 'marvel'. Outside the office, she breathed without a burning throat. Now, she would... she did not know what she would do. But she had to breed her beetles and they had to fight and then—

'Aris, wait.' Vernon put a hand on her arm. She looked down at it. Small, damp, scarless. He withdrew it without apology. 'Show me,' he said. 'Show me your new beetles, and perhaps we can sort out this mess.'

'It is not mess, Vernon. It is my business. My family's business.'

She did not wait to see if he followed her through the tunnels. She did not slow her pace in case his short legs struggled. She was aware he followed because she could *feel* him behind her. And sometimes he tried to talk.

'What did you breed together?' he asked.

'Trumpet and ash.'

'Trumpet? But they're so big!' Then, after minutes of silence, he said, 'Do you have a name for your new beetles?'

A name. She stopped, abruptly so he almost collided with her. She did not have a name for her new beetles. Somehow, she found herself laughing. What would she have written in their foolish ledgers, had they let her?

'Aris?'

'I do not know,' she said. 'But I will, when they hatch. I will see and then I will know.'

He was not impressed when they came to her cavern. He tried to hide this, but even with his face masked he failed. And perhaps he was right. The fences were not straight; how could they be, when made from the cast-offs of a broken cart? The gates barely closed. Poorly put together shrines, ash inexplicably inside, and a pile of rags he did not realise were a bed. Before he had seen, he had called it a mess, as if he had known. Was the beginning of every tale that way? As she walked Vernon to Doari and Dalla's enclosure, the guilt of not bringing her father to the cavern lifted from her.

Vernon looked from one beetle to the other many times. 'Is that really a trumpet?'

'She is small, deliberately made so.'

'They're so different.'

'In some things yes, more important things no,' Aris said.

'And she... doesn't mind?'

'At first. But beetles are pragmatic. Everything needs to survive.'

Vernon turned to Aris. 'Perhaps she sees him as something new, something exotic.'

'How would that help?' she said.

'In many ways.' For the second time that day he touched her. This time was soft, less sure, his hand looking for hers. 'We both do such lonely jobs, Aris. You down here with only beetles for company. Me up there with only those who work for me. Do you feel lonely?'

For some reason, perhaps the slip of hurt in his voice, she answered truly. 'There are times, yes.'

He moved his hand up her arm, and he pulled her closer. 'Your new beetles deserve a chance. It's just a line on a form in a ledger. A box. I can do that for you, Aris.'

When he reached for the hem of her blouse she understood. More, she let herself acknowledge what she had understood for a long time. She had known what Vernon wanted in courting her. But what she wanted in return, that came now. Not marriage. Something more useful.

But these thoughts were slow. They came from somewhere deeper.

He pulled up the blouse and she lifted her arms by instinct. The blouse fell to the floor. He was so short she looked down at his hair's parting, and he stared straight at her chest. His hands were smooth, scarless, oiled and perfumed. Strange how she had not noticed the smell of them before. She did not know what would make such a perfume, but knew it did not grow in the Tear.

This northern man touched her breasts.

Over his head, she saw her beetles. Doari walked the enclosure, his wing-casing spread, but did so silently. His voice his sacrifice. Dalla was checking her eggs. Aris could, and did, imagine many feelings for the little trumpet beetle. Good feelings. Bad feelings. Every one of them built on lies. Every one of them filled Aris with regret.

'Stop,' she whispered. 'Stop.' Louder this time. She pushed away his small hands.

'Aris—'

'No,' she said. She picked up her blouse, noted his look of guilt, and fled.

She wandered through Hadun-Har. When she stopped, she drank. She smiled and someone else paid. At one barroom not even that was necessary; the owner recognised wreckage when he saw it. He gave her one drink and sent her on. Lower, Mid, Upper. She covered aimless miles, caught between wanting to be away and needing to stay. Between needing to be away and wanting to stay.

The more she drank, the less she felt his hands on her. But the drink did nothing for other pains. Her own guilt was too big, too layered to mutter her way through.

'Who builds love without the lies?' she asked one stranger.

Another barroom, another stranger: 'Is marriage a story's ending?'

'How c— can anyone name anyone else?'

'Palmi, that not you, then?'

'You with me?'

'A *box*?'

If they answered she did not hear, did not remember, did not care. She stumbled on, until she did not know where she was. She did not know that she had, in fact, not entered a barroom but a private celebration. A house full of people but only one that she recognised. Of course. What else would please the Audience?

He was shadow dancing. He had told her he liked to dance.

A tornstone lamp was in the centre of the dark room. She flinched at the sight of it.

'Wit can keep his lamps,' she hissed at the person next to her and to no one at all. The tornstone bulged and pinched to form faces. Always changing faces, it would not be still. From their eyes and mouths came light. In that light Palmi danced. His own eyes closed, he danced. He was oblivious to the impossible shadows behind him.

She gazed at this in awe. To not look back, nor forward. To move but to do so for yourself, no one else, even as they watched.

Though she had not wanted to, had not asked to, she came to understand where Palmi's self-indulgence came from. He danced when the rest of them worked, loved, drank, bred. Would marrying such a man be the worst fate? All other choices were being taken from her. How long until this choice abandoned her too?

'This is the last thing that is still ours,' a man said to her softly.

She recognised him, drunk as she was, but could not place where from.

'Everything else we send north,' he said.

'Lamps,' she said. 'We send the lamps.'

'And your beetles. And my cloth.'

She reeled. From the market, loading his trumpet beetle with rolls of cloth. And from Palmi's group of friends at the bath house.

'But,' he said, 'we do not send our shadows. When we do?' He shrugged, and somehow that spoke of catastrophe.

'I have a thing...' She swayed, struggling against the day's drink. 'I cannot send it north.'

'Good,' the cloth seller said. 'Keep it for us.'

'But—'

He was gone, lost in a darkness thick with Palmi's admirers, if he had been there at all.

Aris found a corner in the strange house where no one stopped her from sleeping.

She woke with vomit down her front and Palmi smiling at her.

'Aris,' he said.

She groaned. 'Hello, Palmi.'

He said nothing more, simply helped her up and helped her home. There, she changed her clothes and rinsed her mouth.

'I saw you dance,' she said.

'Then you saw *me*.'

'I did.' She reached to touch him, but stopped. 'When I tell the Drunkard of last night, I will tell a tale of a room full of men. That I was the only woman. He will know what that means. So do I.'

'Does my preference worry you?'

Aris had not considered such a thing directly before. She was not so naïve that she did not know some men preferred the company of men, that some women preferred the company of women. But in her small part of the world, in her wanderings between beetle fields and home, in her small life such knowing had not made an impact. She found herself... unconcerned.

'We are Torn. We have enough worries,' she said.

'My offer still stands,' he said. 'It could benefit us both. And better now that you know.'

The days that followed were busy and filled with new routine. Aris went home for evening meals, slept in a bed, and left early for the cavern. The eggs hatched and Dalla lost interest in them, in Doari, in anything except food. But she did not cause trouble.

Aris moved the dozen larvae to a new enclosure and fed them as best she could. That meant borrowing money. Natalia Geirsdattir agreed to lend without any stake in where that money went. She also agreed not to tell Father.

As Aris shovelled yet more rotting fruit, rodents, and fresh horse dung into the larvae enclosure she wondered if Natalia's coin would be enough for the Commission. If Vernon would accept something other than her in trade for a new line in a ledger. Such were the things she thought on as the larvae ate and grew, grew and ate, at a speed she had not seen before.

They were big, too. Torfa Barasdattir said as much when she delivered the dung. Not so big as hers, but big. And feisty – that was the word she favoured, feisty. If Aris did not feed them regularly enough they would fight with one another. It took her some time to realise that was what they were doing; so slow, with nothing but teeth, there was not much to see.

On occasion Aris would go to the lower market under one pretence or another. She was looking for the cloth seller, but he was not there. What he had said that night as Palmi danced with the shadows, about keeping something for the Torn, she wanted to speak to him about that. She remembered little of the words but much of the feeling. It was driving her now. Her beetles – still nameless – were not for the north.

The north. Quick in its anger, and as relentless as Wit's Blood in its vengeance. It did not overlook Aris.

When half the imagos emerged from the pupa, Aris called for Natalia Geirsdattir. Then for Torfa Barasdattir. The two women who had helped her get so far, and would help her further. But she did not call for her father. She came close, turning towards home when the tunnels twisted that way. She found other ways. Father had said to come to him when 'yet was ready'. It was not. She was not.

Natalia came willingly, as if indulging her own daughter. Torfa was more excited than Aris and left her business in the hands of a hired man. He was new to Aris, but not so new otherwise.

'I should have retired years ago,' Torfa said as they walked. 'And I like it when he bends over.'

Natalia laughed at her old friend. They exchanged promises of drinks and social events neither expected to keep.

'How many of these new imagos?' Natalia asked.

'Six, with six more to come,' Aris said.

'All twelve from egg to adult?'

'What is to stop them? No tatterwings, firecats, or Wit's Blood.'

'You are breeding the wrong beetle, Natalia,' Torfa said. 'Perhaps I am also? But then I have never liked to see them fight.'

'You have a weak stomach.'

'My third husband thought so. Why so much spice, I asked

him? Expensive. And then he choked to death. Next husband, not so expensive.'

They laughed, but Aris was too nervous to join them.

She had helped her new imagos into the last enclosure she had managed to build. It was too small for them all, but what could she do? And what would she do when the others emerged? Despite what she told Natalia, she did not expect all twelve to survive. It was a horrible hope that they would not. A hope she did not have to live with long.

Aris noticed the smoke first – the smell. The others were too distracted with their discussion of husbands. It was wood smoke; a heady smell, rich with a life lived above ground. That was how it was so different to smoke from Hadun. Aris picked up her pace.

'Aris, where—'

And then Aris was running and the women did their best to keep up.

It was too late.

Standing in the tunnel, surrounded by smoke, were three men in northern masks. Two big, one small.

'Ah, here she is,' Vernon said. He stepped back between the other men. 'I have the misfortune of informing you, Aris Rafnarsdattir, that the Commission has ordered the termination of your business activities in accordance with Regulation sixty—'

Aris grabbed his throat. Natalia punched the man in front of her and he dropped without a sound. The last looked to his sharpened staff, then to the three women, then decided to be somewhere else.

The smoke billowed out of the cavern. It was starting to sting her eyes, but Aris ignored it. 'Why?'

Vernon wheezed, and she loosened her grip just a little. 'Not a... registered species.'

'No box,' Aris said.

He tried to nod, but found it difficult.

She remembered the look on his face as she put her blouse back on. 'You live a petty, lonely life, little man. You will die that way.'

His eyes grew wide and white. Piss ran down his leg. He was terrified that this would be his final story for the Audience.

But Aris threw him to the ground. Even in the heat and the dark she knew that to kill such a person would end not just his life, but the life of her and her family.

She turned to the smoke and the flames that were feeding on her dream. They licked the shrine to the Bailiff, testing, tasting, then devouring. She started forward. She wanted to be with them at the last, as the Widow welcomed them together. Natalia stopped her, engulfing her in thick arms. Aris could not fight the woman.

The three of them watched until the smoke was too much. There was nothing they could do; there was not enough water in all of Hadun-Har to put out a fire. It would consume everything in the cavern and then die surrounded by black, pitiless stone.

The three of them watched until the smoke was too much. They said nothing. Aris's tears silently carved their way down her face. She did not have many to give.

The three of them watched until the smoke was too much. Vernon slithered away.

Eventually the fire was finished. Aris would not leave until it was, and the others would not leave her. The ground was hot beneath her boots. Everywhere was ash. Her fences gone, her rags gone, her shrines gone.

Where the ash was thickest she found her horrors.

Beetle husks, some of which bore the marks of a death before the fire: a hole on the top of the skull. Aris shook away images of unsuspecting beetles and a northern man with a sharpened stick. Aris sobbed. She sought the touch of another, and Torfa was there. Her friend tried to pull her away but she had to see it all.

Where the ash was thickest she found her hopes.

Two pupa. Huge, blackened, but unbroken. Vernon's stakes must have missed them. Aris brushed away the ash and the soot and, at her touch, the casing cracked. She cleared the space as best she could, risking her hands on the hot stone. Two imagos slowly emerged. Two males.

'I am sorry,' Natalia said. 'They were always too big to fight northern birds.'

'I wanted something else. Something for us. I wanted *them*.' She gazed at her red beetles, her survivors, tall as her waist, with the horns and pincers of their forebears.

The two males flexed their wing-casings, steadied themselves on their feet, and tried life as an adult for the first time. Curious, they seemed to taste the air, taste the ash, even the three women. When they found each other, a different instinct took them.

'Feisty,' Torfa said, as the beetles set themselves.

'We should...' Natalia said. They gave the beetles the floor. 'At least you know they would have fought for you.'

Circling each other with their wing-casings out they were a thing to behold. Then one male tried its horn; casing down, it shuddered and shook and Aris readied herself for a noise that did not come.

'Not everything is passed down,' Torfa said. 'I would count that as a blessing.'

'Perhaps, but—'

A spout of green flame tore through the air. Aris ducked, far away as they were. Then another spout. And another, as both males tried their horns. Fiery green light danced with shadows on the cavern wall as the three of them looked on in awe. Green, in that place of only black and orange. The beetles turned their horns on each other and the flames flowed over their shells like blood over rock. But still the rock remained.

'How?' Torfa aired the question they were all thinking.

'The fire,' Aris said with a sudden certainty. 'It woke something in my new beetles. The northerners wanted to destroy. Instead they were a part of creation. Born in ash, fire came.'

'This,' Natalia said, 'this changes everything.'

'This is for us. No one will watch a bird again.'

'You will need help,' Torfa said.

Aris looked at her friends. 'I have help.'

'And a name.'

'My fire beetles have a name.'

'The northerners will not like it,' Natalia said. 'They do not like change.'

One of the beetles bashed into the other, then fired its horn. The other slunk away to the cavern wall. Aris went to him.

'They do not have to like it,' she said. 'They just have to see it.'

Twenty

With the final words, the Torn storyteller closed his eyes. He swayed on the sandstone rock he'd stood on for hours, a slow weave. Someone in the public gallery shouted, *No – help him!* And then with a jerk the Torn toppled backwards from the rock.

People were running over at once. Purple tunics swarmed the rock, and in the haze of leaving the world of the Torn story, Cora found herself thinking the rock looked like it was in the middle of a surging purple sea, rather than in the middle of First Wall, itself in the middle of Fenest. She shook herself awake: was the storyteller ill, or under attack? Not another body. This election had claimed too many already. Was this somehow Tennworth's doing?

Cora hurried to the rock, Jenkins ahead of her. There was barely any light behind it, where the storyteller had fallen, but she made out the Master of Ceremonies in the crush of Commission bodies. People were shouting and the noise bouncing around First Wall became deafening. The storyteller had greyed and was coated with a sheen of sweat that glistened in the weak light. The Master fumbled at the Torn's face. The mouthpiece – he was trying to put it back on the Torn's face. But the tornstone inside it was dark. No embers were left.

'Stand back! Give him some room!' the Master shouted.

The purple tunics leapt away at once and the noise around the rock dropped to near quiet. Beyond, in the seating areas, anxious murmurs continued. Cora pushed people aside to get closer.

'I said, get back!' the Master shouted.

Without taking her gaze from the Torn, she flashed the Master her badge. 'Bernswick division. I need to see what's happening.'

'Death,' the Master said, his voice cracking into a sob. 'After so long without his tornstone. Widow Wel—'

The storyteller gasped. Everyone in sight made a noise of relief as if they'd all been holding their own breath, waiting for the Torn to find his.

He sucked at the mouthpiece and at once the tornstone flared and Cora could smell sulphur. She'd never been so glad of the smell in her life. The Master of Ceremonies gathered the storyteller into his arms and demanded someone get the man some water, a blanket, a stitcher. Looking at the Torn, Cora doubted any of those would help him. He looked in a bad state, his eyes rolling in his head, his back floppy. He was breathing again, but for how long? Even now, his lungs might be turning to water. She turned away from the sight and rounded the rock.

The Audience had gone.

The Commission box, too, had emptied. Only those in the public gallery remained, the noisy listeners hemmed in by purple tunics at the end of each row of chairs.

'The voters didn't hang around,' Cora said to Jenkins.

'I expect the Commission rushed them into the garbing pavilion as soon as the poor man fell. Getting on with the job of the election. The spoked wheel turns...'

'And some are crushed beneath it,' Cora added.

Jenkins shook her head. 'He did what he had to, and now he'll be cast aside.'

A shout went up from the garbing pavilion and a huge wooden chest was carried out by purple tunics, constables forming a guard on all sides. A chest now full of voting stones.

'And all for that,' Cora said. 'The Torn 'teller almost died for those votes. And we don't even know where they go!' She could hear her own exasperation, but she couldn't fight it. She couldn't shake the image of the Torn man falling from the rock, dropping into the darkness of First Wall.

'My mother knows where the voting chests go,' Jenkins said, 'though she's never told me. Says she won't, not even on her dying day.'

'Is she saving it for the Audience?' Cora said.

'I doubt even those rogues will get it out of her. But wherever the chests go, it'll be the safest place in the whole Union, given that they won't be opened until all the stories have been told.'

'Four down, two to go,' Cora said. 'Let's hope the number of bodies doesn't rise any higher.'

'I think you spoke too soon, Detective.' Jenkins gestured in the direction of the rock.

Cora turned.

The Torn was carried by four purple tunics. His eyes were open but unblinking. His white coat was spattered with blood. Following the sad procession was the Master of Ceremonies, the mouthpiece of the Torn storyteller cradled in his hands.

'Will his story be worth dying for?' Jenkins said, as they waited for a gig to take them back to the station.

'Strange as it sounds, I hope so.' Cora lit a smoke and tried not to remember the light of the Torn storyteller's mouthpiece weaving from the dark as he came to tell his tale.

Why had the Torn taken off his mouthpiece and knowingly condemned himself to death? Far as Cora knew, it had never happened before at an election story. It was too great a sacrifice; of all the peoples in the Union, the Torn were the fewest. Life in the Tear made just existing difficult – the election story had been clear enough on that point – and when the Torn left their home, they never travelled in large groups in case they were harmed. The massacre at Burlington Palace must always be on their minds. And even when they *did* leave the Tear, they couldn't breathe.

But the Torn 'teller had removed his mouthpiece. Making sure the Audience heard his realm's story properly, with nothing between him and them, had been more important to the Torn this election than ever before. It had been a story of change. Just like the Wayward story was meant to be. There was more to this election than just the usual reshuffle of power. More was at stake – much more. Two storytellers dead. Ruth returned *as if* from the dead. People following Cora in the streets. Plague. The Hook barge destroyed. When would it end?

All at once, Cora couldn't breathe. The streets around

First Wall were still jammed with people. She caught sight of a gig at the crossroads ahead, but it looked to be making little progress in their direction. She needed to get away. Get far away from everyone.

'Four stories told and two 'tellers dead,' Jenkins said, and shook her head.

Cora was glad of Jenkins, of the distraction, anything to help ease her rising panic. 'The Audience has never known an election like it.'

'Never known such good stories either,' Jenkins said.

Cora was keeping one eye on the gig, hoping it would reach them. 'You like the Torn's chances?'

'It's my favourite of the election so far.'

Cora felt the same. Seemed to her to be about survival when things around you were changing, about being *able* to change.

'A tale of triumph over adversity that surely got the voters on side,' Jenkins said. 'As for the Perlish—'

'But both stories were about the same thing really, weren't they? The Perlish want to keep the southern foreigns out,' Cora said. Where was that gig?

'Yes…'

'And the Torn *are* southerners but they don't want to be anyone's foreigns. They want to stay in the Tear and make it work for them.'

Jenkins looked to be deep in thought. So deep, the constable didn't notice when she was nearly knocked over by a group of Seeders leaving First Wall.

'I suppose so,' Jenkins said slowly. 'But the Torn story was about knowing your own worth, not settling.'

'True.'

'And the Perlish story was about knowing your worth *and* thinking you're better than others. That doesn't sit right with me. Such hostility.' Jenkins sounded like she was still recovering from hearing the Perlish story, though it had been days ago.

'And yet the Perlish tale was the funny one!' Cora said.

'There's often cruelty in the comedies, Detective,' Jenkins said firmly. 'That story was cruel for judging people just because of where they're from.'

'Easy, Jenkins. Tell it to the Keeper if it bothers you so much,' Cora said. 'At least the Torn managed to get in a dig at the Commission. If the Torn win this year, there's bound to be grumbling at the Wheelhouse.' That was the first cheering thought she'd had in a while. 'We're getting nowhere fast here. Might as well walk back.'

'Is your leg—'

'It's fine.'

It wasn't, but the constable didn't need to know that.

On the way, Jenkins bought the most recent 'sheets from a seller shouting the freshness of her stories: 'The Torn tale – fire and fights! Fire and fights!'

'But we've only just heard the story!' Jenkins said as they left the pennysheet seller behind.

'They must have presses set up nearby,' Cora said. 'Gone to print as soon as the story ended. All that ink now on your hands – can't get much fresher.'

Jenkins looked at her inky fingers with distaste.

'Let's hear it then,' Cora said.

'Well, there's no mention of the 'teller's death in *The Daily Tales* so I think you must be right, Detective.'

'Any exit polls there?'

'Looks like *The Fenestiran Times* have included one.' Jenkins riffled through the sheets. 'Odds on the Torn story winning have shortened, even with those of the Rustans and the Wayward still to be told.'

'I can believe it,' Cora said. The young Torn woman, Aris, she had faith – faith in her realm. Cora had never seen the Tear with her own eyes but after listening to the storyteller's words, she felt as if she had seen it, smelled it, felt its heat on her face.

Heat.

The heat of the south. What was it Sorrensdattir had said before she died? *South for the hottest season.* And the hottest season was always... Cora pulled out the scrap of paper Jenkins and Marcus had found in the archive.

'Detective, what is it?'

'The season...' As Cora read the list of names again, the five names who likely paid money to Tennworth, one word seemed to gleam on the page. 'She meant Summerleaze. The Torn who died on the barge. She was trying to tell me where I should go.'

'You're going to *the Tear*?' Jenkins said in alarm.

But Cora barely heard the constable. Thoughts were crowding in. Sorrensdattir wanted her to go south to find Summerleaze. Whatever that was, it had to be connected to Tennworth. And it wasn't only the Torn aide who'd told Cora to go south. So had Ruth. Finnuc, too, had tried to help her: *the south is falling apart.* And there was somewhere particular in the south that kept coming up.

'The stitcher, the one who came to the barn in East Perlanse to see to the prisoner transport,' Cora said. 'She'd left the Lowlands because of trouble there, and Beulah...'

'Yes, Detective?'

No need to go into the detail of that bargain. 'Let's just say Beulah has had some trouble with the Lowlands too. I don't know what Summerleaze is yet, but I think I know the realm where I'll find it.' Cora started to run, much as she was able. 'Come on, Jenkins!'

The station's maps were kept in a cupboard at the back of the briefing room. She told Jenkins to find all those of the Lowlands and spread them on the long tables, shooing away the snoozing constables.

'Look for anything marked "Summerleaze",' she told Jenkins, and joined her in scouring the maps. But the job was too big, the maps too many, the Lowlands too vast – all those field names and farm titles. Streams bore names, and so did woods. They were getting nowhere. But she wouldn't give up. They were close. Sorrensdattir had used her dying words to tell Cora about Summerleaze. It *had* to be the place to find Tennworth.

Tennworth. That was it – the way to find Summerleaze.

'We need to look at the Lowlands in the *far* south, close to the Tear.'

'Why there?' Jenkins said.

'Do you know what grows well in all that ash-rich soil?'

Jenkins shook her head.

'Grapes, Constable.'

'The winery!'

It was Jenkins who found it. Cora hurried over to the map the constable was using. It showed the desert on one side of the Tear, the Tear itself, and, to the north of that mighty divide, the Lowlands that bordered it. Jenkins pointed to a small square along that border, which was surrounded by other squares, and curving round *them* was the word 'Summerleaze'.

'It's a farm,' Cora said.

'Looks like the others are too. The names on the paper we found – they're all here: Robinsons, Fimmons, The Larkhouse, Salter. Summerleaze is a bit further north than the others, but they're all marked the same way so they must be farms.'

Cora stabbed her finger at the map. 'Farms sending payments to Tennworth.'

'So Tennworth's a landlord?' Jenkins said.

'Could be. Right on the edge of the Tear. I'd bet a year's salary that we'll find Tennworth somewhere near here. Sorrensdattir said to go to Summerleaze. That's where I'll start.' Cora rolled up the map and jammed it in her pocket.

'I'm not looking forward to being back in the saddle,' Jenkins said, reaching for her jacket.

'You'll be spared that.'

'You're going on your own to find Tennworth?' Jenkins' eyes had widened. 'Is that safe, Detective?'

'I'm not going alone.' Cora made for the door.

'Oh?' Jenkins said, and there was no hiding the disappointment in her voice. 'Who are you taking with you?'

'Someone I used to know. You're better off here in Fenest, Constable. I need you to keep an eye on our three Chambers.'

'But the chief inspector—'

'I'm sure you'll manage.'

Twenty-One

The sky had lightened to a deep blue by the time Cora's gig arrived at South Gate. Ruth's note, the one slipped under Cora's bedroom door, had given quite specific instructions about where and how to meet, once Cora decided she was ready to make the trip: South Gate, a coaching inn, ask for the Washerwoman. So much had happened since that note, she wondered if Ruth was still waiting for her – if Ruth still had something to show her in the south. Regardless, Cora had her own reasons for going now. Maybe she'd show Ruth a thing or two.

She had set off from her boarding house early. She left herself time to change gigs, and her route across the city, more than once, should anyone be following her. At Murbick she was slow counting out the driver's pay and became aware of a shadow in the alley opposite. That feeling of being watched again. She got in a different gig and barked out her destination, making sure she was loud. When the gig was well down the road she looked back. The shadow was gone. She got out at the next gig stop and dived into a jolly house. No one about that early except the poor wretch emptying the slops. Cora helped herself to a sinta juice from behind the bar, found a coat on a peg to swap with her own, then set off again, sitting low in her gig seat, her new coat's collar pulled up. She was certain she was on Tennworth's trail now, and just as certain there were those who didn't like it.

It had taken her a while, but she'd reached the coaching inn. Thankfully, it was already busy when Cora arrived. It probably always was, given it stood at the edge of the city, the gateway to the Lowlands. A good choice to meet someone and slip away without being noticed in the constant noise and bustle of other people's journeys.

Cora knocked at the back door and an old man answered. She asked him for the Washerwoman, as Ruth's note had instructed. The old man shut the door, with no sign he'd even heard her. She waited, and had smoked two bindleleafs by the time a voice called her name from across the yard. It was Ruth, already mounted on a tall bay and holding the reins of a stockier grey.

'That all you brought with you?' Ruth said, looking at Cora's small pack.

'I didn't know… I wasn't sure…' Cora took a deep breath. 'I don't do much travelling.'

'Better light than heavy. We should get going.' Ruth handed Cora the reins of the grey.

With less grace than she was hoping for, Cora swung herself into the saddle. At once, the aches of the journey to Perlanse were back, as if she hadn't been off a horse for days. Her pack sat awkwardly in her lap and she wondered what she was meant to do with it. She couldn't ride all the way to the far Lowlands like this.

'Here, let me.' Ruth took the pack and tied it to some

metal rings on her saddle. There were all manner of things already there, hanging down the horse's flanks. Water bottles, a roll of canvas.

'Isn't it too much for him?' Cora said.

'Her. And no.' Ruth patted the bay's muscular neck. 'She's bred to carry all that a Wayward needs.' She urged her horse forward, under the archway that led out of the yard.

And so they were off.

The Partner knew how long Cora would be stuck with her sister. *Sister*. Might as well say *stranger*. As they joined the road that led south, leaving the sprawl of Fenest behind, they rode next to each other, and Cora took Ruth in through sidelong glances.

She was wearing breeches and a Wayward cloak, both of which were stained and worn. Her long brown hair was tied up, severely so, pulling at her temple so the lines there vanished. She was comfortable in the saddle. But even as she moved in time with her horse, there was something in the set of her shoulders, the way her hands tensed and released on the reins, that made Cora wonder. Something had happened to Ruth. Something terrible. Cora had seen the same look on people who had lost loved ones.

'Got your fill?' Ruth said, without taking her eyes off the road.

Cora looked away, embarrassed, and annoyed, too, that Ruth could still make her feel like a twelve-year-old, as if none of the years lost meant anything. They rode on.

If there had ever been an actual south gate, it was long gone, only remembered in the name of the coaching inn. Like the address of the archives: Mutton Fold, where sheep were nowhere to be seen. Fenest's past was in its place names. That was a kind of story, too.

The morning was shaping up to be warm, and the horses tossed their heads to rid themselves of the flies that drifted about. The land immediately beyond Fenest was scrub, set with ditches to drain rainwater from the city. There seemed to be a lot of people gathered here, sitting around the remains of small fire pits, talking in low voices or simply staring into space. The children, too, were mostly silent as they lay on grubby-looking blankets. Their shelter was canvas propped on poles that leaned drunkenly in the muddy ground. It put Cora in mind of the people camping in the grounds of Burlington Palace while Black Jefferey raged. People who had had nowhere else to go, but they'd come to the capital anyway. Now, as Cora and Ruth picked their way through, Cora could feel the gazes on them, and she could smell the filth of a nearby latrine.

'What are they doing here?' Cora said.

'Living,' Ruth said, with a world of weariness in that single word.

Cora turned to look at the sad huddles. 'Doesn't look much like living to me.'

'When did you last come south of the city?' Ruth asked.

Cora opened her mouth to answer but no words came out. She couldn't remember. Ruth shook her head.

Spread before them were the neat, green squares of managed fields, all the way to the horizon. The Lowlands. They rode all morning and the view altered little. Only the varieties of plants on either side of the road marked any kind of progress.

'What changed your mind about coming south with me?' Ruth said, as they passed a field that lay fallow. 'Was it the Torn story?'

Cora made a fuss of resettling in the saddle, stretching her back, while she considered telling Ruth about Summerleaze Farm and the connection to Tennworth, and decided against it. There was still too much she didn't know about this stranger sister.

'I had time to think about it,' Cora said, 'and decided it wasn't such a bad idea. And when we met at the stables, you said you had a story for another day, about you being with the Wayward.'

'You're coming south just to hear my story?' Ruth said, waving a fly from her face.

'You gave me little choice. And there's something for me down here.'

'Is there now?' Ruth muttered.

The bitterness in her voice surprised Cora. She glanced at Ruth, but her sister's face gave nothing away.

'What are the odds we stay civil for the next few days?' Cora said.

'You tell me. You're the one who gives all her money to the chequers.'

Cora reined her horse to a stop, forcing Ruth to reluctantly do the same. 'You've been watching me?' Cora said.

'Not me personally. I sent—'

'I knew it. I *knew* I was being watched.' Cora found herself laughing, and though she knew she sounded like she was telling stories to the Drunkard, she couldn't stop herself. The relief. 'It was you – your people. Sent by my own sister! And all the time, I thought it was...'

Ruth was staring at her. 'Who did you think was following you?'

At the thought of Tennworth, Cora's laughter died. 'It doesn't matter.'

Ruth took off her cloak. 'I had to know if I could trust you, Cora.'

'And?'

'The Audience hasn't voted on that story yet.' She fixed her cloak to another of the hooks on her saddle.

Feeling's mutual, Cora thought. She kicked her horse forward.

The day wore on. They kept to the bigger roads, though none so large as the main highways of Fenest. The crops continued to change as they rode by: red bushes, tall leafy stalks, an orchard of low, wide trees heavy with blossom. Cora didn't know what any of them were, and didn't have to. Long as they made it to Fenest to feed the city, that was all that mattered. The sheep, too, whose calls bounced across valleys. Every so often she spotted a mill with huge white sails that seemed almost to glow in the greens and reds of the crops surrounding them. Not enough wind today to turn the sails, but they were pretty to look at. And always there were farmhouses squat and fat in their fields of crops.

Ruth seemed to know where she was going, not that she shared that with Cora. When she could, Cora took out her map to check they were still heading towards Summerleaze Farm.

Few on the roads were going south like Cora and Ruth; everyone else seemed to be going north, towards the capital. Most people were walking, and they looked like they'd been on the road for days, if not weeks. Worn faces, worn out clothes, clutching sacks and pushing barrows. Children crying. Many of them were Seeders, judging by the clothes they were wearing, but there were Rustans, too, and Caskers. Every so often, Cora saw a group of them in a field sharing food or just sitting, too tired to talk, even. On their farmhouse porches, Seeders sat and smoked and watched those who'd taken rest nearby, but always from a distance. Always in silence.

Cora thought about what Finnuc had told her, before he was sent to his death: *the south is falling apart.* Was that what she was seeing here? People in need, those nearby not helping. And then there was Lowlander Chambers Morton's claim, that the Caskers were in trouble – hunger and illness in Bordair. But how did that explain all these other realms looking so hard-up? What made more sense now were Casker Chambers Kranna's actions – sending supplies south, to all who needed them, not just Caskers.

A Wayward came in sight, on foot, which was strange to see. Ruth got down from her horse and had a murmured conversation with him, which Cora didn't catch. She took the chance for a smoke, now she had her hands free. The Wayward nodded grimly at something Ruth said, and then both looked south for what felt like a long time. Ruth produced some coins from her saddle bags and the man took them. She and Cora rode on into the growing dusk, with no explanation. Only a feeling of dread that was at odds with the lush green fields, the carefully tended boundary walls, the washing on the lines.

'Friend of yours?' Cora said.

'All Wayward are. That's what it means to be one.'

'I thought it meant never staying still.'

'There's a lot more to it than that,' Ruth said.

'So tell me, Ruth, tell me your story. It was one of them, wasn't it? A Wayward made you take the papers from our parents' study.'

'I would have done it anyway.'

'Sure you would,' Cora scoffed.

'The truth was all around me – around us, Cora.' She gazed at the horizon, which was now all but lost in the gloom of evening.

'Only some of the truth came out after you'd left, after you'd given the story to the 'sheets.'

Ruth gave a short laugh. 'Let me guess. The money Mother and Father stole from the trading halls – it never turned up.'

'It's like you've heard this one before,' Cora said. The scandal of the missing money had run for years in the pennysheets.

'That tale never changes in the telling,' Ruth said. 'Mother and Father must have kept the money within their reach, somewhere in the Union. The rich never suffer, not really.'

'You were one of them, until you left Fenest. Until you went north to the Steppes.'

'I'd always wanted to see them,' Ruth said.

'Most people try to avoid them. Prisoners, people like Finnuc Dawson.'

Ruth glanced at her but Cora couldn't read her sister's expression in the poor light.

'I was young,' Ruth said softly, 'young and curious. The Wayward man I gave the papers to, he offered to take me to the Steppes. A group were riding north that night and I said yes. I shared his horse for the first part of the journey, into East Perlanse. I slept and woke for days in that saddle, my arms wrapped around him.'

'Sounds like a story for the Devotee.'

'Hardly! My backside ached so much that when I finally dismounted I fell over and all but cracked my head open. And if that wasn't bad enough, the Wayward who took me sang most of the way. He had a terrible voice. I was relieved when I got a horse of my own in East Perlanse so I could put some distance between us. But he was kind, for all his caterwauling. He didn't have to take me with him. By the time we reached the Steppes, all my aches were gone. I felt like I was born to be in the saddle. I had no plan after I got there. The innocence of that age.' She shook her head.

'Then what happened?' Cora said.

'I didn't stay long on the Steppes, but it's a beautiful place. The land up there, it's so open, so unworked.' Her voice changed when she spoke of the Steppes. It grew, expanded, and did so with a sense of wonder. No, a sense of hope. 'The grass grows tall, seeds itself wherever it likes. The birds are wild. Not like here.' She waved towards the fields. 'And the *air*. You wouldn't believe it, how it tastes.'

'I believe these fields keep us all fed, Ruth.'

'For now,' Ruth said.

'What does that mean?'

'You'll find out.'

'Is that why we're heading south?'

'Partly. Are you sure you want to hear this, Cora? The story of life after you?'

'Better than hearing hoof beats for hours on end.'

Ruth laughed. 'That's the story really. Days. Weeks. Months. Years of hoof beats.'

'Then it's a white stone from me.'

'You might change your mind.'

Lights began to appear, candles lit in windows that revealed the houses dotted about the valley. From somewhere, fiddle music. There was hardly anyone else on the road now. Cora couldn't remember when they'd last seen someone. They'd have to find a place to stay soon, surely; she couldn't ride through the night. But Ruth showed no sign of stopping, and Cora found she didn't want her to. She needed to hear this story, and it was better told in the dusk, when Ruth couldn't see Cora's face.

'The caravan I joined to go up there,' Ruth said, 'to the Steppes, they stayed long enough for some big gathering about what our parents' papers showed, that the system is stacked against the southern realms. The Commission, people like our parents, they exploit the people of the Tear, the Rustans, Caskers, Wayward too. Fenest's finest have long been demanding kick-backs to allow goods into the city, to grant trade permits.'

'Kick-backs that kept you in fine clothes and gig rides across Fenest,' Cora said.

'Are you going to interrupt all the way through?'

'Depends how good the story is.'

'As I was *saying*, there was a meeting. I didn't go. I was still a Fenestiran then. Or that's how the Wayward saw me. Yes, they're drawn to the Northern Steppes, take council there and breed the horses, but their view of life is closer to that of the southern realms. It makes no sense to think of them as northerners, especially with the way they travel all over the Union, but they saw *me* as Fenestiran, and that meant I was northern to them. I was starting to wonder if I belonged anywhere at all, but I knew I couldn't go back to Fenest so when some people left the Steppes I went with them. No one stays long there.'

'Apart from the prisoners.'

'Cora!'

'Sorry, sorry.'

'There are always Wayward on the Steppes but who they are changes from week to week as people leave, others arrive, the horses are brought to breed and then to give birth. When the foals are old enough, they're herded south and the next pairs arrive. I've been all over the Union, gone from the Tear to the Steppes and back again I don't know how many times. And in between I've done the kind of work the Seminary didn't train me for – putting up fences here in the Lowlands, digging ditches, tunnelling for the Rustans. Stringing vines for the Perlish.'

'See any vines in the far south?' Cora said. 'I'm told the ash is good for grapes.'

Ruth glanced at her, and there was something in her look, some small warmth, that meant Cora knew she was on the right track. She urged her horse on, and Ruth continued her story.

'But one part of my Seminary training *did* stand me in good stead: knowing the elections. The Wayward haven't won in decades, and they were determined to change that. Not long ago there was a gathering on the Steppes, with Wayward Chambers Arrani and the Council of Riders. I happened to be there, waiting for a herd to give birth. I'd been married for a long time by then and—'

'Married!'

'Wayward do *get* married, Cora.'

'It's not that,' Cora said quickly. 'I just never imagined you having a family.'

'Why?' Ruth said. 'Because you don't?'

That stung. It shouldn't have, but it did. Cora gritted her teeth. This woman at her side, she wasn't Cora's sister anymore. She was just someone Cora was on the road with, until they each reached wherever they needed to go. Which could turn out to be two very different places; way this journey was going, that might not be too bad a thing.

'This big gathering,' Cora said. 'What happened?'

Ruth sighed. 'Some in the Council demanded change.'

What was it the Torn storyteller had said? *That singular constant, change.*

'A new way of doing things was needed if the Wayward were to take the Assembly,' Ruth said. 'And this year they have to win. Everything depends on it.'

'This thing you want me to see,' Cora said, 'it's what the Wayward story is about. Why can't you just tell me, Ruth, and save us all some time?'

'Because you wouldn't believe me,' Ruth said simply. 'And you don't trust me. You might be able to hide a good hand of cards, but you can't hide from me. I've known you longer than anyone else. I was there the day you were born.'

'Missed a few years though, haven't you?'

Cora let that sit for a while. Silence take her if Ruth was right – that her sister knew her better than anyone. A sister who had abandoned her.

Eventually, Cora tired of such thoughts. 'Why are you working for the Wayward now?'

'They wanted an outside voice, someone who understood Fenest and the election.'

'You left Fenest when you were seventeen. They must be short on options.'

Ruth ignored the jibe. 'The Council said I was just what they needed: someone who knew Fenest and who'd committed to the Wayward realm, learned its ways. I was asked to advise the Council on an election strategy, help choose the story, think about the pennysheets.'

Cora stilled, as if she'd frozen to her saddle.

The pennysheets. They had dominated her life these last weeks. So much about the Wayward in them. And then there was Marcus, and her tip about the storyteller, and then Ruth—

'The new Wayward storyteller,' Cora said, struggling to get her words out quickly enough. 'It's you, isn't it?'

Ruth's silence was answer enough. She reined her horse to a stop.

'Will you tell Ento's story?' Cora asked. 'The one that got him killed?'

'Of course I will,' Ruth said fiercely. 'Not a word will be changed.'

'But it's too dangerous!' Cora said. 'Why does it have to be you?'

'Because of Nicholas.'

'I don't understand – what do you owe Nicholas Ento?'

Ruth made a noise that at first Cora couldn't fathom, and then she realised it was a sob. Her sister was *sobbing*. But only for a moment, then Ruth seemed to draw the sadness back inside her, as if she'd done it plenty of times in her life.

'Who was Nicholas Ento to you?' Cora asked.

Ruth stared at her. 'He was my son, Cora.'

Twenty-Two

Ruth couldn't speak for a while after that. Cora rolled two smokes. She didn't know if her sister partook of the leaf. If she didn't, now might be the time to start. Cora was pleased to have something to do with her hands, somewhere else to look as Ruth wiped her eyes. They smoked together in silence.

Nicholas Ento, the Wayward storyteller, the dead man Cora had gone to see in the alley between Hatch Street and Green Row, whose open chest she'd peered into in the cold room at Bernswick, watched the laces pulled from his lips, who Finnuc Dawson had *murdered* – he was Ruth's son.

Ruth's son. Cora's own flesh and blood.

'We should make camp,' Ruth said.

'Camp?'

Ruth unclipped the tight roll of canvas from her saddle. 'Don't expect you've ever spent the night under the stars.'

'Not many out tonight,' Cora said, glancing up at the cloudy sky.

'They're still there, even if we can't see them. Here, help me get a rope over that branch.'

The only words between them for a while were Ruth's

instructions for getting the tent up, and Cora's muttered apologies for getting everything wrong. At last, she couldn't stand it anymore.

'Why didn't you tell me?' Cora said. 'Why didn't you come to the station? You must have known I was working the case. You seem to know everything else about me.'

'I couldn't risk it. You saw what they did to my boy, how they mutilated him.' Ruth drove the peg into the ground with force. 'If I'd come to you, I would have fared the same.'

'I would have protected you, Ruth!'

'Like you did Sorrensdattir?'

'I...'

'This is bigger than you and your constables, Cora. I couldn't risk it. Not for this election, not for this story.'

'Ruth,' Cora said quietly. 'Do you know? Do you know who ordered Nicholas' death?'

'Tennworth,' she said, and smashed the peg with a stone. 'I'm not her, Cora.'

'But you know who she is.'

'It's—'

A snap somewhere nearby; something breaking underfoot. The horses, tethered in sight, were still. Ruth was at once alert, scanning the darkness around them.

'What are you worried about?' Cora said. 'There'll be sheep every—'

Ruth held up her hand and mouthed, 'Quiet.'

They waited, stock-still. Then Ruth's bay turned her head and whickered softly into the darkness. There was someone there.

Ruth drew a knife from her boot and silently motioned to

Cora to find her own weapon. Cora reached for her baton tucked inside her coat.

Another snap. This time on the other side of their tent, and closer. At least two then. If there were more...

Ruth raised her knife and Cora her baton. The horses pulled at the reins tethering them, sidled into each other in their desire to get free. Cora felt Ruth's back against hers.

'Strike as soon as you see them,' Ruth whispered. 'They won't be expecting a fight.'

'How do you know? Who is it?'

But Ruth only shook her head. Cora's horse stamped the ground, once, twice, and then there was a man in front of her. Smiling, holding out his hand.

'Greetings, travellers, you look like you could use some help,' he said.

'Now!' Ruth shouted.

Cora swung her baton into the man's face, then he was on the ground, trying to crawl away from her and making a wet cry that turned her stomach.

Behind her, Ruth wrestled with a woman who was putting up more of a fight than the man. Ruth's knife was against the woman's throat but she was struggling, twisting free. Cora shot a quick glance at the man she'd felled; he was face down in the earth.

Before Cora could reach them, the woman had wrestled Ruth's knife from her and slashed at her sister's arm. Ruth cried out but didn't stop fighting.

Cora swung her baton against the woman's ribcage, but the angle was wrong, and the blow only glanced. The woman dropped the knife, at least. She stumbled away, turned to flee, but Cora caught the back of her coat. She had time to feel the grease worked into the damp wool and then Ruth slammed the butt of her knife into the woman's temple. The woman crumpled, just as the man had. Two bodies at their feet. Ruth and Cora panting. The horses tossing their heads and tearing the ground to mud.

'You're hurt,' Cora said.

Ruth examined the slash in her coat sleeve. 'It's nothing.' But her fingers came away bloody.

'Have you got some cloth I can bind it with?'

'I said, it's nothing.' Ruth turned the woman onto her back then raised her knife.

Cora grabbed her wrist. 'What are you doing?'

'What has to be done, Cora. These people don't deserve to live.' Ruth spat in the woman's face. The woman didn't move or make a sound. Her eyes stayed closed. There was a bead of blood by her nose. Cora wondered if Ruth had already killed her. The man, too, was silent and still.

'Leave her, Ruth!'

'You don't know what you're talking about.'

'I know I'm not going to let you kill this pair.'

They stared at each other, Cora's chest still heaving, Ruth's hand straying to her bloodied arm. If it came to a fight, would Cora take her sister down? But then the moment was gone: Ruth went to calm the horses, keeping hold of her knife. While she murmured to the animals, Cora turned the man over so he'd be able to breathe, if his lungs still worked. She checked his wrist and found a pulse. The woman's pulse was weaker. Ruth had hit her hard, at just the right place to make her drop. That hadn't been luck.

'Neither are joining the Widow today,' Cora said.

'Pity. But we can still change that.'

'In case you've forgotten, you're with a police officer!'

'How could I forget that, *Detective* Gorderheim? Member of the Bernswick division, loyal servant of the Commission of Fenest.'

'Who just knocked out a man on your word. Better start explaining yourself, Ruth.'

Her sister squatted next to the horses and with her knife made circles in the mud. 'You might not like this story. But there's a place, in the middle of the Lowlands. Some say it's a camp, like the one outside Fenest, but it's bigger. Much, much bigger. It's called the Orchard. A prison.'

'For who?'

'People with nowhere else to go, those who've lost their homes, their livelihoods. Desperate, frightened people. They're picked up as they go north, told they'll have food and shelter, good jobs. So they make the mistake of going to the Orchard, where nothing is what was promised and they're not allowed to leave.' Her knife stilled and she looked up at Cora. 'There's Wayward who've watched the Orchard. The things they say… It's disgusting, Cora, to treat people like that. The place is run by Seeders like this pair.'

'Seeders preying on their own,' Cora said. 'And others too – Rustans? Caskers?'

'And Wayward.'

'But why? What's in it for them?'

Ruth snorted. 'Money. What else matters in the Union? They find buyers for the people, as if they're cattle. Those that go think their chance has come at last – a new job, a new life! They go to work only to find they don't get wages.'

'But let me guess. They do have debts,' Cora said. 'From being at the Orchard.'

'Which they'll never pay off. It's a slave camp, and growing by the week. The biggest buyer is Fenest.' Ruth was watching Cora closely. 'That fire in Murbick last year, the warehouse owner who denied his workforce existed until they came running out on fire. Those men were southerners sold by the Orchard.'

The warehouse fire – that was one Serus had investigated. It wasn't Cora's patch, but the scene had been so difficult to manage, what with the warehouse collapsing, the body count so high, that Bernswick had been charged with helping the local force. Some nights, Cora still dreamed about the burned faces.

She looked down at the prone man and woman, and forced her voice to be even. 'I won't let you kill them, Ruth. They should be taken to Fenest to face justice.'

'Justice!' Ruth crowed. 'As if *that* happens in Fenest. No one there's been in any rush to stop this.'

'You're telling me that the Commission, the Assembly, they *know* about this place? And they're doing nothing about it?'

'I told you once, Cora, a long time ago, that Fenest was rotten.'

'*Right through the middle*,' Cora finished.

'And it's what I've been telling you ever since. I haven't changed my story. You just weren't ready to hear it.'

'So what now?' Cora said. 'You're taking us to the Orchard?'

Ruth shook her head. 'It's too dangerous. I've lost three people there in the last month. We're going further south. You need to see what's causing the likes of the Orchard in the first place. We'll start again as soon as it's light. I'll take first watch. Get as much sleep as you can, Cora. You're going to need it.'

Cora pointed at the man and woman still lying on the ground. 'And them? You won't harm them?'

'I won't.'

'And Tennworth?' Cora said. 'You'll tell me who she is?'

'When you're ready to hear it.'

Twenty-Three

When Cora was woken by Ruth to take her turn on watch, she found that her sister had bound and gagged the Seeder pair. They were propped against a tree a little way from the tent; awake but looking warily at Cora. No bad thing.

She sat in front of the tent, her baton to hand, and smoked until the sky began to lighten. Now that she could see the man and woman better, it was clear they'd never stood a chance against her and Ruth. Both were too slight. Made a kind of sense, if what Ruth said was true. Convincing desperate people to believe that life would get better, that didn't need much force. How many had this pair lured to the Orchard and then betrayed?

Lowlander Chambers Morton's theory about the suffering in the south might be right after all. Cora had seen Caskers on the road among the Seeders, and Ruth said they were held at the Orchard too. But why would Morton only mention the *Caskers* as having problems, not her own realm, when it was clear to anyone here that things were bad in the Lowlands too?

After an hour pondering that question, and others besides,

Cora woke Ruth. They made ready to leave. Ruth's bare forearm was wrapped in wet-looking leaves. There was a woody smell to them.

'Something you learned in the saddle?' Cora said, and nodded at Ruth's arm.

'One of many things. Wayward are better stitchers than Fenest's needle-sharpeners.'

When the tent was once more a roll of canvas tied to Ruth's saddle and they'd chewed on some of Ruth's dried meat, Cora was forced to make a decision about the prisoners.

'We can't take them with us, but I can't go back to Fenest yet.'

'You should know, if we leave them, their friends will find them by sunset.' Ruth shoved the man onto his side. His face was a mess of blood from where Cora had hit him. She thought she'd probably taken a few teeth too. 'They'll be back to their lies before long.'

'It's a risk I'll take.'

'Your choice, *Detective*.'

Once daylight had properly arrived, the roads were just as busy as they'd been the day before, with everyone else still going north. After a few miles, Cora asked the question that had been on her mind the whole night.

'With Ento being—'

Ruth winced.

'Sorry – Nicholas. Him being left in a part of the city that Bernswick covers, his death was investigated by his...

aunt.' The word felt strange in her mouth, like it couldn't be attached to Cora.

'It's no coincidence, Cora. Nothing is a coincidence in this election.'

'Then Finnuc Dawson intended for me to be the investigating officer.'

'Of course he did,' Ruth said bitterly. 'Dawson's people wanted Nicholas dead, to make the Wayward change their election story. And, in case his death wasn't enough, they wanted to flush me out of hiding.'

'They assumed you'd come to me.' A cold thought occurred to Cora. 'And that I'd give you up.'

'Because you work for the Commission, you'd do your duty.'

'I wouldn't have. You know that, don't you, Ruth?'

A pause, and then her sister nodded.

'You don't believe me?' Cora asked.

'I guess I'll never know now, will I, because I gave myself away. Took a risk. A stupid one.'

'What risk?'

'Nullan told me not to but I didn't listen. I went to hear the Seeder election story.'

'You were at Tithe Hall?' Cora said, stunned.

'I saw you, at the back among the old fruit crates as if you were ready to leave at any moment.'

'That 'teller kept me hooked. It was a sad one though, the boy forced to leave home.'

'Yes,' Ruth said, her voice all but lost, and Cora saw the whole thing differently. How the story of the Seeder boy Ghen would have been to Ruth: a tale of a lost child. Too close to home, with her son sacrificed for the election. Cora tried to change the subject.

'Your first time back in Fenest,' Cora said, 'after so long away. It must have been strange.'

Ruth wouldn't meet her eye. Cora's hands dropped to the front of her saddle.

'You must think me such a fool,' Cora spat.

'Cora, I—'

'How many times have you been back since you left?'

'A few.'

'And you never came to see me. Not once!'

'What was there to say?'

'Everything.'

'I'm not the same person anymore, Cora. After being with the Wayward, moving around the Union, being free. You and I – I thought we were too different. But now that I'm back...'

'You're wrong,' Cora said, and Ruth turned to her, looking almost hopeful. 'You're exactly the same person you always were, Ruth. Selfish. Heartless. Cruel. Like Mother. There's one for the Drunkard; you're just like the woman you wanted to escape.'

Ruth said nothing.

The road forded a trickle of water that, from the look of its banks, had once run more powerfully. They let the horses drink. On the edge of the water was a wooden carving of the Washerwoman, the marks of high water on her wooden dress – the old levels. She was finely worked, her shape more real-looking than the Audience members in the Seats of Fenest. This was how Seeders saw the Audience – more like them. The Washerwoman's long skirts were pulled up and tucked into the waist of her dress. Under one arm was a basket and in her other hand she held a pole for dunking her cloths. Nuts and leaves littered the ground by her feet. Too neatly done for animals. These were gifts left with stories. The hopes of the people of the Lowlands.

The Washerwoman didn't just hear tales of rivers, but obstacles too. Things that got in the way of smooth passage. Cora glanced at Ruth, who was murmuring to her horse again – a Wayward thing.

Cora filled her bottle and took a long draught. The water tasted strange. Too warm than was right for a stream moving, and brackish. It reminded her of something, but she couldn't think what. Ruth was watching her.

'What?' Cora said, climbing back onto her horse.

But Ruth still had no answers. Once they were on their way again, Cora tried to pick up the thread of the conversation.

'You went to the Seeder election story. What happened?'

'I wasn't careful enough when I left Tithe Hall. The story had upset me. I was distracted.' Ruth sniffed. 'They caught me in an alleyway.'

'Who?'

'The Casker, Dawson, and another. His nose didn't look right.'

'Like it was broken?' Cora said, thinking of the body hidden under a pallet in a barn in East Perlanse.

Ruth looked at her sharply. 'You know him?'

'I know he's joined the Audience. But before he took his own life, he killed Finnuc Dawson on the way to the Steppes.'

Ruth shook her head. 'They deserved each other. When they took me after the Seeder story, I thought the Widow was ready for me, but they only bound my hands and feet and shut me in a crate. When they took me out, I was in a kind of warehouse. The air was bad, burning in my chest.'

'White Rock. It's a stone works close to the winery.'

'The Casker was still deciding what to do, like he was waiting for a message that didn't come. He argued with the other man, kept saying, *she's close, too close*. I think he meant you, Cora.'

'I'd found the old Commission coaches by then, behind Tithe Hall.'

'Everything started happening quickly,' Ruth said. 'He put me in the coach and was making ready to leave. I didn't know where we were going but I knew he was going to kill me. It was just a question of what message he was going to send this time. Cut out my tongue, bind it in black and white laces, and post it to you at the station?'

Cora shuddered.

'But you got there in time, Cora. I meant what I said before. I'd have died if you hadn't been there that day.'

'You didn't stick around,' Cora said.

Ruth reached across the space between their horses and put her hand on Cora's.

'I wanted to, Cora. That time, I wanted to.'

It was two days later that they came to something that looked like a village. Cora had seen plenty of houses on the journey, but they were always separate, surrounded by fields. Each farm its own world. This was four plank-walled buildings together in a kind of square: civilisation.

The largest of the buildings had a sign that proclaimed it *Wod's Hostelry*.

'Here's one for the Relative,' Cora said. 'Let's hope they've got something more interesting to eat than that dried dog you've been feeding me.'

'It's rabbit,' Ruth said.

'Same difference.'

Cora got down from her horse and tied it to the post outside the hostelry. Two other nags dozed there in the hot sun. Ruth stayed in the saddle, looking around the square. Opposite them was what looked to be a shop selling spades and forks, all manner of farming business. The windows were thick with dust. An old man sat on the porch, his head tipped back in a snore.

'Rushed off his feet,' Cora said.

Ruth's hand was near her boot, where her knife was stowed. 'I'll stay with the horses.'

'You sure?'

Her sister nodded.

'If you get bored,' Cora said, climbing the steps to the hostelry, 'I'm sure the Neighbour would enjoy hearing from you.' She gestured towards the shack on the shop's other side, the door of which was carved with wheat ears: a Seat. Needed some looking after, though. The Seat's door was just as covered in dust as the shop windows.

'Don't be long, Cora.'

As Cora turned to give Ruth a wave, she caught sight of something on the shop porch opposite. Something stowed beneath the chair of the snoring man. A pair of shears. Gleaming. No dust on them. Sharp too, she'd put a mark or two on that. Sleeping with those blades close by didn't seem an accident.

Ruth was right: this wasn't a place to hang around.

Cora pushed open the hostelry door. Her fingers came away gritty.

After the bright sun outside, it took her a moment or two to see the place. It was small, no bigger than a dining room in an ordinary house in Fenest, the counter at the far wall. A man stood behind it. Dark clothes, his head shorn. He was mid-pour, and on seeing Cora his hand shook and the liquid spilled.

'Afternoon,' Cora said. 'Looking for some food for those who've been long in the saddle.'

'Food?' the man said, setting down the bottle with such awkwardness it nearly toppled over, steadied just in time by the woman seated at the counter. There were two others in the room – a man and a woman bent over their glasses at a nearby table.

'If you have some to sell,' Cora said. 'Doesn't have to be fancy.'

'Food – that's all you're wanting?' the man stammered.

'I'll take dancing girls and cock fights too, if you've got them,' Cora said, and tried a smile.

But the man looked like he hadn't done much smiling himself in a while. A scar ran across his scalp – fresh enough to still be raw at the edges. Had the man stitched it himself? The woman at the counter was staring at Cora. The other pair were doing their best *not* to look at her, but she knew they were listening.

Cora strode to the counter, the seated couple flinching into each other as she passed. When she got out her badge and said the words *Fenest, Commission*, the man gave such a sigh of relief, Cora thought he might sink to the floor.

'Who were you expecting?' she asked him.

'These days, you never know.'

The counter was dusty too. Grey dust. None too fine.

'Wod, is it?' Cora said. 'The sign...'

He turned to fiddle with the barrels stacked behind him. 'Wod's dead. I've got some bread out the back. Not saying it's fresh, mind, or that there's much to go with it.'

'Whatever you've got, I'll take it,' Cora said, tucking her badge away. Her fingers grazed her baton. Good to keep it close in such a place.

As the man slipped away, there was a noise behind her. Cora spun round. The door swung shut. The man and the woman had left, their abandoned glasses almost full.

'Something I said?' Cora asked the woman at the counter.

She shrugged, keeping her gaze on her drink. She was young, no more than eighteen, and looked like she'd come straight from the fields. Her nails were black with dirt, and her patched shirt was stained with sweat and other things Cora didn't want to guess at. At her feet was a bag.

'You going somewhere?' Cora said.

'Is that an official question?'

'Could be.' Cora leaned back against the counter. Seemed wise to keep the door in sight.

'I'm leaving. Know that much,' the woman said, and sipped her drink without looking at Cora. 'Where I'm going, that's a harder one.'

'Fenest?' Cora said.

'All roads lead there in the end, don't they?'

''Spose they do. Speaking of roads.' Cora took the map from her pocket and laid it on the counter. 'This place.' She tapped Summerleaze Farm. 'How far?'

The young woman finally looked at Cora. 'You're going that far *south*?'

'That a problem?'

'For you. For all of us, maybe, in the end.' The woman took a long swig. 'You on foot?'

'Riding.'

'Three days then. Follow the road from here and don't leave it until you see the mill. Or what's left of it. Then take the right-hand fork.'

The man with the scar came back then and handed Cora a cloth-wrapped parcel. When he told her how much he wanted for it, she nearly called on the Poet. But she had the money – borrowed from Hearst before she left Fenest – and this man looked like he needed it more than she did, so she handed over the coins. He swept them into his pocket with more haste than Cora thought decent.

'See you've got some barrels there,' she said. 'Do your own brewing?'

'My brother. After my father died...' He swallowed loudly. 'My brother does it now. Good stuff too. Hops grown not more than a mile away. You want to try a glass?' He was so eager it was painful.

'Another time. Friend of mine, in Fenest, she runs a bar. Big place, lots of thirsty customers. She's looking for a new supplier.'

The man's face brightened. 'How much a week? I could send some back with you, for your friend to try. I'll get a bottle. No. A small cask. Can you carry that?'

The young woman downed the last of her drink and shouldered her pack. 'Be seeing you,' she said to the man.

He stopped fussing and stared at her back, his shoulders

slumped. Cora felt like she'd walked into someone else's story.

'Take care, Melle,' he said softly, and then she was gone.

Melle. Where did Cora know that name from? The Seeder election story – one of the children. Was this her, grown up and leaving home?

The man was saying something about hop blends.

'You got papers?' Cora said. 'My friend can't sell anything that isn't Commission-approved.'

He licked his lips. 'I can get them, but a note from someone in the Commission would help. If you could see your way to...' He took out the coins Cora had just paid him and slid half back across the counter towards her.

'Well, I—'

'Cora!' It was Ruth in the doorway. How much had she seen? 'Time we were leaving.'

'I'll be right there,' Cora said, without turning round. When she heard the door shut again, she asked the man for paper and ink.

Twenty-Four

Ruth was already in the saddle, her bay right next to the hostelry and practically climbing the steps to the door. As soon as she saw Cora, Ruth threw the reins of her horse at her.

'We need to go. *Now.*'

'What's the problem?' And then Cora saw it. On the porch of the shop opposite, the old man had woken up – if he'd ever really been asleep – and been joined by friends. Not a youngster among them, but the tools they held, they looked sharp enough. A line of grim-faced men and women.

'There's nothing for you here,' a woman called. 'We've nothing to spare.'

'We'll be on our way,' Cora said.

'See that you are,' the woman said.

Ruth urged her horse into a trot and Cora's followed suit, faster than she liked. Cora gripped the saddle. Being thrown from a horse wasn't the ending the Partner wanted. At least they were going in the direction that the young woman, Melle, had said led to Summerleaze.

They rounded a bend and suddenly were beneath a canopy of trees. Only now that the buildings were out of sight did Ruth pull her horse back to walking. Cora's mouth was dry. All that dust. She swigged from the bottle but the water still had that odd taste. It was worse now. Was there something in the bottle besides the water? She peered down the neck.

'I told you not to hang around,' Ruth said.

'I was quick as I could be.'

'Didn't look that way to me. Looked more like you got yourself a bit of business, Cora.'

'Just helping out a friend in Fenest.'

'At whose expense? You're as bad as the rest of them,' Ruth spat.

'I'm just trying to get by,' Cora said, and fiddled with her reins. 'Same as everyone else.'

'That's the problem. But the balance of power is shifting. It's moving the ground under our feet even as we sit here and argue.'

'Who's arguing?' Cora said, and knew she'd said something similar when she and Ruth were children, because it annoyed her sister. It annoyed Ruth now.

Cora glanced behind her. There was a smell. Something was burning. 'The people back there, they thought we were like that pair who attacked us – from the Orchard.'

'Or worse.'

'Worse how?' Cora said.

'Because everything's a threat now. Come on, we need to keep going.'

'What's happening here?'

Ruth began to cough. 'Can't you guess, Cora? You tasted it at the river. It was in every speck of ash in that bar back there.'

'Ash? But what—'

'From the Tear, Cora.'

Now Cora was the one coughing. 'But we're still miles from the Tear.'

Ruth's gaze was set grimly down the road, where Cora could see more endless plains, yellow squares of wheat tucked within them. But they were paler than those she'd seen on the way. The ash? But that couldn't be right. It couldn't.

Once they'd cleared the tree canopy, Cora urged her horse ahead.

'The place I need to go, I'll take us there.'

Ruth coughed into her elbow. 'Lead on, sister,' she said with a choke.

It was hot now they were out from under the trees. Too hot for the crops either side of the road, which were brown and wilting. The earth beneath them had cracked into deep fissures. For every three farm houses that came into sight, one looked abandoned. The people they'd seen heading north, this was what they were leaving behind.

The next few days' riding were a blur of heat, dust, and the constant search for water. Ruth fought thirst by sucking on a dried root she carried in one of the many pockets of her hide cloak. Cora tried the piece Ruth gave her but found it worse than not drinking at all – the root was like a twisted memory of drinking.

Just when she felt so faint she couldn't hold on to her saddle any longer, the road began to climb and at the top were the remains of a tower, a ragged sail hanging over the side. A sad version of the mills she'd seen when they started south. The young woman, Melle, had said to look out for this one. It seemed to take forever to reach it, and a kind of dread settled on Cora, until finally they were beneath the mill.

One wall of the tower had crumbled, as if it were a child's play thing and an angry hand had smashed into it. The stone blocks were coated in ash. Cora stared up at the slumped sail. There were holes in it the size of fists, their edges black and charred. It couldn't be right. She had to keep going, find the farm, find Tennworth. That was why she'd come south, and this spot here, this was where Melle had said to take the right fork. Cora nudged her horse on and Ruth followed without a word.

The road narrowed and sloped down, becoming a winding track between stone walls. The air was hot and dry, and the land was beyond use. When had she last heard the noise of sheep? They came to a gate in the wall on her left, and beyond that was a house. She checked the name carved into the gate's sun-whitened planks: Summerleaze. This was the place. But as she pushed open the gate and led her horse towards the house, she wondered if Sorrensdattir had made a mistake telling Cora to come here.

What must have once been seed beds for fruit and vegetables had grown unchecked, unpicked, and then died back in the heat. The skeletal remains of stalks lay twisted over one another, husks scattered around them. She made her way past the ruined crops to the house. The wooden boards round the doorway had warped so that the door hung drunkenly on its hinges. A chair was on its side on the porch, its white paint blistered and flaking. Cora set it upright and called out a greeting. No answer.

'You're too late, Cora.' Ruth was looking around a cluster of outbuildings, all of which were in the same state as the house, or worse. The roof of a shed had fallen in. 'Looks like they've already gone north.'

Her sister stumbled over a pail left in the middle of the little courtyard, as if someone had dropped it as they were running to the road – a tale for the Builder. The noise rang out, which seemed like the loudest thing Cora had heard in days. A dog barked, somewhere inside the house, and then a floorboard creaked.

Cora called out again, and this time someone answered.

'Commoner take you – I won't go!'

It was a man's voice, caught between rage and pride, but with a definite tremor.

'I'm from the Commission,' Cora said, taking out her baton. 'And I'm coming in.'

But before she could push open the drunken door, it was flying towards her as someone charged onto the porch.

He was a burst of flailing fists, something hard and metal in one hand – a saucepan? And shouting, beset with coughs.

'I've told you, leave me alone! This is my place, Mother's place, *her* mother's before.'

A swipe and the saucepan just missed her head. Cora fumbled the pan from his hand but his face was so close to hers she could feel the spit landing on her cheek. The dog barked and jumped up at her.

'... told that boy 'til I'm blue in the face. I won't go!'

And then Ruth was there and between them they wrestled him into the chair. The fire seemed to go out of him, and he was all at once old and tired. Thin too. His arms spindly as the chair's legs. His shirt was more patches than its original cloth, the stitching on each patch a riot of threads and lengths.

'He's more of a handful than that pair who set on us,' Cora said, panting.

Ruth wiped sweat from her mouth then reached to grab the dog. It was only a yappy little thing, really, and was now snapping at Ruth's boots. More bark than bite, just like its owner who was muttering now.

'I've told him. *Told* him! I can't leave the fields. Ridiculous.'

'Now then, Mr...'

The man glared at Cora. It was then she saw his eyes were clouded.

'Sanat,' he said. 'Now get off my land. It is *still* my land.'

'I don't doubt it, Mr Sanat,' Cora said. 'Tell me, who's trying to make you leave?'

He looked first towards Cora, then at Ruth, as if they were playing some trick on him. 'You mean he didn't send you?'

'Who, Mr Sanat?'

'The boy! Wishaw. Wishum. Some foolish city name like that. My grandparents worked all their lives on this land. If I leave now, someone will take it, and I wouldn't blame them. It's good land.'

'It is,' Ruth said, and knelt by his chair. The dog had stopped yapping and seemed to be enjoying Ruth scratching it beneath a much-scarred ear. 'We could see that when we came in.'

A smile of satisfaction spread across the old man's face. 'As it should be, when the land is cared for.'

'Why does this boy want you to leave?' Cora said.

'Some rubbish about the heat, that it's not safe for me to stay.' He wagged a finger at them. 'Now, it *has* been warm, I'll give the boy that. I won't argue that the last few years have been more sun than rain. I'm not one for petty disputes.' He began to cough.

'Of course not,' Ruth said. 'Can I fetch you a drink?'

Unable to speak, Sanat waved towards the door and Ruth slipped into the house.

'The others,' the old man croaked, 'my neighbours, they listened to the boy. Fools. Things will go back to how they were. I been here long enough to know how the world works. The Lowlands are going to win the election this year, everyone was saying that up to the day they left. Once it's our Chambers in charge, we'll be all right again.'

'Latecomer's luck to you then,' Cora said.

'Oh, we don't need luck, miss,' Sanat said. Cora couldn't remember the last time anyone had called her *miss*. 'We've got the right story. It's the Lowlanders' year.'

The pennysheets hadn't been quite so confident.

Ruth came back then with two chipped cups. She guided Sanat's hand to one and handed the other to Cora, who drank it noisily. Ruth leaned close and murmured to Cora, 'There's barely anything in there. He must have sold it all. And the state of the place…'

Cora cleared her throat. 'Mr Sanat, I can see you're… busy. I'm not here to remove you from your land.'

'You couldn't even if you tried!'

'I just need some information, about your landlord.' Cora licked her lips. 'Name's Tennworth – that right?'

'That's her. And it's *Mistress* Tennworth,' he said.

'I need to find her,' Cora told the old man.

'Well, can't help you with that.'

'Why not?' Cora tried to keep the disappointment from her voice.

'Never met her,' Sanat said. 'Paid rent to the local agent. I've seen a few come and go in my time, I can tell you. Now, in my mother's day the money was handled by a girl from down Lapharen way – hard as nails, she was, and my mother always said—'

'I'm in a bit of a rush, Mr Sanat.'

'Isn't everyone these days!' he said, and then more sadly, 'They all left so quick, my neighbours.'

Cora silently cursed every member of the Audience she could think to name. Then, after a deep breath, asked, 'You have no idea how I might find Mistress Tennworth?'

'Never needed to. The agent handled everything. Mistress Tennworth just took the money, and my mother's money before me, her mother's before that. Tennworths have always owned this land, and my family has lined their pockets for the chance to work it. They never even showed their face at the gate, far as I know. And I would *know*, miss.'

'The agent then, where are they?'

Sanat waved in the direction of the gate. 'Down the road, only a few fields between us. And when you get there, miss.' He grabbed Cora's wrist and his thin hand was like a claw. 'Tell Wishaw, or whatever his name is, tell him Sanat won't leave. Everything will go back to how it was. Just you wait.'

Twenty-Five

Ruth was with the horses at the gate, feeding them something green-looking that she'd found.

'This might be the last living plant we see before we turn north again,' Ruth said. She patted the neck of Cora's grey. 'Better it's eaten than left to dry to nothing.'

'The boy that the old man kept going on about, Wishaw. He's the agent. I need to see him.'

'Then let's go,' Ruth said, and swung herself into the saddle.

'And what you wanted me to see?'

Ruth looked out over the dead fields of Sanat land. 'Don't worry – it's close.'

They found the agent's office easily enough. It was the only building anywhere near Sanat's that still looked like someone used it. Not much more than a shed, set at the bottom of a steep hill. There was a horse tethered to a rail outside. Canvas was pulled over the windows to keep out the sun, and it looked in good condition. The paint on the walls was blistering, but someone had tried to rub it down and make good. Just not very well. Not surprising, given the heat in the air here. Every breath burned.

Ruth hung back. 'I'll let you get on with your *official* business.' She couldn't have sounded more venomous if she'd tried. Cora left her with the horses again. Ruth seemed better with animals than people. Being Wayward likely did that to you.

Cora peered round the open door: rows of barrels lined the wall. The nearest to her had the lid off and there was water inside, a dented tin cup floating in it. No one else around to drink it. Hardly a soul in these parts at all save an old man who couldn't see the truth staring at him from his dead seed beds. A truth Cora didn't want to see herself.

'This is an official agent building,' someone said. A lad behind a desk. 'I work with the authority invested in me by Fenest, capital of the Union.'

'So do I,' Cora said wearily, and showed him her badge.

'Thank the Audience for that,' he said, and slumped back in his chair. There were papers all over the floor and a satchel half-filled. 'I didn't think anyone was coming. I sent the letter weeks ago.'

'Wishaw?'

'Wiltsham,' he said. 'Only person who gets it wrong like that is old Mr Sanat, so I'm guessing you've seen him.'

'He says to tell you—'

'I know, I know. He's not going.' The boy started gathering his papers. 'I've done my best to convince him but he's been here too long.'

'Old man like that, hard time of life to be moving somewhere new. Doubt he had anywhere to go.'

'He'll be somewhere new soon if he stays, I know that much,' Wiltsham muttered. 'We all will.'

The boy wasn't making much sense. Cora drew the cup from the open water bucket and drank. That strange taste again.

He thrust some water skins at her. 'Fill these. We'll give them to Sanat as we go. They won't last him long, but... I didn't have to try to help him, you know, by telling him to leave. That wasn't my job.'

'I know. You're a rent agent. Collect the money, pay the landlord, send the records north to the Commission.'

'Commission doesn't care if people stay here.' He stuffed another handful of papers into his now straining satchel. 'They'd probably prefer it if no one had left at all. Make it easier up north. What's it like on the roads?'

'Wouldn't hurt to keep your wits about you.' She put the water skins on the floor. 'So you're leaving?'

'Course I am. Not much point being an agent when there's no rent to collect. And with what's coming...' He dumped the satchel on the porch then turned to stare at Cora. 'Isn't that why you're here, to take the papers back? I told the Wheelhouse I couldn't move them by myself.'

'No. I'm here to see the landlord you've been collecting for. Tennworth.'

Wiltsham laughed. 'She's not here! No one with any sense *is*.'

'Her place then. You must have sent the rents somewhere. Where?'

'But... the Tennworth place is gone, everyone knows that. It was one of the first, being that much further south.'

An ache was stealing into Cora's temple. Could it be from the heat, the funny-tasting water, or from always being that bit behind Tennworth? And now this boy was saying something she couldn't make sense of.

'What do you mean "gone"?'

The boy looked confused. 'You mean you don't know?'

'Student hear me, know *what*?'

'About the Tear,' he whispered.

The word seemed to suck all the air from the building. The ache at Cora's temple flared and she reached for the water barrel to steady herself.

'Show me,' Cora said.

He backed onto the porch, his hands raised in front of him as if Cora's words were dangerous. 'Are you mad? I'm not going up there! It's too dangerous.'

Cora walked towards him. 'You'll show me, or I'll make sure the Wheelhouse knows you refused to help a murder investigation.'

'But—'

'It's all right, Cora,' Ruth said from beyond the porch, on the cracked earth. 'I'll show you. It's why we're here.'

Cora made for her horse, but Ruth stopped her.

'We won't need them, it's not far. But the water skins. They'll help.'

Cora had questions, many, many questions, but she found she couldn't ask them, couldn't speak. It was the air – so hot she could barely breathe as she followed Ruth past the office and up the sloping, brittle plain that stretched away from it. Dead stalks crackled under foot and then the crackling stopped because the ground was soft with ash that grew deeper as they climbed.

The boy Wiltsham hadn't hung around, just taken what he could carry and headed north. Like so many before him.

How long had they been climbing? Cora stopped to suck at the water skin and looked back. The office was now a tiny square, their horses tied to the rail were barely marks in the dry earth. She couldn't breathe, and she stumbled trying to catch up with Ruth. Her hands pressed beneath the ash layer and the earth there was so dry it cut her with its sharp edges. Ruth helped her up and she had time to think about Ruth's injured arm – was it better? – and then there was a blast of heat in her face, as if someone had opened the door of a bread oven.

Cora shut her eyes and cried out.

Heat rushed into her open mouth and she thought she'd choke. Then a hand on her back and Ruth shouting close to her, though there was such a roaring that the words were muffled.

'Look, Cora. You have to look.'

She opened her eyes, and nearly fell. Ruth kept hold of her and they stood there like that, bound together: a pair of sisters at the edge of the world.

A world of red and orange. A world of heat and smoke.

The Tear.

The earth turned molten and steaming, rivers of it carving the land. They'd called it something in the Torn story. Something different. Something for the Audience.

Wit's blood.

It bubbled and spewed, seeped and sputtered, just like all

the blood Cora had ever seen. Blood from the earth. Where it shouldn't be.

What she *should* be looking at here were fields of figs and sintas, grapes, grown by farmers who rented their land from Tennworth. That's what her map showed. But there wasn't a plant in sight.

The southern Lowlands had been swallowed by Wit's blood.

She could just make out the tall cliffs of the Rusting Mountains on the horizon; those mountains deep in the Tear that stretched all the way to the clouds. How were the Rustans faring in this nightmare? Their peaks were high above the ash, but what of them now? Would those mountain homes sink into the hot blood? And Bordair – the inland lake the Caskers called home. The water would be bad – like the ford, only much worse – and the lake would shrink. She imagined a dried-out lake bed, boats fallen to their sides, the wood warping in the sun. No one left to see it. Everyone gone.

This was the end of everything. The Union a ruin, all their stories lost and forgotten. Everything she had thought important, everything she had worked so hard for, none of it mattered standing there. The Tear would consume it all.

Something landed on her boot. A rock. Then her foot was hot with pain and there was the smell of burning. She shook her boot and smoke puffed from it. There was a hole in the leather.

'Watch out!' Cora shouted, and pulled Ruth back from the edge. Fiery stones rained down where they'd just been standing. When the volley cleared, Cora's other boot was pocked in a few places and Ruth had a charred mark on the shoulder of her cloak.

Ruth pointed to something close by. 'See that?'

Cora's eyes stung but she blinked through it and was rewarded by the sight of a thin stone column sticking out of the orange lake beneath it.

'It's a chimney stack. Stone, so it's lasted longer. But it'll be gone soon, and so much more of the south with it.'

When the air became too bad to breathe, they went back down the slope. The agent had left water in the barrels. Cora drank cup after cup until she felt she'd cleared the ash that lined her throat.

She and Ruth sat on the porch, their backs to the long slope and the lake of molten earth some way behind it. Ruth's face was grimy with ash and Cora guessed hers was the same.

It was Ruth who spoke first. Cora had no words. She poked at the holes in her boots.

'When I was first told what was happening, I thought it was a story. That it couldn't be true. It *couldn't*.'

'*The south is falling apart,*' Cora said. 'Finnuc Dawson told me that, right before he was taken to the Steppes. I guess he wasn't lying.'

Ruth shook her head. 'That it should be him who told you, when the people he worked for have done everything they can to hide the truth, to spin it into lies.' She stroked her horse's nose and the animal whickered.

'He wasn't all bad,' Cora said quietly. 'But I misunderstood him, about too many things. When he said that, about the south, I thought he was talking about the people. A new war.'

'There might still be one.'

'But this is... What even is this?'

'The Tear is widening, Cora.'

Cora coughed, her breath like burning embers in her throat, in her mouth, on her lips. Black seeped into the edge of her vision – black veined with orange and red. Tornstone. The wooden boards of the porch seemed to be coming closer. Ruth grabbed her shoulder and didn't let go. Her sister's grip was hard, painful.

'How— how much?' Cora said. 'How long?'

'Ideas on that vary, but the Rustans are probably closest, given how they can move around their mountains and get a bird's eye view. It's their numbers we've been using to understand the problem, together with what we've seen and heard as we travel the Union.'

'And?'

Ruth's gaze was fixed on the ground. The baked, ruined ground. 'Rustans say the sands of the desert beyond the Tear are now molten. On the Union side, the entire Lowlands will be gone in a year. At most two.'

Cora swallowed and felt the ash still in her throat. 'Can it be stopped?'

'No one knows.'

'If you'd told me,' Cora said, 'I wouldn't have believed you.'

'That's why you had to see it for yourself.'

'You've been trying to tell me all the way, haven't you? The ash in the air. The taste of water. I should have realised. I should have listened.'

'It's not as simple as that. Who wants to hear a story like this one? It's much easier to ignore it, carry on with your life.'

'In Fenest, do people know?'

'Some. Those who would like this problem to disappear. Their stories have been for the Mute.' Ruth kicked at the ground. 'The things the pennysheets have printed – in Fenest it's easy to get distracted. But the election stories, *that's* where there are truths. Told slant, but that's the only way to help people understand. They'll be too frightened to hear, otherwise.'

Cora thought of the stories told so far. 'The Caskers' tale was plague – so many suffering.'

'Which the real Black Jefferey helped to drive home,' Ruth said.

'And the Torn – their story was a changing land, the fire at our door.' Cora shook her head. 'Is that what the story was all about? That if we find a way to adapt to the Tear, to this change, we can survive there?'

'That's the official Torn position,' Ruth said. 'Adapt or die. But the Torn realm is far from united in that view. The Wayward have been working with the dissenting voices.'

'People like Sorrensdattir.'

Ruth sighed. 'It's not without risk.'

'The Perlish made their feelings clear, with all that talk of dangerous "foreigns",' Cora said. 'And the Seeders – an election story about family and duty, sacrifice.'

'About knowing your place,' Ruth added. 'If you step out of line—'

'Don't upset the balance.'

'They've always been a short-sighted realm,' Ruth said. 'Never looking any further than the next harvest. The people begging for food at their porches, sleeping on their roads, dying in their fields – they deserve help, not doors closed in their faces, walls put up around them. But the Tear is coming for the north. The Jittery Wit knows it. And now you do too, Cora.'

'The Wayward story – you're going to tell the truth about the Tear.'

'The Caskers and the Torn helped prepare the way. The Rustan story will do the same. We need to convince the people of the Union to come together, not close their doors on one another.'

'It's the Assembly you need to convince,' Cora said. 'They're the ones who make decisions.'

Ruth managed a weak smile. 'Good job we have a way to choose who's in charge of it then, isn't it?'

'What if we get it wrong?' Cora said softly.

'Bloodshed, starvation, cruelty beyond anything we've known. And it's already happening.'

'The realm we need has to be one that sees beyond its own borders,' Cora said, finally starting to see. 'People are already moving north. But...'

It was then the pieces fell together. A pattern neat as the panes of glass that made up the Assembly building's dome.

'But someone wants to keep things the way they are, to stop those people moving north—'

'Cora—'

'I know who Tennworth is. I came down here to find her farm. But she's not here. She was never here. She's in Fenest.'

'She is,' Ruth said.

Cora stood up. 'You've known all along, haven't you? Why didn't you tell me?'

'Because I had to know if I could trust you, Cora. You work for the Commission, for Audience sake!'

'Is that so terrible?'

'It can be. With the wrong people in power.'

'Morton,' Cora said. 'Lowlander Chambers Morton is Tennworth.'

Ruth nodded.

'I need to get back to the city,' Cora said, and started to untie her horse.

'Wait, Cora. Will you help us?'

'Help you? I can't vote on any stories, Ruth. You'll have to trust the voters of Fenest for that.' She looped the reins over her horse's head and pulled herself in the saddle. 'Aren't you coming?'

Ruth grabbed the bridle. 'There will be hard choices ahead, Cora. I need to know I can count on you.'

'You can count on me finding a case against Morton.'

'So help me.'

'How?' Cora said.

'Help the southern realms keep the Union together.'

Twenty-Six

'So, did you find Tennworth?' Hearst said.

They were on the roof of the Bernswick station. With what Cora was about to tell the sergeant and Jenkins, she didn't want to risk being overheard from her office. Most of the pigeons seemed to be off somewhere, wherever it was they went. Only one or two dozed in the bright sun. Cora envied them their ignorance. That of Hearst and Jenkins too, who were waiting for her to say something. Once they knew the truth, they'd be caught in the same snare of fear she'd known since she'd climbed that slope and looked out over the fiery wasteland that had been the southern Lowlands. But there was no saving the constable or the sergeant. They had to know what was behind everything that had happened during the election. And besides, the truth was coming for them. One drop of Wit's blood at a time.

'I didn't find Tennworth *herself*,' Cora said.

Jenkins' shoulders slumped. Hearst watched the birds.

'But I found something else. Something... What I'm about to tell you, you need to keep to yourselves for now. It's not a secret that's going to last much longer, but in the meantime...'

She told them. Of the Tear, of the devastation she'd seen and that which was still to come. She told them everything, except about Ruth. Cora couldn't risk the life of another Wayward storyteller. Then she gave them a chance to ask questions. The same questions Cora had asked Ruth: how long? Can we stop it? What now? She answered without really being aware of what she said. She was too tired, and the Tear was widening.

Cora had ridden back to Fenest alone. Ruth said she was due to meet some Rustan contacts not far from the new edge of the Tear, so they'd parted at the agent's office. Then Cora had begun the long ride back to Fenest, stopping as little as she could manage. When she reached where she and Ruth had left the pair from the Orchard tied up, they were gone, as Ruth had predicted. It didn't matter. They were a tiny part of this story. An effect, not the cause.

It was Jenkins who brought Cora back to the present, on the roof of the station, the sun shining.

'We *must* help the southern realms,' Jenkins said.

Hearst cleared his throat. 'That sounds like a political stance to me, Constable.'

'And?'

'We work for the Commission, the civil service of Fenest,' Hearst said. 'It's not our job to choose sides in an election. The Commission, the police, are always neutral.'

'But the Tear is widening!' Jenkins said, practically shouting. The few pigeons on the roof took to the air.

'Do you want the whole city to hear?' Cora said.

'Yes,' Jenkins said. 'Don't you, Detective?'

'I want to make sure the story is told the right way, to make sure that those who hear it *listen*. There's a difference.

Look, what I've told you today doesn't change anything about our job.'

'But what about what you *haven't* told us?' Hearst said. 'Tennworth. You found something down there about her, didn't you?'

Cora swallowed. 'Tennworth is Lowlander Chambers Morton. She wants to keep people from the south coming into the north.'

'Including her own people?' Jenkins said.

Cora rolled a smoke. 'Plenty of Seeders being displaced that I saw. And it'll be Rustans and Caskers too who'll need somewhere to live, food, jobs. Some Wayward, perhaps.'

'And it's the Lowlands that'll bear the brunt of that,' Hearst said.

'We're talking about people!' Jenkins said. 'We need to help them.'

'And we will,' Cora said quietly, 'if we keep the election running, give all the realms the chance to tell their stories.'

Jenkins had her back to them and was staring out across the city.

'What are we going to do about Morton?' Hearst said in a low voice. His face had greyed. He seemed to have aged ten years since Cora had started talking.

'I don't know,' she said. 'Chief Inspector Sillian won't let me go near the Chambers.'

'Cora...'

'But even the Chambers aren't above the law. We've worked hard to find out just who is behind all this.'

'Much good knowing does us,' Hearst said.

'We're not done yet.'

'Be careful, Detective.'

'For once, I just might be. But if I'm not back before midnight, start searching the river.'

The Dancing Oak was quiet. For a start there weren't any chequers near the huge numbers-board that hung over the ring. No matter the time of day, there was always at least one of them there, lounging in their black and white coats, keeping track of the day's odds.

'Detective, long time no see.'

'Beulah.'

The old chequers was in her box above the fighting ring, surrounded by betting slips. Nestled amongst the paper was an expensive-looking silver teapot, cup and saucer. The smell of jasmine was heavy in the dusty air of the box.

'You know the rules,' Beulah said, stirring her tea.

'With debts, no bets.'

'So I trust you've come to pay up?'

'In a manner of speaking.'

Beulah sighed. 'We've been here before, Detective. No new lines of credit until you pay what you owe. Not that there'll be much chance of betting today anyway. My people are resting up, before the Rustans tell their tale.'

'You'll want to hear *my* tale.'

After a pause in which Beulah regarded Cora with dissatisfaction, she gestured that Cora should take a seat. From the papery nest at her feet, Beulah pulled out another cup and saucer and poured Cora a cup before she could say no.

'For a start,' Cora said, 'I think I've solved your beer problem.'

Beulah handed Cora a cup of steaming tea. 'Some good news at last.'

'Don't get used to it,' Cora said. 'I found someone in the Lowlands who brews, looking for new customers in Fenest. I told him how much you'd need and how often. Seemed to think he was the man for you.'

'Am I likely to have any problems getting it into Fenest?' Beulah asked.

When Cora hesitated, the old chequers jammed her cup back into its saucer with a loud crack.

'No paperwork, no point, Detective. Commission will need the right forms.'

'That won't be an issue,' Cora said, and handed her a folder of papers. With the hostelry being so close to the Tear, paperwork wasn't going to be Beulah's problem. But then Beulah would know that soon enough. Everyone would. And then proving the provenance of beer would be the least of their worries.

Beulah flicked through the folder. 'The Oak won't go dry for a while, if this works out. And neither will your credit, Detective.'

'I'm spending less time ring-side these days.'

'Oh?'

'I need a favour.'

'*Another* favour.' Beulah frowned. 'Have you forgotten the last time I helped you, the last time you wanted to go somewhere you shouldn't? Doesn't the name *Tithe Hall* mean anything?'

'You're right,' Cora said. 'And this time's not so different.' She took a swig of tea and decided she'd stick to coffee. 'At the back of that folder is a sealed letter. A letter that stays sealed as long as I'm alive.'

Beulah laughed. 'If this is a will, Detective, you have grossly misjudged my profession.'

'Not a will. If I die, that letter goes to a pennysheet – pick your hack, but I'd suggest Butterman at *The Spoke*. He's as loud and low as any of them.'

'I'm not part of the Commission's great postal service, either,' Beulah said.

'No, but I'm short on people I can trust.'

'You flatter me, Detective.'

'You *owe* me, Beulah.'

'Do I indeed?' Beulah sipped her tea. 'Sometimes, among so many losing chequers slips, it's hard to keep track.'

'You once told me the dead don't pay their debts.'

'I can be wise when pushed.'

Cora stood. 'Keep the letter, but post it if I join the Audience. Then you'll see a debt paid in full.'

Twenty-Seven

It was a different man at the front desk of the Assembly building this time. He didn't even try to sound apologetic when he told her that Lowlander Chambers Morton had no appointments left this week.

'The Chambers are very busy people. I'm sure you understand, Detective Gorderheim.'

He knew who she was without her having to show her badge. That wasn't a good sign.

'If you'd like to leave a—'

Cora started for the stairs. He called after her. The people in the entrance hall looked up from their papers and their mutterings, and stared at her. She started to jog.

'Don't worry, I know where I'm going.'

She saw him hurriedly whispering to a messenger boy, saw the note move between them, before she'd even reached the top of the stairs. It would be hardly any time at all until news reached the top floor of the Bernswick division police station. Cora ran down the corridor.

When she reached Morton's door it was already ajar and she could hear voices within. She pushed open the door and just had time to notice the feel of the crossed spades design worked into the gold-painted wood – rougher than it looked, likely to give splinters – before she was face to face with Lowlander Chambers Morton and a cloud of smoke. Tornstone-scented. The Torn Chambers was there too.

The conversation stopped. Whatever they'd been talking about, Cora hadn't caught a word of it. But the look on the Torn's face was easy to understand, even with the glass mouthpiece in place. The Torn Chambers was furious.

'What is the meaning of this intrusion? No knock, is—'

'Torn Chambers Raadansutter,' Morton said, 'let me introduce Detective Gorderheim.'

'I know who this is!' Raadansutter shouted. The tornstone in his mouthpiece flared and Cora's eyes watered as the air worsened. 'I saw you, when the Hook barge burned. You were there with the Rustan, Investigator Serus.'

'I tried to save your advisor, Sorrensdattir,' Cora said, doing her best not to cough.

'Terrible accident,' Raadansutter said, 'according to your pennysheets. According to you too?'

'Terrible, yes. But some stories say it was no accident. Have you heard those, your honour?'

Morton touched the Torn's arm. The gesture looked gentle enough, but then Morton squeezed. 'The detective and I just need a little chat,' Morton said. 'We won't be long.'

Raadansutter looked like he would argue Cora back out into the corridor, but the Torn did as he was bid.

When they were alone, Morton leaned against her desk, her arms folded across her chest. 'You seem to have a habit of barging into my office, Detective. That might be how things are done at Bernswick, but we at the Assembly like to use a little more decorum.'

'There wasn't much decorum getting Finnuc Dawson to sew up the mouth of the Wayward storyteller. Or to murder Finnuc once he'd served his purpose.'

Morton kept her gaze on Cora. 'I don't know what you're talking about,' she said slowly.

'I think you do. Did he call you Mistress Tennworth, like your farmers do?'

'Such a fanciful imagination, Detective. Or have you decided to become a storyteller? We are short a 'teller, I suppose.'

'That was your doing.'

Morton laughed. 'You seem to have become rather adrift from things. *You* arrested the man who murdered our dear Wayward storyteller.'

'I know about the Tear,' Cora said.

'The Tear? Detective, do slow down, I'm struggling to keep up.'

'I know you want to keep people out of the northern Seeder lands. People who need food, shelter. That's what all this has been about. Keeping things as they are, even as the Tear widens and the Union disappears into it. Even as the world changes.'

'Some changes can't be fought,' Morton said, and moved to one of the tall sets of shelves. She gently handled the trailing stems of a plant. 'Did you know, blight can run through a whole season's crops in a matter of days, make the soil unusable for years after? It doesn't matter how careful the farmer was with the planting, the watering, keeping off the birds. It's a tale of luck and unfairness, one both the Latecomer and the Neighbour know well. We in the Lowlands know it too.' Morton snapped off

467

a dry-looking stalk and tossed it to the floor. 'But other changes can be controlled, managed. You'll see, Detective Gorderheim, what we do is for the greater good.'

'The good of who? Not those I saw coming north, those with barely anything to their name, wondering when they'll eat again.'

'And did you give them bread and water? Did you help them?'

'I...'

'We're helping those we can, those who have a *right* to be in certain parts of the Union. People like you. There is a place for you with us, Cora, for now. I owe your dear mother that much.'

'My mother? What did...'

Morton clapped her hands. 'How exciting, to see a detective hard at work right in my very office!'

'The money from the trading halls, it went to you?'

'Land can be expensive. Did you know the far southern Lowlands are a good place for grapes? But then we spoke before of grapes, didn't we? I've always wanted to make better stuff than the Perlish; their wines are just so sweet. Ash from the Tear is an excellent fertiliser. One needs to be close but not too close. And now, well. We're all closer than we'd like.' Morton shook her head.

'Your farms made my parents' embezzled funds disappear,' Cora said.

'You make it sound sordid,' Morton said. 'Your mother was like family to me, Cora, and family looks out for one another. No matter the cost. No matter the sacrifice.'

Sacrifice. All at once, Cora could smell rotten sinta. The stench left behind by Heartsbane. The man with the broken nose who had entombed himself beneath a pallet before drinking poison. She saw him, as if he was there in Morton's office. But his face was Cora's own face. His ruined eyes, her eyes.

'Whatever you had over that man in Perlanse, whatever bargain you made to convince him to do your dirty work and then make himself go away, you won't do that to me, Morton.'

'Come, Cora. Everyone has their price.'

'What was his?'

Morton waved away the question. 'I forget the figures. Enough to keep his daughters from the Orchard.'

'So you don't deny it?' Cora said. 'Any of it?'

'What's to deny? What evidence do you have for any of these wild stories?'

When Cora gave no answer, Morton laughed.

'What will you do, hm? March into the Wheelhouse and tell them a Chambers needs to be arrested? Or maybe it's Chief Inspector Sillian you're counting on? How is dear Adella? Still working too hard?'

'I've worked a lot of cases over the years,' Cora said. 'Muggings, brawls, theft, murder. One thing I've learned – and learned the hard way – is that the truth won't sit still. It can't be corralled. Can't be boxed in. Can't be controlled. Not for long.'

'You're starting to sound like your sister.'

'You might be right.'

'She, I cannot help.' Morton's tone had changed. She was firm now. Cold. 'My offer to you stands, Cora. But leave it too long to join us, and you will also find the door is shut.'

'I'll save you the effort,' Cora said, and slammed the gold, carved door behind her.

Twenty-Eight

Cora took her time going back to the station. There was no point rushing, not now. She knew what would be waiting for her there. Let Chief Inspector Sillian wait.

Cora had done her job. She'd discovered who had murdered the Wayward storyteller, and then who had killed that killer. And now she knew why. That left the smaller matter of how she was going to stop Morton from carving up the Union. A story for another day, and one she'd need help with. Lots of help. Not just the kind that wore a blue constable's uniform. It was time to do things differently.

At the front desk, Lester looked as sorry a sight as she'd ever seen him. 'I'm to send you up, Detective. Soon as I see you. Top floor.'

'I could do with the exercise,' she said, surprised by how cheerful she sounded.

Every step up to Sillian's office felt heavier than the last, almost as if the wound from the Hook barge had reopened. Pruett would love that, being right about her needing to rest it. Pruett. When would she see him again? And Jenkins. Cora tried not to think about the constable.

The door was open, as Lowlander Chambers Morton's

had been. *How is dear Adella? Still working too hard?* Of course, Morton and the chief inspector knew each other. Of course, Sillian had tried to protect Morton, warning Cora to keep her distance. Cora didn't have enough fight left to be truly angry at such corruption. It all felt like the Tear itself: an unstoppable force. It went so deep, Cora's own childhood was riddled with it. No wonder Ruth left when she did. Cora's mistake had been to stay as long as she had. Well, it was nearly time. She knocked.

There was a pause in which Cora felt the air on the landing shift, as if Sillian's anger was like sudden intense heat. The Tear – she couldn't stop thinking about it, seeing the rest of the world through its fiery haze. Then that well-known voice said, 'Come.'

The chief inspector was behind her desk. Her back was straight, her palms pressed onto the wood. Not a hair out of place. Not a scuff on her jacket. How long had she been waiting for this chance?

'Ma'am.'

'You can't say I didn't warn you, Gorderheim.'

'I can't, ma'am.'

'And yet you deliberately went against my orders.'

'I did. And I'd do it again.'

'There won't be any chance of that.'

'I suppose not.' Cora took out a smoke rolled just for this moment, and lit up. Sillian's face was the perfect picture of checked outrage, just as Cora had hoped. She blew the smoke up to the ceiling then reached into her pocket. 'I'll save you the bother of asking for this,' she said, and put her badge in front of Sillian. That annoyed the chief inspector, too.

Sillian got up and cleared her throat: the official business was about to begin. Best get it over with.

'On this day and from this day forward, you, Detective Cora Gorderheim, no longer bear this rank. You are henceforth stripped of all titles and duties, barred from entering all police premises in Fenest and the wider Union, forbidden to speak to, or fraternise with, any serving officers while they are on duty. You may not make use of police resources for your own ends, nor undertake private investigations. Do you understand and accept this decision?'

'Yes,' Cora said, though that last part was not quite true. She had no intention of dropping anything.

'So then it is final, and the relevant paperwork will be completed shortly, which you are legally required to complete.'

'There we are then,' Cora said. 'The wheel turns.'

'You know there's nothing you can do,' Sillian said, her voice sounding quite wild now that she'd slipped out of the formalities. 'The Tear, the destruction of the south – Morton's is the only way.'

'There we'll have to agree to disagree, ma'am. Some of us think helping people might be better.'

Sillian went to the window. 'So you really are as foolish as your sister. I thought everyone was wrong about you, Gorderheim. But now I see your stories are only for the Drunkard.'

'Looks like I've disappointed you,' Cora said, and turned to leave.

'You have. More than you know.'

'Be seeing you, Chief Inspector.'

Sillian sighed. 'No, Gorderheim, you won't. Not if you want to avoid hard labour on the Steppes.'

'Or being murdered on the way.'

Cora had got as far as a different set of steps, those outside the station, when Jenkins caught her. Jenkins in full uniform, and Cora leaving.

'It's true then,' Jenkins said, 'what they're saying in the briefing room?'

''Fraid so, Constable. You'll have to buy your own pastries now.'

'And you were just going to leave, without saying goodbye?'

Cora avoided her eye. 'Thought that might be easier on everyone. Don't want to get you into trouble.'

'It would be worth it to do the right thing!' Jenkins cried.

'You're sure that's what I'm doing?' Cora said.

'I... I could leave too. Come with you, wherever you're going. I... I *could*.' Jenkins cast a look of longing back to the main doors of the station. When she looked back at Cora her eyes were wet. This was no help to anyone.

'You'll be more use to me here, Jenkins. Stick with Sergeant Hearst and you'll be all right. Look out for me. I'll need you. We've still got two stories left in this election.'

'You'll be there, for the Rustans and the Wayward?'

'I'll find a way. Take care of yourself, Jenkins.'

'You too, Detective.'

Cora watched the constable go back inside, and just as she was about to turn away, someone else appeared in the doorway.

'Don't feed those birds too much,' she called to Hearst, 'or they'll never get off the roof.'

'They'll be pleased you're not around to cut their dinner rations.'

'I won't be far away.'

'See that you aren't,' he said.

Then Cora turned and made her way into the maze of alleys opposite the station.

'Leaving work early again?' Ruth said, joining Cora halfway down an unnamed alley. 'The Wheelhouse will have that written down somewhere.'

'And plenty more, after today.' Cora ground out her bindleleaf. 'You told me something, on the night you left, all those years ago. Since we found Ento – Nicholas – it's been on my mind.'

'Oh?' Ruth looked strained at the mention of her son's name.

'You said that there was power in stories, and a story of power.'

Ruth gave a short laugh. 'Sounds like the kind of precocious thing I'd say at seventeen, confident I knew everything about the world.'

'But you were right. Everything that's happened since Nicholas was murdered has proved that, and the story's not over yet. I want to be part of it, shaping it, not just listening to someone else's tale.'

'What does that mean?'

'Means I'm done with the station, the Commission. All of it. I'm with you, Ruth.'

'You know the risks?'

'I know the many ways to be welcomed by the Widow.'

'Better her than the Mute,' Ruth said. 'I want some stories left to tell.'

'We'd better get started then, hadn't we?'

Ruth turned and at once disappeared in the twists of the alley. Cora followed without looking back.

Acknowledgements

Thanks to all at Head of Zeus: our fantastic editor, Madeleine O'Shea, Jade Gwilliam, Clare Gordon, Laura Palmer, and everyone involved in bringing the Tales of Fenest to readers. The Commission has logged you all on the appropriate forms.

Thanks to our agent, Sam Copeland at Rogers, Coleridge and White, for thinking this was a good idea in the first place.

Thanks to all our family and friends who voted on the stories in *Widow's Welcome*, and made us believe the rest of the election mattered too.

From Katherine: thanks to Belinda and Jane, who once asked me to say which realms they would belong to, if they lived in the Union, and made the whole endeavour suddenly – wonderfully – real. Thanks, too, to the Royal Literary Fund once again who awarded me a further year of a Fellowship which helped in all sorts of ways, including securing much-needed time.

From David: thanks to Bev, Jamie, Jo, Jonathan, Liz, Lyndall, and Tricia for parachuting into the Tales of Fenest and giving such excellent advice and encouragement. I'm sorry I never revealed who had the affair, but the Torn owe you all for their black stones. Thanks, too, to my colleagues at the University of South Wales, who support my writing every step of the way.

About the Author

D.K. Fields is the pseudonym for the writing partnership
of novelists David Towsey and Katherine Stansfield.
David's zombie-western The Walkin' Trilogy is published
by Quercus. Katherine's historical crime fiction series,
Cornish Mysteries, is published by Allison & Busby.
The couple are originally from the south west
of England, and now live in Cardiff.